ANY THING FOR YOU

Also by L.J. Diva

NOVELS

Anything for You
Falling for London
The Road to Vegas
Hollywood Dreams
The Billionaire's Dirty Little Secret

THE PORN STAR BROTHERS SERIES

Carlos: Book 1
Pedro: Book 2
Tomas: Book 3
Retribution: Book 4
Porn Star Brothers
Forever
Love Never Dies
Stefan: The New Generation
DeLuca
Spiros & Jenny
And Always

ANYTHING FOR YOU

L.J. DIVA

★ Royal Star Publishing ★

Chances is an imprint of Royal Star Publishing
www.royalstarpublishing.com.au

First edition dust jacket hardcover published in 2022
All Rights Reserved, Copyright ©L.J. Diva 2022

Dust Jacket Hardcover ISBN: 978-1-922307-62-0
Trade Paperback ISBN: 978-1-922307-60-6
Large Print Paperback ISBN: 978-1-922307-61-3
E-book ISBN: 978-1-922307-59-0
Audio Book ISBN: 978-1-922307-63-7
A catalogue record for this book is available from the National Library of Australia.

Cover design: Royal Star Publishing and MiblArt
Typesetting in Minion Pro by Royal Star Publishing

The moral right of L.J. Diva to be identified as the author of her work has been asserted.
This book is a work of fiction. Any references to real people or real locales are used fictitiously, and any resemblance to actual events, locales or persons, living or dead, is entirely coincidental.
No part of this publication may be reproduced, published, performed in public or communicated to the public in any form or by any means without prior written permission of Royal Star Publishing.
Requests to publish work from this book should be sent to:
authors@royalstarpublishing.com.au

DEDICATION

For Oscar, and his partner in crime, Jason Sudeikis, who gave me a *Colossal* idea for a novel…

PART ONE

Chapter 1

"So, how many people are in this group? And how often do you meet?" the man asked the girl who was running it. He watched her flit around in front of him doing not much of anything. *Probably trying hard to not show her excitement*, he thought, his ego giving itself a boost.

"We currently have twelve members," the girl, whose name tag read Belinda, replied. "And we meet once a fortnight on a Thursday evening." She unlocked the door to the IT suite and pushed it aside with shaky hands to roll her trolley in. As a part-time librarian, it was her job to run the writers' group. But this week, their special guest was making her quite nervous.

"Mmm…" He nodded and gazed around the library wondering if anyone there was a member of the group. No one looked remotely interesting, so he had no need to pursue them for his needs. "What are the members like? Active as authors? Are they published? Had success? What?"

"Some of our members are just writers." Her gaze fell upon regulars chatting near one of the floor-to-ceiling windows and she pointed at them. "Those two ladies at that table over there, they're writing some cool fantasy stuff." Her eyes redirected to the entrance. "And the guy who just walked in has self-published a couple of books. A couple of other members have had stories published, some are ready to publish, and then there's one member who's published heaps and even set up her own publishing house to do it, because she writes under three names."

"Really?" That piqued his interest and he glanced up at her from his position on the arm of a lounge chair outside the suite. "Tell me more."

"Well, she's really flamboyant and has been doing it for years, wears a lot of jewellery because she used to be a jewellery designer, and has a lot of colourful clothes. Oh—" She nodded in the direction of the front door. "There she is now. I need to finish setting up."

He didn't notice her step into the IT suite; he was too busy focusing on the woman weaving her way around the other side of the library looking at the latest books on stands. She picked up a couple, read the blurbs, and then put them down before moving on to the next stand.

"Interesting," he murmured, his gaze fixed on her. She wore a bright coloured kaftan top over dark blue jeans, with hot pink cowboy boots. Jewellery adorned her ears, neck, wrists and fingers, and her hair curled lightly around the nape of her neck and ears.

"Average height, average build, but reasonably attractive," he continued, uncrossing his arms and standing as she slowly approached.

The young librarian appeared at the door. "Hey, Ari. We have a new member for the night. This is Jason. Jason, Ari."

Ari glanced from Belinda to the man in front of her. Her gaze moved up his body until it reached his face and her eyes widened in shock and her heart hammered in her chest. "Ah…but you're…"

"Yeah…I am," Jason replied with a slight grin. "Real name Jason, but professionally I go by Jay, and everyone's called me that for decades. So…call me Jay." He shrugged and gazed into her widely curious yet sparkling green eyes and noted her rounded features. "Is Ari short for anything?"

"Arial. But everyone calls me Ari." She regained her composure, put a clamp on her racing heart, and swallowed the very hard lump in her throat. She knew who Jay Daniels, hot shot, big time Hollywood actor, was. And he made her quite breathless. Especially now that he was standing here in front of her, and she could see him in person. Six foot plus and hairy in all the right places, with dimples and twinkling eyes. He was just her type. Yes, he was definitely her type. But what was he doing in her neck of the woods? A slight frown touched her face. "So…why are you *here*, of all places?"

Jay's brows rose and he pointed to the floor as reference. "Here? Is there something wrong with here? I don't see anything wrong with here." His gaze roamed over her from head to toe and back again. "I like it here very much."

Ari took a sharp intake of breath and blushed, trying to keep it together. "I meant here in little old out of the way nowhere." To get out from under his hungry gaze, she scurried into the IT suite and placed her bag on the table closest to the door.

Jay grinned to himself and followed, deliberately taking the seat next to her. "It's hardly nowhere. I'm here filming a movie with Russell Crowe in the outback. But something shut down the production, mechanics, or whatever, and we had to halt filming. I asked the cast and crew if they knew of any author or writing groups around and this one was mentioned. So here I am." He spread his hands out and lightly shrugged. "And I'm glad I came. I think I'm going to find *lots* of inspiration here tonight."

Ari placed her writing folio on the table and her bag on the floor by her feet. "Ah-huh. And why would a big time Hollyweird actor find inspiration here in this little old writing group?" She pulled out her chair and sat down. The gas lift office chair slid down with a thump and she let out a surprised whoop.

"Here, let me help." Jay swiftly moved behind the chair and grabbed both sides of the seat while his long fingers pulled the lever. He lifted her up. "There. That better?" He moved closer so his face was beside hers. "Better?"

She blushed, inhaled his rather tasty cologne, and mumbled, "Yes, thank you." *Oh, what a time to make a fool of myself,* she thought. *The one week an actor you have a massive crush on happens to not only be in your country, but in your state, and now in your writers' group, and you go and make a fool of yourself.* In her peripheral vision, she saw him grinning at her and swinging lazily back and forth in his chair. His legs were spread apart in the crotch display position, a body language term Ari had only recently learned for one of her novels. Jay Daniels was on the hunt and showing his manhood for all to see he was in control and had the power.

The other members filed in, filling up the room, and she thanked God for the distraction.

Once the introductions were out of the way, and they oohed and aahed over the new addition, they went around the room discussing what they'd done in the last two weeks.

"I just finished off the story I was writing. I finally solved the problem I had with the characters, and the rest came really quickly," Poppy said. Blonde and in her mid-twenties, she was the youngest of the group.

"Oh, that's good." Belinda adjusted her glasses. "Did the advice we gave you help?"

"Absolutely." Poppy nodded. "It helped me break through by thinking outside the box. I just had to change the actions to another character."

"Good." Belinda gave a sharp nod of her head and moved on to Fiona. "And what about you, Fi? What have you done?"

They continued until Jay was next, so he launched into talking about screenwriting and the movie he was making.

"And yeah, pretty much anything with Russell is a hit, so I can't wait to finish it. I haven't done a movie in two years, and I'm really excited. Not just to be making a movie;" he put on the Aussie accent, or at least tried to, "but to be making it in the land down under. I'm hoping to learn your language and your Aussie-isms. I've already practised talking like Russell. G'day, I'm Russell Crowe."

"Oh, God!" Ari groaned and rolled her eyes while everyone else laughed. "I know some of our actors have horrible American accents, but you lot just can't pull off an Aussie accent. That was bad."

"I thought it was pretty good," Jay replied in the accent. "It even got a laugh out of Russell."

"Not because it was good," Ari muttered and avoided eye contact. "Because he was laughing *at* you, not with you."

"Ouch!" Jay grinned. "You know how to hurt a guy and cut to the quick." He grasped his chest and gasped for air. "Knife...to chest...must...pull...it out," he muttered, pulling the imaginary knife from his torso and laying it in front of Ari. "I believe this is yours."

She gave him a dirty side-eye and scoffed. "Keep it. I don't need your fake knife with your fake blood everywhere." With a dismissive wave of her hand, she added, "You done?" and launched into talking about the latest novel she was writing. She was having trouble deciding which way to go in a scene, or whether to change it completely.

Jay leaned back in his seat and listened with one ear while googling her on his phone. Ari Travers popped up at the top of page one and he recognised her from the photo in the Google author box on the right. He clicked on a few details before clicking through to her website. After a quick look, he liked what he saw and heard sirens and warning bells going off in his head. That was always a sure sign he needed to do or say something in that moment or needed to know someone he'd just met. He clicked through to her socials and followed her on the ones he had profiles on. By the time he lifted his eyes, the group had moved on to discussing one member's name choice for her character, its meaning, and whether it was appropriate.

After a few minutes, Jay joined in. "This is an interesting topic, because in real life, many people have names they don't like, so they change them, or use their other names. For example, my full name's Jason Oscar Daniels, but I've always been called Jay. J-a-y. So that's what I use for acting. Even my family and friends call me Jay, but does anyone know what Jason means?"

"July, August, September, October, November!" Ari quipped while organising her folio.

"Ha!" Jay chuckled along with everyone else and swung

his chair around to give her his full attention. "And do you know what Arial means?"

"As long as it has no reference to the little mermaid, I don't care." Ari stopped herself from gazing at his rugged good looks that were making her blood boil, her body tingle, and her sexual organs throb. Which was not a good thing.

Several members laughed, Jay along with them.

"Wrong spelling. So do you know or are you just being coy?" he teased.

She finally turned to stare him straight in the eye. "No, I don't."

"Ah, it means sans-serif font." Jay watched closely for her reaction.

Ari groaned, rolled her eyes, and dropped her shaking head. "You bloody bastard."

"Got you!" Jay grinned and swung back and forth in his chair.

The banter continued until the end of the meeting when the members packed up and stood to leave.

"It's only quarter to seven," Jay said to Ari. "What are you doing now? Do we have time to make a video?"

Ari frowned as she looked at him. "*We* make a video?"

"Yeah." He nodded. "I want to tell everyone about this meeting, and meeting you, how cool you are, how crazy talented you are." He held up his phone and she saw her website open on it. "I googled you. You're crazy talented. We need to do a video."

Ari glanced from his phone to his warm, sparkling brown eyes and then caught herself. "No, *we* don't." She slid her folio into her bag and walked out the door.

Jay ran up behind her and managed to steer her over to a

quiet part of the library while they were talking. "Come on, Ari. I could make you famous."

"Wait...how did we get...?" She looked around. "I was headed for the door."

"I know." Jay grasped both of her arms. "Trust me. You're crazy talented, have a tonne of books under three names, and have your own publishing house. You make the jewellery you wear and have incredible clothes. You deserve more than a couple of hundred followers, Ari. Let me help you with that." Gazing earnestly into her eyes, he hoped he conveyed a heartfelt message.

She blinked and tingled and sizzled from his touch. He was so damn hot and the type of good-looking guy she always found herself attracted to. Which she was, because she'd watched a tonne of his movies and TV show appearances, and realised just *how* hot, and how much of her type he was. But now he was standing in front of her, holding her arms, gazing into her eyes with his warm chocolatey brown ones, and his hair was tousled just so, and his beard framed his face and dimples to a level of perfection. A sigh left her, and she licked her lips and blinked. Shit! "Ah…" Her jaw dropped and she gaped at him. "I don't—"

"Don't worry. I'll do all the talking." Jay pulled up the video app on his phone and held up his arm to see if he captured both of them. "Okay, here we go." He slid his right arm around her and pulled her close but turned the camera away so you only saw him. For the moment. "Hey, hey, this is Jay and welcome back to Australia." He stopped at the chuckling beside him.

"Oh, God," Ari sputtered and covered her mouth with her hand. "You don't really say that do you?"

"Of course I do, it rhymes," he said and turned back to the camera. "As you know, I've been posting about my trip down under and that there's been a delay in filming. Well, I decided to catch a writers' group or two, and I want to introduce you to my girl, Ari Travers. Say hello, Ari." He turned the camera to take in both of them.

"Hello, Ari," she replied, hands grasped in front of her.

"Oh, that's cute." Jay grinned at her before continuing. "I met Ari tonight at her local writers' group. She writes under her name as well as two others. Adult fiction, kids, non-fiction, a tonne of genres, so much so she set up her own publishing house to cover it all. But get *this* she also used to have her own jewellery label." He looked at the sparkle that covered her and gave her a short nod. "You make that?"

"Ah…" She glanced down at what she was wearing. "Most of it."

Taking a closer look at what was around her neck, he decided to be cheeky for likes and comments, and added, "Is that necklace a cock ring?"

Ari's head pulled back slightly in horror, but her left brow rose high. "Why? You need one to keep you in line?" popped out of her mouth before she had a second to think about what she would say.

Jay laughed at the comeback. "Hardly, it's not big enough."

"Oh, sweetie," she said innocently. "I'm so sorry. I didn't realise that a man of your size would have such a small penis. It must be *so* embarrassing in the bedroom."

"Ouch." Jay faltered, his jaw dropping at the comment. "You really do know how to cut a man with a quip. Anyways," he turned back to the camera, "just get a look at Ari's style with her amazing outfit." He tilted the phone down to her boots and back up. "She's creative in her art *and* her style. So follow my girl, Ari Travers, on her socials, I have. And check out her website for everything she does. This is Jay and Ari, signing off." His thumb tapped the stop button. "That was great. Don't worry; you'll have thousands of followers in no time."

"You shouldn't have done that," Ari told him and walked off, making it to the entrance before he caught up.

"What do you mean, I shouldn't have? I wanted to. I think you're incredibly talented and deserve some attention." Jay walked beside her as they made their way out of the council centre where the library was located, and down the stairs into the cool night air. "I mean, I didn't have to, but I wanted to. To help you out."

Ari stopped midstride and turned to face him, waiting while the bus went past, and the local hubbub died down. "I didn't ask you to, and I felt pushed into it. You just led me over to that section and whipped out your phone."

"I could have whipped something else out," Jay deadpanned.

"Oh, my God, you don't stop!" Ari's eyes closed and she breathed deeply, despite the congestion of the shopping district.

"Neither do you, apparently," Jay told her. "You have some wicked lines yourself, Ari Travers."

Ari opened her eyes and glared at him. "Okay, you didn't have to…but that's you. It was nice of you after just meeting me, but now, I have to go." She walked across the road to the shopping centre carpark, and over to her car.

"Are you leaving? We haven't talked enough yet." Jay hurried after her, not wanting her to leave, not wanting to lose her. Not yet.

"No." She opened to back door of her car and deposited her library bag. "I need to do some shopping." Locking the car, she started for the centre. "Why?"

"I just…" He fell into step beside her. "Want to keep talking. Get to know you more, talk more, maybe talk about your writing."

"Why?" She glanced at him before stepping onto the curb. "Plan on stealing my ideas?"

Jay stared at her for a moment and considered what he was going to say. "Hardly!" he finally retorted and followed her inside and around the centre before they emerged an hour later. "So really, I just think that chatting to all of you Aussies is giving me great ideas, new perspectives, thoughts, etc. You know?"

"Ah-huh." Even though she'd been busy shopping, Ari had enjoyed his company and opinions on different items in the stores. He was a comedian with a wicked sense of humour, but possibly a better actor as she never knew if he was serious or not. Clicking the alarm for her car, she reached for the boot door, but Jay got in first.

"So…" He pulled the door out of her way. "When can I see you again?"

"What?" She almost dropped her bags. "Why would *I* want to see *you* again?"

"Ouch! Because you have a crush on me, and I have one on you." He closed the door and stared expectantly at her, a grin from ear to ear. "I mean, it's really obvious. Right? I'm incredible and you're crushing on me. And you're incredible and I'm crushing on you. So I want your number and your address."

Ari gathered herself. "How 'bout neither." She raised a

brow and gave him a megawatt smile before manoeuvring around him to the driver's door and opening it.

"Aw, come on, sans-serif font," he pleaded, but received a grim smile and narrow eyes for his trouble. He put his hands up in defence. "Sorry, I'm joking. But seriously, I want to see you again. And the director thinks it's going to be about two weeks before we can get back to the movie. I find you fascinating and want to keep seeing you."

Ari sighed and stared into his eyes. He seemed sincere, for however sincere actors can really be, and he was hot, and she'd be stupid not to take advantage of the situation and get to know him. Who knew what could come of it? Maybe a few thousand new followers, maybe some book buyers, and maybe a hot steamy night together. "Oh…" Her lips puckered and she blushed. "Ah… I guess I *should* give in. Even though seeing an incredibly hot actor will be *such* a waste of my time. God knows how I'm going to get *any* writing done." Ari feigned disinterest and slyly glanced away. "It's not often you have inspiration for stories literally fall into your lap."

"Oh, *I'm* going to be inspiration for your stories?" Jay had already decided to follow her home, so it didn't really matter if she'd said no. He leaned against her car and pulled out his phone. "Number please." He waited for her to give in and tell him, tapping it in as she recalled it. "And address."

"I could tell you to figure it out for yourself." Ari climbed into her seat.

"But I'd just follow you home anyways." Jay shifted so he was blocking any exit from the car, and from her closing the door on him.

"Yes," she muttered, aware of how large and masculine he was. "I bet you would. Stalker!"

He laughed. "Come on, hand it over." She told him and he added the info to her number. "I'll see you tomorrow, unless Friday's not a good day."

"Not really. Unless you want to help with the housework." Ari poked him in the chest. "Get outta my way. I wanna shut the door."

"Twelve good for you? I'll be there then. See you tomorrow." He shut the door before she could answer and walked away.

"What the hell…" Ari watched, slightly stunned, as he crossed four rows of cars to get to his. "What the hell just happened?" Exhaling, and shaking her head, she looked at herself in the rearview mirror. "Seriously, what the hell just happened?" In disbelief, she watched him drive off, and finally did the same.

*****

Ari was up early, had the housework done, and was looking decent by the time Jay turned up in her driveway. It was also bin day, so she'd left the double gates open for him to drive in.

"Hey." She watched him alight from his four-wheel drive. "You found the place okay, then?"

"Absolutely." He gave her his trade mark smile and turned to pull a bunch of flowers from the front seat. "And these are for you."

"Ah…what…wow." Ari was stunned. No man had ever given her flowers. That's how boring her life had been. "Thank you. I'll go and put them in a vase and bring a couple of drinks out."

"No need. I'll come with you," Jay said. "Get to see how you live."

"Ah, no," Ari replied with more force than necessary. She blushed and glanced away from his inquisitive gaze. "I'll take these inside and bring out some drinks. You take a seat on the bench over there and I'll be back in a minute." She hurried inside and found a vase. Taking no time to arrange the flowers; she just dumped them into the water and left them on the sink, then grabbed two ice-cold cans of soda from the fridge, shoved them into can coolers, and hurried outside. "Here you go. Don't know what you drink, but that's what we drink, and it's all we have. Unless you want water or juice." She sat beside him on the bench seat she'd dragged around the side of the house to the driveway earlier and set her can beside her. "Nice day." The bundle of nerves inside of her made her uneasy.

He held up his phone. "Do you mind if I record our conversations? After last night, I have a feeling we'll come up with some wicked stuff to use for TV or movies."

Ari smarted. "As long as you send me a copy and get my permission before using any of it and give me credit for it."

"Of course." Jay grinned and shifted towards her, setting his phone on the bench between them. "You said *we*. I didn't know you had fellow house dwellers. Anyone I need to know about?"

Alarmed, Ari shot around to face him. "Why would you need to know that?"

Jay tilted his head and watched her. "A partner? I'd need to know about that if I'm encroaching on another man's territory. I don't do that sort of shit."

"Oh…" Ari's blush swept over her, and she gulped for air as his words sank in. "No, no partner. Perpetually single. You don't need to worry…" she trailed off. *Jesus, seriously,* she thought and looked up at the sky. *Why did I just tell him I'm perpetually single? God. Fuck me! Wait, did he say he wanted to know if he was encroaching on another man's territory? Encroaching? Who says that in this day and age? And holy shit, he wants to encroach…on me…*

"Perpetually single?" Jay repeated. "That doesn't sound like a good thing."

"Not for me, it isn't." A sad smile crossed Ari's lips and she launched into a list of questions she'd come up with to talk about when things grew awkward. Which they had. They were mainly about his movies and TV appearances, but at least they were something. "You said last night you haven't done a movie in two years. You wouldn't be the first actor to take a break, or not get a role."

"True." Jay drained the last of his drink. "But when you're a washed-up actor like me who hasn't had a decent role in nearly two years, and had to stoop to playing extras, or bit parts on shows to get by, it becomes a lot more than just taking a break, or not taking a role. It's because you're seen as problematic, and no one wants to take a chance on you anymore. I even resorted to playing some douche bag hip-hop dancer wearing a red track suit and a Will Ferrel style wig in the background of some skit on a comedy show."

"Were you good at it?" Ari couldn't recall seeing that one on YouTube.

"Fuck yeah!" he retorted. "I rocked it. Just as I do every role I take because you never know who's watching that can give you your next job."

"Mmm…" Ari thought a moment. "Well, then you can't be too washed up if you're here making a movie with Russell Crowe."

"Yeah, yeah I am. And I'm fucking surprised by that. But maybe it's my redemption, just like meeting you."

Surprised, Ari frowned. "Redemption? Hardly!"

"You never know," Jay replied and licked his lips. "So… who's *we*?"

"Oh…" Her gaze flew downward, and after a deep sigh she told him how her life was taken up with the care of her mother, and jewellery and writing were, in part, her solution to dealing with an incredibly suffocating, lifeless existence.

"Wow, Ari, I'm sorry. I didn't know." Jay laid his hand on hers and gently squeezed. "No one really knows what 24/7 carers go through unless they do it themselves. I have a friend who had to take over the care of her parents for ten years, and it not only aged her body, but she was a bit of an emotional wreck when she emerged from it."

"Yep." Ari felt the weight of his hand on hers and the tingle slowly making its way through her body. "Unless you do it 24/7 no one has a clue and they all ask you about respite, but you don't want respite, you just want a fucking life to call your own." She sucked in air and glanced away. "Don't want to talk about it. Do you want another drink, or lunch? I did the shopping yesterday, but I didn't buy extra for guests. Didn't know I'd be having any."

"That's okay. I can go and get something for all of us. The shops are just around the corner, right? I saw them on my way here." He watched her discreetly wipe her eyes. "Anything in particular you guys want?"

"We pretty much eat everything." Ari nodded and looked down to see her hand was still in his.

"Would you like to go and confer, and then I'll go and get it." Jay squeezed her hand and let go.

"Ah, yeah…" Taking another deep breath, Ari rushed inside.

"Fuck!" Jay sighed. He leaned his elbows on his knees, ran his hands over his face and through his hair, and then stared at the ground between his legs. *Poor Ari. Having her creative and artistic talent subdued by a shitty life. That's not fair.*

He knew the feelings of that suffocating subjugation well. In the last two years of his marriage, his ex-wife had always talked down his role at home, and his abilities as an actor and comedian, trying to make herself look bigger in the process. He was talked down to, walked over, and treated as a second-class citizen in her life. He finally left her and filed for divorce. It only grew worse as that divorce was played out in public, with her as the victor and him as the wimpy doormat. When news came to light that she'd already been having an affair with a much younger man, a singer musician, before he'd even filed for divorce, the tables turned rapidly in his favour. But it only made her vindictive streak worse. She dragged him into court repeatedly for more money, more properties, and sole custody. Judges denied her every time, and that also made her vindictiveness worse. But here was Ari, in desperate need of getting out from under that suffocating thumb, and he knew he had to help her.

"Hey, so it's pizza. There's a pizza shop around the corner. We can go and get some." Ari leaned against the wall and watched him come out of his reverie.

"Pizza it is." He slapped his hands on his thighs and stood up. "Let's go."

They were back in twenty minutes and walking through the back door into the laundry. Ari put her finger to her lips and looked at Jay.

He nodded and placed the pizzas on the kitchen sink. "I

need the bathroom," he whispered.

She nodded and walked through the laundry into the hallway and opened the toilet door, turned a corner and closed the hall door leading to the lounge room. "Bathroom's next to it," she whispered and hurried back to the kitchen.

Jay did what he needed and washed his hands, lingering in the doorway opposite. It looked like a junk room, with boxes and containers piled up to the ceiling on the left wall. There was a built-in wardrobe along the right wall, with a tall boy and two bookshelves next to it, and a table under the window with a laptop, printer and pen caddy. He took in every detail then hurried to the kitchen where Ari handed him a tray with a plate piled high with pizza and another can of drink.

She pointed for him to go outside, and they went and sat on the bench seat.

"I'm not going to meet your mom?" Jay asked between his first and second slice.

"Nope," she replied, and shoved a new slice into her mouth.

They ate in silence for another five minutes and then sat sipping their drinks in the relative silence of the neighbourhood.

"Will I get to meet your mom in the next two weeks?"

"Nope."

"Will we talk about her? It? This?"

"Nope." She turned her head towards him. "What do you mean *this*?"

Jay chose his words carefully. "This situation that you're in?"

She shook her head. "Nope. Already done that."

"Okay." He nodded thoughtfully. "So we'll be sitting out here every day?"

"It's nice enough." She shrugged a shoulder. "Why? You got plans?"

"Well…I'd like to take you out to lunch, the beach, whatever. Get you out of the house, maybe. Have some fun." He watched the reactions fly over her face. "What? Didn't think I'd want to?"

"Didn't think I'd ever meet a big Hollywood actor, let alone sit and eat pizza with him." A small smile crossed her lips. "It's just a bit weird."

"Yeah, I guess it would be." He slid towards her and placed his tray beside him. "I have a confession."

"Oh…" Ari raised an inquisitive brow.

"I devoured your websites last night. Well, not literally," he joked.

Her eyes narrowed. "All of them?"

"All of them." He settled back, leaning against the wall. "Everyone of your author sites, your blog, your publishing house, your social media."

"So you *are* a stalker!" Ari huffed and crossed her arms. "Great!"

"It's not like that. I just wanted to see what you were about, liked, watched, read."

"A stalker!" she said forcefully. "Because that's what stalkers do."

"Well, this stalker also got you over ten thousand new followers on your socials last night."

"What!" Her head swivelled toward him. "What?"

"Yep," he grinned. "That video we did resulted in over ten thousand of my followers following you. Congrats, now you have to entertain them."

"Wait…what! How did…? When did…? Holy baby Jesus!" Ari tried processing what that meant. "I have over ten thousand followers? On what? Insta, Face, Twit, Tok?"

"Mainly on Twitter, because that's where I am, mostly, but I checked your socials this morning and you've gained a few thousand on Insta as well. Don't know about Facebook or TikTok."

"Whoa! Damn! Now I have to engage more. Any suggestions?"

"You've been doing pretty well with your posting schedule, just keep it up."

"Wow…um. Thanks…" She gulped back the lump in her throat. "Maybe they'll buy my books."

"Speaking of." Jay crossed his legs and adjusted his sunglasses. "I bought all of yours last night and will be reading them in the next week or so."

"What!?" Again, her head swivelled towards him.

"Yeah, on Kindle. I plan on starting your kids' stories tonight. They'll probably take me two or three days, and then I'll start on your novels. I plan on reading them before I go back to the movie set. I have no idea when I'll see you after that. We'll have to Zoom or Facetime."

"You bought all of my books?" Incredulousness washed over her. "They're not exactly *your* type of books."

"Yeah, but my kids might like your stories, and maybe I could turn your novels into movies." He scratched a sore spot on the top of his head. It had flared up lately, although usually it only did so when he was stressed, so he didn't know why it was itching now. He was calm and happy sitting there and more unstressed than he had been in years.

"Really?" She dared not even consider that prospect. Dared not dream, dared not hope. "I mean, they're not that good. Some of them are shit, especially my early ones. But I definitely became better the more I wrote. I got used to it, like everything else. You get your own flow."

"Yeah, same with screenwriting. The three-act structure, hit your beats in that structure and you've got a winner." He'd had a smash TV show a decade earlier where he'd not only starred in the lead role, but co-written all of the episodes, directed half of them, and co-produced the entire series. It had afforded him a million dollar a week pay packet and multiple awards.

"Yeah, I guess it is," Ari agreed. "Want another drink? I have to get the washing in."

"I can help with that." Jay handed her his tray and followed her to the back door, where he waited until she came out with the laundry basket and then helped fold the laundry as she unpegged it.

"So what type of grass is this? Is it smokeable?" Jay joked, looking around at the back yard's greenery.

"Ha-ha." Ari rolled her eyes. "It's Couch."

Jay's brows rose at her pronunciation. "Cooch? As in cooch, cooch? You sure about that? You know what that means, right?"

"What what means? That's how we pronounce it here in Aus, even though it's spelled as couch."

"Oh, 'cause that's how we say it. Couch grass. But *cooch* means a woman's downstairs department. Or as you Aussies would say, the map of Tasmania."

Laughter gurgled in Ari's throat, but she choked on an air bubble instead. "Oh for fuck's sake! Seriously?"

"Yeah." Jay nodded, his cheeky grin sliding across his lips. "Weird how different countries have different spellings or pronunciations of words, huh."

"Well, I suppose it's a lot like root and route," Ari replied. "For Route 66 in America, I say it as rout, which rhymes with out. So it would be Route 66. But you guys also say *I'm rooting for you* when it comes to your favourite sporting teams. But we don't say root here, we use *barrack for*, or *go for*, instead."

"Why shouldn't I say root?" Jay asked.

"Because it means sex, fuck, shag, hence the saying *root like rabbits*."

"Oh." His eyes widened and his brows rose again. "Really?"

"Yeah, so you really need to decide which pronunciation you want to use."

"Why's that?"

"Well, do you want to rout the couch or root the cooch?"

Jay doubled over, laughter rumbling from deep in his gut. "Oh, my God, that's hilarious. I'm going to have to use that, so I'm definitely stealing it."

"Just be sure to credit it to me." Ari grinned.

They continued chatting about mundane things until the chores were finished and it was time to leave. Walking towards the driveway, Jay shoved his hands into his jeans' pockets. "Well, I have to leave you. I have a feeling you might need to explain some things. You need me to get dinner before I go?"

"No, thank you. There's leftover pizza and you've done way too much as is." Ari's hand lightly touched his arm. "Thank you. This has been incredibly interesting."

A soft grin slid across his lips. "It definitely has, sans-serif font."

She groaned and threw back her head. "That's *not* funny, *don't call me that*. It just comes off as rude and insulting."

The grin slid away. "Well, I don't mean to be rude to you, Arial Travers, or insult you. I do apologise." Jay placed his right hand over his heart. "I sincerely apologise. Now that I know about your life, that does seem rude, doesn't it. I'm sorry."

She gazed into his eyes and gulped back the lump in her throat. Damn he was hot. Why did he have to be so damn nice, too? "Um…" she managed. "Thank you for your apology. I accept it. Just don't say it again; it's not even funny."

"I won't, I promise. Well, if you're all set here. I'll be off."

"We are. Thank you." She walked him to his car and followed as he backed out of her driveway, waving in return as he did before driving away. She locked the gates and went inside to make as many notes as possible about their conversations for future novels.

And to take a cold shower.

Chapter 2

Jay dropped by on both Saturday and Sunday, with conversations kept to everything but their personal lives. On Monday, Ari was busy with appointments and Jay with interviews via Zoom, but he managed to take her out to lunch on Tuesday.

"This is nice." He looked around at the restaurant and its homey décor. "Simple, easy, casual."

"Yeah, it pretty much is." Ari smiled at the waitress and took the menu offered. "So… What are we eating?" She knew the restaurant had mainly pizza and pasta meals; they were known for them, but since they'd had pizza last week, she wanted something different.

"Whatever you want, my treat." He glanced over the top of his menu at her to take in the colourful earrings framing her face. The bright multi-toned blues highlighted the blue in her green eyes. Her full lips curled into a soft smile. He also noted the arthritis in her hands and psoriasis in her nails, recalling the medical and health issues she'd told him about over the weekend, and he wondered how she managed to handwrite hundreds of thousands of words in her novels and stories. Her curvy figure wasn't a disappointment, nor was her love of carbs or food in general. He'd often gone on binges of loving carbs, but he had regretted it. Unfortunately other vices had got in the way in recent years.

"Guess what? I've finished reading all of your children's stories. I'm not going to bother with your non-fiction books because jewellery, styling, and song lyrics don't interest me, but I'll start on your novels next."

She looked up in surprise. "What? Did you just—"

"Yeah. I've devoured forty-nine stories in the last three nights." He laid the menu down and grinned. "I told you I'd bought them, and I was going to read them."

"Ah…" She choked. "Yeah, but I didn't think you'd get through them so fast."

"They're only short stories, some shorter than the others. And I'm a fast reader from years of working as an actor. You gotta get stuff read and learned in quick time."

Her mouth gaped and she blinked a few times. "Wow. Ah…okay. What did you think?"

"They're good," Jay said, his enthusiasm coming through in a rush. "You have a talent for writing kids' stories that's for sure, and they're all safely tucked away on my Kindle in case I get the opportunity to read them to my kids when I have them."

"Oh…" She nodded. "That's nice. How old are your kids again?"

"Eight and ten."

"Ah, there's a couple that's too old for them," Ari replied. "You might have noticed the language. Some are for twelve plus."

"I did. And they will be kept aside for my nieces and nephews. But you'd be surprised at how much kids know

Anything for You

these days. They're like adults in small bodies."

Ari chuckled. "Yeah, I guess some are."

"You'll find out when you have your own." Jay smiled and turned to the waitress who took his order.

Ari ordered and handed over her menu, turning to gaze out the window at the passing traffic as her mood slipped.

"You okay?" Jay asked and straightened the placemat in front of him, then the salt and pepper shakers, then the serviette stand. He wasn't OCD, just liked everything in its place, in every aspect of his life, and tried to make sure that happened. Except he never seemed to be able to. "Did I say something wrong?"

"I doubt I'll be having children, so saying *you'll find out when you have your own* to a woman my age is just a tad insulting and ignorant." She took a sip of her drink and held the frosty glass to each burning cheek before putting it down.

Jay switched to caring mode. "Oh…Ari… I'm so sorry. It didn't occur to me. Can you not have children? How old are you? I thought you were only mid to late thirties."

Ari's brows rose. "Mid to late thirties? Wow. Either you're incredibly blind, or incredibly kind. But no, I'm late forties, so not having children any time soon."

Jay's hand paused at his mouth, the glass of fizzy cola popping bubbles onto his top lip and into the three-month-old beard that covered it. He considered his next words carefully, drank a mouthful, and set the glass down. "I'm so sorry, Ari. I didn't know you were older than me. I didn't think that it wouldn't be happening for you one day."

"Yeah, well. You know my situation," she answered coolly. "So…definitely won't be happening."

"Could you adopt?" he asked softly, seeing the pain on

her face.

"And what?" she scoffed. "How am I supposed to take care of a parent *and* a child by myself?"

The waitress brought the food and Ari inwardly sighed and thanked God that the conversation was over. They ate in relative silence; except for the occasional *oh this is good* every few minutes.

Jay knew he had made her uncomfortable. She kept her eyes down, didn't look up except for out the window every now and then, and the conversation was dead. He waited until they had finished and were having a breather before dessert. "I didn't mean to upset you. I'm sorry."

"It's not that you upset me…" She finished off her drink and finally looked at him. "It's the topic, the subject. I hate talking about it because it depresses me."

He gave a slight nod. "I understand. It can't be easy not getting the life you want, but always dreaming about it, hoping for it."

"No, it isn't." She adjusted herself and sighed. "Can't be easy for you, in your position either."

Jay's eyes narrowed and he kept his voice neutral. "*My* position."

She watched him. "Being so happily in love, adoring each other, speaking highly of each other at every turn. *Looking* so happy in love when you were together, and you had the perfect life. A wife, two kids, busy careers, money, fame. Then it all fell apart and went to shit. That must have hurt."

He kept his breath even, despite his racing heart, and inhaled and exhaled slowly, hating the witch of an ex-wife who made his blood boil. Talking about her made him want to ram whatever object he had at his disposal into the eyeball

Anything for You

of the person asking about it. But Ari was different. There would be no ramming of objects. He kept his breathing even. "It was at the time. But things change. They always do. Relationships change like everything else. Not every couple gets to be happy for the rest of their days."

"No." She bit her lip. "But you two looked like you had the real deal. I'd see videos or TV shows and see the way you looked at each other adoringly and feel envious."

"Envious!" His left brow rose and a half-amused smirk lifted the left side of his lips. "Believe me, there was *nothing* to be envious of, especially in the last two years of the marriage. It was as fake as hell, and I couldn't wait to be out of it which is why I filed for divorce."

Ari's eyes widened in surprise. "*You* filed for divorce?"

"Heard it was the other way around?" Jay crossed his arms and leaned them on the table. "Let me tell you about that supposedly happy marriage you think I was in the middle of—"

"Here's your dessert." The waitress set the tray on the table and put two plates of chocolate mousse cake, and two fresh glasses of drink, in front of them. "Enjoy."

"Thank you." Jay smiled up at her then turned his attention back to Ari. "My ex-wife is the biggest bitch I've ever known. Of course she didn't start out that way. Yeah, sure, it was all lovey-dovey, madly in love, wild fucking every day when it started." Ari blushed and he waved a dismissive hand at his memories. "But once we were married and she popped out the kids, she felt as if her life and career was fading away while mine was still running along. But once our youngest was two, she couldn't wait to get back to work. So she hired the nanny and away she went, taking every role thrown at her.

And some of them were damn good, too," he said, almost enviously. "She earned a couple of awards and kept on working while my career started nosediving, which is why I'm a washed-up hack."

He stabbed his fork into the cake and ripped a chunk off, holding it in front of his face as if inspecting it. "And she reminded me of it every single god damn fucking day. That I was a washed-up, has-been hack, and that she was now the star of the family and the relationship, and I'd better learn my position, which was way back in line, even behind the damn dog, eating her dirt. I ended up hating her so much I left and filed for divorce."

He slammed the fork down into the cake, smashing the first piece into the second. "As you might know, she blamed me, and I became the bad guy. Until…" He looked Ari full in the eye. "My private eye dug up the information about her boy-child toy boy and her cheating before I'd left. And suddenly, voila," he snapped his fingers, "the tables had turned, and I was no longer the bad guy. *She* was." Jay leaned back and sighed from his gut. "But only in the opinion polls, because in court, I was still the bad guy every time she dragged me back for more money, more belongings, more possessions, or over the kids. I was *always* the bad guy, and still am."

The silence between them lasted a few moments, and the dessert went uneaten.

"I'm sorry," Ari finally murmured. "I didn't know."

"Why would you?" Jay stared at her under hooded eyes. "She made me out to be the bastard and the press ate it up until she was outed."

With a shake of her head in sorrow, Ari went on. "It's sad. That women, or men, can do that to the person they claim to love. It always surprises me how people can go from saying I love you, I want to spend my life with you, have children with you, grow old with you, and then one week, one month, one year later be gone and seeing someone else they're saying the same things to. Your actions make a liar out of you. Make lies out of your words. It's sad and it sucks and I'm sorry."

"It is," Jay agreed and took a sip of drink. "Promise me something, Ari."

Puzzled, she cast her sad eyes his way. "What?"

"Promise me you'll never do that to the man you love. And promise me that you'll never let a man do that to you."

Ari exhaled and let her eyes drift shut. "I promise."

*****

When Jay turned up at Ari's on Friday morning, he was all set to help with the housework and told her what he thought of her novels while he did it.

"Wait…you've read all of them? The stand-alones?" She stared at him in shock for a few seconds then shoved the laundry basket at him. "But that's like, four hundred and eleven something thousand words."

"Is it?" Jay held the basket while Ari pulled out the first towel to hang. "It's taken me three nights, so a novel a night, and because we didn't see each other yesterday, I read the shortest one during the day, and then the longest last night."

"Jesus!" Ari hung another towel over the line. "Okay, tell me. I already know they're pretty crap. They were the first four novels I ever wrote."

"Actually, the first *was* crap. Extensive fucking in graphic blow by blow detail, which, in my opinion, was unnecessary.

But the next three weren't too bad. The rom-com's kinda funny, the romantic drama's fairly good, but that reverse harem one was…" He shook his head and let out a rush of air. "Whoo, wish a woman would do that to me."

Laughter bubbled out of Ari. "Yeah, right."

"No, I'm serious." Jay shifted positions as his left arm was starting to ache. "I wouldn't mind some female billionaire paying me a hundred grand for a month on her island as a sex slave. Sun around by the pool all day, fuck all night. I'm still in pretty good shape for being on the wrong side of forty-five and I've never had any complaints from anyone other than my bitch of an ex-wife towards the end."

Ari finished pegging the last towel and checked him over from head to toe. "You are pretty hot still. Certainly not Henry Cavill beautiful, but middle of the road average looking who's either going to attract women or not. I think you're pretty hot." The words slipped out before she could stop them, and red-faced, she grabbed the basket and dashed inside for the next load.

"Pretty hot, huh," Jay said through the screen door as he leaned against the door jamb. "*You* think I'm pretty hot? That's good to know, Ari, because I think I'm pretty hot too." He heard her snort and the screen door opened, her face hovering beside his.

"You've got tickets on yourself. Just the other day you were calling yourself a washed-up has-been and now you're talking about being hot and pulling chicks. How many have you had if your ex was the only one who ever said you weren't good?"

Jay thought about all of his exes and counted on his fingers. "I've dated, and that's *dated*, about twenty women, and had two long-term relationships. Only one ever complained about my sexual prowess and yet I managed to knock her up twice, so I couldn't have been that bad."

"Did you have sex with all twenty that you dated?" Ari asked, curious.

"Yeah." He nodded. "All twenty of them. They were women I went on multiple dates with, and they probably lasted a few months each. So yeah, I fucked all of them."

"And *none* of them, besides your ex, complained about your prowess?" Ari questioned.

"Nope." Jay shook his head. "*None* of them."

"Bullshit artist." She shoved the basket at him and walked over to the line. "So, obviously it wasn't your prowess that made them leave."

"Nope. I'm the one who moved on in all dating relationships, and in the long-terms, the first one left me, and I left the second. Yours, I presume." Jay saw her hold up a slinky nightie and wiggled his brows, making her blush.

She choked. "You presume," she replied and quickly grabbed a dress. "So, you're a year younger than me, putting you in the late forties category. What now? Do you see yourself getting married again? Having more kids?"

Tilting his head back, he looked up at the semi-cloudy blue sky and sighed. "No. Yes. I don't know. It's hard, getting over someone that hard, that close, that intimate. We were together for ten years as a unit. We were almost one, we moved so well together. And when you're that entwined and enmeshed with another person, it's hard to be completely done with them. Don't get me wrong," he righted his head and looked at her, "I'm definitely not in love with her, haven't been for years. I have no love for her whatsoever, but I definitely have other emotions, like hatred, anger, resentment."

"I know the feeling," Ari muttered, and hung the last piece of clothing on the line.

"Yeah…" Jay's brows furrowed. "Yeah. And as much as I love my kids, I sense that she's turning them against me more and more. But even *though* I love them, I'm actually glad when I don't see them. I'm much happier because all I hear from them is *Mommy says you're this,* and *Mommy says you're that. I hate you, you won't let me have this, I'm telling Mommy.* Jesus!" he growled and kicked at the concrete path. "I'm so sick and tired of her and what she's doing, and I'm so much happier when she and the kids aren't around."

Ari stood on the back concrete step, watching the angry outburst. Sadness washed over her. She knew those emotions, for another reason, and so identified with what he was dealing with and going through, albeit, on another level. "I'm sorry. It sucks when a parent turns the kids against the other because they have a vendetta against them. Kids should never be used like that."

"I absolutely agree." He thrust his finger at her. "But that bitch doesn't care. She's out to ruin my life and she doesn't care." He waved his arms in angry motions, pointing and thrusting. "But this is what I've put up with for the last few years, and nothing I do seems to stop her. Hell, she even ran off the woman I dated after I left her."

"What about the person she was seeing when you left her?" Ari didn't want to be nosy, but she figured why not since they were talking about it.

"Oh, he loves the kids, and they love him. Didn't you see the happy snaps on social media of their holiday to Italy?"

"Ah…" she muttered. "Yeah, it made the magazines here."

"Yeah." He placed his hands on his hips and his head

Anything for You

dropped. "They made the tabloids everywhere. Didn't they look just *so* happy," he spat and ran a hand through his hair, tousling it into odd angles.

"I'm sorry." Ari shook her head. "I shouldn't keep bringing her up. It clearly still upsets you, so we can stop talking about her. It'll probably make you a lot happier."

He stared at her for a few moments, at her sad green eyes, full lips, and fuller figure, and felt better. "I am happier. I'm happier than I've been in a while. But you know what would make me *really* happy?" He stepped over to stand in front of her. With her on the step, it made them eye to eye.

"What?" Her breath caught in her throat as his masculine scent wafted over her. All she wanted to do was kiss him and breathe him in. Her lips puckered.

"Is if you let me read that novel of yours."

"My what?" She frowned in confusion. "My novel? Which one? You said you'd bought them all, so you'll be reading them anyway." Staring into his eyes, she found herself swaying slightly, captivated by his aura that was slowly sucking her in every time she saw him. Just a little more each day.

"No, you're right," he hastened to say. "I did buy your novels. The ones you've published. But I want to read the ones you've written this year. You were talking about them in the group. The one you want to publish this year sounds incredibly interesting. I was hoping you'd let me read it." Jay put on his best seductive smile and laid a gentle hand on her arm. "The psychological thriller. You sounded incredibly excited about it. You want to release it next. I was hoping to get an early read." He followed his smile with his puppy dog expression that he knew sucked women in. "What do you say? Can I read it?"

Shocked, Ari couldn't even string a sentence together. "Ah…why would…I…wow…" She grasped her hands to her chest. "Really? I mean, you've already read the others." His soft puppy eyes were sucking her right in and all she wanted to do was say yes, and not just to him reading her book. Catching herself, she breathed deeply and tried to get a grip on her emotions. "I guess. I mean, I could use you as a proof reader, or beta reader, or something. I've finished the edits, and just have to send it off to my editor. But if you can give me some pointers and tips, it might make the story even better."

"Great," Jay enthused. "Would you be able to print it out today so I can read it tonight? That's if you need to print it out; you may already have a hard copy."

"Ah, no, I'd have to print it out. It's about three hundred pages and I'll need to keep adding paper, so I'll have to watch it and it'll take a while," she rambled.

"That's okay," Jay placated. "I have no problem waiting. Are we done with the washing?" His phone beeped and he pulled it out of his jeans pocket. "Oh, it's my director. He wants a Zoom meeting in twenty minutes." He glanced up in alarm. "Ah, I don't have my laptop. I'd have to go back to the hotel."

"Got Zoom on your phone?" Ari asked. "Just take it in the car or sit around the side."

He almost stared straight through her. "Ah, yeah. I do. Great idea. And you can print out your book while I'm taking it."

"Yeah, I guess I could." She smiled. "But you still have time to help with one more load."

They finished the laundry and while Jay went to the car to set up for the meeting, Ari set up her laptop and printer.

Anything for You

While it was booting up, she placed a thick stack of paper into it, and two minutes later it was printing her future novel last page first. Thirty minutes later she snapped a bull clip onto the bundle of three hundred pages and shut down her electricals. She found a spare Amazon box to store it in, taped it shut, and went to find Jay. He was still in the car with his meeting, so she sat in the shade at the back of the house and knocked back an ice-cold Pepsi Max. Ten minutes later, she heard the car door, and wandered around to the driveway. "How'd it go?"

He made his way over and they sat on the bench. "Good. They have most of the things fixed, so they're going to refilm Russell's scenes because they didn't come out well, and that means I'm still not needed until next week." He looked around her. "Printed it out yet?"

"I did, and it's in a box for easy storage so it doesn't get ripped. The pages are bound with a bull clip, and I've used up as much blank space as possible to keep the page count down. So, if you have any notes, asterisk or bracket the section and make notes on the back of the page."

"Sounds great." Jay grinned. "I can't wait."

Hours later, before he left, Ari handed him the box.

"You're giving me something from Amazon?" Jay looked suspiciously at the box, turning it around in his hands.

"No." Ari scowled. "I told you the book's just in there for protection."

"Oh, cool." Jay's fingers tried to lift the flap. "Did you tape it down?"

"Yep." She grinned. "Didn't want you peeking until you get back to your hotel."

"Cheeky!" Jay gave her a quick kiss on the cheek. "I'll get

this read and see you tomorrow." He climbed into his car and placed the box on the passenger seat. "I can't wait," he sang, and backed out of the drive, illuminating a blushing Ari in his headlights.

The kiss had taken her completely by surprise, and she was still holding her hand to her cheek as he drove off. "What the hell…?" murmured out from between her lips. She hadn't been expecting it and was shocked by it. If only his lips had landed two inches to the right.

*****

"Oh, my God, Ari." Jay stood in her driveway the next morning, clutching the manuscript to his chest. An expression of shock and awe was on his face and his mouth gaped open.

"What? You didn't like it? It sucks, right?" Her spirits fell, having hoped that she was finally on the path to being an author who wrote as well as those with BAs in English and Creative Writing, compared to her year 10 English skills. "It sucks, doesn't it?" Her mood slipped farther.

"No," Jay gasped. "Not at all. It's fucking brilliant." He thrust both hands forward, holding the manuscript like a prized award. "Sure, there are a few sections that need tightening up, and an editor can help with that. But the twists and turns and red herrings kept me guessing. I…" His breath became ragged. "I love it. I want it," he managed. "I… remember a few days ago I said that the movie I'm working on was probably my redemption? Well, I think meeting you and reading this book is too."

Ari's jaw slowly dropped, and her eyes widened in disbelief. "What?"

He became serious. "I want this book, Ari. I want to turn it into a movie and a best-selling novel, and I'll star in it, and it'll be my big comeback piece and I'll make you famous."

"What?" Ari barely believed what she was hearing and in all seriousness, didn't believe it at all. A big time Hollywood actor wanted her book? No way was that happening. "Oh, I need to sit down." She turned and tripped over her own feet. He grabbed her from behind before she could smash into the wall and helped her to the bench seat.

"Here. Sit and take a break. I've clearly surprised you." He sat beside her and laid the bound stack of papers on his lap. "But I'm serious, Ari. This book is incredible."

Finally getting her breathing and brain under control, she turned to him. "You really can't be serious? *You* want *my* book?"

"Absolutely." Jay nodded enthusiastically. "It's one of the best psych thrillers I've ever read. You laid it out well, there are plenty of red herrings and twists and turns. I *did not* see that last bit coming. Although…" He looked down at the pages. "I did notice that it kinda paralleled my life a little bit. The actor with the ex-wife and kids, plus the new love interest. I kinda felt for him, for the love interest, for them. Ari…" He looked at her squarely. "Did I…*inspire* any of this? I mean," he held the pages up, "the male lead even kinda resembles me."

"Ah…" Ari glanced away, guilt bubbling to the surface. "*Well*…it could be *any* guy who looks like you or who has an ex-wife and kids. Millions of men do. It's just a trope."

"Ah-huh! Ari… Was I the inspiration for this character?"

She inhaled and murmured on the exhale. "Maybe…"

Jay snorted with laughter. "Oh, that's hilarious. Was it all me or did one of my movies or TV roles inspire this?"

Ari grinned and cast a quick glance at him. "That weird thing where you blew up fireworks in a bar and were a bit of a psycho." She pulled a face. "A drunk psycho."

"Well, I've played a couple of those," Jay said.

"Yeah, true," Ari agreed. "But you play *really* hot psychos, and I was inspired after watching you."

"Good to know I inspire something in women," Jay drawled and leaned back against the wall. "I play hot psychos, huh? Maybe I'd better play some more." He waved the manuscript in the air between them before placing it on the bench. "But what I really want to play is the psycho in this novel. I'll say it again, Ari. It's a hell of a book and I want it. I want to take it to New York and Hollywood and get it made into a blockbuster movie. I can help you get a publishing deal, or help you get it published through your own imprint. I've got followers, friends, and people in the business who still give a shit about me, so I can get it done and make you famous." He nodded as each idea came to him. "And I get my big comeback. Maybe you're on to something. Maybe I should take on more serious roles that have chops, you know. What I mean," he clenched his hands to emphasise his words, "is meat on the bones of the characters. So I can push myself more as an actor. To emote and bring emotions to the face of my performances." He relaxed back into his seat. "Maybe playing psychos in gritty movies is the way to go."

"But won't that typecast you?" Ari asked, interested in the inner workings of an actor's mind. "Or doesn't that worry you?"

"Ah…" Jay moved his head back and forth as he weighed up his thoughts. "It does, and it doesn't. I think I've been lucky enough to show off my comedic skills and my serious side.

And I've done my share of both, as a lot of actors do. And yeah, some have been typecast, especially if they've started young and only played the same roles. But I've done a lot of genres, so you can't really stick me in the corner and say, oh he's just a comedian, or; he's just a serious actor. I'm both, and I've had massive success at it. Massive success at both genres. Take this movie I'm filming with Russell." Jay waved his hand around. "It's not a comedy, but there are funny parts. It's a bit of a drama, so has dramatic parts. It's set back in the 1950s, so a bit of a period piece. I get to play a wide scope in it."

"Sounds interesting," Ari told him. "I guess it will be a couple of years before it's released."

Yeah." Jay nodded and crossed his legs. "But that's the way it goes in movies. There are many layers of people making decisions from start to finish. I even had a movie once, where the release date was pushed further and further back until it wasn't released at all. Damn pity that was." He adjusted his sunglasses and ran a hand over his mouth and beard. "'Cause it was a damn good movie and probably one of the best performances of my acting lifetime and no one's ever gonna see it."

"That sucks," Ari sympathised. "It's like the publishing industry. I've heard so many horror stories about traditional publishers, and some of them are about the houses not even releasing author's books. That's why I decided I wasn't letting anyone else control me or my books, so I published them myself."

"And what's the paygrade like?" Jay had never written a book, but figured it was a lot like writing screenplays for movies and TV shows, which he'd done. And even though a publisher had paid him for his biography, he hadn't written it. An in-house ghost writer had done that after interviewing him extensively. That was the way of the celebrity memoirs that publishing houses put out.

"I make enough to buy books on writing and cover small expenses." Ari shrugged. "My own fault, really. I suck at advertising myself. I'm so bogged down dealing with the books I have, getting different formats done and released, paying business expenses, etc., that I don't have the energy or the money to put into advertising. Or the time to learn about it."

"So you make a few sales a month," Jay murmured. "Do you know if that's gone up in the last week? I've done a few videos recommending your stories and books. Now that you have over ten thousand followers, it should have changed things."

"Haven't looked," Ari replied. "But if sales are coming in, great. If not," she shrugged, "I don't worry."

"Why not? Isn't that the point of making money? Worrying about sales?" Jay asked. "Ari, you and I really need to have a chat about publicity and marketing. And we can do that after you decide to let me make you and your book famous."

She snorted with laughter. "And how do you plan on doing that?"

"Well, I guess by helping you out with everything. I have friends in New York that are editors and used to work for the fancy publishers but went out on their own. They could help you whip it into shape. I know designers who could do your covers and book trailer. We could print out a thousand copies and send them to my friends in the industry and get them talking about it on social media. Get copies to producers and book reviewers."

"And how much is all of that going to cost me?" Ari questioned. "I'm not made of money. I already have an editor, so I just need to find a cover designer. My budget will only allow around five hundred per month, and I know it's expensive to print copies off, let alone a thousand or more."

"Well, that's where I come in," Jay said. "I want this book so badly I'll foot the bill."

"What!" Ari's expression crumpled as she stared at him. "No, no, I can't ask that of you. And I don't expect you to do it. This is my book, my business. I need to pay for it."

"Ari, I want to help you here." Jay laid his hand over hers. "This book needs to be published. It needs to be out there, and I can help you with that. Let me pay for it. Let me help you."

"No." Ari shook her head in defiance. "Everything I've done I've had to do for myself. Pay for myself. Make happen myself. No one else has done anything unless I've paid for their services. It's all been me and me alone. I don't expect anyone else to pay for it or to help me out. It doesn't feel right. I've done everything independently and that won't change now."

"You won't even let *me* help you?" Jay queried. "Is your pride getting in the way of being helped?"

"What! No!" A scowl crossed Ari's face. "I've had to do everything myself for so long. I feel as though I couldn't accept anyone's help *or* offer of help. It feels weird."

"How about for once you let it happen?" Jay leaned towards her and saw the blush creep over her cheeks. He gently stroked her arm. "Ari, I could make you, and this book, famous. I could help you get on that path to fame and fortune as an author. And if the rest of the books you've written lately are like this one, then you have absolute hits on your hands.

Millions in sales, best sellers, movies made out of them. Listen to me, Ari," he took her hand in his and gave her his puppy dog expression, "you are on the cusp of stardom, Ari. Let me help you get this book out there and help publicise it. I'll get it into the right hands, and you'll be on your way."

The words floated through Ari's ears and into her mind, but her gaze was focused on Jay's eyes and lips, and she knew full well he was seducing her into it. *Oh, what I wouldn't give for those lips*, floated along through her mind. *I'd get to kiss Jay Daniels, hot psycho movie star.*

"Ari..." her name whispered from between his lips, so perfectly encased by the brown hair of his full beard, tinged just so with grey. It framed his smile and dimples, and she found herself falling...drowning...

"Ari, let me help you and get everything you need," he whispered.

Her stubborn streak came speeding back to the fore, and her long-held independence came out. "No." Thrusting herself upwards, she turned and stormed away. "I think its lunchtime," wafted on the breeze behind her.

Jay sighed, irritated but somewhat amused. Ari was going to be one hell of a challenge.

*****

"Ari," Jay said the next morning. "I'll keep harassing you until you say yes."

"And I'll keep saying no until you're blue in the face from harassing," she replied. "Seriously, how many times do I have to tell you I'm not comfortable with you paying for what you're offering to help with? I can't accept that level of help.

It's weird and wrong and makes me feel icky. I'm not a user, Jay. I don't use people. I never have. It's the wrong thing to do even though times have changed and apparently that's all younger generations do and get by on. Using people."

"Yeah, these days it's who you know, not what you know," Jay said. "I agree with you on that. And my ex seems to be one of them." He sighed and unconsciously rubbed his head. They were sitting outside again. The only times he was allowed in the house was to get food or use the toilet, and even then, Ari had told him to take a leak in the garden instead. "Look, Ari, I don't want to come off as this control freak pushing you into something you don't want to do. But I believe in this book and believe in you, and I think with my help I could make it sell millions, *make* millions to help you get out of here. It won't cost much, my friends will do it for a lower wage rate, and that just leaves the copies to be paid for. Let me do this for you." He grasped both of her hands. "Let me do this for you when *no one* else has done *anything* for you. Let me in and let me be the first."

Her mouth opened, ready for the word no to come out, but nothing came out. She heard her muse behind her, telling her *don't say no, just say you'll think about it, or you'll regret it*. Ari breathed out. "Ah…fuck! I'll think about it." That surprised her. Normally she ignored her muse outside of writing.

Jay sat back; surprised he'd actually got one step closer. "Good."

"I said I'll *think* about it," Ari repeated, and pulled her hands from his. "How much longer are you here?"

"Ah, it's Sunday today, I think I have to leave…" Frowning, he pulled his phone out and checked. "I leave Thursday morning, so I can't make it to the writers' group. But that's okay." He shoved his phone back into his pocket. "I've been there once and found what I was after. So…" He shrugged a nonchalant shoulder and puckered his lips. "I just need to get you to say yes."

Curious, she asked, "And what were you after? What did you find there?"

A slow, sexy grin slid across his lips, and he eyed her up and down. "Everything," was all he said.

A tiny little something went off in Ari's mind. She didn't know if it was worry, an alarm, or a shot of adrenaline. Hell, it could have been purely sexual considering Jay was puckering his lips at her and telling her he was going to get her to say yes to him. But regardless of what that niggling little feeling was, she just knew she'd say yes to him anyway.

*****

On Monday morning, he was at it again. "I'm only here for three more days, Ari," he begged and slid off the bench seat to kneel in front of her. Grasping her hands, he added, "Let me do this for you."

Ari gazed into his eyes. He seemed sincere, he really did, and regardless of his current rough exterior, and, she suspected, low self-esteem, she found him charmingly sexy and a little boyish. A sigh left her. "Look, Jay. I've been thinking about this. I really have, oh, get back up on the seat, don't kneel on the ground." She helped him up and watched him brush off his pants legs. His longer than usual hair, meant for the current role, ruffled around his neck and jawline. It actually made him look sexier than usual. "I've been thinking, and I'll

Anything for You

repeat what I said the last few days. I'm *not* a user; I don't feel comfortable with using people to get what I want. It's cheap, tacky, and quite frankly, says you have no integrity or self-respect if you go through life using people."

"Can't disagree with you there," Jay said, resting an elbow on his leg and his chin in his hand.

"So, I don't want to use you just to get my book out there or to get free publicity. Although you've already done that after reading my books, so yeah," she gave him a half-hearted smile, "I've noticed quite a few book sales at Amazon, and I have a few more followers on social media and you did that off your own bat. And it's sweet and kind and generous of you. I can't expect you, or ask you, to pay for a cover designer, editor, or a print run without becoming a user or feeling like one."

"Ari—" Jay started.

"No, let me finish." She dismissed his interruption with a wave of her hand. "While I refuse to accept that offer as you've presented it, and I refuse to be a user, I think I've come up with an alternative solution."

"Ari… What?" Jay frowned. "Did I hear right? Wait… you're going to accept my offer?"

She sighed at his antics. "If you'd shut up long enough you'd hear what I've come up with."

"Okay, okay." He ran both hands through his hair, pushing it back and behind his ears. "My eyes are open; my ears are more open. Tell me."

Chuckling, Ari went on. "I came up with a plan. A *business* plan."

"Oh…" Jay's eyes widened, and his lips turned into an o. "Okay. I'm intrigued. Go on."

"Right." Ari took a deep breath and wiped her sweaty palms on the legs of her shorts. "I will accept your offer of payment for a designer, editor, and printed copies. But *only* if it's considered an investment which will be paid back double when sales reach a hundred thousand." She paused. "*If* sales reach a hundred thousand and I'm hoping they will."

"Okay." Jay nodded and gazed at his surroundings while thoughts ran a million miles an hour through his head. "Okay. This is good, this is good. Me paying for everything will be an investment in you and your creation. Good. Great. That's really good thinking, and that investment will be paid back upon sales of a hundred thousand." His fingers drummed against his open lips as he thought some more. He was desperate for the book to be a hit so it could be made into an even bigger hit movie. "Okay. But I suggest an amendment." His eyes found hers. "That you pay me back when your sales hit one million."

Her eyes widened. "Oh, I don't think I'll sell a million."

"Bullshit!" Jay thrust to his feet and paced back and forth in front of her, hands gesticulating in time with his words. "When I come up with a plan, and believe me, I will come up with a plan, it will be the best plan out there. I have millions of followers, thousands of friends and colleagues. I'll come up with a plan to get everyone on board and by the time I'm done with this book, it *will* sell millions, Ari, because I will *make* this happen for you. I'll make this happen for *us*. Come here."

Ari was yanked to her feet. "Whoa! Hold up there." But the feel of Jay's hands on her, and her hands on his muscular chest, sent pulses through her body, so she didn't mind so much.

"So the deal is, I'll invest money in you and your book by

covering the costs of cover designer, editor, and copies. I'll also pay to ship those books to everyone I know that will be on the list." He nodded as his plan became clearer in his mind. "And we need to make that list. Right, okay. And upon selling your one millionth book you'll pay me back double. Okay." He laughed, psyched that he was getting what he wanted. "I'll make you and your book famous and then make me and the movie famous, oh…" He bent until his face was level with Ari's. "What about you personally?"

She frowned and gave a short breathy huff. "What *about* me personally?"

"You're going to be famous, Ari. Is there anything you'd like to do for yourself before you're on TV and in interviews? You mentioned your health issues the other day. Would you like to get those fixed before the book comes out? Do yourself up physically?"

"Oh…" Her mouth worked up and down. "Well, you've sprung that one on me. I certainly wasn't thinking about stuff like that."

"If I'm going to invest in you, Ari, then let's go the whole hog." Jay went back to pacing. "Anything you need done, or fixed, to make you look good, feel good, and think good. Anything to fix your low self-esteem and insecurities about your—"

"Excuse me!" Ari's hands slammed onto her hips and her brows rose. "You wanna try that line again? But this time to my face and not while you're pacing. How dare you insult me after raving about everything else."

"Ari, sweetie—"

"*Don't call me sweetie*, it's patronising," she spat.

Jay gently laid his hands on her upper arms, but she took

a step back. "I'm sorry. I'm just going by what you've told me about your health issues and all of the things you'd like to fix about yourself if you had the money. Like from book sales or winning the lottery."

She relaxed. A little. "That is true; I would get those things done if I had the money. But it doesn't mean I have low self-esteem!"

"No." Jay shook his head, his tone serious. "But you did tell me your looks made you insecure."

"I said I'm insecure *about* my looks," she said tersely. "Doesn't give you the right to twist my words and claim I have insecurities about everything. I don't!"

"I'm not, but I'm sorry if my words came out that way. My point is," Jay licked his lips and lowered his voice, "my point is, I'm willing to invest in your book, your company, your business. Why can't I invest in you while I'm at it and help you fix all of the problems you wish you could fix yourself? So by the time the book comes out and it's a hit, you'll be physically well and ready to take on the world, looking the best you've ever looked. I'm investing in *you*, Ari. The *whole* package deal. Deal?"

She'd smarted at his tone of voice with the insults, and even though the smooth baritone of his speaking voice titillated her to her core, she wondered if there were more smart-arse comments to come. *Or maybe I'm just overthinking and over reaching*, she thought. *He is the first person to offer me help and I am the one suggesting the business deal instead. So why do I now have this nagging feeling that I've made the wrong choice?*

The words popped out of her mouth before she could think further. "Deal!"

Chapter 3

By the time Jay left to go back to the movie set, they had a plan in place. But it wasn't something Ari wanted to talk about in the writers' group when it came around Thursday night. She knew Jay hadn't mentioned the other members on his socials, even though he'd mentioned the name of the group, and she didn't think bringing up how he was helping her was appropriate, so she kept quiet most of the night, until she was asked about him before they wrapped up.

"Ari…" Fiona zeroed in on her. "That hot piece of arse actor wasn't here tonight. Guess he didn't want to face the rest of us about why he's only been promoting you on social media." At fifty-three, Fiona had been writing for only a couple of years, more for herself than anyone else, and she was nowhere near ready to publish, or be a published author. Her insecurities about her stories got in the way of her moving forward, and she'd always shown Ari disdain for being the most advanced of the group.

"He flew back to the movie set today," Ari casually replied while packing up her folio. "And whether or not he mentions anyone else is up to him. I don't control him. Everything he's done is his choice. Nothing to do with me." Keeping her temper in check, she just wanted to get out of there as soon as possible and didn't want to be ganged up on.

"Oh, come on, Ari," Bethany chimed in. "He clearly took an interest in you, and you've barely spoken all night except to say you're editing your book." At twenty-nine, Bethany had once been published, but one book that didn't sell well hardly made her an author. She'd turned to the writers group to see what she could do about producing more.

Ari slid her folio into her bag and cast a glance at her. "Yeah, he took an interest, something that he took upon himself. A grown arse man made a choice to take an interest in me. A grown arse man made a choice to read my books and promote me on his socials. A grown arse man made a choice to promote me because he found me interesting and applauded all of the hard work I've put into this. If a grown arse man making these choices about me pisses you all off so much, I don't fucking care. Get over it and behave like fucking grown-ups. Because, Fiona," Ari turned to her stunned face, "I don't fucking care for your snide remarks borne from your envy. Grow up and get over it. I'm not fucking interested." With that, Ari spun on her heel and strode out of the room, leaving them all shocked in her wake. She was muttering under her breath as she continued towards the entrance. "Fucking bitch. Who the hell does she think she is? Jealous old cow. I'll fucking show her how interested in me he is. She's going to choke on her words when he makes my book famous and turns it into a movie."

*****

Over the next few weeks, she heard from Jay sporadically,

but he had put her in contact with his friends in New York before he'd left.

Edith, the editor, to whom Ari sent her manuscript off to for analysis, marked off the sections in need of help, and Ari edited them, making each scene stronger and adding a few scenes along the way.

Chuck, the cover designer, who conferred with her on designs, came up with such incredible covers that she gasped when she saw them. "Oh, my God. They're stunning," she told him via email. "I'll sit with them and let you know."

By the time Jay finished the movie and made it back to Ari's, the editing was finished, and the covers completed.

"They did turn out well," Jay complimented the covers Ari had printed out. "Was it what you were thinking for them?"

"I don't really know what I was thinking." Ari looked at the different formatted versions on the printed sheets so she could see what each book was going to look like. "The cover for the special edition will look awesome with the gold font. They'll be brilliant." The designs had turned out better than expected. The idea she'd seen in her mind paled in comparison to what Chuck had created on his computer software.

"I told you he was good." Jay studied the different covers. "The guy is magical. He can listen to what you're trying to describe to him or take your childish scribbled drawings and make magic out of it. I definitely think this suits the story." He exhaled a deep breath and handed the papers to her before leaning back against the wall. He turned his face up to the sun, closed his eyes behind his glasses, and crossed his legs. "So the covers are done and the editing's done."

"The covers aren't quite done," Ari told him, putting the papers into the folder beside her. "I still have the interior formatting to do so we get the page count for the spine width. I'm doing all three formats."

"Trade, large print, and dust jacket hardcover." Jay nodded. "Are you using the same trade interior for the special edition?"

"Yep." Ari leaned back beside him and listened to the local hoon drag his car down the street beside her house. "Dickhead," she muttered and sighed. "How long are you here for this time?"

"I've got a week left." Jay scratched the top of his head and smoothed his hair back. "I'd like to get those special editions printed before I go, so I can take them with me and get them sent off when I get back."

Ari shook her head. "Won't be possible. The book will need to be proofed first with one final edit, and then we can get it printed. I don't think that printer will do one for proofing."

The delay angered Jay and he started to arc up but caught himself and tried to keep his tone neutral. "How long will the delay be?"

"I'll do the interiors this weekend and get them uploaded. Once reviewed and approved, I can order copies and should have them by the end of next week. Once read, and checked over, we can contact the offset printing company for the copies. Oh…how are we getting them? You said you'd order enough for us to have personal copies. If you're gone, I wonder if they'd send the bulk to New York."

"Don't know." Jay swung his leg absentmindedly, running through the scenario in his head. "But if they can't, get them sent to you in two parcels, your copies and the rest, and send them on to me. I'll put the money in your bank if they're not paid for before I leave."

"And the plan's still the same?" Ari's stomach twisted into knots at the thought of having a best-selling book. While the books she did have out had seen a sales spike thanks to Jay talking about them, they had taken a nosedive after a couple of weeks. She'd been talking about her soon to be released novel on socials to draw up interest.

"The plan is still the same. I take the books home; package them up with instructions about when to read, when to post a review, and when to post to social media."

"And that will be September when the book is up for pre-order and then released."

"Exactly." Jay nodded. "You keep one hundred of the special editions for giveaways," he glanced sharply at her, "you have added the special ed number to the interior, right?"

"I have the layout and will add it to the second copy I make especially for it. Don't worry." She grinned at his frown. "I've written it all down."

"Good, good." Jay relaxed and watched the coloured lorikeets screech overhead as they flew past and headed for the trees in the park a couple of houses away. "You've got a lot of wildlife here. Those birds are beautiful."

"They are," Ari agreed. "Always a pleasure to watch when they're in my yard munching on the weeds or flowers. They especially love the rain and come out in droves. All of them. Parakeets, lorikeets, magpies, miners, the dirty little shits. You'll see red, green, blue and yellow varieties. Just stunning."

"Oh, yeah, did I tell you about the snakes and spiders we came across this time round?" He pulled his phone out and flicked through the photos. "We had brown and red bellied snakes and look at this motherfucker of a spider. What the fuck is that?" He held the phone closer to her and with two fingers on the screen enlarged the photo.

"Ugh!" Ari shuddered and slid along the seat away from him. "Don't. I hate spiders. Even looking at pictures of them."

"I think one of the crew said it was an Australian tarantula, or bird eating spider. And this one," he flicked to the next photo, "this big grey mother's a huntsman."

"No." Ari madly waved her hands at the back of her neck. "No. Whenever I see a real one or a picture, I think there's one on me. Gross."

Jay chuckled and put his phone away. "Seriously? You live in a country full of massive things, and killer things at that, but you can't stand them?"

"That's because they can kill you," Ari objected. "I'm not ready to die. Besides, I don't think huntsmen kill. They just bite, but it's not poisonous or something."

"What about the others?" Jay slowly danced two fingers up Ari's arm to imitate a spider.

She shivered and swatted his hand away before rubbing her hand over her arm. "Stop it. You're freaking me out. Besides, you guys have killer gators in Florida, pythons, rabid skunks or squirrels, or something, bears, all sorts. It's not just us."

"True." Jay uncrossed his legs and stretched them to their full length. "But all of yours seem much more dangerous."

"Sharks travel around the planet; they don't just live here. Same with snakes and spiders, they also live in other countries," she reminded him. "And other countries have their own killer animals, so the world, or specifically you yanks, needs to stop picking on us with your snide remarks and unfunny jokes. Because it sure as hell doesn't stop you from coming here." Her brows rose in amusement. "You can't get enough of the place. So much so you're all moving here."

"Makes up for all of the Aussies moving to L.A. and New York," Jay joked. "We're trading with you."

"Meh." Ari pouted her lips. "If only you'd send your best-looking actors our way."

"Ouch!" Jay gripped his heart and feigned choking. "And what do you call me, pray tell?"

"Middle of the road average?" Taking in his looks she gave a sharp nod.

"Excuse me!" Jay removed his glasses and leaned towards her. "Middle of the road average?"

"Yeah." She gave an uncaring shrug of her shoulder. "You're not the ugliest guy on the planet, but you're not Henry Cavill beautiful, either. You're just an average looking guy women will either think is hot, or not. I've already told you this."

"And since *you've* already said I play hot psychos, then *you* think I'm hot." Jay leaned closer, licked his lips, and puckered them as if he was about to kiss her.

Mesmerised, Ari stared at them, wishing they would kiss her. "Yeah well, only when you're in psycho mode."

"So I *should* play psychos more often or be in psycho mode more often." He leaned closer still, his gaze holding hers, and his voice lowered. "Because I will be when I bring this character to life on the big screen. And I do plan on playing him, Ari, and would like you in the movie, too. It's based on your book after all, brought to life."

Her hooded eyes blinked as she took in his words. "What!" She pulled back and her eyes flew open. "I'm not an actor. How could I be in—?"

"Of course, you could be in your own movie. If M. Night

Shyamalan and Stephen King can make appearances in their movies, and Stan Lee did for the Marvel movies, then so can you." He grasped both of her arms and turned her towards him. "I think you need to play the female lead opposite me. We'd blow up the screen."

"Hardly!" she scoffed and pulled out of his hands, swiping a stray hair off her forehead. "Not with the way I look and all of my issues. I suppose they'd want some big Hollywood actress to play the role, which I get. I'd prefer an unknown, as with most of the cast, to give new actors a chance, but I guess it doesn't work that way."

"Not really, no." Jay leaned his elbows on his knees. "I've been talking to producers about this book. Some loved it and would want to do it, but with names to draw the people in."

"Besides you?"

He gave a half laugh. "Besides me. They want big names for the big roles and smaller names for the smaller roles."

"Understandable." Ari thought about all of the characters in her novel. "I could play a really minor role just to say I was in it."

"Maybe you could be the shrink, or the psychic." Jay stroked his chin; his beard was fuller after months of not shaving it. "Something flamboyant." He looked at her as she looked at him and they said the same thing at the same time.

"The psychic!"

Laughing, Ari considered it. "Yeah. Maybe."

"Either way, I've got Hollywood interested so we just need to get those proofs and special ed copies. We're already in July and you want to publish it in September."

"Yep. I better get those formats done and uploaded. Don't come around until next week and then I've got the weekend

Anything for You

to concentrate on it."

"That's fine," Jay agreed. "As long as you give me another novel or three to read over the weekend."

"What? Do you mean the other ones I've written this year?" Ari looked at him in surprise.

"Whatever you've got, let me read them. I've read your family saga series as well, so I'm finished." Jay stood to stretch out his back. After months of sleeping in caravans or on cheap motel beds, his back had become quite inflexible.

"I guess I could." Ari quickly thought through which novels were edited. "There's a couple. Maybe you'll like them as much as this one."

"Oh, I'm sure I will, Ari Travers." Jay's gaze was steadfast as he watched her face and the suspicious emotions that fled over it. "I'm sure I will."

*****

After spending the weekend perfecting the novel's interior, Ari uploaded them Monday morning to the printing company she used to distribute her books. The three formats only took a short time to be reviewed, and after approving the online proofs, she ordered a copy of each.

She and Jay spent the week eating out, talking about her other novels, and ways of getting publicity until the paperback versions of the book arrived on Thursday afternoon.

"Okay." Jay rubbed his hands together in anticipation and watched her pull the large print paperback out first. He held out his hand. "I'll proof this tonight for any spelling mistakes that we might have missed. You check the others and make any corrections. If we can get the books finished tonight, we can contact the local printer tomorrow about getting them printed and shipped." He turned the book over a few times, read the blurb, and slid his fingers over the cover. "It looks great. Very psych thriller."

Ari stared at the trade print in her hand as rolling coils of excitement filled her body. She always loved seeing her books in print for the first time until she found what needed to be tweaked. The first copies were always proof versions to be dissected and examined. "The cover image is incredible."

Jay held the larger sized large print version next to hers. "Chuck made it work. What about the hardcover?" He looked into the box. "That didn't come?"

"No. Hardcovers always take longer." Ari thumbed through the interior. "It printed well, but there's always something to tighten or change. Always something I missed. So mark up that copy with a pencil, not a pen, and then I'll fix any formatting issues. I'll get this one done tonight."

*****

That night, Ari read through her book and marked off any corrections to be made and did them Friday morning before Jay arrived. "I've completed the trade format and it's ready to go for upload at the local printers," she told him as he handed over the large print edition. Her face dropped. "Shit! I forgot you were also doing corrections." The energy drained from her. "I'd better go through it and see if I missed anything."

"Don't worry. I didn't correct too much. I think we caught most of the issues before you did the formatting." He glanced at his watch. "How long will it take for you to make the corrections?"

"An hour or less. I just flip through the pages," Ari replied. "Can you find something to do while I get to it?"

"Sure. I've got some of your fellow writers' books to read. So far none of them have come close to being as good as yours. Have any of them complained that I didn't follow them or promote their books?" He shoved his hands into the pockets of his shorts and rocked slightly on the balls of his feet. "I bet they did."

Ari huffed. "Oh, yeah. Some did. Told them you are a grown arse man who makes his own choices, and if you chose to follow and help me, then that's nothing to do with me, or them. Better go fix this." She waved the book and walked three steps before she stopped and turned back. "So they're not very good? I've never read them."

"Not the ones I've read so far. I even read some of the excerpts they put on social media." He sighed and shook his head. "Absolute shite."

"Ouch." Ari grinned and hurried inside. Finished in half an hour, she uploaded the newer versions to her distributor, and once done, they called the local offset printing company they were using for the special editions and chatted to one of their reps who helped them with every step. With the online form filled out and detailed shipping information added in, Ari uploaded her files and hit the send button. She received the 'thank you for your submission' email in her inbox, and then she turned to Jay. "Done and dusted! Twelve hundred books to be printed and posted."

"Excellent." He gave a sharp nod and rubbed his hands together. "Step four of the plan has been executed. Step five will be to get these books to New York and sent off. Oh…" Jay half crossed his arms so he could still wave his hand around.

"I've already typed up the plan, so when I get the books we'll print the letters out and ship them with the books."

"A thousand books will cost a lot to ship off individually." Ari frowned. "God, this is expensive."

"But I'm paying for it, so don't worry about it." Jay took hold of her arms. "Look at me." When she was looking at him, he continued, "This is *me* investing in *you*. It's a drop in the bucket in an ocean. I can afford it and you'll be paying it back once you sell a million copies. And I *know* you'll sell more than a million."

"If I do, that'll be awesome." Ari clasped her hands in front of her. "I don't think I will, but it's nice that you have faith in that and are supporting me and helping me with this. You're going so far out of your way to do it."

"It took a business contract to get you to accept my support, so yeah; I had to go out of my way to get you to do this." His grin slid ear to ear. "But it's worth it. I know the book's going to be a massive bestseller, and your other books will be too. Once you have them edited by Edith and get Chuck to do your covers, you're really on a roll with those psych thrillers you've written. And I'll get this one turned into a movie and make sure it stays faithful to the book, because I hate how Hollywood takes a book and makes the movie completely different.

"So do I," Ari interjected. "And some of them turn out shit."

"Exactly. So I'll see to it that it's as faithful as possible. And with our plan in place, there's no way that won't happen for you, for me, for both of us."

The corners of her lips turned up into a wistful smile. "I hope so. It's every author's dream to have a successful book, and then, maybe, a movie made out of it." She eagerly looked into his eyes. "And how many of us authors can boast that a big time Hollywood actor has literally had a part to play? And I don't mean in the movie."

"Not many, I expect," Jay said. His plan churned over in his head, knowing he had Ari exactly where he wanted her.

*****

On Saturday morning, Jay dropped in to say goodbye before leaving for the airport. He was going back to New York on the midday flight.

"Oooh, I'm going to miss you." He hugged Ari fiercely. Sleep had eluded him the night before because he'd been planning out the multiple steps of what he would be doing with Ari's next book. He'd tweaked the plan until it was time to pack the rest of his luggage for the flight home. "I don't want to go without you. I want to take you with me. Mwah!" He planted a big kiss on her cheek before loosening his grip. "Maybe that can be the next step. Once your book is released, and you get the publicity circuit here out of the way, you can come to New York to promote it. And you can stay with me, and I'll show you around and—"

"Whoa, wait up there." Ari was still recovering from the kiss, even though it was on her cheek. "I'm a long way from even selling the book, and then it has to be a massive seller to warrant anyone in the media noticing and wanting interviews. But going to New York?" She put her hands up and stepped back. "That's a massive thing that I'm not prepared for. I've never been overseas. I wouldn't know how to get a visa or anything. I have no idea what paperwork I'd need to fill out."

"From what I know you don't need a visa for a visit. I think it's something like a six month stay on your passport where you can holiday or work before returning home. So you could come for a snowy Christmas; something you've never had before." Jay had it all planned to a T. He just needed to convince Ari it was a good idea.

"It sounds lovely, Jay, but that's a long way off and I won't get the money from the sale of the books for a few months. It's not straight away." Ari swept her hair aside and looked up at him in the overcast glow of the day. "I've never been on a plane, let alone overseas. And what about my stuff, and my situation here? How long do you expect me to be there for? A couple of weeks? A couple of months?"

"Don't worry," he soothed. "This is all something we can work out in the next couple of months. But once news gets out of your book sales and it hits all of the charts, especially in the U.S., and with me helping you, everyone will want to know the story of how it came to be. So coming to the U.S. is a must for publicity."

"And where would I stay? And who'll pay for my airfare and accommodation? I won't be able to yet." Ari paced nervously and bit on a fingernail. "It's all well and good to suggest this, Jay, but I just want to get the book out first."

"And I get that." Jay watched her intently. "They're all just thoughts and suggestions, and I could put you up and pay for it until you get your money. All part of the investment."

Ari had made Jay lay out a contract between them to sign and going to New York and staying with him was not part of that contract. "I can't ask you to do that. You've invested in the book, not paying for me to travel to New York."

"It's all part of the package, Ari," Jay said. "Getting the book past a million in sales, getting it produced, getting you

Anything for You

done up to look good…it's all part of investing in you and this book." He stopped her pacing. "Be ready for success, Ari. Be ready to go out and grab onto it and run with it because it's coming. And if that means coming to New York for a few months, or a year, or more, to accomplish your dreams of being a best-selling author, then prepare for it. Besides," his gaze caught her surprised one, "you've mentioned a couple of times about wishing you could live in New York for a year. That's why you asked me a lot of questions about it."

"Yes, I did, but I never expected you to suggest paying for me to go. I figured if the book was a success, then I'd pay my own way over."

Jay shrugged. "Why can't I make it happen sooner?" His watch alarm went off and he checked the time. "Shit! I gotta go. I gotta check in two hours before my flight and it'll take me an hour to get there. Ari, just think about it, okay. Let me help you until those millions roll in and then if you want to pay me back, you can. But don't let go of your dreams because of your stubbornness. Think about it, okay?" He cupped her face and planted a resounding kiss on her lips before gazing into her stunned eyes. "Think about it. I gotta go." In seconds he was in his car, backing out of the driveway, and leaving her behind.

*****

Ari didn't hear from Jay for two weeks. This was just as well as she was still reeling from his kiss.

"Ari, my girl, how are you?" Jay's face filled the screen when they Facetimed.

"Fine," Ari replied, not wanting to give her excitement

away. She'd missed him, missed talking to him, missed seeing him every day, missed his lips on hers. Missed everything about him.

"Only fine?" Jay frowned. "How can you be only *fine*? You should be nervous and excited. Your book's coming out next month."

A butterfly bolted around her insides. "I know. I know. I'm trying to stay calm about it and not freak out. Did you get the books? I got mine. Aren't they gorgeous with the gold foil?" She held up a special edition in front of the camera. "I think people will be sorry when they get a plain one but see this one all over social media."

"Oh, I know they will be." Jay held up one of his. "They all came yesterday. The company printed and shipped them really quickly. They're stunning." He turned the book over, looking at the blurb, the foil, and Chuck's name at the bottom of the cover before turning it back to the front. "The bits of foil absolutely make it."

"So when are you sending them out?" Ari placed hers on the desk beside her laptop. Her personal copies were already on display on her bookshelf, and she'd taken dozens of photos ready for posting to her socials.

"They're all going out the last two weeks of August, but I'll hand them out personally to my friends and family here in New York. The plan is for them to have the books by the first of September. Read it, then post to socials and leave reviews. By the time the book's released, you should be number one from sales from followers." He leaned closer to the camera. "You okay? You look a little white."

"Nervous." Ari's head nodded slightly. "Normally I'm not when releasing a book. But this time is different. This time it'll have star power behind it." She noticed how smooth his skin looked after shaving off his beard and wondered what it felt like. "When did you shave?"

"Basically the minute I got home." Jay ran his hand over his jaw. "I don't mind growing it and having something there, but that was way too much for way took long, so off it came along with the hair." He turned his head left and right for her to see. "Got a trim and a shave at the local barbers. I've been going to him for a good couple of decades, so he knows my hair and my face well. Why…" He peered into the camera. "You don't like it?"

"Oh, I like it," Ari hastily replied. "I was just used to the extra hair and beard. You look a lot different when you're clean-shaven and tidy."

"A lot of people tell me that." Jay adjusted himself in his chair and leaned back. "And I can definitely see the difference in photos. I bet you look different with long hair. Looks like you've had a cut as well."

"Yeah, I have. And yeah, I do." Ari slid her fingers around her right ear to her neck. "I was getting a bit sick and tired of all the curls. But I used to have it down to my waist when I was younger."

"When was that? Last year?" Jay joked.

"Cute!" She chuckled. "No, a couple of decades ago. I've had short hair for about fifteen years now."

"Ever thought of growing it back?"

"Sometimes. But I also figure it would just be easier to wear a wig."

"There are a couple of good wig shops here in the Big Apple. Maybe when you get here you can get some and we'll go out in disguise so no one will recognise us."

Ari sniggered. "Yeah, that will be rip-roaringly hilarious."

"Why?"

"Well for one…me in New York. And two, me wearing wigs. And three, us going out."

"Ari." Jay leaned forward and pulled his laptop closer. "Why is any of that funny? I've already told you you're coming to New York to promote your book. And who knows, maybe to live. And it would be fun to dress in disguises. I'd like to go out without being recognised for once."

Ari glanced away. "Well, I still don't believe I'm moving to New York, so I've put that idea out of my mind. I need to concentrate on the plan for September, but also my plan for a cover reveal on social media in the days leading up to publication. I'm thinking about one thing at a time."

"Fair enough," Jay said. "You think about that. I'll think about getting you to New York to publicise your book and to stay for a year."

"Jay," Ari protested. "Don't do that. Can't you just let this take it natural course?"

"Ari, there's been nothing natural about this since we met. It's all been planned," Jay argued. "And there's nothing wrong with that. Planning out a book launch, which is what this is—"

"With how many celebrities helping to launch it?" Ari interrupted.

"It's still a book launch," Jay continued. "Regardless of the fact some big Hollywood actor is helping you launch it by using all of his big Hollywood friends. It's not really different from the book launches that happen when actors, singers, or politicians launch a book. It's all about who you know that can help you out. And I have a lot of friends who'll help me out. And you." He pointed at the camera. "The plan is in motion, and ready for phase two."

"The sending out and reading of books." A chill rushed down Ari's spine and she shivered. "This is just..." Glancing around her office, she tried to register what was happening. Because she still couldn't. "Far more than I could ever imagine happening."

"And I get that." A soft smile showed off his dimples. "This is a once in a lifetime opportunity, Ari, and you're taking it. Have you fixed any of your health issues yet? I told you this was an investment in you as well as your book."

A creeping blush found its way up her neck to her face. "And I told you not to do that. My health issues are my thing to deal with, not yours."

"Have you done anything?" he persisted. "You want to look good for the press, Ari. You're already gorgeous, but you were worried about a few things. Have you had your head shots done yet?"

Glad for the change of subject, she nodded. "I did. Last week. They look pretty good."

"Great. I can't wait to see them, but in the meantime, get your health issues sorted."

Ari refused to take the bait. "The photos will go up on the website on September one, to coincide with the book's pre-order release, so they'll be new, too."

"That's great." Jay's phone buzzed and he picked it up. "Ugh, my ex. Probably wants more money." He declined the call and placed his phone face down on the desk. "Back to you. Have you got everything ready for the big reveal?"

"I have."

"In the meantime, I'll start packing up the books for shipping and let all of my friends know they're coming. And also deal with my bitch of an ex-wife. Are you uploading the book on the first of the month, your time?"

"Yep, my time will coincide with your early morning."

"Great. We'll Facetime again then because I have some legal issues to deal with. In the meantime, go and get yourself fixed, Ari. I'll see you then."

The screen went blank, and Ari clicked out of the app. Sighing, she leaned back in her seat and thought about the money Jay had put in her account for her as the investment. Although she was sure he'd paid Chuck and Edith personally, or they did the job for free, he had given her money for whatever else she needed. Upload fees, proofs, and for any medical issue she wanted to fix.

With help from Jay's Aussie assistant that he'd rehired for her in the weeks after he'd left, she'd had her teeth whitened before the photo shoot for her headshots. Then she'd had dermabrasion to fix some skin issues and had her first round of sclerotherapy for the painful veins in her legs. Both the dermabrasion and sclerotherapy would take several rounds, but she'd already seen an improvement in everything.

So while she didn't really like spending someone else's money, it was all part of his investment in her. And he wanted her to look and feel her best, so he'd given her what she needed to improve herself and her looks. She wasn't a user, but since she had it sitting in her account, she may as well use it. Right?

Chapter 4

In the twelve days leading up to the first of September, Ari set in motion her social media plan. On Instagram, she posted three white squares, one per day, to make a space between what was to come, and what had already been published. Then, day by day, she revealed a square of book cover, so after nine days it revealed the entire picture.

On Facebook and Twitter, she posted different photos of 'coming soon' covers, as Instagram's white squares would not work on other social media platforms. And on the first of September, not only was the last square revealed on Instagram, but she uploaded the e-book and two paperbacks to Amazon, and then set both to publish.

Within two hours, they'd had been reviewed and were live.

The game was on!

Ari went into the backend of her website and uploaded her new header with one of her new headshots into the widget. It too went live. She updated her bio and timeline and added three more headshots to her about page. Within ten minutes, that too was live.

By early evening, Australian time, Ari was live everywhere. Her book was on socials and her headshots were on her websites. She was sitting at her desk trying to combat the butterflies in her stomach when she saw a couple of reviews had already been posted to Amazon.

The Facetime app popped up and she saw it was Jay calling. She clicked him on. "Hey."

"Hey, Ari, my girl. It's live I see, with a couple of reviews. Good ones at that."

She stared at his tired face and saw the beard was back full force. "Yeah. Any idea who left them?"

"Don't know. But the plan was simple. Read it, review it, and roll it out over social media. I saw all of your posts. The cover reveal looked great."

"I think it turned out well," she said. "I'll post about it every couple of days and get some other things in there, so I don't drive people nuts over it. I don't want to turn them off before they read it."

"I see you have over twenty-five thousand followers on Instagram now." Jay's gaze darted back and forth to the social accounts he had open on his laptop. "More than double what you got after I first posted about you."

"Yeah, that's been freaky. I don't even know where they came from, although I do see a couple of your friends. Did you tell them to follow me?"

"I did." Jay clicked onto Twitter. "You've doubled your Twitter followers too. Part of the plan was to follow you if they liked your book. But I did ask my nearest and dearest family and friends to follow you to get the buzz going. They'll start posting on socials in the next week as we planned. It's rolling out in waves."

"Am I the type of person they normally follow?"

"Well…" Jay's head did a little bounce left to right and

back again. "No. I did ask them to follow you to help you out as a favour to me, but they don't have to reply to any of your posts, or care about what you post."

The hair on the back of Ari's neck bristled. "Well, gee, thanks so much."

He gave her a half-arsed grin. "Sorry, Ari. It's just to help the book get launched and to get you some of their followers."

She changed the subject. "You look like shit."

"I feel like shit," Jay's deep voice rumbled, and he leaned back and rubbed his weary eyes.

"The ex?"

"Oh…the ex, the kids, the lawyers. But the bright side is some of the people who've read the book already love it as much as I do, and I think it'll make a great movie. The excitement is building."

"I hope it keeps building so I can hit the top spot, and the psych thriller charts, on Amazon. Not that it means much, but it'll be a massive boost to sales of my other books, I hope."

"You hope?" Jay almost scoffed and clicked through to Ari's publishing house website. "You've updated your pub house, too. Right there on the front page under new release."

"Of course," she replied. "As if I wasn't going to update that."

"You also gave it a makeover. New theme, I see."

"I could hardly let it look like crap with the new release. So yes, new theme."

"Everything looks great and it's now on a roll." His phone rang and his eyes darted towards it. "I'm almost scared to see who it is."

"Go on. It might not be her," Ari encouraged, and glanced at her own phone to see a couple of notifications from different social media sites.

Jay reluctantly turned his phone over and groaned. "It's her."

"See what she wants and deal with it like a grown arse man," Ari told him. "A formerly-hot-psycho who now-looks-like shit man."

"Hey!" He leaned towards the camera and pointed at his face. "This is what she's done to me just in the last three weeks. Sucked me dry of all energy and my youth."

"Ha! Youth! That's hilarious. You're forty-five. You ain't that young anymore, Daniels."

"I'm not that old either, but I'll soon be a withered old piece of flesh with the way she's going. She's a succubus."

Ari's laughter contained multiple snorts. "A succubus. That's even more hilarious. But isn't there a way to kill a succubus? I know they had a few on *Supernatural*. Probably *The X-Files* too."

Jay sighed and ran a hand over his face, into his hair, rubbing the spot on his head that was aching and itching at the same time. "I hope there's a way to kill them because I'm done."

The phone rang again, and he glanced at it. "It's my lawyer. This call I'll actually take."

"Okay, see you next time."

"Bye, Ari, my girl. I'll call on the nineteenth to see how sales are going." He clicked off and took the call. "Merrick, I need to get Ari here where she belongs. So how in the hell can I get rid of my ex-wife?"

*****

Anything for You

For the next three weeks, Ari went about business as usual and watched the social media posts from Jay's friends who'd read the book roll across multiple platforms. She watched their reviews grow on Amazon, and saw her followers grow on her social pages.

By the time September the nineteenth rolled around, Ari hadn't even wanted to check the pre-order status of the book, and simply basked in the glow of it all. Plus, she was a teensy bit afraid that Jay's plan hadn't worked and that no one had ordered the book at all. She now had over fifty thousand followers, likers, or subscribers on each of her platforms and many had even commented on her blog posts about her book release, but would that translate into sales?

But, at some point, she knew she'd have to bite the bullet and check. So with trepidation, she logged into her dashboard and went in search of her pre-orders. Before scrolling down the page, she checked the clock on her phone and saw there was only five minutes left until it was September nineteenth in America. "Five minutes," she muttered. "Nearly live time." Placing her left hand over her eyes, and splitting her fingers enough to look through, she scrolled down the page and looked for the numbers. She found a series of ones.

The Facetime app beeped, and she hastily opened it.

"Ari, my girl. D-day for your book. What the hell are you doing?" He saw her covered face.

"I don't want to look," she replied, but looked back at the number anyway.

"But it's release day. You need to." Jay leaned closer and adjusted his glasses. He was near-sighted, and without glasses or contacts, he saw nothing clearly. "Besides, you need to take screen shots of it all so you can have the memory of it. It should hit the number one spot almost upon release, shouldn't it?"

Ari's hand slowly slid away, and she stared at the number of pre-orders for her book. Her brows furrowed and she muttered, "Ah yeah, I suppose…not quite sure how it works, or how fast." Leaning back, she quickly took a screenshot of the page seconds before it went live. "Wow!"

"Wow what? How many? Ari…?" He squinted at the screen. "What's wrong? Are there no pre-orders? What's happening?" He clicked onto the book's Amazon page but didn't see anything about where it had fallen on the book charts. "Is it too soon? Ari?"

She seemed whiter than normal and was staring at a spot on her laptop.

"What's going on? How many pre-orders did you get?" He raised his voice. "Ari!"

She breathed in and swallowed the lump in her throat, then moved her gaze to the camera. "Ah…" A deep sigh left her and her eyes closed. "Enough to pay you back double like we agreed on."

"To pay me…oh, my God." Jay covered his mouth with both hands and rocked back in his chair. "Ari! You did it. *I* did it. *We* did it. That means you sold over one million copies on day one. The day of release. Oh, my God. How many?"

Ari stared from him to the number. "I…I don't even know if this even means something numerology wise. But it's kinda bizarre."

"Why? What's the number?" Jay leaned in.

"Well, 1,111,111 copies were on pre-order. So that means 1,111,111 copies just went out to 1,111,111 Kindles and laptops and other devices. Holy shit!" Ari leaned her elbows

Anything for You

on her desk and covered her face with both hands. "Holy fucking shit," she mumbled from between her hands.

A guttural laugh came from Jay, and he exploded out of his seat, his fists flying sky high in triumph before he began clapping and dancing in front of his desk. "We did it, Ari. We did it. Woohoo." Wiggling his butt, he twerked and looked at the camera, beat-boxing as he sang. "We did it, Ari, we did it. We did it, Ari, we did it."

"Okay, God, don't do that," she complained, but couldn't stop herself from laughing. It felt good. Really good. To not only know her book had sold well, but to laugh at Jay and what he was doing for a brief moment before getting back to business.

"Woohoo, we did it." Jay pulled his chair back to the desk and sat down. "We did it. God, what a number to sell." He refreshed her Amazon page, and his eyes grew wide. "Oh, my God, Ari. Check Amazon."

"I am checking Amazon."

"No, I mean your book page. Check your book page and take a screenshot."

Ari refreshed her book page and scrolled down to see she was number one in not only psych thriller, but romantic suspense, and the whole Amazon store. "Holy shit." She took a screen cap and scrolled back up. The number one banner was under the book's title. "Holy freaking shit! I'm number one." She saved a second screen cap and kept scrolling up and down the page. She had hundreds of reviews from Jay's friends, just over eight hundred of the thousand who'd received a book. He'd told her some hadn't liked it, and part of the plan was if you didn't like it, don't review it or promote it, as they knew bad reviews would change her ranking.

"I can't believe this." Ari shook her head. "I just...I..." She gave a hysterical laugh, quickly threw her hands over her mouth, sighed, and looked at Jay. "I can't believe this has happened. That you've done this for me. That you went out of your way to do this for me. I..." She was unaware that her head was shaking *no* the whole time. "I can't believe that someone has helped me so much. Helped little old me from little old nowhere, to become a successful author. Because that's what I am now." Tears sprang to her eyes, and she tried to blink them away.

"You're a best-selling author, Ari," Jay said, his soft grin in place. He'd shaved for the occasion, knowing that while Ari liked his scruff, she preferred him clean.

"Yeah..." Her mouth gaped as she tried to put words together. "But it's just one book, and what if the others don't live up to this hype? What if the others bomb, like all that came before them?"

"That won't happen," Jay assured her. "We can use the same plans for each, but now that people know your name, or your author name, and you start doing interviews, they'll read your other books and chomp at the bit for your next one which is just as awesome."

Ari shook herself to snap out of the shock she was still reeling in. "God, I hope so. Okay, Ari," she said. "Snap out of it. Shit just got very real." Sitting up straighter, she leaned towards her laptop and refreshed all of the pages. Her book page, social media pages, and her dashboard all read the same as they had sixty seconds ago. "Okay. Guess I'd better blast it across social media, then." She took a photo of her dashboard with her phone and posted it to Instagram, connecting it to Facebook and Twitter. TikTok and Pinterest came next. She then whipped up a blog post and set that for seven-thirty the next morning. "Okay, socials are all set." Gazing at the dashboard where the pre-order numbers still sat, she sighed. "I can't believe it."

Jay was leaning his elbows on his desk and cupping his face with his hands. His lips turned into a smile. "Believe it, Ari. You're now a best-selling Australian author who just sold over one point one million copies of her new novel. How many Australian authors can claim that record? How many can say they've sold over a million with one book? Let alone a catalogue."

"Very few," Ari replied, and tried to focus on the situation at hand. "So what now?"

"What now is you make yourself available for interviews, both from here and Aus. I can help set up your ones here, and that might have a side effect for Aus. If they see you doing interviews here, they'll want in on it because you're Australian. And, considering you just posted your pre-order status, that's going to show everyone you're a best-selling author, no matter where they are."

Ari's head bobbed along with his words. "True, true. I'll keep an eye on my inbox to see what happens. What will you do on your end?"

"If anyone gets in contact with me about having a chat with you, I'll pass along your details. I'll also put feelers out, as I said, to anyone who's interested in doing interviews."

"Okay. I'll stand by for the barrage. In the meantime, I owe you ten grand."

Jay's lips slid up on both sides. "You do. But I know you don't get paid yet, so I can wait. You can pay be back for Christmas."

"With what? A Rolex?" Ari quipped, and picked up a copy of her book, marvelling at how damn good the cover was, which she knew would have helped immensely.

"Ha!" Jay snorted. "They're around fifty thou, I think. But no. December's about the time you get your money, isn't it?"

"Probably, yeah." Ari set the book down and leaned back. "I still can't believe this has happened. I mean," she threw her hands up in the air, "never in a million years did I imagine a big time Hollywood actor doing all of this for me. No, scratch that, never in a million years did I imagine *anyone* doing all of this for me. Let alone any of my books selling well or selling over a million copies. I just…" She gazed out the window in front of her and sighed at the world passing by. "I could never have imagined any of this happening. I am so beyond grateful, and astounded, and unbelieving, that you did this, that anyone did this." Swiping her hands across her face to get rid of her tears that were sliding down her cheeks, Ari licked her lips and sat straighter. "Really, Jay. I really don't know how I can repay you except for repaying the investment as planned."

Jay crossed his arms and laid them on the desk in front of him, leaning towards the camera. He'd known this day would come, had planned it just so, right down to the paperwork he'd had his lawyer draw up. He knew she was going to be grateful. She'd talked about being unable to repay him back. But down to his planning, today was the day to collect. "Well…I have an idea about that."

"What?" She leaned her elbows on the desk, linked her fingers together and rested her chin on them. "Anything. As long as it doesn't cost me a fortune."

"Oh, it's not going to cost you anything except time."

"Oh…" Her interest was piqued. "Not going to cost in dollars but time? How?"

"Well…" Jay drawled and gave her the smile he knew she loved. "You can repay me for my generosity and help by moving to New York."

Ari frowned. "What?"

"That's right. You heard correctly." Jay nodded. "I want you to move here to New York to gain acceptance as a newly crowned best-selling author. Think of the knowledge and history that this city holds, and all of the things you'd learn. All of the people you'd meet."

"I can't move to New York." Ari leaned back and breathed. "You know my situation, Jay."

"And that's a situation you need to get out of, Ari," Jay argued. "Let me bring you here."

"No. That's out of the question," she said. "You know I also have plans in place for when my money comes in."

"To move to the Gold Coast in Queensland," he said. "I remember those conversations. You also told me you'd love to live in New York for a year to experience all four seasons and everything it had to offer. So why can't you do that first? Why can't you let me move you here to New York for the year you've dreamed of so you can experience all of those seasons? Why can't you do this now? Wouldn't it be better to do it now?"

Silenced, Ari breathed a weary sigh. There was no reason why not. When she finally had enough money from her book sales, the plan was always to move to the Gold Coast. Even if she won the lottery, or an RSL Art Union home, the plan was always to move there and have a nice house, a great life, everything she'd always dreamed of having. But the two most important things that she wanted could not be bought with money; love and a family. And not even Jay could give her that. They weren't in love, and weren't a couple, and she didn't even know if she could have a child at her age which meant she knew that any man she met, or fell in love with, or into a relationship with, would either be childless, or have children, which Jay did. But they were his kids and not hers. Just like Jay. He wasn't hers. She finally spoke. "I don't know. I could think about it."

"Well, that's one thing you don't have to do." Jay pulled his laptop closer. "Ari, I've already sorted it out."

Weariness overcame her and she didn't have the energy to argue. "Sorted what out?"

"I've already planned for you to move here. I've sorted it out already. You'll come and live with me in my new brownstone—"

Her ears perked up. "You have a new brownstone?"

"Since last week, but that's not important," he continued. "You'll come and live with me here as my guest for the year. I'll pay for you to pack your stuff and ship it over. You can have the second-floor bedrooms for an office and bedroom suite. Your stuff that you don't need can be stored in the basement so you can get what you need when you need it. I'll show you around town, the best places to eat, to party, to dance, to have fun. And there are so many places that'll give you inspiration for your books. It'll be great."

Reluctance fled through Ari's body. "It does sound great, it really does…" Her voice trailed off and she was silent for a few moments. "But you know my situation." Biting her lip, she noticed Jay had stayed silent and just watched her. "I'm not sure I'd feel right being a guest who stayed for a whole year. I feel as if I'd wear out my welcome at some point and I'd become the guest who never leaves, and you'd have to throw me out."

"Ha! I don't think so," Jay replied and then had a thought. "Would you feel better if we made a contract for it? That you get to stay in my house until the year after next, giving you just over a year to be in New York and after that it's up to you?"

"Ah…" Ari went back to biting her lip. "Maybe…it's an idea, anyway."

"Okay." Jay nodded and scribbled something down on his notepad. "I'll have a contract drawn up, just like the last one, that says you can stay in my house for just over a year until you make a decision about your future." He slashed a question mark next to it. "Anything else?"

"What about the legals?"

"Ah, got those sorted as well. You have a passport, don't you? And I've set up a visa for you as well."

"Wait…you've already done that?" Ari's brows furrowed.

"Of course." Jay watched the expressions fly over her face and waited.

"So…you already planned *all* of this?" The light dawned. "*All* of this without asking me first?"

"Pretty much," Jay replied. "Ari, think about it. Without help, your book may not have sold, which it has. And without help, you may never get out of the situation you're in. I'm here, Ari. I'm here to help you. Maybe that's why I was chosen for the movie role with Russell. Maybe that's why I was in Australia, and maybe that's why it occurred to me to attend some writers' meetings after the set was shut down. So I could meet and help you. Don't you want help, Ari? Don't you *need* help? Help to get you out of the situation you're currently in? Help to get you out of your current life and into a better one?"

"I don't know. Are you saying the universe did this?" Ari deflated. Here was Jay, a perfectly nice guy offering to help her once more and she was fighting him *and* the offer. "I don't want to be a user. I told you that when you offered help with the book. I am *not* a user, Jay. I don't like using people to get free stuff."

"It's hardly free stuff," he replied. "Yeah, I'll pay for you and your things to be shipped over and yeah, stay in my house as my guest—"

"That's free!" Ari argued.

"Okay, then what?" Jay spread his hands in defeat. "What do you want to pay for? You don't have your money yet, so can't come over yet—"

"I can wait until next year when the money comes in—"

"But why wait when until then? Until January or February when I can bring you over now. Next month, in fact."

Another frown slid over Ari's face. "Why next month?"

"Because that's when I'm free to come and get you."

"What?" Ari's eyes widened. A surprise a second, he was.

"I've got it all figured out." Jay slid his sweater sleeves up and turned serious. "By the time I get there in four weeks, because I can't come sooner, you'll have done a whole host of interviews, packed up your small bits and pieces, and had a clear out ready to go. My lawyers have organised for your visa which you'd get when you arrive, and you'll stay with me. So your travel arrangements, legal papers, and accommodation are taken care of. I'll be your tour guide until January when you'll get an assistant to help out, and then you can explore

Anything for You

the city while I work."

"Work? What are you working on?"

"On getting your best-selling book turned into a best-selling movie," Jay retorted. "Isn't that the next step in your world domination?"

That scored a soft laugh out of her. "Hardly, but a movie would be nice as we've discussed."

"Nice! Nice!" Jay playfully mocked. "What's this nice business? Your book's going to be a movie and we're starring in it. We've already talked about it."

"Yes, I know. And I remember saying that the lead role was not for me, but you'd make the perfect psycho. I think we said I could be the flamboyant clairvoyant."

Jay laughed. "That rhymes and you absolutely could be." He paused for a long moment. "I'm coming to get you, Ari, my girl. Whether you like it or not."

"Do I have a choice?" she demurred.

"No, you don't." Jay grew serious. "I want you here, Ari. I want to give you everything that you want, everything that you need. Everything you've always dreamed of and desired."

Little did he know that she wanted and needed him and his arms around her, and his lips on hers. Her heart had beat for his since he'd kissed her months earlier, before leaving to go home to New York. The city was now calling out to her via him.

"I helped you with your book, so now let me help you with this. With your career, your *burgeoning* career as a best-selling author," he added. He could see the look in her eyes. A desire to follow her dreams, a wanting to say yes. She could live out one of her dreams by living in New York. With him. But he also saw something else. A desire *for* something else that he couldn't put his finger on. He sent a silent prayer out in the hope he'd find out what.

Ari let go of a deep breath. "I guess I could," she said slowly. "But—" She cut him off when he opened his mouth. "I'm not going to be seen as a user, using you for accommodation. So I'd like to put in towards rent or board or food or something. And put that in the contract."

Jay's grin flew across his face. "Deal! You will not be sorry you're doing this, Ari."

"I think I already am," she replied and glanced over her shoulder at the door, hoping no one had heard the conversation from the hallway. Turning back, she added, "You know my situation. It won't be easy."

Jay sobered. "I know. I know it'll be hard on both of you, but you deserve this, Ari. You deserve to live life your way, for you, and not for other people. And you have me to help you with that. I'll be there every step of the way, helping you, freeing you from the situation you're in and have been stuck in all of the adult years of your life. I'm coming to take you away from that, Ari. I'm coming to get you and free you, Ari, my girl. I'm coming to free you."

Hot, fat, overwhelming tears rolled over Ari's lower eyelids and quickly slid down her cheeks. Her eyes pooled with more while spilling the previous over. She covered her face with both hands and wept silently. The feelings of despair, that she'd had for so long, were longing for freedom, longing to shuck off the chains of her life to finally live life. But they knew that until Jay was actually there helping her pack, and until she actually set foot in New York, in Jay's brownstone, they would not believe it was actually true, that what he was saying was actually true. The feelings of despair and heartache that she'd

Anything for You

felt for so long would not believe any of this until it happened. And until then, she had work to do. Not only work because of her situation, but work for the publication of her book. So for now, she had to shove all feelings aside and get to work. Not let them feel, not let them rise, not let them exist in the real world.

Ari set Facetime to mute and laid the phone face down on the desk so Jay could not see her. She breathed deeply through her clogged nose to clear it and wiped her red face free from tears. Once she was free from all traces of depression, she pushed up the screen and took him off mute. "I needed a moment there."

"Understandable," he said softly. "Especially since your situation affects you enough to do that. It's time to live, Ari. It's time to live your life. With me."

Her puffy red eyes gazed at his face. Perfectly smooth with dimples, tousled hair, and a soft boyish smile that melted her heart. Oh God, how she wanted him. If only he wanted her. *But that will never happen if I don't take the chance*, she thought. *I can either live in the place I want to live most, and be happy that I'm there, but maybe also go without love, life, or the world. Or I could take the chance and move to New York for a year and have new experiences, a new life, maybe new loves, and maybe with Jay. And if not with Jay, then maybe he has friends to introduce me to. Single friends. Without exes and kids.* She sighed. "It won't be easy, you know. Living in your life."

He frowned at her turn of phrase. "How do you mean?"

"It won't be easy living in your life." She felt her energy being sucked from her. "Because that's what I'll be doing. Living in *your* life with you, Gloria, and the kids, all in a new city. I'm walking into *your* life. I'm moving into *your* life. I'll be living in *your* life. Everything there will be about you. I'll be immersed in *your* life, living in *your* home, dealing with *your* problems like they're my own. I might end up drowning in it."

His ego attempted to calm her. "Is that such a bad thing to start with? Living in my life with me? Once you settle in you'll be making your own life, Ari. You'll make friends, go to new places, meet new people. It won't be about me all the time, just to start with until you settle in and get the lie of the land and find your feet. And believe me; once you do you'll be off and running. I just know it. So is it really such a bad thing?"

She gave another sigh, wearier than the last. "Maybe. Maybe not." She paused a while before speaking again. "Okay, Jay. I'll live my life with you."

"Yes." He fist pumped the air. "I'm coming for you next month, Ari, my girl. I promise. I'll be there around the third week, but I'll let you know the closer we get. I still have a lot of stuff to sort out here, like getting new furniture for the brownstone. But I could leave some of that until you get here and then you get to have a say on what furniture you'd like to live with for the next year."

"Something homey and comfy," she replied. "And a big desk."

"A big desk it is. And you can decorate your bedroom suite and new office how you like."

A soft smile slid across her lips. "Sounds nice. I'd like to be able to put all of my stuff out on display. I've never been able to do that."

"Well you can do it now. We'll do up the office just how you want it."

"Again, sounds nice. But I'll believe it when I see it happen."

"It will happen, Ari, my girl. Just you wait."

*****

Over the following weeks, Ari gained followers and readers, and had networks wanting to do interviews with the world's hottest new author. But, as she explained, she wasn't a new author. She'd been writing for over fifteen years, and publishing for just over ten. So, it really was a matter of taking ten years to become an overnight success. TV hosts from around the world were reading the book and making it their book club find, or book of the week, or the one book to read, or the one must have read.

Ari did Zoom videos to many TV shows in America, half of Europe, and Australia. Days of phone interviews with radio stations followed days of Zooming to TV stations, and by the time Jay turned up in her driveway, she was exhausted.

"I'm so tired," she complained and fell into his warm, strong embrace. Her head bowed to his shoulder and rested. "So damn tired." Inhaling, she found his scent came through strongly. Masculine, with a touch of soap and a spray of cologne. A spicy, sexy cologne. "You smell good. You feel good too. Can you do all the work for me?"

"Ari, my girl." Jay held her closely, having missed her like crazy. "I've missed you and your humour, and your warmth." His chin rested gently on her head. "I've missed you so much and I wanted to come back so much sooner."

"I wish you had." She finally lifted her head to gaze into his chocolatey eyes that she always drowned in. "I wish you had. There was a fight the other day."

"Oh, Ari." Jay rubbed her back. "I'm so sorry. You can't stay. You're coming to New York with me and that's final."

Ari sighed, depression oozing from every pore. "I know.

But at least the last few weeks have also been good. Lots of interviews, more sales, more followers, more readers. That side of things has been great, and more money will be coming in, so I can definitely survive in the Big Apple, financially."

"The sales of your other books have been good?" Jay slid his hands to her arms and escorted her to the bench at the side of the house where he sat her down. "Are your other books still selling?"

"They were already selling, but in dribs and drabs after your Twitter reviews of them. The novels and the kids' stories, they've all sold consistently, but in low numbers. It's the new novel that's the best seller."

"And how many have sold now?" He hadn't spoken to Ari for most of the last month. Just a quick call to say he was coming and a photo of him getting on the plane. Most of his time had been taken up with dealing with his ex, his kids, and future movie, and TV gigs he was lining up. Plus, furniture shopping for their new home.

"Over two million, now. Can you believe that?" The shock of the whole thing hadn't worn off, and Ari was still in disbelief one month later. That she had a best-selling novel on her hands, and that she was a best-selling author with over two million in sales. "Obviously the 800,000 plus sales came in the last four weeks with all of the appearances and radio interviews. My followers on social have skyrocketed, my videos have taken off, everyone wanted to know who dressed me, who was I dressed by, where did I get my clothes and jewellery from. Every time I did a TV interview the hosts all wanted to know where I got my stuff from, so I always wore my own jewellery, and now I have thousands of orders of my jewellery. I have to keep telling everyone that I don't make it anymore, and still, they put their orders in. But I do have leftover stock that I could sell off when I settle in New York."

"Maybe you should keep some and rent it out to TV shows and for events," Jay suggested. He'd seen Ari's creations the last time he was there, and thought they were stunning.

"Mmm, that's an idea." She nodded and ran a hand through her hair. "When does the moving company get here?"

"Tomorrow." Jay leaned back against the wall and crossed his legs. "I'm glad I managed to get here today. My plane landed this morning and I drove straight here." He glanced at his watch. "Oops, need to change the time."

"Just use your phone," Ari said. "Then you'll see New York time as well. What *is* the time there at the moment?"

Jay pulled his phone out and clicked on the clock app. "Eight-thirty last night."

"Right." Ari nodded in thought. "It's about thirteen and a half hours." She remembered googling all things New York and had collected multiple travel brochures from the local travel agent.

"Yeah, about that." Jay scratched his stubbly chin. He'd shaved before the flight, but he could feel it starting to come through, so he made a mental note to shave again later, or tomorrow morning.

"How long are we still here for?" Ari shifted to the left, so she was partially facing him. "If the movers are coming tomorrow, how long are we staying after that?"

"The plan is to get back in time for Halloween. So we have about five days before our flight. That will give them time to pack and get it out, and time for us to get the rest of your things ready and a have a couple of days before we leave.

Unless you want to leave sooner?" He watched her closely.

Her gaze met his. "Maybe we should."

"Or maybe once we leave this house, you'll need a couple of days to destress. We could get a hotel down the beach for a couple of days, or a hotel in town."

Ari thought about it for a few moments. "The beach sounds nice. We could go for walks along it and hit the local shopping centres before we go. I haven't been there in years."

Jay saw some light come back into Ari's eyes. "We absolutely could. I'll call my assistant and get him to book us a suite for the next few days."

"You can't do that yourself, Jay Daniels?" Ari joked. "Are you that famous you can't even call a local hotel to book a room?"

Jay's face lit up with a grin. "Actually, I am, and you will be too, very soon, if not already. You're massive."

"Oh, God, I hope not." Ari quickly checked over her body. "I don't think I've gained any weight."

"Ha-ha. Not physically massive," Jay retorted. "Physically you're just fine. More than fine. In fact, I'd say hot. Have you been doing yourself up, Ari?"

"Well…" she drawled and shyly glanced away. "I did end up spending some of that money on myself."

"So you finally got your health issues sorted? Good." Jay's eyes perused the view and noticed her hands and nails were still the same. "You look fantastic, but then you always did." He sent a quick text off to his assistant about booking a hotel suite and shoved his phone pack into his pocket. "Have you packed up a lot of your stuff? You were supposed to pack up small stuff and what you didn't need straight away."

"Done that, in my new luggage. Figured I'd splash out on

a set and a few travel cubes to help out." Ari considered what they could have for lunch.

"Great. That'll make it quicker and easier. And hopefully, we'll be in our suite by tomorrow evening." Jay's phone beeped and he checked the message. "My assistant has made the reservations and sent through the details."

"That was quick," Ari observed. "You only just texted, what, five minutes ago?"

Jay's lips slid into a grin. "No point having an assistant if they can't be efficient."

"So…" Ari sighed, wondering if she needed an assistant of her own. "Lunch?"

*****

When Ari went to bed that night, for the last night in that home, the weight of the world had finally lifted and was no longer on her shoulders. But she wasn't free yet.

*****

The next day, the movers came and packed up her belongings. They labelled everything, and carted it out to the truck, and after five hours, her bedroom and office were almost empty except for the furniture she didn't need to take.

During the day, Jay had kept telling her to take one last look around to make sure she'd got everything while he packed her life into his car for the trip home. Six suitcases and two bags. That's what she'd packed with clothes and accessories for her move to New York. She rolled and folded and packed as tightly as she could get everything she'd require immediately upon arrival in her new home. The rest of her belongings could take weeks to arrive, so she'd packed as many essentials as possible.

When it came to her mother, it had been decided that Ari's sister would take on the care in the interim until they found a permanent carer. So Ari was finally free to go and live her life.

After spending a few days down by the beach for a quick holiday, they drove to the airport for the long flight to America. Jay's home and Ari's *new* home. It was her first time on a plane, and her first time going to a new country. And while she was excited, she was also incredibly nervous, holding Jay's hand for most of the flight.

PART TWO

Chapter 5

The view of the city from the plane window dazzled Ari, and she used her phone to take as many photos as she could. New York was a city she'd longed to visit. A city that never slept, that was always alight, and had always called to her with its siren call. Bright lights and gritty streets had always looked exciting, and now she was thrilled to be visiting, finally, even if it was for only one year. And it was going to be a year she packed full of tourist attractions, strolling each street, exploring each store, stall, park, and borough. Yes, New York was the place she currently wanted to be. Especially since that's where Jay lived, and right now, she wanted that year with him in this city more than anything. The Gold Coast could wait awhile.

They disembarked from first class, strode through the terminal, and found Jay's assistant waiting for them.

"Bobby," Jay called to the tall man waiting for the passengers to disembark.

"Jay, Ari." Bobby nodded his brunet curly head to both. "I've got the luggage cart. You get your luggage. The car's waiting out front."

"Good to know, thanks, Bobby." Jay led the way to the

luggage claim carousel to collect their bags and when the cart was full, they showed their paperwork to the officials, Ari got her passport stamped, and then they walked outside into the brisk, crispy Big Apple air of October.

Once the car was loaded, they settled back for the ride home. But Ari found it too exciting to sit still for long, snapping pictures through her window, then leaning over Jay to snap pictures outside of his. Her eyes took everything in as they drove along the highway from JFK. She was dazzled, and there was no denying it.

They arrived at Jay's brownstone twenty minutes later. It faced the East River and the downtown area of the city, plus its bridges. It was a hell of a view, one that was broken by the woman banging wildly on Jay's front door.

"Oh...fuck!" Jay eyed the woman through his window. "Bobby, what in the fuck is she doing here? Get rid of her. I don't need her bullshit right now, especially if she sees Ari."

"Who is she?" Ari queried, peering out the window past Jay.

The woman, as if hearing the question, spun around as the car pulled up and leaned over the brick wall of the high front stoop. "Jay Daniels, you fucker! Where have you fucking been?"

"Bobby!" Jay warned. "Deal with it."

Bobby was out of the car and racing up the stoop stairs as the woman was racing down.

"Get out the way, Bobby. I'm not dealing with you. I want Jay." She shoved him aside and stormed over to the car. "Jay fucking Daniels, get out of that fucking car and fucking face me, you dead beat piece of fucking shit." She banged her fists on the window and tried to see into the car.

"Fuck." Jay leaned away from the door, hanging on to the

inside handle, trying to keep her from getting in. Fear flitted through his eyes. "Ari, move to the seat opposite us so she doesn't see you."

Ari pulled off her belt and shifted to the other seat. "Jay? What's going on? Is she going to do something? That's Gloria, isn't it?" Ari's chest tightened in fear. She'd heard a few stories from Jay about his ex-wife and had seen photos of her, but this woman was looking on the mentally unhealthy side of life.

"Just lie low," Jay told her, and then spoke to the driver. "Once I'm out of the car, take Ms Travers on a drive around town, and show her the sights. Ari..." He squeezed her hand reassuringly. "I'll call when it's time to come back." He gave her one of his award-winning smiles, a fake one that didn't reach his eyes, and pushed his way out the back door, keeping his body between the door and the car so his ex couldn't see into the back seat. He slammed the door, and the driver took off.

"What do you want, Gloria?" He shoved his hands into his jeans pockets so she couldn't claim he'd touched her, and gave a slight nod to Bobby, who was filming the whole episode of rage Jay knew well after these last few years. The rules where Gloria was concerned were to always have a witness and film whatever was done in public. And most of all, to *never* touch her.

"You filthy stinking bastard." Gloria slammed her fists into his chest.

Jay baulked and stepped back out of her way but kept his hands in his pockets. He hardened his tone. "I said, what do you want?"

"I want the money you owe me," she screamed. "You

stinking deadbeat. You dumped your kids on me for the week when I told you I couldn't take them."

"They're *your* kids too; don't pretend they're not since you have custody." Jay kept his tone firm and tried not to yell as his temper flared. "I told you I'd be gone for a week or so and would be back in time to take them for Halloween. *You* agreed to that plan last month. As for the money I owe you…" He stood firm, but leaned towards her, towering over her by a head. "That automatically goes into the account that was set up, which we *both* agreed upon. To come here demanding to know where it is, when it's automatically put into the account is just one more excuse for you to have a go at me. To *attack* me, which is what you're doing. So since you have your money, and I'm taking the kids tomorrow as planned, you have no right to be here harassing me. Leave, or I'll call the police."

"The police," she spat. "What are they going to do? I'll tell them *you* hit me and *you're* a deadbeat dad."

A movie star herself, she was used to getting her way, used to people saying yes to her, used to having what *she* wanted. But since Jay had left her and asked for a divorce, and the proof of her infidelity had come out, she'd been on the back foot and didn't like how that felt. That was why she always took him to court to try and get ahead. But the idiot judges kept letting him win and she hated it, hated them, and hated her ex for not giving her what she wanted. Her singing toy boy certainly did, doing things to her in bed her ex certainly hadn't. Her anger boiled and something clicked in her head. "Why did the car drive away?"

"Because it's a rental and I didn't want you smashing anything." Jay kept his gaze and tone directed at her. No

Anything for You

need to give things away and make the situation worse.

"Ah-huh." Gloria stared directly into her ex-husband's eyes. "Was there a *woman* in the car? Did you pick up a whore at the airport, or wherever the hell you've just come from? Aren't you done bouncing rebound whores on your dick, Jay?" She hated not knowing what he got up to, regardless of the fact it was technically none of her business, but not having as much control over him as she used to pissed her off. She couldn't control who he saw, where he went, what he did, or who he did it with. She had no problem taking him to court when he did. Every time he had dated someone she went to court for full custody. But once again, those idiot judges threw her claim out. Stupid bastards, they had no idea.

"I have my luggage in the car, which is now being driven around waiting to come home so you don't damage anything. Leave, Gloria, it's time for you to go. You're not welcome at my home."

"*Your* home," she shrieked, waving an arm at the five-storey red brick brownstone. "That you bought with *my* money. Money meant for *me* and *our* children."

"Hardly!" Jay pulled his phone out and typed in 911. "Leave now, Gloria, or I'm hitting the call button." He showed her the screen. "And if you don't think I'm serious, just try me. Because I was done with your bullshit when I left and filed for divorce. And I am *beyond* done with your bullshit now. I will not have you stalk me at my new home."

"Stalk you!" The anger seethed in her veins. "Maybe if you'd done your damn job as my husband we'd still be together, and I wouldn't have to track you down just to get what I'm owed by my *ex*-husband."

"That's right, *Gloria*, I'm your *ex*-husband, and you have been paid enough." Jay's finger hovered over the call button. "*Leave now.*"

"Oh, I'll leave when I want." Gloria spun around to walk back up the front stairs but she finally noticed Bobby who was holding up his phone. "Are you filming this, you snivelling little toe rag?" Gloria started towards him, right fist in the air, but he darted out of the way and kept on filming.

"Come back here," she screeched, unaware that a patrol car had parked at the kerb.

Jay looked at them in surprise and lowered his phone. "Oh, this is gold," he muttered. "And not my doing."

"Sir, what's going on?" a tall African American officer asked. He prepared to draw his weapon. "We've had several calls about a commotion."

"Not from me," Jay replied. "Must be from the neighbours, because my ex-wife was here when I got home, and I haven't called you yet."

Gloria was still screeching at Bobby who kept darting out of her way and they were now several houses down the street.

"She's your ex?" the female officer asked. "Do you know why she's here?"

Jay's gaze darted between all four of them in amusement. "She wanted more money and to have a bitch. Look, I have a guest being driven around in the limo we arrived home in. Can you hurry and get her out of the way?"

"And what do you want us to do?" the male officer asked, looking from Jay to his ex and the man she was trying to beat up. Both were headed back as Bobby scurried down the street.

"Thank God you're here," Bobby gasped at the officers and stopped beside Jay. "You don't pay me enough to deal with this," he told him.

"Remind me to give you a bonus," Jay replied dryly and watched Gloria slow to a halt as she realised what was going on.

"You bastard, you called the cops." Diving for Jay, her fists managed to pummel his chest before the officers hauled her off and cuffed her. "What are you cuffing me for," she shrieked, and struggled to get out of the restraints. "He's the one who should be arrested."

"For what?" Jay frowned in disgust. "*You're* here at *my* residence making a scene. And I'm not the one who called the cops, my neighbours did that before I even got home."

"You bastard, you'll pay for this," Gloria screamed as she was led to the patrol car. "You'll pay for this Jay fucking Daniels. You and that whore you have in the car wanting to move into your house." Struggling, she was rewarded by being slammed across the hood and having her cuffs tightened.

"Calm down or we'll have to spray you," the female officer told her. "Now get in the back seat." She placed her hand on Gloria's head and pushed her into the back of the car.

Jay saw his new neighbours loitering with their phones in hand. "I am so sorry everyone." He held his hands together, prayer style. "I am so sorry for the commotion. Thank you to the person, or people, who called the NYPD before I even got here. I'm sorry this happened only a couple of months after I moved in. I hope it won't happen again." He turned to the officers and shook their hands. "Thank you so much for attending. We have it all on film if you need the evidence. I'll get my lawyer to contact you. Thank you so much."

When they asked for a photo with him, he obliged then leaned down to the back window to talk to Gloria who growled at him. "You've been arrested, Gloria. And you'll more than likely be charged with a few crimes. How do you think this will look in the press? Or in the court the next time you drag me there?"

It was only then that the situation hit her, and her eyes grew wide at the thought of bad publicity and losing *another* court case which was chewing through her money. The publicity she'd get for being in the back seat of a patrol car in cuffs and taken to a station to be charged with various offences, was not going to be good. She narrowed her eyes and growled. "You're not going to get away with this, Jay Daniels. If it's the last thing I do."

Jay and Bobby watched the car drive down the usually quiet street, waving at her as she plastered her face against to window, teeth bared in a snarl. They watched the neighbours finally go back inside now the commotion was over, and watched the car turn left three blocks down.

"Now." Jay pulled out his phone. "Send that video to my lawyer and keep it in a safe place. I'll call Ari." He dialled her number and heard her pick up on the first ring.

"Jay?"

"Ari, my girl. Problem solved; you can come back now." He watched Bobby send off the email and did a slow pace on the footpath. "Where are you?"

"Not far, I think." Ari glanced out the back passenger window. "It's been a nice trip around town, but I haven't really enjoyed it because my stomach's been in knots about what's happening."

"It's over now, so tell the driver you can come home. We'll wait outside for you."

"Okay. Be there soon." She clicked off and told the driver

Anything for You

to take her back. The muscles in her shoulders relaxed a little and the view of the lower Manhattan skyline took her breath away. *Everything will be all right, Ari. You just have to believe that*, she told herself. *Jay can deal with his ex, he'll keep her away from us, and you can go about living your best life here in the Big Apple.*

While Jay waited for the car, he took a call from his lawyer.

"Do you want a restraining order on the bitch?" he asked. "I can get one within the hour."

"I don't know. Would that just make her worse?" Jay went back to pacing on the tree-lined street.

"Worse than what? What I saw in the video?" Merrick Statton esquire asked. All of his clients were millionaires; actors, singers, musicians, social media app makers. If you earned less than a million after tax each year, he wasn't interested unless you were a long-standing client. "We could petition for full custody of the kids and use this video to prove she's off her rocker. You'd get it, too."

"Do you know if she's being charged, or will she get off because of who she is?" Jay hoped for the former as it might knock some sense into his bitch of an ex.

"*Do you* want to lay charges?" Merrick asked. "It was you and Bobby she beat up."

"How would that go down?" Jay inquired, seriously considering the prospect of getting rid of her behind bars for a while. "Actor Jay Daniels lays charges against former wife, actress Gloria Hannaford, for assault and battery."

"Probably not good," Merrick replied. "But it *would* make her look bad. Just like the cheating scandal did when you divorced. Although…" He leaned back in his chair and tapped his meaty fingers on his rich oak wood desk. "We could make her grateful that you *didn't* press charges *and* still make you look good."

Jay stopped pacing, excited by the news. "What? How?"

"I could have a chat with her lawyer, and while the charges could be dropped, she would have to sign a document similar to a restraining order. If you *don't* want a full restraining order on her, that is. But she would have to stay away from now on unless invited to your home, in order for the charges not being filed. That would be the deal. And she would have to play nice for her alimony and child support to continue."

Jay glanced at Bobby. "Would that be for just my charges, or for both of us?"

Bobby cocked his head and watched him in return. "Burn the bitch!" he told him.

"Tell him I heard that, and you can have a chat with him." Merrick swung his chair on the 60th floor of one of Manhattan's most prestigious buildings towards the East River. It gave him views of four bridges, and the boroughs of Brooklyn and Queens, which was quite a sight. "Make her grovel to you for once. And think of it as the first step, the *soft* step, towards keeping her out of your life. Especially if you don't want to look bad."

"How about I just look like the battered ex-husband?" Jay suggested. "Is a full restraining order something that would make me look good at some point?"

"It could. But this might also show you're still a caring, generous man who wants her to stop, but also doesn't want to see the mother of his children in jail."

Jay's ego bristled. It always wanted him to come out on

top. It always wanted him to better his ex and make sure she looked worse off. Damn Merrick!

"Okay. Let's do that and I'll talk to Bobby. Tell her lawyer the video will be released—"

"I'd say it's too late for that." Merrick watched Gloria pummel her fists into Jay in the video his assistant was showing him on her tablet. "It's already out across social media, thanks to your neighbours. I'd say I'll be hearing from her lawyer any minute." The phone on the assistant's desk rang. "That's probably him now. I'll get you ahead of the game by drawing up a statement. You don't want the mother of your children to go to jail, yada, yada, even though she cheated on you while married, yada, forgive, forget, yada, yada, fucking yada."

"And that's why I pay you the big bucks." Jay grinned and watched the limo pull up. "Gotta go." He clicked off the call and said to Bobby, "We need to hire a bodyguard for Ari, or maybe an assistant who knows martial arts." He reached out and pulled the back door open before the car could fully stop at the kerb. "Ari. Let's get you inside. Bobby, start pulling out the luggage." He held his hand out for Ari and helped her out of the car. "Here we go, home sweet home. I'm sorry that your homecoming was marred by my bitch of an ex."

Ari's boots crunched the lightly dropped snow on the footpath and she inhaled the crisp air floating off the river and across the street. Giving a quick glance to the autumn-filled tree-lined street, she shook her head and hugged him. "Is she gone? It's not your fault."

"She's gone." Jay kissed her temple and pulled away, holding her by the arms. "But hopefully things will be better. Let's talk about it inside." He closed the back door and they helped unload the luggage from the trunk before carrying Ari and Jay's multitude of bags and cases up the front stairs to the door.

"We have a lovely vestibule where you can wipe your feet or hang a raincoat before entering the house." Jay led the way into the warm interior and set four of Ari's cases by the stairs. "Welcome home, Ari. For the next year, anyway." He saw Bobby trailing behind them with his bags before closing the door. "Bobby, can you lug this stuff up to the bedrooms and I'll show Ari around?"

"Ah…sure." Bobby shrugged and hauled his boss's luggage up the stairs.

"Okay, so you can see the hallway goes all the way to the back of the house which is the dining room and kitchen. And through this door here…" He showed her into the room on their right which was a cosy sitting room. "We have a couple of lounging areas that also lead to the kitchen." He clasped his hands and spun around to face her. "There are bedrooms on the next two floors, and then the master above those. There's a bathroom under the stairs on this floor, and a laundry, storage room, and gym in the basement along with another half bath. So…" He watched her expectantly. "What do you think?"

Ari glanced around in wonder. "Except for the lack of furniture, the bones look good."

The hallway was lined with black and white tiles. Most likely they were representative of the ones that had been originally laid. The rooms down the side of the house had light wood floors, varnished to a shine. Small fireplaces sat either side of the lounge room with sliding doors to divide the two areas. What she could see of the kitchen was modern and silver. The walls were the colour of soft yellowy cream, and the curtains were light enough to let the sun through.

"You haven't bought much, have you?"

Jay shrugged. "I bought beds, side tables, lounge suite, electricals, and the dining table and chairs. It was all I needed. But now we can go shopping and you can pick some things out. I mean, come on," he grabbed her hand and spun her around, "this is where you'll be staying for the next year and I trust your taste. Bring this place to life with colour."

"Is there food in the fridge?" Ari asked. "I suppose I should learn about all things supermarket while I'm here and all of the delicacies New York has to offer."

Jay dismissed that suggestion with a slight wave of his hand. "Worry about that later. Let's get you up to your room and settled in. You're going to be here for a year and can decorate how you like." He led the way up the light-coloured wooden stairs to the light and bright second floor which had a view of the river and took her into the bedroom facing the front of the house. "Here's the bedroom. You have a king-sized bed, a view of the river, and a walk-in closet." He moved her through the doorway to the left to see the closet. "And there's a small bathroom that both bedrooms share." It was decorated in white, yellow and blue. He continued through the adjoining door. "You can use this closet for storage, or the rest of your clothes, and then here's the back bedroom you can use for an office."

The room was bare, approximately the same size as the front bedroom and had views of the back garden and the house behind them.

"It's plain, and I figured you wouldn't want to be disturbed while you're working, so a plain office with no distractions would be good." He turned around, put his hands on his hips, and took in her wide-eyed expression. "I can't tell what emotions you're feeling right now."

"Ah..." She pulled a face as she tried to figure it out. "Wonder, excitement, disbelief, and a little bit of fear and trepidation."

"You know those last two basically mean the same thing, right?" Jay grinned and gently pulled her into his arms. "There's nothing to fear, Ari, my girl, I promise. *Especially* from my ex."

"What happened?" She gazed into his eyes and saw nothing, but knew fear was in hers.

Jay measured his response. "She became physical, but as I keep telling you, she's not your problem to worry about. Yes, you will most likely see it on the news or social media, but she's not your problem, Ari. Okay?" He planted a kiss on her forehead. "So, what do you think you'll need for this room? Do you want to make this room your office?" Looking at the bare walls he considered a few layouts. "We could make it your bedroom and switch them around if you prefer. Make the front room your office, to get a bit more light during the day."

Ari sighed and unwrapped her scarf, unbuttoned her jacket, and took a good look around. "I guess it would come down to which room has the most light. I'm only going to be sleeping at night, but possibly working all day. I'll need light to work."

"But you won't be working immediately," Jay told her. "I want you to take the rest of the year off and just breathe, relax, and be a visitor in this city. Sightsee, take a holiday, and let your soul rejuvenate, and regenerate, and revitalise."

He moved his hands with his words, creating movement and flow. "Let yourself be free, Ari. Free to roam, to go out and come home whenever you want, do what you want, see and be what you want."

A small chuckle passed through her lips. "Cute." Sliding her coat off and folding it over her arm, she added, "I think for now I'll unpack. It shouldn't take long, and it'll help me feel settled."

"Okay." Jay gave a nod. "Need help?"

"No." She shook her head and gave him a soft smile in return. "It'll be therapeutic to do myself. Besides," she looked at her watch which she'd changed to NY time, "it's already afternoon and we haven't eaten lunch, so it could be dinnertime by the time I finish."

Jay took her hand and checked her watch. "Okay. It's three. Do you want a snack, or a drink? And we'll eat later."

"A drink would be incredibly appreciated," Ari said, and they walked back into the front bedroom where Bobby had deposited her luggage. "And unpacking shouldn't take long. It's the packing that takes forever."

"Yes, but…" Jay raised his forefinger in dispute. "You'll take forever deciding where to put everything because you get to use both closets."

A small smile slid onto Ari's face. "Yes, true. But," she raised her forefinger and butted it against his, "I have two closets to use, one for summer, one for winter. So all of my coats and jackets will be stored quickly, as will everything else. But I saw there was no island for jewellery so…" She glanced towards the wall dividing the bedroom from the closet. "Maybe some tallboys for jewellery storage would be good."

"Let's leave that until you're unpacked and have a think

about what you'll actually need, and which bedroom you're taking. You get started and I'll go and get us a couple of drinks."

While he was gone, Ari pulled her two small suitcases off the handles of her two largest cases and set them on the bed. They were full of her jewellery and accessories that she'd need for the winter months. Then she placed all four large cases on the bed and opened them. Full of clothes and shoes, they were going to be easy to unpack because most of the clothes were in travel cubes.

Downstairs, Jay grabbed two cans of Pepsi Max from the fridge and said to Bobby, "What do you want to do about Gloria? If you want to sue her, that's up to you. But have a chat with Merrick first." He cracked his can open and sculled, waiting for his assistant.

"As much as I want hazard pay, I also want to see that bitch burn." Having just turned thirty-five, Bobby had been Jay's assistant for ten years. He'd been through the cheating scandal, the divorce scandal, and the demise of his boss's career. But these past few months he'd noticed the change. He nodded his curly head. "Let's burn the bitch where she lies." The hate he had for her emanated from every pore and Jay knew it.

"Okay," Jay agreed. "If you're finished, you can head home and take the rest of the day off. It's the weekend tomorrow, so I'll see you next week," he paused, "unless I absolutely need something I can't do or get myself."

"You've become so damn lazy," Bobby complained and picked up his jacket from the back of the stool at the island bench. He slid his arms into it and pulled it around himself. "I mean, seriously. You'd be completely lost without me.

And pretty much screwed every which way."

"I am screwed, Bobs. But Ari is my saviour." Jay leaned against the kitchen bench and took another swig of drink.

"Not by me, you're not." Bobby slung his messenger bag over his head and around to his back. "And yeah, I can see you've perked up since you met wonder woman upstairs."

Jay's grin lit up his face. "Yeah, she is. Shit!" He held up the other can. "I better get her drink to her and help unpack."

"Don't worry about *your* unpacking. I already did that." Bobby headed for the front door. "Seriously, you don't pay me enough to deal with your shit. Ex-wife *or* dirty laundry."

Jay's laugh was hearty as he followed Bobby to the front door and slapped him on the shoulder. "Just hang on until next year, Bobs. You'll get your raise then."

"Oh, an extra two-hundred and fifty in my pocket," Bobby mocked and stepped onto the stoop. "That won't even cover the cost of getting here with the way prices are rising."

"Oh, boo-fricken-hoo, Bobs. See you next week." Jay closed and triple locked both front doors and raced upstairs to Ari's bedroom. "Got your drink. It's not as cold, sorry. Had to talk to Bobby."

"That's okay." Ari walked out of the closet and took the can Jay cracked open. She sculled it back and winced. "Whoo," she gasped, "still cold." Placing it on the bedside table, she shut one of her large suitcases. "One down."

"Already? That was quick. Need help?"

"If you don't mind." They made light work of the rest of the unpacking. It was easy enough, with her toiletries in the bathroom and her office bag with laptop and notebooks by the bedside cupboard.

They sat heavily on the bed. "Done. For now." Ari checked

her watch. "Just on 5:30. What time do you normally eat?"

"Not until around seven." Jay rubbed the sore spot on the top of his head. It had been playing up since he'd seen Gloria. "But if you want to eat earlier…"

"No, seven's fine." Ari slumped back on the bed and lay staring up at the ceiling. It was the same soft teal colour as the walls. As pale as could be, but still noticeable. "I guess I should make a list of what I need."

"No rush. We'll need other stuff as well." Jay was comfortable there on the bed beside her. It felt natural to be in that position. "I have the kids for Halloween. We'll be trick-or-treating. Did I tell you?"

"Yeah. I guess I'll meet them then." Ari wondered what they were like. While she'd seen photos and heard stories, she also knew Jay felt he could no longer be a proper father to them.

"You will. But I'm not holding out that they'll love you as much as I do. I know their mother will make them spy on us and tell her everything."

"And then use it against you," Ari murmured, swinging her legs a little. "That sucks. No parent should ever do that."

"No, they shouldn't. But that's not your problem to worry about, Ari, my girl." Jay rolled onto his side and leaned up on his elbow, his head on his hand so he could look at her. "My ex is my business to deal with, as I keep telling you. Don't worry your pretty head about it. And if the kids don't like you, then…" He sighed and looked into the distance. "Then they don't like you. I don't have them often, thanks to her, as you know. I don't think anything will make it better, and I don't think anything you do will change things. Just be yourself, be polite to them, for my sake, and leave their shitty behaviour to me."

"I'm not going to tolerate any bullshit," Ari told him and slid her hand over his stubbly face. "From them or you. I may be a guest in this house, a contracted guest at that, but that contract said nothing about tolerating anyone's bullshit. Yours, theirs, or your ex's." Her hand fell to the bed. "Hell, even Bobby's."

Jay chuckled. "Yeah, yeah. I know, okay. Feel the need to defend yourself verbally, but for the love of God, don't touch them. If they touch you, tell me and I'll deal with it."

"That could be a problem," Ari argued. "If someone hits me, I hit back. Your kids are old enough to know better. If they hit me, I'm defending myself."

Jay studied her face for a moment and deemed her to be serious. He also realised it would piss Gloria off. And to that, he just didn't give a fuck. "Okay," he agreed. "Hit them back. But remember, I have cameras around the place, so don't hit first. And then I can use it to show they were abusive."

"You have cameras? Where?" Ari frowned. "Not here in the bedrooms, I hope."

"Oh, yeah, I'm so going to perve on you at night," Jay joked. "No, no, not the bedrooms. Main rooms downstairs, and hallways upstairs. Let them hit first then strike back."

"Your kids sound as fabulous as their mother." Ari sighed.

"You don't know a quarter of it. But she's taught them well, according to her standards, unfortunately."

"So I don't have to like them, and I won't tolerate their bullshit," Ari agreed. "Done!"

"Okay. If you're done let's head down and find something to eat." Jay pulled her to her feet and led the way.

Chapter 6

The next few days was a flurry of furniture shopping, Jay dealing with his lawyer *and* his ex, and making Ari feel comfortable in his home. Which was now also her home.

Ari took pictures of everything and documented it all on her social media pages, inbetween unpacking all of her jewellery and accessories into her new tallboys built for jewellery storage, being shown around by Jay, and taking afternoon walks with him along the river.

Halloween came along on Monday and Jay went to pick his kids up at four o'clock, so they'd have the time to change into their costumes.

He rang the doorbell. Barely a second went by before it was flung open.

"Jay."

"Gloria."

"The kids are ready. Make sure you have them back by nine-thirty at the latest." She could barely look him in the eye. A far change from the previous week.

"Ah…calm Gloria," Jay mused. "An at home Gloria." He stayed put in the doorway, hands in jeans pockets. "See, isn't it nice being civil?" He glanced past her sullen face to see her toy boy lover in the lounge room at the end of the hall. The lounge room and hall he'd paid for with the divorce settlement. Once, it had been theirs. Set in the heart of New York City, it boasted views one would die to own in the Big Apple. Their retreat had been the old brownstone standalone mansion out in the burbs of Brooklyn, but neither had lived there since, so it was on the market and waiting to be sold. Gloria had demanded the apartment and half his money. What she got was the apartment and one third of his money, as a lot of it had been made before they met. They also split their business dealings and sold off antiques, paintings, and art neither of them wanted. But she'd still wanted more, regardless of how many times the judges said no.

She glared at him under hooded eyes. Eyes that sparkled with anger and hatred that clearly emanated from her core. "What do you want me to say?" she said through gritted teeth. "I will *never* thank you."

"Of course you won't," Jay replied. "Because you're never thankful. To me or anyone else it seems except the boy child you're with." He nodded at the lover standing at the end of the hall, casually leaning against one wall, and received a nod in return. At least Denver had the decency to never get involved in their issues and kept his mouth shut when Jay turned up. "You seem incapable of playing nicely, of being generous, of being grateful or thankful. So while I know you, Gloria, I also know I'll never get any of the respect, love, or decency I got when we were first together and first married. But even then, I'll concede it didn't last long in our marriage, either." His gaze moved from her face to Denver's. "You learned how to disrespect me pretty damn quickly."

"You made it easy," she spat, and glanced over her shoulder.

Anything for You

Denver made her heart skip a beat, and when he smiled in return, it made her want to jump him right there. She turned back to Jay. "You made it easy to disrespect you. But then again, you never deserved my respect in the first place."

"So why bother marrying me? Why bother having kids with me?" Jay asked earnestly. "Why bother making babies with a man you so clearly didn't love or respect, but who wanted to spend his life with you and give you the world?" His gaze travelled her body. Her brown hair was in a neat topknot, she had a full face of make-up, a grey sweatshirt teamed with a pair of black sweatpants, and pink bunny slippers on her feet. If she didn't look angry and hostile all the time, she'd still be the attractive woman he'd fallen head over heels in love with all those years ago.

"Why do you think?" she tormented, her brows rising in detestation. "Career, money, opportunities. You offered the world and I took what I could get." Her cold eyes swept over him. "And ten plus years ago your DNA was pretty damn hot. I knew our children would be beautiful. That's the only reason. To procreate and get beautiful children." A sneer lifted her top lip. "It's not like your dick could do anything else."

Cutting remarks about a man's penis were always a low blow. It didn't matter who said it, or who it was said to, that was the ego, the foundation of a man's masculinity. You cut that, you cut deep. And he still felt it deeply. So deeply he wanted to bite back, but refrained. He went in the opposite direction.

"I feel sorry for you, Gloria." He watched her expression change to one of puzzlement. "You're so full of hate and bitterness over *me* ending the relationship, that you don't see what damage you're doing. You don't see that you're playing right into the hands of your mother who did the exact same thing to you. And when your boy child down there," he nodded at him, "stops doing exactly what you want, you'll dump him and move on, not even caring about what any of this is doing to the children."

"Dad."

Jay's attention turned to his children. "Hey kids. I'm here to take you trick-or-treating." Under the costumes, he saw unhappy faces and knew his relationship with their mother had taken a toll on them. "You ready to go?"

Andrew, aged ten, growing tall and lanky like his father, glared from parent to parent before looking at his sister, Marisol, aged eight. She was dressed as Anna from *Frozen*, as she was every year, and he was dressed as The Joker from *Batman*. Last year he'd been Batman, the good guy; this year he was the villain. "Yeah, I guess," he finally replied, watching his mother.

"You two have fun, my babies." Gloria took his face in her hands and kissed his cheek before doing the same to his sister. Her beaming face contradicted her thoughts. "I've told your dad to have you home by nine-thirty, and I don't want you eating a lot of candy before you get home, or you'll be sick. Okay?" She adjusted Marisol's dress. "Have fun, you two."

"Come on, kids." Jay held out his arm to round them up. "Let's go and see how much candy you can get this year. Think you'll beat last year?" Jay ignored Gloria as he watched the kids leave the apartment and walk off for the elevator. He followed and stopped behind them. "I thought we'd go somewhere different this year."

The lift doors opened, and they stepped inside. He pressed the down button and saw Gloria standing in the hallway, arms crossed, scowl on her face, watching. Jay turned his back to her and waited for the doors to close.

"Why are we going somewhere different?" Andrew asked, staring defiantly up at his father. "And why are we going with you?"

Jay inwardly cringed. "Because I thought somewhere different would be good. And you're going with me because that's what your mother and I set up."

"But I want to go trick-or-treating with Mama and Denver," Marisol piped up.

Jay looked down at her and saw his own eyes reflected back at him. "Sorry, Mari, your mom didn't want to. She hasn't been trick-or-treating with us since we were a family."

"Why?" Mari asked as the doors opened.

"Well," Jay started as he led the way outside. "Because she just doesn't want to. I don't know of any other reason, Mari. I'm sorry." He saw Bobby and flagged him down. After helping the kids into the back seat of his car, he climbed in after them. "Okay, Bobby's going to take us to my new neighbourhood so you can see where I live now for when you come to visit. And if we have time, we'll fit in a trip to the old neighbourhood."

"Can we go there first?" Andrew turned from the window. "I can see my friends."

Jay thought about it few a few seconds. "Ah, sure. Bobby, the old neighbourhood, please."

It took twenty minutes to get there and Bobby parked outside of their old house.

"I wish we still lived here." Marisol climbed down from the four-wheeler and stood staring up at the red brick mansion. "Do we still own it, Daddy?"

"We do, for now, sweetie." Jay closed the car door and glanced at the house. It held a lot of memories. Still. "Mama and I are trying to sell it because we don't want it anymore."

"Why don't you want it?" Andrew asked, antsy to get going. He could see groups of kids down the street. "The same reason you don't want us?"

At some point in the visits, comments like that always came up.

"I've told you before, Andrew, your mom and I never said we didn't want you. It's just that houses cost money to run, and your mom doesn't want to live here anymore, so we're selling it. A house is just a possession; it has nothing to do with not wanting you."

"Tell that to Mama." Marisol brushed her wig aside. "She leaves us with the babysitters all the time so she can go out with Denver."

"And you rarely want us." Andrew scowled. It was an exact replica of his mother's. "I'm going to catch up with my friends." He took off down the street after the group of kids.

"Andrew," Jay yelled. "Don't run off." Sighing in frustration, he grabbed Marisol's hand. "Come on, Mari, let's try and catch up." They walked quickly down the street to meet up with the group which contained the neighbourhood kids and a couple of parents.

"Hey, Jay's back in the hood." One father greeted him with a hearty handshake. "What are you doin' here?"

"Oh, the kids wanted to come back to see their friends," Jay replied smoothly and watched the kids compare costumes with their friends.

The conversation continued down the street and back up the other side.

"Why don't you come in for a beer before you go?" another father asked, but he received a shake of the head in return.

"Sorry. I gotta get the kids home by nine-thirty and I want to show them around the new house first." Jay rounded up his children. "Thanks anyway, though." They walked back down the street to the car. "Did you get lots of candy?"

Andrew shrugged a shoulder. "Got a bit. Some things I hate." He climbed up into the car and slammed the door.

Jay bristled and led Marisol around to the driver's side to let her in. "And you, Mari?"

"I got some gummy bears." She popped two into her mouth and climbed up. "Where to now, Daddy? I want to go home soon."

Jay checked his watch. "I'll have you home by nine-thirty, Mari, don't worry. We're going to my new neighbourhood now so you can see how they do Halloween."

Andrew slumped down in his seat and sighed. "We don't care about your new neighbourhood." He stared out the window and munched on candy.

"There's no need to be rude, Andrew," Jay said. "People move all the time. Your mom moved into the apartment, and I moved into a new home. The house is being sold because we don't want it anymore. It's just a house."

"It's *our* house," Andrew argued, glaring at his father. "*We* grew up in it."

Jay glared back and raised a brow. "*We*, and that also means *you*, haven't lived in that house for nearly four years. You had only six years of your life in it."

"Doesn't matter. I hate the apartment and I hate your new neighbourhood," Andrew grumbled and shoved more candy into his mouth.

They pulled up out the front of Jay's house.

"Okay, everyone, here we are. I thought we could walk around the neighbourhood before I show you what the house looks like."

"I need the toilet, Daddy," Marisol said, and quickly unbuckled her belt.

"Oh, okay, well I guess that means we'll be seeing it now." Jay opened the door and helped Marisol down and waited for Andrew to slide across. Instead, he stormed out of the other side and slammed the door. "Andrew!" Jay reprimanded. "Stop slamming the damn doors."

"Daddy, you swore." Marisol popped another two gummies into her mouth. "And I need to pee."

"Then let's get you inside and you can both meet my house guest while you're at it. Her name is Ari, and she's a best-selling author from Australia."

"Is she your latest whore?" Andrew asked before sticking a hard-boiled candy into his mouth. A second later he was choking on it as Jay grabbed him forcefully by both arms. He was roughly shaken and swallowed the candy in a breathless gulp.

"Don't you *ever* say that about *any* woman, let alone Ari," Jay warned in a low and deadly tone. He bent over far enough so he was eye to eye with his son. "We raised you to *never* use language like that against a woman, or any other human being. How *dare* that word even pass your lips." Jay shook his frightened son. "Don't *ever* use that word again, do you understand me?" Another shake. "Andrew."

Andrew gulped and stared back at his father; the father who had never hit him, and rarely raised his voice at him. But, thanks to his mother, this father was a man he was

Anything for You

coming to hate.

"Where did you get that from?" Jay demanded, and tightened his grip. "Your mother?"

Andrew's breathing was ragged. "That's what Mom said."

"Just because your mother says it doesn't mean you should. Understand me?" Jay moved his face towards his son's so they were nose to nose. "Don't *ever* use a word like that against another human being again. Do you understand me, Andrew Jason Daniels?" When he didn't reply, he shook him harder. "Apologise!"

Andrew gulped at the pain in his arms. "Sorry," he managed through gritted teeth. "I won't." He couldn't wait to get home to tell his mother about this.

"Daddy, I really have to pee now," Marisol called from the front door as she danced in place.

With one hand, Jay dragged Andrew up the stairs to the front door. "Okay, sweetie, let's get you inside." He reached for the door knob with his other hand, but it opened first.

"Hey," Ari said brightly. "Happy Halloween." She waved them inside. "I saw you pull up."

"Andrew, Marisol, this is Ari, my house guest. Say hello."

"Hello, I need to pee." Marisol looked up to the sparkle-covered Ari. "Sparkly jewels."

Ari smiled at her. "Hello, Marisol. Let me show you to the bathroom." She led her down the hall to the bathroom under the stairs and opened the door. The light automatically came on. "Here you go. Let me take your pumpkin bucket."

Marisol handed it over and stepped inside the small room. "Some privacy, please."

Ari's grin grew. "Let me know if you need help, and I'll pop your bucket on the kitchen table." She walked into the kitchen and set it on the table next to platters and bowls of Halloween food and candy. She also noticed Jay hadn't followed and found him in the hallway, hands in pockets, talking to Andrew. "You guys want anything? Drink, candy, cupcakes?"

"I'll have a quick drink, but Andrew's waiting for the bathroom," Jay said. "Andrew, this is Ari, my houseguest."

"Hello, Andrew, nice to meet you."

She was met with silence as Andrew sullenly stared at the floor.

"Andrew's in trouble because he used a bad word to describe you," Jay told her. "He was swiftly told off and he told me it's what his mother had said."

Ari's brows rose. "Oh…well. That's unfortunate. Unfortunately it's not the first time I've been called bad names. But it is unfortunate that men can't be friends with women without someone accusing them of something. How sad that your ex had to be so rude about someone she's never met and has foisted that upon her children."

Marisol came out of the bathroom and Andrew walked in.

Jay sighed and bowed his head in frustration.

"Mari, your bucket is on the kitchen table along with some Halloween goodies. Would you like a bite of something before you go?" Ari asked her.

"Yes, please."

Ari led the way into the kitchen and poured drinks for all of them. "We have cupcakes in the shape of pumpkins, marshmallow ghosts on sticks, spider and goblin gummies." She handed a fizzy purple drink to Marisol. "Grape soda with snakes."

Anything for You

Marisol giggled and drank from the snake straw Ari had put in the cup.

Jay accepted his glass and checked his watch. "Only seven-thirty. We should be able to get around the neighbourhood in an hour." He heard Andrew come out of the bathroom, but he didn't enter the kitchen. "Andrew, do you want a drink and some food before we continue trick-or-treating?"

He was met with silence.

Jay walked over to the hallway door and saw Andrew sulking by the front door. "Andrew. I'm talking to you. Do you want something to eat or drink before we go?"

Andrew refused to raise his eyes, but he did say, "No, thank you."

Heaving a deep sigh from the pit of his gut, Jay turned away. "He's not interested," he muttered and finished off his drink. "Do you want to see your bedroom, Mari? I bought both of you beds and side tables, with desks and bookshelves you'll have to fill up with your stuff when you come over." He picked up a gummy snake and bit its head off. "Or do you just want to get back to trick-or-treating?"

Mari sucked the last of her drink through the straw, making a lot of noise in the process. "I don't care about my room, Daddy. We hardly spend time with you and probably won't be staying here unless Mama wants to dump us to go away with Denver."

Jay glanced from his daughter to Ari in surprise and watched as Marisol shoved a whole cupcake into her mouth. Luckily, they were small ones, otherwise she would have choked.

"Well..." Ari took a sip of drink and continued. "Guess you'd better get going then. Quite a few groups have already been around. This is what's left." She waved a hand at the table. "I guess we get to feast on it for the rest of the week." Resting her left hand on her hip, she noticed Jay's worn-out expression that was quickly turning into exhaustion.

"Guess we'd better get going then," Jay agreed. "Mari, you finished?" He watched her lick her fingers.

"Can I have some more drink to wash that down with?" she asked.

"Sure." Ari poured her a quarter cup of grape fizz and Mari downed it in seconds.

"Ah…" Mari gasped and handed the cup back. "Thank you. Time to go." She collected her pumpkin bucket and wandered down to the hallway.

"She looks like her mother," Ari murmured. "And Andrew looks like you, but definitely takes after *her*."

"I don't think I've ever called a woman a whore because I heard my mother use the word, though," Jay replied and raised a brow. "I'll call you when I drop them off."

Ari's brows rose. "Ah, so that's what it was… Okay. See you later." She squeezed his arm and followed him down the hall.

"Okay, here we go. One trip around the block and then I'll get you home." Jay opened the door and ushered them through before glancing over his shoulder. "Bye. I'll see you later."

"Bye." Ari watched them hustle down the stairs and down the road to the next house. She knew they'd be taking the side street to circle the block as the street behind them had been closed off to cars for the evening and folks had gone all out with decorations. She closed the door and hurried back to the warmth, wondering what Jay had dealt with. "How

Anything for You

bloody sad that she had to call me names in front of her children without even knowing who I was or what I'm here for?" Ari collected the empty dishes and moved the leftovers into containers with snap lids so they stayed fresh, and then remembered she'd seen Bobby in the car. Quickly whipping up a container of goodies, she hurried it out to him, knocking on his window.

He jumped in surprise and hit the down button on the window. "Hey."

"Hello, Bobby. I made you up a container of Halloween goodies and added a can of soda. Unless you want a coffee?" A shiver fled down her spine as the chilly October air wound its way through the fibres of her Halloween print wool cardigan. "Do you want anything else?" She handed the items through the window.

"Oh, no thanks, Ari. I wasn't expecting anything. Thank you." He placed the drink in the console and opened the container. "Ooh, gummy snakes."

"It's just a bit of everything that was left. Would you like a cup of hot soup instead to warm you up?" Ari rubbed her arms and stood up straight. Her lower back was aching and straining against the cold, as were her arthritic hands.

"Oh, no, thank you. I had a late lunch before I picked up Jay." He held up a Thermos. "I have my coffee, and I'll be going to dinner once I drop them off at Gloria's."

"Okay." Ari nodded and glanced down the street. Not seeing them, she figured they had already turned the corner. She turned back to Bobby. "Need the toilet or anything? It's cold out."

"Um…" He gave her a guilty look. "Now that you mention it…"

She grinned. "Grab your keys and come on in."

Bobby returned her grin and exited the car, dashing after Ari, down the hall and into the bathroom.

Ari closed the front door and stood staring into the lit-up skyline of Manhattan. The way it sparkled and twinkled illuminated her heart and soul, and every night she'd sat in an easy chair at her bedroom window gazing out across the city, still unable to believe she was actually there, and not getting into bed until the early hours. And even though she was sadly lacking in sleep, she didn't really care.

"Thanks for that." Bobby stopped beside her and shook his keys. "Better get back in the car in case they come back in a hurry."

"Are the kids always like that?" Ari studied his face for an answer.

"Little toe rags?" Bobby cocked a brow. "Andrew definitely has been the last four years, more so the last two. Gets it from his mother. Mari, not so much, but—" He quickly checked the window to see if they were coming. "She's generally okay. I think she was always a daddy's girl at heart, and her dragon of a mother hasn't turned her. Yet. But I've seen days, and tantrums, that aren't good. So who knows?" Bobby deflated and rubbed his arms. "He used to be a good dad. They used to be good kids. *She* used to be a decent human being before she became an arrogant asshole. The kids loved him, and he loved them, but the more time they're with their mother…"

"They take in her hatred for him," Ari supplied and shook her head in sorrow. "How sad. That one parent can do that to their kids, let alone the ex."

"Jealousy, anger, hatred, it's definitely a curse," Bobby agreed. "I have a feeling that by the time they're teenagers,

Anything for You

they'll want nothing to do with him, and he'll want nothing to do with them."

"Which is even sadder," Ari murmured. "I…" She paused, unsure if she should even say anything.

"Go on," Bobby urged, waiting to hear what she had to say.

Ari glanced guiltily at him. "I've sometimes wondered, during our conversations, if he even wants to be a father anymore. Especially to them. Andrew, I get, believe me, but Marisol seems sweet. You shouldn't just give up, you should try harder, maybe get them away from undue influence."

"As in their mother," Bobby quipped.

"Yes," Ari said. "Do you think they'd be better off with their father? Or at least spending more time with him?"

"Probably." Bobby glanced out the window before continuing. "But I don't know if his heart's in it as much as it used to be. He could try with Marisol, but personally I think Andrew's a lost cause. He was a grumpy shit right from when we picked him up. And after what Jay did outside when he called you a whore—"

Ari's brows rose. "Yeah…I heard that's the word that was used."

His eyes widened. "Oh, he told you—"

"I was simply told Andrew said something that he was repeating from his mother, but not what," Ari told him. "Until Jay mentioned he wouldn't say that himself."

"Well, then you'll be glad you didn't see Jay shake the shit out of the kid. Grabbed him by both arms and shook an apology out of him. I bet the little sod will blurt it out the second his mother answers the door."

"Not that I condone violence against a child, but I hope Jay gets in first." Ari saw them coming up the footpath and opened the door. "They're back. You'd better go."

"Oh, thanks." Bobby dashed outside and unlocked the car. "Ready to go?"

"Just about." Jay had both children by a hand. "Do either of you need the toilet?"

Marisol replied no, but Andrew just shook his head.

"Then say goodbye to Ari, and I'll get you off home." He looked up at Ari. "I'll call you when I drop them off. I need to do a couple of things afterwards. Okay?"

She shrugged. "Fine by me. You can do what you want. Any idea when you'll be home?"

"Ah…" He let go of Mari to check his watch. "After eleven. Kids, say goodbye."

"Bye." Marisol waved and opened the back door.

"Bye," Andrew grumbled in her direction and then said, "Just wait, Mari, I'm getting in first, you have to sit in the middle." He yanked the door from his sister's grasp and pushed her aside.

She fell backward and her pumpkin bucket scattered its contents over the snow-covered footpath. Bobby and Ari rushed to help while Jay grabbed his son.

"Hey!" He stuck his finger in Andrew's face, while using the death grip on his arm. "You don't push your sister. What's wrong with you? That's the third time you've played up tonight, Andrew. You've been a shit all night. Now you can get your punishment. Hand over your candy."

Andrew's eyes widened. "What? What did I do? You can't do that."

"You just pushed your sister, *after* using a bad word, *and* being a grump all night. I'm punishing you. Give me your candy." Jay was done with Andrew's antics.

"But I—"

"Now!"

The tone of his father's voice made him hand the bucket over. "What are you going to do with it?" He gulped.

"I'll keep it. And the next time I see you, *if* you behave, you can have some." Jay turned to Marisol. "Now apologise to your sister. Mari, you okay?" He saw Bobby and Ari standing behind her.

"I have a sore bottom and a wet costume, Daddy. But I'm okay." She brushed herself off.

"Andrew." Jay physically moved him towards his sister. "Apologise."

Andrew had the decency to look ashamed. "Sorry, Mari. I shouldn't have pushed you."

"Don't expect any of my candy now Daddy has yours," Mari said. "You're getting none of it."

Sullen and embarrassed, Andrew looked up at his father under the street light. "Can we go now?"

"Absolutely. And I'll be telling your mother what you did and that I took your candy as punishment." Jay let him go and waited for him to climb inside. He lifted Mari up behind him, took Mari's pumpkin bucket from Ari and got in behind her. "Bobby, let's go. Ari, see you later." He shut the door.

Bobby exchanged raised brows with Ari and quickly got in and started the car. Ari waited until they were out of sight before going inside. "Oh, I wish I could be a fly on the wall in that conversation."

*****

The ride into the city was a silent one. But Jay knew that wouldn't last. Once they arrived at the apartment building, both kids ran inside before Jay could shut the door, but he caught up with them as the lift doors opened.

He grabbed Andrew by the arm. "You are not getting off scot free. We're going to tell your mother exactly what you've done."

The doors opened and Marisol skipped ahead, Jay and Andrew following up the rear. Jay banged on the door. "Gloria, I've got the kids."

About thirty seconds later, the door flew open, and she appeared dishevelled. She had on different clothes than before, and her once neat topknot was falling loose and carefree around her face.

Marisol skipped inside. "Hello, Mommy, I got lots of candy." She held up her bucket for her mother to see.

"Okay, sweetie, that's nice, go inside." She turned to her son and saw Jay's grip. Her face tightened. "Why do you have my son in a death grip?"

"Oh, let's see why I have *our* son in a death grip," Jay replied. "Because *his* attitude sucks. He called a woman a whore because you did, so it must be okay. He was rude to people during trick-or-treating because you are, so it must be okay. Then he pushed his sister over so he could get into the car first. We didn't raise him like that, Gloria, so he can only be getting it from one place."

She coldly glared at Jay. "Andrew, go inside."

"He kept my Halloween candy," Andrew complained when his father let him go. "I got nothing."

Gloria's already pointed brows rose higher. "Is that so, Jay?"

Jay stared at her in amusement. Without make-up, she wasn't that attractive anymore. "Yes, Gloria, it is. I took it as punishment, and when he comes again, he can have some if he behaves."

"Andrew." Gloria crossed her arms, her eyes still glaring at her ex. "Go inside, I need to talk to your father."

"But my candy—"

"Go inside," she yelled at him.

He jumped back and skulked off down the hall dragging his feet.

Gloria turned back to her ex, her eyes firing up ready to throw daggers. "Who the hell do you think you are?"

"Now, now, Gloria. Remember that agreement you signed *just last Friday*," Jay reminded her, and watched her physically back off. "Now, you calling anyone who's female in my life a whore is now being said by our son. How will *that* look at the next court date you drag me to, huh? Teaching your son not only to swear, but to disrespect women like that. Naughty, naughty." He wagged his finger. "The judge might even decide that our son needs his father more than his mother right now." He watched her eyes widen in fear, or hate, he couldn't tell, and she opened her mouth to attack. "Your agreement," Jay warned. "I can still void that and have you for assault and turn it into an *actual* restraining order. So watch what you say next." He saw the daggers fly from her eyes. "Yeah. You hate me. Even though you're the one who did, and keeps on doing, the dirty on me. And yes, I grabbed our son by his arms and took his candy. But I would *never* use my kids against you or turn them against you. So, Gloria," he stepped back and saw Denver in the lounge room, "be *very* careful what you do next."

The door slammed in his face.

"And there's the whorish little cunt," Jay muttered and wearily walked down the hallway to the lift. Downstairs, he climbed into the driver's seat. "You want me to drop you off, Bobby?" He gunned the engine to get the heat going and glanced at his assistant. "Restaurant, home, boyfriend's?"

"Are you going to *The Chop Shop*?" Bobby strapped himself in.

A sigh from the pit of his gut left Jay. "I think I need to after everything that's happened."

"Then drop me off at *El Gardos*. Max is working tonight. I'll stay until closing and go home with him." He and Max Sorbodine and been a couple for seven years. Max was the manager of one of New York's hottest restaurants, having climbed his way up the ladder over the last couple of years.

"Then I'll drop you off on the way." Jay drove in silence as he wound his way through the city, dropping Bobby off fifteen minutes later. He then drove across to Brooklyn and headed for *The Chop Shop*, coming to a halt in the car park ten minutes later. He sighed, picked up his phone, and found Ari's number as it was first in his list.

It rang twice before she picked up.

"Hey, I won't be home until after eleven as I said earlier. I need to vent after tonight."

"Okay." Ari shrugged and glanced around the new homey looking lounge room. "I'll just watch TV until you get here. Where are you?"

"At *The Chop Shop*. It's an old warehouse where you pay to beat shit up. It's a great way to vent."

Ari chuckled. "Okay. I'll see you later. Bye."

"Bye, Ari, my girl." He clicked off the call and checked for messages before going inside where he paid the fare and dressed in the overalls, hard hat, and goggles they supplied. For the next hour and a half he smashed everything they gave him, venting his anger towards his ex on everything before him. He smashed china to smithereens, beat metal to a pulp, and even thrust his fist into a wall which wasn't planned, but happened at the height of his anger. Once he'd vented, and was drained to the core, he changed and left, arriving home ten minutes later to find Ari on the couch watching late night shows. "Hey," came wearily out of him.

"Hey." She popped a cheese ball in her mouth and watched him slump onto the couch beside her, laying his head on her shoulder and his feet on the ottoman in front of them. In that moment, every bit of the last two years of his mid-life crisis concerning Gloria looked as if it had worn him out and aged him by decades. She popped a cheese ball into his mouth. "Rough visit?"

"And that is why I don't have the kids that often." Jay sighed and ran a hand through his hair, ruffling it in the process. "It's too much of a mind fuck."

"Marisol seemed okay. She's cute and perky. Andrew... not so much."

"Andrew's definitely the worse, takes after his mother that one does." He stared blindly at the TV, not really seeing the show that was on as they had all become a blur.

"When do you see the kids again?" Ari munched on another cheese ball and licked her fingers before changing the channel to *The Late Show*.

"Not until Thanksgiving, thank God. I know I should see them more often, and sometimes I do. I'll take Mari out for a daddy daughter day, and sometimes I've taken Andrew for a father son day, but that never ends well."

"How was she considering the whole incident on Friday night, and proceeding legal contract?"

"Oh, when I brought it up she backed right off. Otherwise she would have exploded." He toed his shoes off, crossed his legs, and grabbed a handful of cheese balls which he fed himself one by one, distracted by the evening he'd had.

"Well, it's all over for now, until you have the kids again, at least. You won't have to worry about her until then."

"Yeah," Jay mumbled, his eyes glazing over. "I hope so."

Ari turned the TV up as the show came back from an ad break.

"Okay, let's get to my first guest for this evening. She did some pretty stupid things on Friday night and we're going to get to the bottom of it. Please put your hands together and welcome actress, Gloria Hannaford."

"What!" exploded out of Ari.

Jay's eyes widened and his head lifted from Ari's shoulder. "What the fuck!"

"When did she do this? Is this today?" Ari turned the volume up further and watched a glammed-up Gloria wave to the audience before sitting down.

"Well…hello, Gloria Hannaford, Happy Halloween," Stephen Colbert said.

"Happy Halloween, Stephen." Gloria crossed her legs and smiled brightly for the audience. "Happy Halloween, everyone."

"Okay. We need to dive right into this," Stephen said and rested his arm on his desk. "We've seen the footage, we heard what you said, and you were arrested for it. You went to your ex's house and screamed down the neighbourhood when he wasn't even there. When he did get there, you beat him, and

Anything for You

his assistant Bobby, and were arrested. What happened?"

"Well, Stephen." Gloria gave a guilty smile. "I was a bit of an asshole last week."

"A bit!" Jay huffed and stared at the screen.

"Okay, so you admit that." Stephen leaned closer. "Tell us, in your own words, what happened."

"Well, I was pissed off at some things that had gone wrong that day, and even that week. You know how it's just one thing after another that goes wrong, and it all built up, and so I was in an asshole mood, and then the child support didn't come through to my bank account, and I very stupidly went to my ex's to take it out on him. So yes," she nodded, "I was an asshole and did some pretty bad things last Friday night."

"Bitch is owning it on TV," Jay mumbled. "She's trying to get ahead of me."

"Okay, so let's show the footage that made it to social media of you being arrested." Stephen pointed at the camera and the footage from Friday night rolled. When it finished, they cut back to them at the desk.

"Now, you were arrested, but not charged, and it's all because Jay Daniels, your ex-husband, is not pressing charges. Nor is his assistant, Bobby Flannigan, pressing charges."

"That's right." Gloria's smile dimmed a little. "Regardless of how much animosity is between Jay and me, he's always been a fantastic dad. He's even got the kids tonight, taking them trick-or-treating."

"That's fantastic, and good for him." Stephen nodded.

"Backhanded compliment said to make her look good," Ari muttered.

"But let's read the statement he released this weekend."

Stephen picked up a piece of paper to read from, but the graphic of it showed on the screen. "As much as I resent the animosity that has occurred between my ex and me these last years, the last thing I want is to put my children's mother behind bars. What good would that do my children? None. We have come to a resolution that best suits the fractured family unit we are, so that my children will always have both parents in their lives caring for them. I will always try to resolve the best solution to our situation, even though I don't have full custody of our children, and sadly, don't get to see them as often as I'd like. My children are my number one priority and always will be."

The audience applauded wildly, and Gloria's smile fell right off her face.

"She's trying hard not to lose it," Ari said, shaking her head in disbelief. "My God, look at her."

"I wondered why she was dressed up when I first got there and then dishevelled when we got home," Jay muttered. "And wearing different clothes. I suppose the boy child's there in the green room."

"Probably." Ari raised a brow of distaste.

"So that was Jay Daniel's statement. How do things stand after the abuse you verbally and physically hurled at him and his assistant?" Stephen asked.

The camera zoomed in on Gloria, showing the weak smile that barely covered her underlying emotions. "Things are… *okay,*" she said. "*Manageable.* Obviously our divorce was painful, and sadly," she flinched, "made worse by my cheating, which I do own, absolutely."

"Bullshit!" Jay spat.

"And while things haven't been the best the last couple of

years, we're now in a moment of understanding, and he was incredibly understanding that I was having a very bad day. It was one of the neighbours who called the police, and I don't blame them. I was behaving like a maniac, and I own that. I'm very grateful to Jay and Bobby for not pressing charges and me not being in jail. I'm extremely happy to be out and home with my babies." Her lips spread open in her widest smile, and she played to the audience.

"That's fantastic and it's over and done now," Stephen said. "Did you apologise?"

"Absolutely." Gloria primped for the viewers at home. "They both accepted my apology."

"The fuck we did," Jay yelled and sat up in his seat. "She did no such thing."

"Great, so let's move on and talk about you and Denver. He's here tonight to play his latest song."

A collective groan came from Jay and Ari.

"The two of you are as loved up as ever. How's it going?"

"Oh, fantastically well, Stephen. I'm so in love, happier than I've ever been."

"Bullshit artist," Jay grumbled. "She said the same about me."

Gloria continued, "Denver's great, vibrant, creative, amazing."

"Good in bed?" Stephen asked.

"Fuck!" Ari's brows rose again.

"The best." Gloria gushed. "He's the best lover I've ever had. Virile, passionate—"

"I hate you, you bitch!" Jay growled, glaring at the screen.

"And does he write you love songs?" Stephen pushed. "His latest is about you, isn't it?"

"Yes, it is." She blushed. "He wrote it after we met and then kissed for the first time."

"Didn't take you long, you whore." Jay shot daggers at the screen.

Ari studied his face before turning her attention back to the show.

"So, Denver's the guy you cheated on Jay with, right? But you're still going strong," Stephen pushed, knowing he was getting gold.

Gloria faltered and visibly swallowed. "Ah, yes…yeah. He was. Which was unfortunate timing for us, with Jay and me still being married. But Jay wanted the divorce, and I decided to give it to him so I could live my best life and take a chance on something new."

"It's clearly worked out, so congratulations." Stephen turned to the camera. "And after the break, we have Denver with his latest song that was written for the stunning Gloria Hannaford. Don't go anywhere."

Jay angrily switched off the show and flung the remote. It smashed into the TV, making Ari jump.

She silently watched him run his hands through his hair, stunned by his vitriol.

"Cunt, you filthy fucking cunt. Who the fuck do you think you are?" Jay muttered, feeling the grittiness on his fingers. He looked at them, realising he had cheese ball dust on them, and licked them one at a time. Finally remembering Ari was there, he turned his head to look at her. "One day, that bitch is going to get everything she deserves, but until then, I'm going to bed. Have a good night's sleep." Jay patted her knee and wearily got to his feet. "I'll just grab a drink before I go." He stumbled into the kitchen, grabbed a beer from the fridge, and cracked it open. Sculling back half the can, he waved goodnight before walking down the hall and up the stairs.

Ari silently made her way over to the remote and turned the TV back on. Her heart was pounding in her chest, scared by Jay's outburst.

The show came on, and she turned the volume down so she could still hear Denver's new song. Regardless of what she thought of the situation, it was a good song, and she watched the performance until the end. She could understand Jay's anger with Gloria; she just couldn't understand Gloria's four year-long anger and hatred. But then, none of it was her business to understand anyway.

She returned to the couch and watched the rest of the show, following it up with *The Late, Late Show*, wondering all the while if living with Jay was going to be a problem she just didn't need.

Chapter 7

The following weeks flew by, with Jay showing Ari around the city and her new neighbourhood. They bought more furniture and furnishings, Ari found clothing and accessory shops galore, and she posted about it on social media.

And it was because of those posts that she scored herself spots on several morning shows to talk about her novel.

"And now we come to our next guest. She's the Australian best-selling author thanks to actor Jay Daniels, and her latest novel, *So Red the Rose*, is still in the top ten of book lists everywhere. Please welcome to the show, Ari Travers."

Ari nervously took a deep breath, saw the stagehand wave her onto the set, and walked over to the hosts of *The Maury and Maureen Show*. She shook their hands, turned and waved to the studio audience, and when the hosts indicated for her to have a seat, sat down, adjusted herself, and blinked under the blinding lights of the studio.

"Hello, Miss Ari Travers." Maury said. "Welcome to New York from the land down under." He unsuccessfully pulled off an Australian accent, but smoothly sat back in his seat and crossed his long, lean legs. At six feet tall with grey streaks in his otherwise black hair, he still came off as a well-dressed forty-something, even though he was actually sixty-something.

Ari's left brow rose critically. "Oh, trying the accent." She gave a slight nod of her head. "Not good."

Maury's laugh was deep and rolling. "I thought I'd try." He rubbed his hands together in glee. "Tell us here in the studio today, how did you come to be here in New York?"

Ari rubbed her sweaty palms on her jeans and recounted her months with Jay in a quick bullet point dialogue. No point boring them with long stories and dragging things out. "And so I flew over with him and here we are."

The audience applauded and Ari gave them a smile and nod of acknowledgment.

"And where are you now, Ari?" Maureen asked. At thirty-two she was the young half of Maury and Maureen, but also held her own, having graduated journalism school with top honours, as well as sociology and human science. She knew exactly what to ask and how to ask it.

"I'm staying with Jay while I'm here," Ari replied, keeping her tone even. She and Jay had discussed what to say in interviews without giving away too much. "I'm a paying guest in his house as I didn't want to overstay my welcome and didn't feel right being a freeloader. I pay to stay with him and it goes towards what I use or need."

"Interesting co-habitation plan, Ari," Maury uncrossed his legs and leaned towards her. "Sure you're paying to stay in his *guest* room?"

The crowd snickered and Ari raised her left brow again, narrowed her eyes and sighed. "*Yes*, Maury. I'm not a freeloader, or a user. I'm paying my way to stay in his *guest* room and if you continue to imply otherwise, I'll get up and walk out."

Maury leaned back in surprise. "Feisty one, aren't you."

"You don't know the half of it, so don't push it," Ari warned, her eyes flashing.

To defuse the situation, Maureen cast her critical eye from Maury to Ari. "Why don't you tell us about the novel? We did a satellite interview with you last month, when the book hit the top of the best seller list, and we spoke about it. But what's happened since?"

Ari turned her attention to Maureen. "A lot, as you can see. Jay's plan worked. The book reached the top spot on Amazon for weeks; sales crept up and up and up, everyone who read it, reviewed it, bought it, liked it, or loved it, and I hit the top of many book lists." She shrugged a shoulder. "It surpassed one million in sales on the day of release, and as each celebrity jumped on it, more and more people bought it, so now it's slipped over two million, which has definitely surprised me."

"I'm sure it has." Maureen smiled and her laser whitened caps sparkled like diamonds. "It's not often an indie, or self-published, author becomes a best seller by publishing their own stories."

Ari lightly bristled. "Actually, Maureen, thousands of indie, or self-published, authors who publish their own stories have massive success and sell more books than many traditionally published authors combined. You'd know that if you'd bothered doing any research on it. I just happen to be one of them."

A few sniggers and chuckles went through the audience and Maureen arched a perfectly groomed brow, while Maury casually put his hand in front of his mouth to hide his laughter.

L.J. Diva

"But either way, I've done the hard yards for over ten years, set up my own publishing house, and bizarrely, managed to meet an actor who took an interest in my writing," Ari continued, feeling beads of sweat form on her back, brow, and top lip from the heat of the studio lights.

"Is that *all* he took an interest in?" Maury asked and his lips curled into a smirk.

Ari's brows rose in anger. "Yes, Maury, and I did warn you." She turned to the audience. "Seriously, is his mind always in the gutter?"

The audience laughed and applauded, cat calling to Maury.

"Now, now." Maury put his hands up in defence and laughed. "My mind is not *always* on sex, *or* in the gutter. I just find this whole situation to be a little…" He paused while trying to find the right word. "Weird…"

"That's the *best* word you could find?" Ari asked. "That a male and female *still* can't be friends, or business partners, or flat mates, without something sexual going on? What decade do you live in?"

Whoops of delight came from the crowd.

Maury chuckled. "Okay, okay. You've got me there. Not weird at all."

"Unlike this situation where a sixty-something male host has a thirty-something female co-host because men can age on TV but women apparently can't," Ari continued.

"Oh, yes, thank you!" Maureen applauded along with the audience. "He gets to keep his job because he's been around twice as long as I've been born, but I'm the one with the university degrees, and *I'm* told to make my skirts shorter, my boobs bigger, and to get Botox."

"What!" Ari's brow furrowed in shock. "Who the hell told

you that? Dirt bag must be blind." She took in Maureen's perfectly coifed long brown hair, maroon skirt suit, matching silk blouse, legs that went on forever, and feet that were swathed in maroon suede pumps. "You're gorgeous. What dick for brains thinks you're not?"

The audience cheered her again and she shrugged and put her hands out, palm side up. "Seriously, who?"

"The bigwigs at the network that make all the rules." Maureen carefully uncrossed and recrossed her legs, making sure to keep her knee-length skirt down so she didn't flash anyone.

"Well, that sucks," Ari said and smoothed out her crystal covered cape. She'd dressed up in her usual creative clothing style—this time a crystal covered top with a cape over it, navy jeans, coloured boots that matched her top, and plenty of jewellery.

"Certainly does," Maureen agreed and saw the floor manager winding them up. "So, Ari, how long will you be in New York?"

"A year, which is the plan," Ari told her. "And then we'll see whether I stay longer, especially if I'm enjoying myself, or I'm ready to fly back to Aus and settle down on the Gold Coast. It'll all depend."

"And if you and Jay do end up getting it on," Maury got in right before the floor manager waved them out, "we'll be right back with more after the break."

The audience cheered, the floor manager yelled *break*, and Ari seethed.

"*Really, Maury?*" Ari rose and straightened herself. "Just couldn't bloody help yourself, could you." She nodded at Maureen and ignored Maury's sly grin. "Nice chatting to you. It's time to go." She walked back the way she'd come and was shown to the green room where Bobby was waiting. He was acting as her assistant until she got her own. "Well?" she said and sighed. "Did that go well…or not?"

"Could have been better," Bobby conceded. "Not much talk of your book, *but…*" He grinned. "Considering what *was* talked about, you just might get a whole new set of fans and followers."

Ari chuckled. "Yeah, that did take a turn, didn't it?"

An assistant came in to remove her microphone and said they could go, so they gathered their bags and left.

"Okay, what next?" Ari watched Bobby hail a cab while checking his phone. The car screeched to a halt barely an inch beside his leg, and Bobby still didn't look up. He just swiftly opened the back door.

"You okay, Bobby?" Ari slid into the back and moved over.

He climbed in beside her and slammed the door. "Sure, why?" He gave the driver the address of the next interview.

"You could have been run over."

"Nah, I'm used to New York traffic. Been here my whole life. The next interview is a magazine interview. The photo shoot is set for," he quickly checked the appointment app on his phone, "three days' time."

"Why's that?" Ari glanced at the scene around her, at sky high buildings and bustling people.

"It's because the shoot will take longer than the article, and it's set up in the studio. Although they usually ask a lot of questions at the shoot, as well. Now, we've gone over your website, and you've removed incriminating items and updated other stuff."

"Not really incriminating," Ari retorted. "Just some old blog posts that might not come across well in this day and age fourteen years later."

"Well, in this day and age, they were incriminating." Bobby swiped through social media looking for any hashtags to do with Ari, and *The Maury and Maureen Show*. He found them and clicked on. "You're already trending."

"What? From the show? I just finished it, so how's it trending already?"

"Probably the audience, or crew. But your segment is definitely being talked about."

"So…is that good or bad?" Ari covered her eyes with her hands and peeked through her fingers at him.

Bobby scrolled some more. "So far so good, by the look of this."

"Whew!" Ari lowered her hands. "As long as I'm not trending in the same hashtag as Gloria, or Jay, I'm good."

Bobby grinned. "Oh, just you wait until they take Maury's comments to social."

Ari groaned and her head dropped back. "Has he always been such a dick?"

"Oh, yeah." Bobby clicked off his phone and looked at her. "For every second he's been on TV he's been a dick. So much so he's on his tenth partner in thirty years."

"That's what…one every three years," Ari said. "Seriously? He's gone through them that fast?"

"Well you said it; he's a dick and thinks women are beneath him. But who knows after today? Oh…here we are."

They pulled up out the front of a typical New York skyscraper, paid the fare, and alighted; doing a quick check of the taxi in case they'd left something behind. They hadn't, so closed the door, hurried inside, and up to the fifteenth floor.

The doors opened and Ari held her stomach. "Ugh, I hate lifts like this."

Bobby took her arm and escorted her into the office of *Flash*, one of New York's biggest fashion magazines. "Give it a moment; you'll be fine." They stepped over to the front desk. "Ms Travers for Genevieve Tommers. Ms Travers is here for an interview."

"Of course, take a seat and I'll buzz her." The girl behind the reception desk picked up her phone.

Ari pulled from Bobby's grasp and wandered over to the floor-to-ceiling glass window that showed off a fairly decent view of the city. Her breath caught in her throat. "Wow," came softly from between her lips. Her eyes greedily took in all the view she could see, the tops of the most glamorous hotels, office buildings, bridges, the Empire State Building.

"Ari Travers?"

Ari turned around to see a woman looking for her. "Yes?"

The woman's eyes darted to her. "Ah, Ari Travers." She extended her hand and walked forward. "I'm Genevieve Tommers. I'll be doing the interview in our meeting room. This way." She shook her hand and led the way down the hall to their left and into a room that had an even more expansive view of the city. "Please, take a seat. Would you like something to eat or drink?"

"Ah, just a juice, if you have one," Ari replied and turned her back on the view, so she wasn't distracted during the interview. She took a seat with her back to the city and Bobby sat opposite her on the other side of the table.

Genevieve handed out the drinks and sat down. "Okay. I've organised this interview for an hour, and then if I have follow-up questions I'll be at the photo shoot to get some more information." She pulled out a small black recording device from her jacket pocket, along with a square of folded white paper. She unfolded it and Ari saw it was at least three sheets.

"I have your questions here." Genevieve clicked the record button on her device and placed it between her and Ari. "Tell me your story first and then I'll ask them."

"Ah, okay." Ari glanced at the device and leaned in a little. She retold the story from start to finish, something she'd done multiple times since the book had exploded onto the book charts and Jay's plan had made it go viral. She was also sick of it. When she finished, she had a few sips of juice and watched Genevieve scan her questions.

"That covers a few things I wanted to ask but let me go through the rest." She asked about Ari's time in New York, the flight over, packing up and moving, moving into Jay's house, and had she met Gloria and the kids yet.

Ari glanced at Bobby before seeing his shrug which meant she could answer if she wanted, and she gave honest answers. Her time had been great, so far, she was scared but excited about flying and moving, glad that she had somewhere to stay upon arrival, and didn't have to search. Sad for Jay's circumstances; and was looking forward to more traditional holidays she hadn't celebrated in Australia.

"Ozzies don't celebrate Thanksgiving?" Genevieve asked.

"No, we don't," Ari replied, noting the way she'd pronounced it, and leaned back in her seat. "And you have a few other holidays we don't celebrate, but we do have some equivalents."

"Fascinating. Looking forward to celebrating them?"

"Sure."

"With Jay and his family?"

Ari took a slow breath. "I don't know. He hasn't mentioned anything about any upcoming holidays. And I haven't made plans for any."

"But Thanksgiving's next week," Genevieve pushed and leaned forward.

"And at this stage, it hasn't been mentioned," Ari repeated. "I personally can't wait for Christmas and New Year's. It'll be great."

"And have you and Jay grown closer over the last few months?" Genevieve was hoping for some dirt. After thirty years in the business, she knew how and when to get it.

Ari flashed Bobby a look. "We've become really good friends, but then I think we were from the start. We clicked, we made each other laugh, tried to out-joke each other, would have deep and meaningful conversations with each other, *about* each other. We're really good friends and I owe him a lot."

"Did you pay him back for the loan?"

Ari's brows rose and her lips lifted at the corners. "I did. Double as promised."

"And you've mentioned that the two of you have another contract now?"

"We do. I'm not a user and didn't want to be the guest who overstayed her welcome. So I offered another compromise."

"Some would say you *are* using him." Genevieve stared at Ari, almost daring her to something.

"And Jay and I had *those* conversations as well," Ari replied coolly. "I would be called a gold digger, a user, etc, etc. If I *was* using him I wouldn't be paying rent and board.

I'm paying my way, paying to live as a tenant in his house for a year. And if I can inspire him to get into filming again, it's a fair deal, I say."

"And how are you inspiring him?" Genevieve turned her body and leaned her right elbow on the able, her fingers resting against her chin. "Does *he* inspire *you*?"

Ari became even more guarded. "My novel inspired him to make it into a movie. And he loves the next few novels I'll be releasing. As for him inspiring me..." She shrugged lightly. "Who knows what will turn up in the next thing I write? Maybe he'll inspire me to write about an actor again, or a serial killer, or a bitch of a magazine writer." Ari raised a brow and saw Bobby's eyes widen in alarm.

Genevieve lowered her hand. "Touché. But it *is* my job to get dirt."

"Then go and dig in a yard or go to a garden shop; you won't find any here. Are we done?" Ari picked up her glass and drained the remains of her juice. "I need to go and raid a stationery shop for notebooks and pens."

"Planning on writing something new?" Genevieve crossed off the last question on her papers.

"Who knows?" Ari left her glass on the table and slid her chair back. "Maybe something about throwing a nosy reporter out of a fifteen-storey window." She stood and grabbed her bag. "I'll be back for the photo shoot. Do I bring my own clothes and accessories?"

"No, we supply them." Genevieve stood and carefully placed the paper and recorder into her pocket. But Ari saw that she hadn't turned it off. "One last question if you don't mind. Are you in love with Jay, or do you see yourself falling in love with him?"

"Okay, that's enough," Bobby finally interjected. "She's already told you they're just friends."

"It's just a question." Genevieve pleaded innocence. "A simple one at that. Off the record."

"No, it isn't." Ari swung her bag onto her shoulder and walked around the reporter. "I know you didn't turn the recorder off, but I will say this…*again*." Ari turned back to Genevieve who eagerly stepped forward. "I owe him a lot and we've become really good friends, and I hope," she leaned towards Genevieve, "he'll keep helping me have number one selling novels. Bobby, let's go." She marched out the door, with Bobby trailing after her. Genevieve stood in the doorway watching them leave.

Back in the reception area, they waited for the lift, backs to everyone, and once the lift arrived they ignored everyone else until they had hailed a cab and were on their way to lunch.

"What the hell!" exploded Ari. "I was too scared to even speak in case someone was listening in and recording it. I mean, did you notice that she didn't even turn off the recorder when she put it in her pocket? Sneaky bitch." She slumped in the back seat. "And then, thinking that I thought it was off, she asked those questions. Double sneaky bitch!"

"Some reporters are like that. Just like Maury this morning. They want dirt on the people they interview."

"But there *is* no dirt." Ari sighed. "We're just friends."

"Are you?" Bobby asked without looking up from scrolling through socials.

"Ugh," she scoffed. "Not you too?"

Bobby shrugged and finally looked at her. "He's my boss, you're his guest, and we're all on Gloria's hit list."

A groan came from Ari. "That's all I need."

Anything for You

*****

On Sunday, Jay and Ari were in the lounge room relaxing on the couch in front of the TV. They spent the day of the Sabbath at home, relaxing and gearing up for each week.

"So…" Ari said during the ad break. "What's happening for Thanksgiving? You going to your parents? Having the kids? And what is there for me to do around town at this time of the year?"

Jay absentmindedly played with his hair as he lay back on the sofa, zoning in and out of the show, and the ads, they were watching. "Mmm?" He rolled his head to the side. "The kids? I have them for lunch at Mom and Dad's house. My sisters and their families will be there, and so will you. I'm not letting you miss out on your first Thanksgiving here in the good old US of A."

"Do your parents know that?" Ari nudged him with her sock covered foot.

"Know what?" Jay's eyes glazed over at the TV.

"That you're not only bringing the kids, but your house guest."

His lips turned into a half grin. "Yeah. I told them. But we're only staying for lunch. Once I drop the kids off we're back here to set up the Christmas trees."

"Trees?" Ari's expression turned to surprise. "Didn't think you were the type of guy to put trees up for no reason."

He turned his head to her. "I usually do, especially since the breakdown of my marriage. I'll have the kids for Christmas lunch, so we'll have our party Christmas Eve."

Ari thought about it. "I'll have to go and get myself something to wear then."

"Please do. Dress up to the nines. But until then, this Tuesday is Thanksgiving at my folks' house."

"With your kids..." Ari contemplated what World War III was going to look like.

"With my kids," he replied dryly.

"And then home to put up trees. Yay!"

"And decorate the place. Which you will be a part of since it's your first Christmas." Jay warmly grasped her hand. "It's your first Christmas in New York, Ari, my girl. Your first Christmas away from your old life."

At that, Ari sobered. "Yeah...it is."

"Hey, I didn't mean to upset you." Jay pulled himself up beside her and slid an arm around her. "I'm sorry."

"I'm not upset." She shook her head. "Things are just different to how they used to be. Everything's happened so quickly, and now Christmas is coming, and for the first time in over three decades I'll be doing something different and doing it *somewhere* different."

"New state, new country, new year, new life," Jay told her. "Welcome to your new life, Ari."

She gazed into his sparkling eyes. They were eyes that had no irises to see, eyes that were nothing but blobs of brownness. Sometimes, she could read him by the emotions coming from his eyes. Sometimes not. Now she could see he was relaxed and happy. "Yeah, I guess."

"You guess?" he scoffed in shock. "How can you not be?"

"Because each day is new, each week is new, each month will be new, and that means each holiday and festivity will be new too. I'll just have to take it one day, one week, one month, and one festivity at a time."

Jay studied her and nodded. "Good point. So, we deal

with Thanksgiving first. And Christmas and New Year can wait until next month."

Ari snorted with laughter. "Considering they *are* next month."

"See, your spirits have risen! My job here is done." He slumped back on the couch and slid down to get comfortable.

Ari smiled and shook her head. "Next stop, Thanksgiving."

Chapter 8

On Thanksgiving Day, Jay and Ari picked up his kids and travelled a half hour upstate to Jay's parents' house.

Marisol chatted off and on, but Andrew sat sullenly in the backseat, put out by Ari intruding on his day. As if he needed his father's whore having lunch with them.

Ari chose to ignore Andrew's sulkiness and gazed out the window to watch the brown leafy trees go by as they passed house after house, all looking the same, old colonial, or brick mansions from eras gone by.

When they pulled up to the Daniels' old colonial home, Marisol saw her grandparents waiting for them and jumped from the car. "Grandma."

"Marisol." Melinda Daniels held her arms out for her granddaughter to run into. "How is my little Marisol this Thanksgiving? Enjoying your day?" She smothered her in hugs and kisses.

"Good, Grandma. And you?" Marisol let her go to hug her grandfather. "Grandpa."

"Is little Marisol ready for turkey with all the trimmings?" Ben Daniels asked her.

"Yes, Grandpa. Is everyone here yet?"

"Andrew." Melinda hugged her grandson then watched as he hugged her husband. "Go inside you two, your cousins are waiting. Go and get warm." She watched them rush inside then turned to her son and his guest. "How have they been? But more importantly, how have *you* been?" Her gaze darted from her son to Ari.

"They were little shits for Halloween." Jay shrugged and put his hands in his coat pockets. "And this here is my guest, Ari Travers. She's the author I've been helping, and absolutely raving about, these last few months."

"Of course, hello Ari, nice to meet you. Call me Melinda, and my husband is Ben. Come inside and warm up." She waved them in and slid her arm around Ari as they entered the quaint two-storey cottage to the scent of warm roasting turkey and pine cones.

"A lot warmer than outside." Ari slid her coat off and handed it to Jay who hung it on a hook next to his beside the door. "Quite a chill going on."

"Do you not have such cold weather in Australia?" Melinda ushered her into the spacious lounge room that connected to the dining room at the back of the house.

"Oh, we definitely have freezing weather, but we only snow in certain places, it's not everywhere. Although it's been quite a treat to hear it crunch under my feet all the time." She rubbed her arms and stood in front of the large stone fireplace. "It's just a lot colder here."

"We'll get you warm in no time," Ben said, going to the liquor cabinet and pulling out two glasses and a bottle of amber fluid.

"None for me, thank you," Ari called. "I don't drink."

"And I can have two drinks tops, since I'm driving," Jay

added from beside her in front of the fire. He held his hands out to the flames to warm them. "Save mine for later so I can savour it."

"Oh…" Ben's hand faltered in mid-air. "Looks like I'm drinking alone, then."

He poured himself a drink and closed the cabinet.

They heard the kids screaming in the backyard and glanced towards the back window.

"Good, they can burn their anger off," Jay muttered and shoved his hands into his jeans pockets to keep them warm. "They'll wear themselves out in no time."

Ari turned to look at him and a soft grin curved her lips. "Andrew will, anyway."

Jay groaned and rubbed his eyes. They were red and puffy and tired from the stress of today before it had even begun. "I can only hope."

"So, Ari, tell us how you met Jay." Melinda indicated for Ari to sit beside her.

"Mom, I've told you a few times," Jay complained and leaned against the fireplace mantel. His hands may have thawed, but his legs had not.

"But I haven't heard it from Ari, and it's our first time meeting her, Jay," his mother replied.

"In all fairness, I'm tired of telling it," Ari said. "Only because I've had dozens of interviews the last few months and they all asked the exact same thing. They couldn't come up with an original question if they tried. But…" Ari sat beside her. "I'll make an exception just for you." Seeing Melinda glance at her son, Ari started the story of how they met, how Jay had helped her to have a best-selling novel, and how he'd helped her to move to New York. "And since being here, we've sightseen, shopped, and I've done radio, TV, and magazine interviews. I've been here about a month and so much has happened." She'd also collected multiple copies of every magazine and newspaper she'd been in.

"That does seem like something out of a novel," Michelle, Jay's younger sister, said. "Does it give you any ideas for books?"

Ari remembered back to the *Flash* interview. "I had a magazine writer ask me the exact same thing last week. But I have the next few books lined up ready for release, so I'm taking a break from writing and playing tourist instead. Who knows what ideas I'll get for future novels and stories?"

"It does sound rather intriguing. Being a writer of novels and kids' stories," Jessica, Jay's elder sister, piped up. "It must be fabulous having a bestseller? Are your other books selling just as well, or is it just the latest one?"

"It's been a side-effect of Jay's plan for *So Red the Rose*. That sold well, and people found my other books, then they bought them to see how they were, and they ended up selling well themselves." Ari shifted in her seat and watched Jay sit on the arm of his father's chair. Five sets of brown eyes, so similar, were fixed on her and it made her a little uneasy; as if she was the prey for five hungry tigers.

"Must be nice, being rich," Michelle said. "Jay's been rich for a couple of decades and spreads it around, which is great, thanks bro." She grinned at him, and Ari noticed it was the same smile as Jay's, and that her looks were the female version of him. "But it must be new for you, Ari."

"Wouldn't know," Ari replied. "It hasn't started rolling in yet. I'm still waiting to be a millionaire."

"Why's that?" Melinda asked. "Are they not paying you?"

Anything for You

"Not yet. They make payments three months after the sale," Ari told her as a horde of children came screaming into the house.

"When's lunch, Grandma?" One girl stopped in front of them.

Melinda glanced at the clock on the wall. "Not for another hour. Go back outside and keep playing. Burn up your energy so you'll be really hungry and eat lots of turkey and all the trimmings."

"Okay." The girl, all of about ten with long brown hair, ran back to the kitchen to join her siblings and cousins for a drink. "Grandma said an hour."

A chorus of "aws" came wafting along on the same air as the aromas of roast turkey. But once they'd had their drinks, they ran back outside and started screaming again.

"Oi!" Jay stuck his finger in his ear and shook it. "Now that that cacophony is gone, I'm going to show Ari my old room. Unless you've turned it into something else?"

"No, darling. Unless you include a storage area," Melinda told him. "Otherwise it's still relatively the same."

"Okay, cool. Come on, Ari." Jay stood and held out his hand. "Come and see where the acting genius first started and was cultivated from."

Grinning, Ari took his hand. "Is it going to be bad? Do I need a hazmat suit?"

His family laughed at the horror on his face.

"Hardly!" Jay retorted. "It's testosterone central, comic central, actor central." He led her into the hallway and down the stairs into the basement.

"The basement," she mocked. "They cultivated you and kept you hidden in the basement?"

Ha-ha!" he replied dryly and flicked on the light. The room was a clean version of the way he'd left it. "Ta-da! My life before fame."

Ari let go of his hand and stepped into the room. Her gaze darted around taking in everything. She saw shag carpeting in a shade of coffee cream, and wallpaper in shades of coffee cream and brown with a pattern she couldn't quite pick out. An old bed barely looked long enough for him to grow in, accompanied by a desk, wardrobe, bookshelves, a couple of bean bags, and a stereo unit from the '70s that sat on two old milk crates. Another crate held records, while another held old electronic gadgets and computer equipment.

"Wow." Ari wandered over to the shelves. "So much history. Comic books, trophies, toys. The making of an acting genius." She heard a chuckle and turned around. "What?"

"Look at you." He smiled, hands in pockets against the cold, body language loose and calm. "Getting a kick out of where I lived as a kid and teen."

Shyly, Ari smiled and moved over to the wall. "Certificates, photos, pictures. Quite a history of your life, Jason Oscar Daniels." She leaned closer to get a clearer image of Jay in the photos.

"But just a small part." He leaned against the wall beside her and crossed his arms, a soft smile playing on his lips. "I wanted to show you what I was, what I used to be."

"Aren't you still who you were, who you used to be?" she asked softly.

He thought about it and glanced around at his former life. "A small part of me is. This is the foundation of who I am. The foundation up until life as an adult." He walked slowly around the room, gently touching his things. "And then I left home and had to live as an adult and do adult things and *be* adult about things." He paused and picked up his Rubik's Cube from the bedside table. "And then *those* things change you. And you're not really who you used to be."

"A better version of it," Ari said and walked over to the bed.

"Or worse," Jay muttered and threw the cube into the air. He caught it and spun it between his hands.

"Are you worse?"

"Well…" He stopped spinning the cube and looked at her. "I married Gloria Hannaford."

Ari snorted with laughter. "True…true…"

Jay set the cube on the side table, his fingers lingering on it. "Bad relationships can leave bad residue in a person."

"Bad juju," Ari muttered.

Jay's face crumpled in amusement. "Where'd you get that from? Do Aussies say that?"

"Bobby, and no." She sniggered. "Isn't Gloria bad juju in general?"

Laughter came from him. "Oh, yes. She is. Worse than that, probably."

Ari sat on the end of the bed, and it sagged lightly beneath her. "So…your relationship with her has changed you for the worse?" The bed sagged beside her.

"In many ways I think it has," he said. "As much as I try to not let it, I think it has on many levels, and that's a damn shame because I like the person I used to be before her, when I met her, and during most of our marriage. But when I look back at it…" He shook his head at the memories. "When I look back on it, things changed around the time her affair would have started, and that's when she changed and so I changed. The fights, the arguments, the shouting." He shrugged, tired of thinking about it. "I don't even know when I began to recover, but lately, all of my friends have told me I got my fire back around the time I met you."

Her heart pounded at the way he looked at her and she felt the heat radiating from him. She knew she was falling, but gallantly tried to fight it.

He gently took her hand and held it between both of his, looking down at it. "I'd say you've been good for me, Ari, my girl. Gave me something to do, to look forward to. You made me laugh again, cry from happiness instead of anger and frustration, came up with plans and celebrations." He thought through what he was going to say next. "You've helped me a lot, Ari. Without even trying, without even knowing. You've helped me get back on track to being me and I'm starting to see the old me come through again. Not all the time," he added, "considering Gloria, and the kids, and all. But the old me's getting there. Getting back, coming back."

"That's good to hear." Ari squeezed his hand. She really liked the Jay she knew. She knew she would have liked the Jay he used to be and hoped more of him came through.

"Yeah," Jay murmured and smiled at her. "It is. And it's all because of you."

Ari's heart fluttered, her stomach quivered, and her blood sang in her ears. Jay Daniels changing because of her. Becoming better because of her. Becoming his old self because of her. She was floating on cloud nine. A soft smile slid across her lips.

"I'm glad you're in my life, Ari," Jay said. "I'm glad I convinced you to move here to New York. I'm glad you came. I'm glad you're here with me."

A blush swept over her at the intensity of his gaze. "So am I."

"Lunch!" was yelled down the stairs breaking the spell around them.

"Mmm, okay then." Jay laughed. "Lunchtime."

They walked upstairs and gathered around the already crowded dining table that had been extended for all of the family.

Lunch went for two hours, as they languished over multiple servings of turkey with stuffing, cranberry sauce, and various pies for dessert. After the kids ran outside to burn off all they'd eaten, the adults did the cleaning up. But before long, they started leaving, one by one, packing up the kids, containers of leftovers, and gathering their coats.

Jay, Ari, and the kids started their trip back close to five and arrived just before five-thirty at Gloria's apartment.

"I'll take the kids up and then we can go," Jay told her, and slipped a small bag from the glovebox into his coat pocket before alighting. He took the kids inside and once in the lift, he told Andrew, "Since you've *reasonably* behaved today, except for the silence on the road trip, I've decided to give you some of your Halloween candy." Jay pulled the bag out of his pocket and held it up. "This is one fifth of your candy, around five hundred grams. Here."

Andrew's eyes widened at the sight of the bag and he hesitantly took it. "Really?"

Jay smiled at him. "Of course. I told you you'd get it back in instalments if you were good."

"Thanks," Andrew muttered shyly, and shoved it into his coat pocket.

"That's right. Hide it from your mother so she can't have any," Jay said. "Good idea." They walked up to the apartment and he banged three times. They waited. And waited. And waited.

The door finally opened, and Gloria stood there ruffled from head to toe.

"The kids are home," Jay told her. "Happy Thanksgiving. Bye, kids."

"Bye, Daddy." Marisol waved and skipped off down the hallway.

"Bye, Dad." Andrew followed and ran for his room.

"Gloria." Jay's smile was wide. "Now you can deal with them." He walked off, the door slamming behind him, and went downstairs to take Ari home.

*****

"So we have two trees, copious boxes of decorations, and what the hell is this?" Jay pulled a battered looking green ring from a box. "What the hell *is* this?" Turning it over, he saw the wire holder. "Oh, I think it's the wreath for the front door."

"And it's clearly seen better days." Ari stared at it. "Can it be fixed? Revived? Do we need a new one?"

Jay examined the leafy branches wrapped around the plastic ring. "I think they just need to be reset in place. It's only wire. I'll do it last." He placed it on top of a decoration box and then handed the box to Ari. "You start with the decorations, and I'll bring up the trees." They carried everything up the stairs from the basement where Jay had dumped all of his belongings when he'd moved in. His plan was to organise them at some point, but he dealt with it only when he was looking for something in particular, and then he unpacked just that one box or bag where he'd found the item he wanted.

Once all of the decoration boxes were upstairs, they set to work. Jay set up the two trees to be either side of the bay window in the lounge room. During the day they would frame the glorious view of the snowy city, and by night they would light up the house.

"Do you want to go for a theme?" Jay opened all of the boxes to see that they had. "I think I just bought whatever the store assistant told me I needed."

"There are two boxes of tinsel, two boxes of balls, and looks like…" Ari dug into another two boxes. "Two boxes of other decorations. Plus, a container of lights you clearly did not fold up properly."

Jay chuckled and stared down at the black wire mess. "Yeah, looks like."

Ari set her hands on her hips and stared at all of the boxes. "I doubt you'd have anything theme related, and it looks like the tinsel and balls are all colours, not just one or two, so I'd say it's going to be whatever you've had for the last couple of years. *And* since I'm a bit of a picky person, we'll even everything out between the trees and what's leftover can go elsewhere."

Jay had nodded as she spoke. "Yeah, that pretty much sounds like the last couple of years." He clapped his hands once and rubbed them together. "You divide, and then we'll conquer."

Ari grinned and dug into the first box of baubles. "Ten for you, and ten for me. Let's decorate." With each one decorating a tree, and Ari handing out the baubles, the boxes were quickly emptied. She stepped back and admired their handiwork. "Right. So far, so good." The overhead lights bounced off the coloured spheres. "Let's have a look at the ornaments next." They pulled out the ornaments from the next two boxes to see what they were, and Ari divided them up.

"Are these for the mantel?" She held up an ornament of Santa on his sleigh being pulled by his reindeers. "These don't have hangers."

"Ah…" Jay glanced up and studied the piece. "Yeah, I think some were." He quickly checked the others. "Oh, so are these." He picked up two more. "Ah…I think there were five in total, from vague memory."

"Is it these?" Ari picked up two ornaments. "They don't have hangers, either."

Jay looked at the group of carollers, and a snowman piece. "I guess. I didn't really take much notice. But if they don't hang, then we'll put them somewhere."

"Mantel?" Ari looked over at the fireplace. "It's high enough to not be knocked off."

"Coffee table?" Jay countered. "We'll do a little scene."

"Easily smashed, especially by kids, or some yobbo."

"Yobbo? What's a yobbo? Is that another Aussie-ism?" Jay asked.

Ari grinned and stood up to brush off her hands on her knees. "Slang for idiot, dope, dipshit. Okay. You put these five on the mantel, and I'll keep decorating."

They made quick time of it then Ari pulled the tinsel from one box.

"These are really long pieces. Are they for the tree or something else?"

"I think they were for the stair railings and door frames."

Jay pulled smaller pieces from the other box. "I don't really know. I had Bobby organise the decorating for me."

Ari smirked at him. "You went and bought the decs, but had someone else decorate the house you were in. You lazy sod."

"And now I'm a sod. First a yobbo, now a sod," Jay bemoaned. "Well just for that, you can take those longer pieces of tinsel and wrap them around the stairs and leave some for the main door frames. Hurry along now." He flicked a dismissive hand and turned his back.

"Oh, I'm gonna call you more than a sod and a yobbo in a minute if you keep that up." Ari carried several pieces into the hallway and started with the stair railing.

While she did those, Jay fixed the wire leaves on the wreath, wove through two strands of tinsel, and added a big red bow he found in the ornament box. "There. I think that will suffice." He held it up to make sure everything was evenly spread, and Ari walked through the door. "What do you think?" he asked.

"That looks good." She held up several strands of tinsel. "The stair railings have this stuff twisted around them, just need to do the main doorways and since *you're* over six feet, you can do those."

Jay groaned. "Always down to the tall Jay." He set down the wreath and took the tinsel from Ari. "All door frames?"

"Only those along the hallway and if there're any left over, we'll hang them in this room."

"And you're doing what?" Jay held up one piece and slung the others over his shoulder.

"I'll divide the tinsel for the trees and start laying them on. Off you go." She waved a dismissive hand and turned her back.

"Oh, you cheeky sod," Jay said. "Throwing my actions back in my face."

"Suck it up, buttercup," Ari replied and tucked a strand of tinsel into the tree.

"And now I'm a buttercup," Jay quipped and hung the first strand over the door frame. "Is this how we're doing it?"

Ari glanced over her shoulder. "No. It needs to drop in the middle."

"And we're using *what* to hold it in place?" Jay lowered his arms. "Tape? Tacks?"

Ari dug through the boxes to see if there was anything to hold them up. "Oh, here." She straightened and read the pack. "Pin clips that push into the wall or door frame and hold tinsel in place." Handing them over, she added, "Don't forget to hang them evenly."

"Yes, boss." Jay saluted. "Three evenly hung door frames coming up."

Ari chuckled. "Oh, for God's sake." She was tingling from the exchange of quips, warmed by more than the interior of the brownstone, by more than the ease of which they conversed. She knew her attraction to Jay had grown and not just in a small way. After they'd met it had been hard to not let herself fall for him. They were from two different countries, and two different worlds. So Ari had pulled back on her attraction to him and made the decision to feel friendship on her part. But after the kiss back home, and then Jay moving her into his house, it was getting harder and harder to deny that her feelings had grown into more than attraction. She was falling for him and falling hard. And keeping a check on those emotions was even harder. She had no idea if Jay felt the same. The fact he held her hand sometimes or rested his head on her shoulder while watching TV didn't prove anything.

"One down, more to go." Jay hurried to the next doorway and tacked the strand in place.

Ari finished with the tinsel on one tree, and quickly started on the other.

"Done," they both said after ten minutes.

Ari turned from the tree. "All the door frames done?"

"Yep. Both the trees done?" Jay hurried over.

"We just have the lights and the wreath left." Ari picked up a strand of lights. "Not too knotty. You really should take care to wrap them properly each year."

"I didn't un-decorate last year." Jay picked up a strand. "The decorators did, and it looks like they tied this set up."

"Let's plug them into a power point to see if they're coloured or white," Ari suggested. "And we need to know so we can spread them around."

"I think there was a set on the mantel and front door last year." Jay thought back. "But it was in the old house, and again," he shrugged, "I didn't do the decorating."

"Oi." Ari rolled her eyes. "The rich are so out of touch. Let's check these lights because we also need to see if the bulbs need replacing." They spent the next few minutes plugging in the lights and separating them into coloured and white before wrapping them around the trees. They had four strands left and placed them along the mantel, around the lounge room door, the inside front door, and along the kitchen island bench.

"And we just have the wreath left for the front door." Ari held it up as Jay packed up the now empty boxes.

"And we'll do that after I take these boxes downstairs." He

hurried to the basement storage room and deposited the boxes, then raced up to see Ari opening the inside door. "Do we need coats?"

"Don't know, but I'll hold this door closed while you hang the wreath up." Ari handed it to him and held the door closed behind him.

He opened the front door of the vestibule. "Whoo, it's chilly." As he tried to hang the wreath, he realised there was no hook for it. "Shit, can't hang it." He quickly closed the door and handed it back to her. "Need a hook and hammer. Back in a minute." He rushed inside and downstairs to rummage in his toolkit. After finding what he needed, he made his way back up and was banging a nail in the front door in seconds. "And we are done." He exchanged the hammer for the wreath and hung it in the centre of the door. "Perfect. What do you think?" He fully opened the door for Ari to see.

"Perfect. Now get inside because it's cold and I need a pee."

He closed and locked the front door and hurried past her.

"I'm going to freshen up." She locked the interior door and dashed upstairs.

Jay glanced around the open plan living area at all of the decorations and walked into the kitchen for a beer. He downed it in seconds, belched, and sighed. *Christmas might not be so bad after all*, he thought, and rinsed the bottle under the tap and left it upside down on the dish rack to drain.

Ari came down and found him. "So, what now? It's like ten, or something."

"And neither of us have anything to do tomorrow, so we can stay up late and sleep in later," Jay replied. "You want something to eat or drink?" He opened the fridge and scanned the shelves. "We have Mom's leftovers from today." He pulled the container out and lifted the lid. "Lots of turkey, potatoes, peas, beans, carrots."

"Sounds good." Ari slid onto a bench stool. "Heat 'er up, chef."

Jay raised a brow and popped the container into the microwave. "One gourmet Thanksgiving meal coming up, milady."

A grin lifted the corners of Ari's lips. "Technically it's for two…"

Jay waved his finger at her. "You know that's—"

"Yeah, yeah." Ari's grin grew. "Just joking. And what do we have to drink, *garçon*?"

Jay's laugh rumbled out of him. "Well, I've just had a beer, so you can have one of those, juice, water, your diet drink, or a Pepsi."

"I'll take a Pepsi on the rocks, thank you, *garçon*." Ari took the napkin he handed her and whipped it across her legs. "Don't forget the cutlery."

Jay shook his head. "Yes, ma'am. He handed over cutlery before getting a glass and filling it with ice, then cracking an ice-cold Pepsi Max over it.

"Ooh, look at those bubbles," Ari enthused and accepted the glass. "Thank you, *garçon*." She sculled back several mouthfuls before pausing. "Whoo, that's cold," she gasped. "But it hits the spot."

Jay topped up her glass. "We also have pie for dessert, and I think there's popcorn from today, too, if you want something else to munch on."

"Maybe later, although I doubt we'll need it."

The microwave dinged and Ari took a sip of her drink while Jay removed the container and peeled back the lid. The steam slithered into the air and the scent of meat and vegetables wafted after it. "Mmm…"

Jay dished the food onto two plates and slid them across the island before walking around and sitting on a stool beside Ari. "Dig in."

They ate in silence for a few minutes except for a few murmurings here and there over the flavours invading their mouths, and when they were done they laid their cutlery on their plates.

"Still tastes good." Ari dabbed her mouth and took a couple of sips of her drink. "But I think I'm too full for pie. We can leave that for tomorrow."

"Fine by me. I'm full up as well." Jay collected their plates and rinsed them under the tap. "I won't bother with these until tomorrow." He left them and picked up the kitchen towel, slowly drying his hands while contemplating what he was going to do. "So… Is there anything in particular you want to do now? Watch TV, a movie, listen to music… dance…?"

Ari's brows rose. "You dance?" She slid off the stool and finished the last of her drink. "Since when? Have I seen it?"

"Well, I mean, the only dancing I do is that weak-ass hip-hop dancing thing I did in that comedy skit all those years ago." Jay swung the towel over the oven door handle and reached for her hand. "Milady."

A small blush crept over Ari's cheeks. "Sir." She took his hand and he escorted her into the lounge room. "You're not going to hip-hop, are you?"

"No, no." Jay walked over to the music system on the

wall. "Just let me get some old-school music going on and we'll dance all of that turkey off." He selected a particular decade and waited for the first song to start. When it did, he put his arms out to his sides, clicked his fingers in time with the music, and turned around. "Can I pick 'em or what?" He grinned as the beats of Michael Jackson's *Thriller* burst out of the speakers.

"Cool. Turn it up." Ari clicked her fingers and rocked out to it.

Jay adjusted the volume and they danced until the next song came on.

"Oh, I love this one. How'd you know?" Ari removed her sweater and threw it on the couch. She spun around and did some fancy footwork she'd learned back in the '90s when she'd line danced.

"Hey, how'd you do that?" Jay pointed at her feet. "Show me."

Ari slowly went through the foot motions and taught Jay how to do them. It was simple enough; the left foot toes had to move left while the right foot ankle followed. Then you do it in reverse.

After he learned the dance step, he showed her his hip-hop moves and she picked them up quickly.

Eventually, she called time out. "I'm hot and in need of a drink." Ari wiped her brow. "Whew, it's warm in here, or is that just me?"

"Not just you. We've been working up a sweat from all the dancing. What do you want?" Jay headed into the kitchen and opened the fridge door. "I'm having another beer." He pulled one out and cracked it open, sculling it back while Ari came to his side.

"I'll do the same with a Pepsi." She pulled out a can, cracked it open, and sculled it back. They stood in front of the open fridge, trying to cool down while drinking their refreshments.

"Ah." Jay exhaled. "That was good." He rinsed the bottle and left it beside the other one on the sink.

Ari let out a gush of air. "Ooh, that's cold. But so good." She closed the fridge and looked at the wall clock. "Just after midnight. Guess we'd better turn the music down and calm down after that."

"Meh, don't be a party pooper," Jay told her, but went and changed the volume anyway. He clicked through the different genres he'd had Bobby set up and came across ballads. "Okay, time to slow things down a bit." He waited until the first song started, nodded his head slowly in time to the beat, and held his hand out to Ari. "Come dance, Ari, my girl."

Blushing, Ari took his hand and he twirled her into his arms and over to the space between the Christmas trees.

"We've got rock ballads, sparkly lights, a night still young," Jay murmured into her hair. "Dance all night with me, Ari."

Cocooned in his arms, she felt the blood slowly heat in her veins. Felt the tingle slowly start in the pit of her stomach, and the throb slowly start between her legs. His touch, his taste, his smell was what she wanted. His hands on her, his flesh against hers, his tongue dancing in sync with hers while they danced around the floor. She sucked in a shuddering breath and her left hand slid from his shoulder.

"You okay?" His head lifted from hers and his brown eyes stared intently into her green ones. "Ari?"

"Ah…" She managed to break her gaze away and found

they were standing in the doorway to the hall. "How'd we get here?"

"We danced our way here." Jay's voice was soft as he continued gazing at her, knowing he'd danced them to the doorway for a special reason.

"Oh, well, I guess it's time for bed, then," she managed. Her heart thundered in her chest and sang in her ears, not to be obliterated by the music that still blared out of the speakers.

"I hung some special decorations up when you weren't watching."

"Huh?" Her gaze darted back to his and saw him look up at the door frame. "What am I supposed to be…oh…?" She saw a small bundle of green leaves. "What's that?"

"*That* is mistletoe," Jay told her. "It's very special this time of the year and has special properties."

"Such as?" Ari had heard of it, but it wasn't widely used at Christmas in Australia.

"Well…" Jay dragged the word out. "Its special property is that it seems to be able to make any couple standing under it, kiss."

The realisation hit her, and her eyes closed. "Oh…" Her head fell forward and the blush sped up her neck and across her face. "Oh…"

"Mmm, oh…" Jay smiled tenderly. "Ari…"

"Mmm?" She couldn't look at him, even though she was still in his arms.

"I want to kiss you, Ari."

"Mmm…" she mumbled. "Ah…" Her eyes flew open to see him hovering.

"Ari…" whispered from between his lips before they landed on hers.

They were soft on hers and opened for his tongue to pass through. It danced with hers in time to the ballad playing and made her dizzy with emotions she had never felt. Passion, desire, fireworks going off somewhere overhead, people cheering, even though they were the only ones there. His tongue caressed hers, teased hers, made love to hers, and her arms slid around his neck, pulling him closer.

His arms slid around her, pulling her closer, harder against his body. He didn't want to let her go, didn't want it to stop, but he knew he needed to take things slowly. He needed to bide his time even though he didn't want to, and the way he was feeling in that moment, he so desperately didn't want to stop. But he had to. So he did.

"Mmm…" His lips tore from hers. "Oh, God, Ari. I don't want this to stop. I don't want this to stop." He breathed heavily, his lips against her cheek. "I've fallen for you, Ari. I'm in love with you even though I've fought with myself not to, tried to stop myself from falling for you."

"What?" Ari pulled back, still breathing hard. "What? What are you saying?" She was dizzy, her head, the room, and the world was spinning.

Jay swallowed the lump in his throat. "I've fallen for you, Ari. I've fallen in love with you." He didn't let go, kept her caged with his arms locked in place around her. "I love you."

Unprepared for those words, Ari could only stare at him. Stare from his eyes to his lips, to his beard, the dimples, the ruffled hair. This was a man who had just declared his love for her and what was she doing? Panicking. Even though she felt the same way. "I…really," she breathed. "You really…"

"Yes, Ari," Jay said softly. "I've fallen in love with you, and I hope you feel the same."

Anything for You

"Oh, God." Her head shook side to side and her eyes closed against the onslaught of emotion. "So many people have asked that, or asked about it, and I kept saying no, that's not what we are, this can't be…" Her breath left her in a sigh. "Ah…"

"Well, maybe they saw what we were yet to see," Jay suggested. "Maybe they saw what we've been fighting against since we met. We clicked, we connected, we got along like a house on fire and I'm relaxed and myself around you and I haven't been myself in so many years. Ari, this is it. This is happening. We're falling in love."

"I…oh, Jay…I…" Ari shook her head. "I don't. I…"

"You don't love me? You don't have feelings for me?" he almost demanded.

"I do," she whispered, and rested her right hand on his chest. "I do, but is this such a good idea considering that's happening with your ex and our contract and—"

"I don't give a God damn fuck about my ex," he exploded. "She's my ex and a pain in my fucking ass, but she doesn't dictate who I date or fall in love with. And I've fallen in love with *you*, Ari. I can't deny it any longer." He placed his lips on hers.

For a moment she gave in, but then came to her senses and pulled back. "Jay this is sudden, and I can't breathe. Let me go." She struggled from his arms and closed her eyes. "Just need to breathe."

"You okay? Are you going to faint?" Jay placed his hands on her hips to steady her. "Ari?"

"A little lightheaded from all of this emotion," she said, breathing deeply. She opened her eyes but couldn't look into his. "Look, Jay. I do feel the same, but is it a good idea to give in to our feelings with everything going on? Our contract. I'm only here for a year and we have no idea what to do after that because the plan was to go—"

"I don't care about the plan anymore, Ari. I love you." Jay cupped her face with both hands. "I love you. I want you in my life, in my house, in my city. I want you here with me."

"And your wife…" she muttered, sadly staring into his eyes.

"My *ex*-wife," he reminded her and kissed her gently. "She's my *ex* for a reason. I'm not going to stop living life because of it, *or* her. She moved on before the divorce. I'm moving on after."

Ari's eyes slid closed. "I'm so overwhelmed right now. I just…we need to slow things right down and just sit on it a bit and let it all sink in because I certainly wasn't expecting this tonight. Or to have all of these feelings come rushing to the surface." Pulling out of his embrace, she pushed her hair back with both hands. "I just need time to calm down and we can talk about this rationally in the morning."

"I am being rational, Ari," Jay assured her. "That kiss made it real. Made it *all* real. My feelings, my thoughts, this moment, this situation." He grasped her arms. "Everything, right now in this moment is very, very real."

Ari sighed and closed her eyes. She wasn't stupid by any means and felt the exact same way about Jay. But something just didn't sit right in her gut, and she knew it had to do with Gloria. "We need to take our time with this. This is just going way too fast for me and I need to breathe and think. And then I think we need to talk about where all of this is going and how it's going to get there." She opened her eyes and looked at him. A soft smile was lighting up his lips. "I'm

Anything for You

very overwhelmed at the moment."

"Understandably." He gave her a nod, "So, how about this. We pack up for the night, go up to bed." He saw the alarm fly over her face. "I mean our *own* beds, of course, and try and get some sleep. And when we wake tomorrow, we can sit and talk about it, and if you have any questions, I'll try and answer them. Okay?"

She nodded. "Sounds okay. I hate being overwhelmed. It does my head in. It's a complete mind fuck."

"Okay, come here." He pulled her in for a hug, wrapping his arms around her and stroking her hair while he rested his chin on her head. He felt her arms around his waist. "I love you, Ari. I want you in my life so we *will* talk about this all you want. But we *will* make this happen."

*****

When Ari woke the next morning, it was after barely a couple of hours sleep with all the tossing and turning she'd done, wrought from emotion from Jay's declaration of love.

Do I love him? Of course I do. But how did I expect this to go?

Throwing her arms above her head and around her pillow, she wanted another ten hours of sleep, but she knew that wouldn't solve anything. It would just be her hiding from Jay, from his feelings that he wanted to talk about, from the real life that was going on outside her bedroom door. Could she deal with that? With all of that? Deal with Gloria and the kids? Because that's what that would mean. If she allowed herself to fall for Jay openly, she would have to deal with his life, his ex-wife, and the kids. And after seeing Gloria the day she arrived, she definitely didn't want to deal with her.

So what do I do? she asked herself.

A knock at the door interrupted the conversation with herself.

"Ari," Jay called. "It's after ten. You okay?"

Sighing, she rolled over and buried herself under the covers.

"Ari." Another knock, and then the door opened. "Ari, you awake? It's after ten." Jay saw the bundle on the bed, and, walking over, he saw her nose poking out from under the quilt. "Ari." He gently pulled at the covering.

"What?" She sighed. "I'm tired, and nice and warm." She pulled the quilt back.

A soft smile lifted Jay's lips. "It's half ten. If you don't want to get up, I'll let you stay in until twelve and I'll just join you here until you wake." He crawled over her and lay on the bed, throwing his arm over her and snuggling into her back. "I could do with another hour or so. I barely slept all night. All I thought about was our kiss, my love for you, finally admitting it to you and myself, and what it was going to mean for our future."

Future!

Ari's eyes flew open. She'd been clamping them shut since he'd walked in, barely able to breathe, unwilling to move, even when he'd climbed up beside her. But now he was talking about the future. With one another?

"Okay." She flung back the covers and stood up. "Get out and I'll have a shower. I'll be down soon." Not looking at him, she hurried for the ensuite, unaware of the smile on his face.

"And she's up," he muttered, and rolled off the bed. Not that sleeping in the same bed as Ari would have been bad; in his books it would be the best night ever. He flung open the curtains to reveal a snowy landscape and hurried downstairs to get brunch going. *Something light and easy, like scrambled eggs and bacon*, he thought.

Ari finished her shower and dressed, dreading the conversation she knew was coming. A shuddering breath left her, making her uneasy. "God, girl, get it together," she murmured. "You gotta get it together and be an adult about this. And be honest while you're at it." Breathing deeply, she waited until her nerves had calmed before going downstairs.

"Hey." Jay saw her. "The eggs are almost done, the toast is in…" The toast popped. "Nope, toast is done. You wanna get those?" He kept mixing the eggs in the pan.

Ari breathed in the aromas wafting around them and grabbed the toast which she buttered and set out on each plate. "That it?"

Jay glanced at the table. "Juice is done, coffee for me, and the eggs are ready to go." He turned off the cooktop and dished out eggs onto their plates. "That's yours, milady, and mine…" He set the pan down and they walked around the island bench and sat at the table, eating in relative silence until they were done.

Jay had watched her in between mouthfuls, wanting to say something, but also figuring it was best to wait. "How was it? Did I put enough salt and pepper in?"

"Did you put any?" Ari frowned and swallowed the remnants. "I didn't taste any." She washed it down with a sip of juice. "I'm not a pepper girl and try not to add salt to anything. Besides, it had bacon. That's salty enough."

"It was just a sprinkle of each." Jay finished his coffee, watched her nervously glance at him, and then blush and get up to take her dishes. "Since we have nothing else to do, we're going to have that conversation about last night."

Ari dropped her plate in the sink. "Shit. Slipped out of my hand." The lie slid out easily from between her lips as she tried to cover her nerves. "Not broken, though." She finished rinsing and piled everything into the dishwasher, including the dishes from the night before.

"Here." Jay rinsed his plate and cutlery and Ari stood aside for him to place them in the dishwasher. He loaded it up and set it to wash. "Don't need to worry about these, but we do need to worry about us." He watched Ari wander into the lounge and continue to the bay window overlooking the city. He followed. "Ari."

She tilted her head slightly.

He stopped behind her and lightly rested his hands on her shoulders. "I think I've tried denying it since that kiss all those months ago in Australia. When I had to leave to finish filming the movie. I had no plan to kiss you then, it just happened. But I haven't stopped thinking about it, or you, since. And I think, in part, that's what drove me to help you. That, my feelings, and because of your situation, you needed to get out of there and I could help you with that. I came up with the social media campaign, so you had sales and money coming in. I wanted you here so you could start your life as a best-selling author and get on with your life in general. You deserved that, Ari, you really did, and you still do. Being away from you all those months just made that clearer each day. Even after our Zoom and Facetime calls, it made me want you more."

Ari was silent, listening, feeling, digesting. His hands were light and comfortable on her shoulders. His voice was soft

Anything for You

yet charged with emotion. His touch felt right, just as his lips had last night.

"I can't help that my feelings have grown into love, Ari," he murmured into her ear. "I can't help that I've fallen in love with you."

She turned her head, so her ear met his lips and he nuzzled her cheek. "But would this work?" Melting back into his body, she knew she was letting go. Letting herself fall. And in that moment, she didn't care.

"Why not?" Jay asked and slid his arms around her. "Why wouldn't it?"

"Your ex, your kids."

Anger flared in Jay's chest, but he kept it in check. "I hate my ex, and as you know she causes all manner of trouble. And she probably would cause a whole lot of trouble for us. Me in particular. Although I'd like to think that contract she signed to keep her out of jail worked to some degree."

"Any chance of her marrying Denver?" Ari dared to ask.

"Probably not. Not in the near future. He's ten years younger than her. I doubt he's anywhere near ready to get married and settle down, or have kids, especially to an older woman *with* two kids. I don't see him doing anything that remotely resembles that until he's in his forties. And besides, if she did, she wouldn't get anything out of me except child support. The money train would grind to a halt and stop delivering her monthly alimony."

Ari's brows furrowed. "You still have to pay her alimony even though she earns a tonne of money from everything she does? If you haven't had a movie role in two years, besides the one with Russell, why would the judge make you pay her?"

"Oh, it's not that much, in all fairness. I was barely working, so it's a limited payment. She gets the child support, but she can afford to look after her own kids just as much. If anything, several of the judges have actually said she should be paying me alimony since she's earning far more than what I am, but that's not the point here." He turned her to face him. "I'm happy with you, Ari. I feel good, and carefree, and comfortable. We have fun when we go out, and you don't put expectations on me, or demand things. You're the complete opposite of Gloria and I find that refreshing. And all of that is why I've fallen in love with you. You're smart, and talented, and creative, and tell a mean story and I love that. You're not a user or abuser and you find it hard to accept help from people. Or money. And Gloria has no issue taking, which makes her the complete opposite of you, believe me."

"But how is she going to affect *us, this, you and me*?" Ari desperately gazed into his eyes, hoping to find the answers she sought.

A sigh left him. "I don't know, Ari, I really don't." He slowly rubbed her arms in comfort. "All I can say is that I will try and protect you from her at every turn, and if we keep this on the down-low, she may not find out at all. Her ego is too busy setting up the lies she tells the world about me, and having her fling with the toy boy. She may not even realise that we're happening. Besides, even when we have been out, we've exhibited nothing more than friendship towards each other."

"I know." Ari licked her lips and glanced away. "But I don't want trouble. I also don't know how this will work out. You have your kids; I have my timeline. I'm just here for a year. Is it really that wise to hook up when I'm not here for long?"

"Who said you'll be here for a year?" Jay gently tipped her chin up, forcing her to look at him. "That's *your* plan. My plan was to keep you here longer, so you'd have a tonne of inspiration to write more books. And," he gave a slight nod, "so I could have you here to see if a relationship would form. It's you that wanted to spend a year in New York. It's you who made the choice to come here for a year instead of going straight to the Gold Coast. So maybe *you* had a secret plan underneath all of those other plans? Mmm?"

A blush crept over Ari's cheeks. "I wanted to spend a year here, yes. I wanted to see the sights, experience the atmosphere, and soak in all of the inspiration I could. It also meant I could promote the book and get the next two out as well."

"And…" Jay prompted when she stopped.

The blush deepened. "And…it also meant I would be spending time with you." Ari clamped her hands together and held them to her abdomen, trying to keep a grip on her raging emotions. "I'm actually overwhelmed by everything, and it's only been what, four, or five weeks since I got here." She pulled from his arms and turned to the window. "We've been out most days exploring the city." Her eyes took in the snowy view of Manhattan. "And it's been great, and my stuff has arrived, and most of it's in storage downstairs, and I've unpacked what I need so far. I have all of my clothes and jewellery and accessories. We've been shopping for whatever else I've needed, and you've bought me stuff I didn't. And the last four or five weeks have been hectic and exciting and inspiring and overwhelming. And now this…" She spread her hands. "I just…I don't know what to do with it."

"With us? Our unbridled, burgeoning love?" Jay shoved

his hands into his pockets and stood beside her. "This is happening, Ari. Our feelings for each other are growing, whether you like it or not. Whether you're overwhelmed or not. It comes down to what are we going to do about it."

"I don't know if I want to do anything about it," she replied, still staring out at the view. "I think it will ruin things and Gloria will add to that."

"And I think that will be time wasted when we could be loving one another and making love with each other."

Ari looked at him in alarm. "I'm hardly ready for that. Except for last night, we hadn't kissed since months ago and this is happening way too fast. We haven't even had an actual date."

A smile raised Jay's lips. "You want to date? You want to take this slowly? Is that it? Not rush into it, just take it one step at a time?"

Ari thought about that. "That would help me to not be so overwhelmed. Everything's happened so fast, I barely have time to breathe some days, and now you're talking love and sex when we've kissed twice. I just need things to…"

"Go slowly, one step at a time," Jay finished for her.

"Yes," she replied and relaxed into a deep breath. "One step at a time."

"Okay, well I'd say the first step was the kiss, and the second was me telling you I love you," Jay stepped closer. "It's time for you to tell me how you feel."

Terror gripped her and she froze, and then chided herself for being so stupid. *Relax*, she told herself, *it's not the end of the world*. The terror melted away and she closed her eyes and allowed herself to feel everything she did for Jay.

"Ari?"

"I feel the same." She kept her eyes closed. "I kept my feelings in check in Australia because we lived in different countries, and it wasn't going to work. But now that you've changed my life and I'm here, it's hard to keep a rein on them and they're growing, and I don't really have a say in that. But—" she finally opened her eyes, "the biggest problem and road block to all of this is Gloria."

He turned her towards him. "And I'll deal with her, don't worry. She's not your problem. Neither are my kids. What's important is we explore our feelings and let ourselves fall in love and everything that comes with that."

She gave him a half-hearted smile. "Everything *includes* Gloria."

"The hell it does!" he said. "It's *us, just us*, Ari. *Just us.*" He gently cupped her face and lowered his lips to hers.

The fireworks exploded in her head, and she responded.

They didn't stop until they gasped for air.

"Well." Jay breathed rapidly. "Does that prove the point?"

Ari leaned her forehead against his lips. "Yeah, I guess it does."

"Do you still want to take things slowly?" Jay hoped the answer was no.

"Yes," she managed and tilted her head back to look into his eyes. "At least until Christmas, so we can give this first stage of our romance a chance to settle in. And for me to get used to it."

"Until Christmas, huh?" He nodded and raised a brow. "Well that just gave me an idea for making our first night together magical."

She blushed and he placed his lips on hers.

Chapter 9

The next two weeks were a flurry of shopping, expeditions around the city, ice-skating at Rockefeller Plaza, parties at Jay's friends' houses, and more sight-seeing.

Ari had also scored two radio interviews, both of them on the same day.

One did not go well.

"So, Ari, you're an author who's here for a year; tell us how that happened," Ken J. Jamison asked her as she sat in his studio at *KYJ Radio*. "But, more importantly, tell us about your relationship with Jay Daniels." He watched her expression change from calm to mildly camouflaged terror.

"What relationship?" she asked, a nervous tinge to her tone. "We're good friends. He's helped me with my book, and he's letting me stay in his guest room for a year. We have a great friendship, and I'm sick of being asked about it. Geez, anyone would think that's all there was to talk about. I do have a best-selling book, you know." The twist in her gut tightened, and she sat a little higher in her swivel chair. "Seriously, it's all anyone wants to talk about, but nothing's going on, and I don't know why no one's listening to me when I say that. You're all obsessed with making up a relationship where there is none."

"That sounds like a ton of denial to me," Ken said, staring intently across the console at her.

"Not denial, just pissed off that everyone wants to make up lies about me and gossip," Ari replied tartly. "I'm here to talk about my book, if you don't want to, there's no point me staying." She swung around in her chair to look at everyone out in the office. Bobby was there, giving her a slight shrug, as if to say, *it's up to you.* She swung back round, feeling riled. "Does anyone at home want to hear about the book?"

"If it's not denial, Ari Travers, what is it?" Ken pushed. "Jay Daniels hasn't done this for anyone else. He hasn't helped an unknown author—"

"Do you know that for a fact?" she bit back and rested her palms on her thighs to subtly soak up the sweat they were leaking. It was warm in the studio, the glare of the lights didn't help, and neither did the glare coming from Ken. "Do you *know for a fact* he hasn't helped an unknown author before? Or anyone else for that matter?"

Ken slowly nodded in thought and knew he wanted the dirt, not the truth. "No, I don't know that for a fact—"

"Then don't spout things as facts if you don't know if they are. It makes you look like a shoddy interviewer. Now, if you want to talk about my book, fine, let's do that," Ari pushed. "Otherwise there's no point me being here, because I'm not giving you dirt that does not exist."

"But the dirt has already been splashed across the tabloids and on the internet." Ken held up three trashy magazines which had pictures of Ari and Jay out and about in New York.

"And they mean that he's showing me around as my tour guide and friend. Don't make something out of it that's just

Anything for You

not there. What *is it* with you gossipmongers? Always making up garbage because you want the likes and follows, but all it does is hurt the people involved. Again, Ken, if we're not talking about the book, there's no point me being here." Ari raised her brows and gave a slight shake of her head. "Are we talking about my book or not? I'm not here to make up gossip or give you more fodder for it. I have a book to promote which is what this interview was set up for. If you're not interested…" She removed her headphones.

"Wait, wait, wait, just a minute." Ken slammed down the tabloids and thrust his thick forefinger at Ari. "You don't get to make the rules on *my* show, *Ms Travers*, that's *my* name up there on that sign." His finger redirected to the wall behind him.

"So what!" Ari spat and set the headphones down. "The *station* booked me to talk about my book, I'm sure your *listeners* want to *hear* about my book. I'm not here to talk about anything else. You may run this show, but you don't run the network." She swung around and saw Bobby's wide eyes.

"You're pathetic," Ken said, hoping to get a rise out of her.

Bobby shook his head at her.

Ari breathed deeply and swung back round. She picked up her headphones and put them back on. "*I'm* pathetic? You're the misogynistic pig who wants to verbally batter a single woman because you believe she's dating an actor who helped her. Because *you* don't know how to handle women any other way. Because *you* want to believe the trash rags instead of finding the truth, because like real men, the truth doesn't exist, especially in *your* mind. You are useless at your job, and yes, while this might give you ratings, just like with

Maury from *The Maury and Maureen Show*, I'll get even more followers, and likers, and attention because I stood up to your sorry, piss weak arse." Ari watched his jaw grind and the briefest flicker of something cross his eyes. "I came here to talk about my book. We either talk about my book, or I leave. Which will it be?" She raised her brow in defiance. "The clock is ticking *Mr* Jamison. But I'm sure you're loving this, as are your bosses."

"What have my bosses got to do with it?" He sniggered. "Okay, *little Ms Travers*. Let's talk about your book." He held it up and read off the cover. "*So Red the Rose*, by Ari Travers. A so-called psychological thriller with some fluffy romance thrown in, but all it really is is hard core porn sex and some guy killing off his wife and kids. The characters are piss weak, the storyline's piss weak, and the premise is piss weak. Just as *Ms Ari Travers* is piss weak when it comes to answering questions about her *relationship* with Jay Daniels."

Ari removed her headphones, laid them calmly on the desk, and swung around in her chair. In one brief movement, she stepped over to the door, opened it, and walked out, not even bothering to close it behind her. Bobby scurried after her, and they heard Ken on the overhead system as he continued slandering her.

"That's right. Ms Ari Travers just huffed her way out of our interview, *and* the studio, over her book, simply because she didn't want to talk about what a piss weak book it really is. God knows why Jay Daniels wanted to help her try and sell such a pile of piss weak shit. Unless she has something he wanted. Like in the pussy department. Maybe that was why Jay helped her. He got lots of pussy in exchange for it. Either way, I actually read this piss weak drivel to find out what it was about, and that's three hours of my life I'll never get back. Though I'm sure Jay gets more than three hours every night. Unless she's good at doing blow jobs. Maybe that's why he's helping her? He gets blow every night, both the drug *and* sex varieties."

"Fucking hell what a shit head," Ari exploded when the elevator doors closed behind them. "Who the fuck does he think he is? Pushing for trash that's not true and then saying such things about me and Jay. Seriously, who the fuck does he think he is, and can I sue his arse off for it?"

Bobby considered it a moment. "You can definitely get the lawyers on to it. All of that was just a low blow and completely unnecessary. He's known as a tough interviewer, but that was just downright misogynistic and gross. Jay won't be happy either. Talk about slander and defamation." The doors slid open, and they walked outside and hailed a cab.

"Who the hell *is* that douche, anyway? Another Maury?" Ari wrapped her coat around her but kept her scarf loose. She was seething mad and wanted to kill him. Wanted to kill something, someone, preferably him. "Do I tell Jay, or do you? And who calls the lawyers?"

"Already on it." Bobby was furiously typing away on his phone. "Text to the lawyers sent. But you might want to see Jay and tell him yourself, although I'll try and get a copy of the show via their website, unless the lawyers do. He won't be happy." He finished on his phone and slid it into his coat pocket.

"I bet Gloria's chafing at the bit, if she's heard it." Ari watched the city go by as she boiled on the inside. "Who knows what she'll do."

"Nothing, if she knows what's good for her." Bobby pointed out the window in front of her. "We're at the next interview."

"I hope this one goes better," Ari grumbled and climbed out. They went upstairs to the *K-Rock* radio station and were led to the green room, where Ari slid off her coat and scarf, and gave her make-up a quick once over in her compact mirror. "How do I look? In control of the situation? Or should I not even bother?"

Bobby gave her an appraisal. "You look fine. And don't worry about motor-mouth Jamison. He's like that with a lot of people."

"Or just women?" Ari asked.

Bobby gave her a wry grin. "Or just women. But Zennith Williams is completely different. She has a book club, which is why you're here. *She* actually read your book and loved it."

An assistant came in to escort Ari to the door of the studio, and Bobby held onto her things while she was prepped. When the news of the hour was playing, Ari was led inside and introduced to Zennith.

"Hello, Ari, welcome to my show." Zennith walked around her booth to shake hands. "I'm so glad I could get you on. I love your book and can't wait to talk about it."

"Thank you for having me, and I hope it will be a better time than the one I've just come from with Ken J. Jamison." Ari raised her brows and gave a weary grin as she took in Zennith's appearance; an almost shaved, cropped hair style, full red lips, and a flamboyant yellow and purple floor-length dress that looked like a toned-down ball gown.

"Ah." Zennith nodded knowingly. "Yes, I've had many authors and guests who have war stories from appearing on

Ken's show. Let's talk about them. Take a seat and we'll be on in a few minutes." She grinned and waved at the chair beside Ari, then collected some papers from her assistant and settled back behind her console. After donning her headphones, she pressed a few buttons, indicated for Ari to put on her headphones, and went back on-air.

"Hello, again, ladies and gentlemen. We are back to introduce this hour's guest, Ms Ari Travers. She's the Australian author of the best-selling novel, *So Red the Rose*, and she's just come from Ken J. Jamison's show, so we'll have a lot to talk about. Let's get into it." She flicked a button and the station's jingle played.

"Let's get into the elephant in the room. Ken J. Jamison. Ari, tell us about your interview with him. Was it even an interview?"

Ari chuckled half-heartedly and spoke clearly into the microphone. "Not so much as a gossip session. All he wanted was the dirt on Jay and me, because there've been tabloids claiming more than what there is. Jay's a guy who helped me out in an incredible way, and now he's playing tour guide in this incredible city. We're friends. Nothing more."

That wasn't a complete lie, as nothing *had* happened. *Yet.* They had only declared their love for one another and kissed. *A lot.* But nothing else. They barely touched in public, except when Jay put an arm around her to escort her across the street, or into establishments, or held her hand as they walked down the street. And that was only on the odd occasion.

"Ken does like to dig up the dirt on people," Zennith said. "Did you speak about your book at all?"

"Not really. The only thing he mentioned was the title.

Once. Nothing else. He just wanted dirt and pushed it to the point where I walked out. I had to. He was being misogynistic and only got worse when I did walk out. The things he said about me were revolting, as were his comments about Jay, so Jay's lawyers are on the case since I don't have any lawyers of my own."

"You involved Jay's lawyers?" Zennith's hazel eyes grew wide. Rings of purple eyeshadow that butterflied out to her temples, made them look larger than they were. "It was that bad?"

"Incredibly sexist and revolting, so yeah, Bobby, Jay's assistant, who's acting as my assistant for the rest of the year, contacted them about it. I really don't know how that guy still has a radio show." Ari adjusted her earring under the headphones and shifted to get more comfortable.

"He has a radio show because his bosses are just as bad as him." Zennith raised her brow. "Just as bad. But enough about our rival. Let's talk about the book. *So Red the Rose.* Where did the title come from?"

Ari settled in to tell the story, and before they knew it she'd stayed a second hour just to answer questions from callers.

"Are you and Jay dating?" one woman asked.

"No, we're not," Ari replied. "We're friends and he's showing me around the city."

"Then why do the tabloids have you dating?" the caller continued.

"Because the tabloids are bullshit artists who get off on lying and making up stories about people, especially celebrities," Ari told her. "They don't care who it hurts, or who it's about. They just want to sell trash rags. I mean, seriously, why can't a male and female, celebrities or mere mortal normal folk, be friends without being romantically linked to each other?"

"Why would the tabloids lie?" the woman persisted.

"Because they get off on lying about celebrities," Ari repeated. "*And* to make money."

Zennith moved on. "Okay, next caller, what's your question for Ari?"

"Ah, yes, I want to know what you think of Jay's wife, the incredibly beautiful and talented actress, Gloria Hannaford?" the female asked.

Ari glanced at Zennith and rolled her eyes. "I don't. And she's the *ex*-wife."

"Excuse me?" the woman said.

"I *don't* think of her. Why would I? And she's Jay's *ex*-wife."

"Oh, well, it's just that she was on *The Late Show* talking about what she did to Jay and his assistant, and that footage was shown of her on Jay's doorstep. I figured out the timeline and I think it's when you got here to New York. So you would have seen her on his doorstep."

Ari frowned and spun around to see where Bobby was, shrugging and raising her hands, palm side up. *What the fuck?* she mouthed and turned back to Zennith, giving her a look. "Well, I don't know what *you* know, or *think* you've figured out, but I've never met the woman, and I don't think of her. At all. She's Jay's ex to deal with, and not for me to talk about. So…not my business."

Zennith shook her head and changed to the next caller. "Okay, I think we have time for one more question. Hello, what's your question for Ari?"

"Um, yeah hi," a male voice said. "I just wanted Ari to

know that I loved her book and thank God Jay helped her get it out there, because the world is better off with it being known. And that Jay must think she's pretty all right if he's helping her, so people shouldn't be so rude, like Ken J. Jamison was. The book's really great, and what does it matter if she dates Jay? He's single, she's single, they're two single people who can date if they want. Why's it anyone else's business?"

Ari glanced over her shoulder at Bobby. *Is that Jay?* she mouthed.

I think so, he mouthed back.

"That's very sweet of you to say, caller," Zennith replied and watched Ari grin to herself. "You don't happen to know Ari, do you? Have you met her at all?"

"Um, yeah, at a small writers' group gathering back in Australia."

"Jay, you sod!" Ari exclaimed. "You know you're on the air."

"Ha! Yes, Ari, my girl, I do. Hello, Zennith, it's Jay Daniels here folks."

"Hello, Jay, how are you?" Zennith warmed to him immediately. "How nice of you to call in to the show. Have you been listening?"

"I have. I also heard Ken's interview earlier, so guess how that's going to go? But I had some time today to see what was happening and have been listening to the praise for Ari's book. Thanks for having her on."

"Thanks for finding her *and* her book." Zennith glanced at the clock on the wall. "We only have a minute or two, but I agree with what you said. Thank God you found her and helped get this book out to the world. It's incredible, and I think the world is better off for having it out there."

"Absolutely," Jay agreed. "When I finished reading the draft Ari gave me I was in shock. I knew I had to have it, especially to make a movie out of it. The next few books she's releasing are just as good, so I can't wait for you all to read those either."

Zennith glanced at Ari's red, but smiling, face. "Oh, fantastic. That's something we haven't yet mentioned, Ari. Are you writing anything, or do you have another book ready for release?"

"I do. The next book is ready for a March release next year, and the sequel will be out next September." Ari's stomach grumbled and she checked her watch. "There are a few others that are due for release the year after."

"And are you doing any writing now?" Zennith asked.

"No, just taking time out for a holiday and downtime. I'll think about writing something new sometime next year."

Zennith's finger hovered over a button. "Well, I can't wait to read the next book, as I'm sure our listeners can't, and your readers can't, and Jay, thanks for calling in. Say goodbye to Ms Ari Travers, the Australian author of the best-selling novel, *So Red the Rose*. Thank you, Ari."

"Thank you, Zennith. Great name by the way."

Zennith's face lit up. "Thank you, Ari, and goodbye listeners. You have been listening to the *Creative Arts Show* with Zennith Williams. Until tomorrow." She clicked the switch and the *on-air* light turned off. "And there we have it." She removed her headphones. "Thank you so much for coming in. I really did enjoy your book."

Ari stood and shook her hand. "Thanks for having me. I didn't realise Jay was listening, and would phone in. Clearly he needed to have some fun."

"I think some of the other listeners were having fun too, except for those who got personal. The woman who asked about Gloria…" She paused and held her finger to her chin. "I have a feeling I know that voice."

"I had the feeling it *was* Gloria," Ari replied and opened the door to the office. "She clearly wanted dirt that was not forthcoming because there is none." Bobby handed her coat and bag over. "Thanks. I think it's time for lunch because I'm starving, and my stomach is growling. I hope you couldn't hear it over the airwaves."

"I didn't hear a thing, but lunch does sound great." Zennith handed some papers to her assistant. "I highly recommend *El Gardos* downtown if you're going that way. Jay lives over in Brooklyn, right?"

Ari glanced at Bobby, knowing his partner was the manager, and wondering why Zennith was asking. "He does. Why?"

"Oh, no reason." Zennith laughed. "Just figured you might want something close to home. Well, thank you so much for the show; it was a blast, and so much fun. Will you come back when the next book comes out?"

"Sure." Ari nodded and slung her bag over her shoulder. "It'll be up for pre-order on March the first, and on sale March 19th, so book me in."

"Fantastic. Thank you so much for coming in today, Ari." She rested her hand on Ari's arm. "Have a good Christmas and a happy new year and I'll see you again in March."

"Thank you, Zennith; you too. We're off to eat. Let's go, Bobby." She led the way to the lift, and they entered. "So *could* we get into *El Gardos*?"

"Probably. But Jay texted and said he's got lunch sorted. He'll meet us downstairs."

When they exited the building, they found Jay waiting for them in his four-wheel drive at the kerb.

"Hey," he called out the window. "Quick, get in, it's cold out." He waited for Ari to climb into the front, and Bobby in the back, before zooming away into traffic. "I've booked us a table at a restaurant in Rockefeller Center since we're nearby. Figured you'd be hungry after your radio interviews."

"Hungry *and* angry. You know about Ken J. Jamison, right?" Ari asked.

"Oh, I not only know, I heard with my own two ears, and then gave my lawyers an earful about how we're going to squash that asshole like the dog turd he is." Jay clicked on his blinker and merged into the right lane, successfully avoiding the car behind them.

"That was sick, and so is he." Ari adjusted her seatbelt. "I hope something can be done."

"Slander, defamation, anything we can throw at him. He not only said those things about you but he said those things about me as well." Jay turned the corner and slid into the right lane before a car could come up behind him. "I'm not going to let assholes like Ken J. Jamison get away with speaking about you like that, Ari. It was disgusting, degrading, vile, and filthy, and if I met the guy in a dark alley, I'd be the one walking out. He's a disgrace to manhood."

Ari glanced at him in surprise. Although considering how he always reacted to Gloria, she really shouldn't be surprised that his temper often got the better of him. "So I just have to wait and see what your lawyer says?" Ari glanced at the couple trying to cross in front of them. They stepped back just in time, and she saw their startled expressions in detail right outside the window as they drove past.

"Pretty much," Jay replied and pulled up outside the Rockefeller Center. "Here we go. Lunchtime. Hope you like grilled burgers and steak."

"Oh, hell yes. You know I love food, especially cow." Ari slid out of the car and waited for Jay to hurry around to the footpath before entering the restaurant.

Once shown to their table, they were handed menus and chose what they were having. When the waiter left, they continued the conversation.

"How long does it take lawyers to deal with arseholes?" Ari asked, glancing around at the steakhouse décor. "I was so seriously disgusted by him and what he said."

"So was I. To the point where my blood boiled," Jay replied just as his phone rang. "Oh, let's see, it's Merrick." He answered the call. "Tell me what you can do."

"I've heard the show, spoken to the owner, manager, and all accounted for who are in charge, and there will be an apology issued to you and Ms Travers forthwith. If not, I suggested we sue him as we would win, but it could take a while. I then suggested that they force him to apologise live on-air and give both of you compensation to save on time and money for a court case. Because we'd win. They were ever so enthusiastic about that and have offered you both one hundred thousand dollars."

"That's nothing!" Jay burst out and he shifted in his seat. "Except for absolute bullshit. He set out to humiliate her, demean her, and attack her when she didn't comply with his questions and then dragged me into it. He was an absolute asshole who needs to be brought down a peg or two. A hundred grand for the misogyny Ari had to deal with is nothing. Pig fodder."

Anything for You

"And I thought that too, which is why I said no. What's the number you're thinking of?"

Jay glanced at Ari and saw the interest on her face. "I'd say five million. No less. They regularly have a million listeners, so how about five dollars per listener? And they pay your fees, of course."

Merrick smirked. "I like where you're going with this, Jay. Tell Ms Travers I'll get her five million out of *KYJ* as soon as possible. Same with you."

"And a public apology out of Ken, which I'm sure their lawyers will write," Jay added dryly. His head nodded slightly and his gaze drifted to Ari who was frowning. "I'll let her know."

"You do that, and I'll go and get you both five million dollars each."

Jay hung up and slid his phone into his pocket. "That was Merrick. He's heard the show, spoken to all he needed to, and they offered one hundred thousand dollars as compensation to not go to court which would cost them more."

"Not sure it was worth that," Ari argued. "It feels like it's worth more. He was sick."

"And that's why Merrick is going back to them with five million *and* his fees, plus an on-air apology from Jamison himself." Jay leaned back as the waiter set his drink in front of him. He sculled it back, ordered a second, and waited for the waiter to leave before continuing.

"Five million..." Ari's voice trailed off. "Wow..."

"You're worth it, Ari, my girl." Jay gripped her hand. "Absolutely worth it. And let me tell you, it's not the first time the station has been sued for what motor-mouth Jamison has said. He's done it many, many times."

"Yeah, but, *five million*." Ari's head spun. Her money from book sales hadn't even started rolling in yet, and here was she about to make five million dollars from a radio station for the misogyny of the host. *I'm in the wrong business*, she thought. *I should be suing people to make money instead.*

"Don't worry about it. Merrick works wonders, and that's why he's my lawyer." Jay nodded as the waiter placed his second drink in front of him.

"What about what Gloria said?" Bobby piped up. "Did you hear that?"

"Gloria?" The colour of Jay's face slowly changed colour. "What's she got to do with it?"

"We think she was the caller before you." Bobby looked at Ari and sipped his daiquiri. "The caller was asking about her and what Ari thought of her."

"Oh, *that* caller." Jay nodded. "I did hear her while waiting my turn. What's it to her if you've met Gloria or not, if the caller *wasn't* Gloria, that is. If the caller *was* Gloria, then it's none of her damn business and the bitch can fuck off along with Jamison. They deserve each other." His blood had boiled for most of the day; first with what he'd heard Ken say about his beloved Ari, then what his callers had said on-air. Most had been nice, but on Zennith's show there was that one woman who kept mentioning Gloria.; the woman who made his blood boil for a living, and who tormented him to the point he really wished she were dead.

"How long do you think it will take Merrick to finish the deal?" Ari changed the subject from Gloria back to Ken and sipped her soda as she watched Jay's face redden. She didn't want him blowing his top, as he often did when Gloria came up in conversations, in the restaurant.

"Are you angry?" Jay asked her, leaning on the table towards her. "Are you angry at what he said?"

Ari thought about it. "I was this morning when it happened, but by the time I got to Zennith's show and things were so much calmer and more peaceful, the anger dissipated. But if you get me riled up, it'll be back. Besides," she squeezed his hand, "Bobby took care of the legalities and you're finishing it off. I have two saviours looking out for me."

Ha!" Bobby chortled. "If only Jay said such nice things about me."

Jay gave him a scornful raised brow before he squeezed Ari's hand in return. "Yes, you do, Ari. Because I'm looking out for you, and that means Bobby and Merrick are looking out for you too. We're a package deal."

"Oh, is that what we are?" Bobby quipped and sipped his drink. "Good to know."

Ari chuckled and leaned back for the waiter to place her plate in front of her. A sizzling steak with roast vegetables covered in thick, rich gravy greeted her. The aromas wafted into her nose, and she inhaled them deeply. "Oh, God that smells good." She became dizzy with the scent and closed her eyes against the flood of senses working overtime.

"Mmm, that looks good, but I don't eat red meat." Bobby glanced from her meal to his. A stir-fry vegetable platter was the only thing the steakhouse served other than red meat. "Mine's just as good."

"Looks good too," Ari replied. "I might have that as a side next time."

They chatted through the meal and had just finished when Jay got the call from Merrick.

"Five million each, all expenses paid, and an on-air apology written by the lawyers will be happening tomorrow," Merrick said. "It's all done and dusted."

"Great. Get the deal done and we'll be listening tomorrow." Jay turned off his phone and said to Ari, "The deal is done."

*****

The next day, they listened to Ken J. Jamison's radio show and heard the on-air apology. Clearly written by the lawyers, it was brief, but to the point. He never really took the blame, and it was an apology only big stars got to get away with without being cancelled.

"That's a piss weak apology if I ever heard one," Ari said, and flicked the radio off.

"True," Jay agreed. "But we are five million dollars richer." He looked at the cheque in Ari's hand. The station's lawyers had turned up that morning to deliver it in person and they were off to deposit it into Ari's bank account. She was now a millionaire, and things could only get better for her. "Things are looking up, Ari."

Ari stared at the cheque and couldn't wait to get to the bank. "They certainly, are, Jay, they certainly are. I'm not a multi-millionaire like you just yet, not until I bank this baby and see it in my account. But not long now."

"Great, then you can start paying for our meals out," Jay joked. "Let's go put that in your bank account and get you some money."

Chapter 10

By the end of the third week of December, they were getting the house ready for Jay's Christmas party.

"So, do you have one every year, or just this year?" Ari watched him move the kitchen table around. "And why are we moving the table now when the party's on Saturday?"

"I want to see where the best place for everything is." He pushed the table lengthways along the wall. "This could be the bar with tubs of ice and drinks. And the chairs can go into the lounge areas for extra seating." He turned around and pointed both hands at the island bench. "The food will be laid out here by the chef I've hired, and the staff can hand out drinks and such."

"How many staff will be here?" Ari was excited at the prospect of her first Christmas in New York, and her first Christmas party in Jay's house as a couple. Well…soon-to-be couple. They hadn't consummated their relationship, and until they did, they were casually dating. In Ari's eyes, that meant they were technically not a couple yet.

"Six. Two for food, two for drinks, and two to serve and let in guests." He looked around the space and waved his hands as if judging the placement. "I think that's all in the right spots. It'll give them some room when they come in for munchies or a drink. Besides," he wiped his hands on the butt of his jeans, "I'll have about thirty guests and this place is not that big, so we'll be full up. But I don't think we need more staff."

Ari looked at the placement of the table. "Is that the right place for it? What about lengthways against the doors to the back porch?"

"No. That'll be in the way there if anyone needs to step outside for some air or a cigarette. With the table against the wall opposite the kitchen bench, there's plenty of room in the middle for people to move around and get outside."

"And do we need any more decorations, or do we have enough? 'Cause some of your friends went all out with theirs."

Jay grinned at her. "Yeah, they do. We tried to outdo each other for years, and when I was with Gloria, we used to throw massive parties for like, two hundred of our friends. No one could top it, but since then, since the separation, and the divorce, I haven't really given a fuck about it. I do the basic decorations, have a few of my friends over and that's it. No hassle, no trying to outdo everyone. It's just a quiet, intimate Christmas party for thirty people." He shrugged. "You cut down as you get older. I guess."

"Realise what is and what isn't important," Ari murmured. "I haven't celebrated Christmas like this ever. Just the two of us with a few nibblies, Christmas lights, and the carols on TV."

"So it's been completely different for you this year, then." Jay took her hands in his and kissed them. "You've seen New York at Christmas, got to meet a bunch of my friends, finally, and now you're the hostess of this year's Christmas party."

"Oh, I don't think so." Ari blushed. "I'm not throwing it, so I'm hardly the hostess."

"Oh, you definitely are," Jay corrected. "You live here with me; we're presenting this party together. You are the hostess, and I am the host."

With her insides tingling at the prospect, Ari chose to change the subject. "Do we have anything else to do before the party? And what time are we starting?"

"It starts at seven, and I don't think there's anything else to do. Bobby organised the caterers and menu months ago, even though I was in a different house. But as for the rest of the week, I don't have any plans except for continuing what we've been doing. Which is me showing you around New York."

"Yes…about that," Ari replied slowly. "Have you noticed there've been a few photographers hanging around? As if they know where we'll be and when?" She hadn't wanted to suspect Jay or Bobby of telling the paps where and when they'd be, so had taken the other road of believing they'd just happened to be in the area taking shots of other celebs when they spotted Jay. It was the easiest option *to* believe.

"Hanging around here?" He pointed a finger towards the front of the house. "Outside? They've been hanging around outside? Well that's not right."

"No, not here." Ari watched him, but he didn't seem overly concerned. "They've turned up at the places we've gone. I noticed a couple at Rockefeller when we went ice-skating. And then the photos ended up online saying we were out on a date because we were holding hands and hugging while ice-skating. And we were only doing that so I didn't fall over."

"But we were," Jay countered and rested his hands

casually on his hips. "We *were* on a date, and that's what we've been doing the last two weeks. *Dating.*"

"Have you been telling the paps where we'll be?" blurted Ari. "Because if you have, that's not fair to me, Jay. Are you stirring up your ex?"

"Gloria? Pft! What's she got to do with anything?" Jay huffed. "And for the record, no, Ari, I haven't been telling the paps where we'll be or where we're going. Why would I?" He saw she wasn't convinced and took her by the arms. "Ari, look, paps are everywhere in this city. It's New York; thousands of celebrities work and live here. We're everywhere, so the paps are too. Not to mention all of the celebrities who visit. There's probably a hundred paps per celebrity, if not more, so if one caught us at Rockefeller, then there were probably other celebrities there as well."

"Did you see any?" she asked, still not convinced.

"Yeah, I saw some I used to work with. It's Rockefeller Centre. TV shows are filmed there, so there's always someone coming and going. The paps were probably there for them and found us in return. Ari…" He pulled her close and stole a kiss, making her blush. "You're a celebrity now. A famous author with a massive number one book in the whole country, and me…well…" He shrugged. "I've been one for decades. But they've pretty much left me alone these last two years."

"Until that scene with Gloria." Ari's brows rose in amusement.

Jay groaned and his head dropped back. "Until that scene with Gloria *and* the movie with Russell. They've both thrown me back in the spotlight. So yeah…" Another shrug. "I get to deal with it all over again."

"Not to mention the fact I've denied it up until now. They probably think they've caught me in a lie, considering the online headlines and all. *No one* thought we weren't lovers from the start. They all lied and claimed we were and ignored my comments that we weren't."

"What does it matter now?" Jay nuzzled her neck. "It's all happening so what does it matter? Besides, I have something very special planned for Christmas. Once everyone's gone, expect a surprise."

She snuggled into him as the nuzzling continued. "Like what?"

"Like never mind until it happens. Give me a kiss…" He planted his lips on hers and she melted into him.

*****

The Christmas party roared to life four days later, with guests turning up from seven.

Thirty or so of Jay's friends and their partners came along dressed for the holiday festivities and hit the bar soon after arriving.

Jay and Ari mingled for an hour as he introduced her to those she was yet to meet.

"Ari, I want you to meet Tad Reardon, an actor buddy of mine. He's also written a few shows and produced others."

Ari took in Tad's tall, dark, good looks. She guessed him to be around mid-forties, like Jay, but unlike Jay he was nowhere near going grey. "Hi. Nice to meet you. I'm not familiar with your name or face. What have you been in?"

Tad's brows rose in amusement, and he looked at Jay. "How can she not know about me? Have you told her nothing?" he joked. "How am I not famous everywhere on this planet?"

Ari glanced between him and Jay. "Is there something…"

"No, no." Jay shook his head. "Tad just likes to think that because he's done the shit movies and TV shows he's done that everyone in the world knows who he is. So when someone doesn't know him, he gets upset."

Tad laughed and slapped his friend on the shoulder. "Hardly. Just joking with you, Ari, it's nice to meet you. Jay's plan for your book worked, huh? That's when I first heard about you and what you did. Jay's made you a massive best seller."

"So everyone keeps saying." Ari shrugged a nonchalant shoulder. "And I guess it's true, but I'm still getting used to it. And now I finally get to meet some of the friends he posted my book to. What did you think?"

"Oh, don't ask Tad what he thinks of books, he never reads them. The only thing he reads is his own stuff which is why he's illiterate when it comes to others," Jay told her.

"Oh, you're…" Ari's eyes grew wide. "I'm sorry."

Tad roared with laughter. "Oh, Ari, you need to stop believing everything this douche says." He grasped Jay's shoulder. "He loves to tease and torment, and put his friends down—"

"Hey, we all do the same thing—" Jay interrupted.

Tad shushed him with a finger to Jay's mouth. "Quiet, you, you've said enough. Now Ari," he turned to her, "You have to understand something about us comedians, we talk shit about each other all the time. It's just fun, no harm intended, and most of it's not true."

"Most?" Jay queried.

"I said most." Tad kept on going as he waved his fifth drink of the evening around. "And it's true. We do. Let it go in one ear and out the other. No harm, no foul."

"Ah, okay…" Ari appraised both of them. Slightly drunk, but at this stage harmless. "Okay. Well, it was nice meeting you, Tad. I'll see you throughout the night and since you're already enjoying yourself, continue to do so."

Jay slapped him on the back and escorted Ari to the kitchen for a drink. "He's right, we do talk shit, let it go in one ear and out the other. Hey, here's Wendy. Wendy, babe, how you doin', you look great. Ari, this is Wendy, Wendy this is Ari. I sent her book to you." He kissed her on both cheeks as he introduced them.

Wendy Gallagher was a comedian and actress with a thirty-year career. She was willowy and tall, and her dark auburn hair glowed as it perfectly curled around her face and shoulders. Her porcelain skin made her brown eyes look like black holes in her head.

"Wendy, nice meeting you." Ari shook her hand. "Thank you for your review of my book."

"Hello, Ari, you're more than welcome. It was a great book." Wendy's voice flowed smoothly from between two sets of perfectly placed white veneers. You never would have known she'd lost her real ones due to smoking like a chimney for twenty years, or that she'd had her nose almost replaced for snorting so much through her youth. But the doctors had worked wonders.

"Thank you." Ari nodded her appreciation. "I've seen some of your movies, they were great. *Divine Intervention* especially."

"Thank you. That was one of my favourites." Wendy picked up a glass of champagne from a passing waiter. "It took long enough to get to the big screen, but it was worth the wait."

"It certainly was," Jay said. "Thank you for coming, Wendy. Enjoy the food and drink, and the many festivities." He moved Ari on, and they grabbed a few hors d'oeuvres from the waiter and kept on moving into the hallway where it was relatively quiet. "Whew, it's crowded, even with, what, sixty people, now."

Ari swallowed her food and took a couple of sips of cola. "You did say they could invite their other halves, so thirty was going to grow to sixty pretty quickly."

"Yeah." Jay sighed and rubbed his eyes that were red from wearing his contacts. "I know. I was just hoping that I'd keep it around thirty."

"Then you shouldn't have added plus one to your invites." Ari chuckled. "What did you expect was going to happen? Did you cater for sixty?"

"I think we catered for a hundred to be on the safe side." Jay slid his arm around her and escorted her down the hall. "I know you're meeting all of my friends, and I think I told you this before, but you don't need to make small talk with them all night. Just move on, and chat. You can even sneak away if you like."

Ari frowned at him. "I can't do that. This is your party, although you said it was *our* party, and they're your friends that helped make my book go to number one. I should be mingling and thanking them. You also said I was the hostess, so I need to mingle to make sure they're getting what they want. Drink and foodwise, that is."

"Yeah," Jay mumbled. "But I'll warn you now; they might end up getting other things that they want."

"Such as?"

"Such as I know some of them are into weed and other

substances. I'll try to direct anyone wanting to smoke to the back terrace, and if anyone's going to snort, inject, or swallow, then they had better be discreet about it."

"Or how about you tell them not to do it at all," Ari suggested. "If Gloria found out, she would use it against you in another court case."

Jay shrugged. "Gloria snorts and smokes as much as anyone else. She knows all of my friends would attest to it because we used to do it at our parties. Not much she can say, really."

"Well then..." Thoughts floated through Ari's mind. "Stop them from doing it because I don't. I don't care to have people snorting or injecting in my presence. Hell, I don't even want anyone smoking in my presence, but this is not my house, and I don't have a say in that. So please direct them all to the back porch, and they can do it out in the cold air and not in the house."

"Ari." Jay took her hand in his and licked his lips. "This is my house, I'm not about to tell my friends they can't enjoy themselves."

She gazed into his eyes. "I'm not telling you to tell them that, just to direct them outside if they wish to do it. I don't want to be around marijuana, or whatever the hell it is you guys smoke here. I also don't want to be around injectables or snortables."

Laughter rolled out of Jay. "Snortables. I don't think I've heard it put that way before."

"Yeah, well, it's not funny." Ari pulled her hand from his. "I know I'm just a guest in this house and yes, you can do what you want in your house, but please show some respect for what I want. I don't want to be around drugs."

Jay's laughter died down and he became serious. "You're right. I need to show you some respect when it comes to substances you may not have an interest in. So yes, I will direct everyone outside." His arms slid around her and he pulled her close. "I love you, Ari. I don't want anyone hurting you. And I don't want you being around anyone or anything that might hurt you, or you might feel disrespected by. I want you to be happy." He lowered his head and his lips gently laid themselves on hers.

Her lips melted into his, and her body pressed against the frame that was Jay Daniels. The man she was madly in love with. And she *knew* she was madly in love with him, because she wanted to spend the rest of her life with him. And all plans of moving home to live on the Gold Coast were rapidly fading into the background every day that she kissed him.

He pulled back and gasped for air. "Okay…that was um… time to mingle again."

She sighed and rested her forehead against his clean-shaven chin. "Yeah…mingle…"

They walked back into the living area, and he introduced her to some of the cast members of the hit show he'd written and starred in some years before.

The bell rang and one of the waiting staff answered it, letting in Mack Ellington, Jay's best friend.

"Mack," Jay yelled across the room and went to greet him. "Good of you to finally make it to my party, you fucking bastard, come on in. Can you get him a beer?" Jay directed the staff member and escorted Mack into the lounge room. "I want you to meet someone. Ari, come and meet Mack."

"Hi." Ari watched them walk over and shook hands with the good-looking actor. "I've seen your show, *Night Moves*.

It's good."

"Thank you, thank you." Mack gave a small bow. "It's a pleasure to meet you, Ari Travers. Jay's told me everything about you."

"Oh, has he now." Ari's left brow rose, and she looked at Jay. "That would be impossible since he doesn't *know* everything about me. Just as I don't know everything about him."

Jay chuckled. "Oh, you know what I mean."

"Jay could not stop talking about you once he'd got back from Australia from that movie," Mack continued. "It was Ari this, Ari that. Every phone call was about you."

Ari's right brow rose in sync with her left. "Oh, was it now?"

Jay blushed and gave another chuckle. "Again, you know how it is."

Mack accepted his beer and sculled it back. "Ah, that's good. I needed that."

"Hard night on the set? Are you still filming?" Jay asked and ordered a drink for himself.

"No, we stopped two days ago and don't go back until next year. It's just been a hard few weeks, few months, few years." Mack deflated with a sigh. "The show's getting harder to do, and I'm not into it anymore. I'm thinking of ending it."

"Ending *Night Moves*?" Jay was shocked. "That's a massive ratings hit; you can't stop that."

"Why not?" Ari asked, glancing between them. "If it's exhausting him, and he's mentally done with it, then why not?"

Mack pointed a finger at her in agreement. "Exactly! My thoughts exactly. I'm taking the next few weeks to try and recharge, but the thoughts have been coming for some time now and I may not need to think too hard or long about it. I think I'm done and it's time to have a break and then move on."

"Jesus." Jay swiped a hand over his mouth. "Quitting a hit show is nothing to take lightly. I mean, sure, sometimes you know as the creator when the show is going to be done because you plan out the timeline and number of series to tell the story. But you didn't do that with the show. You just said it would go on and on."

"Until I was done," Mack said. "And I think I'm done."

"Wow." Jay could only stare at him in shock. "But you're up to a million an episode. That's big bucks to throw away."

"A million an episode!" Ari's eyes bulged. "Are you kidding? I can't even imagine earning that every week, let alone in a year."

Mack shrugged an uncaring shoulder. "Yeah, that's what I'm up to. It's been going for four and a half years, so I doubled the salary every year because the network was desperate to keep it going. It ranked in the top five every week. But no, I wouldn't be throwing anything away. I don't think I care about it anymore. The money, the show, none of it. I'm mentally exhausted and I think it's time to go."

"Can you wrap up the show at the end of the season?" Ari asked. She didn't know much about the behind the scenes of TV, but she knew what it was like to suffer from burnout.

Mack considered the question. "I could. We'd have to re-write some of it, but it could be done. There's half a season to go and the finale was going to be complete anyway because you're always left wondering if your show will even be renewed for the next year, so lots of questions were going to be answered throughout and storylines wrapped up. But yeah, I could change it to reflect a show finale and not a season finale."

"Man." Jay shook his head and ran a hand through his hair in disbelief. "I think you're bat shit crazy at one mill an ep, but if it's what you want to do, or need to do, then it's your choice to make, and you know I'll support you whatever you do."

"Yeah, man, I know you will. Just as I helped support you and what you were doing with Ari." Mack looked from Jay to Ari. "It was a great book. I can see why Jay was so gung-ho about it."

"Thank you." She nodded. "He certainly was, and I wouldn't be here if it wasn't for him. And thank you for liking it and leaving such a glowing review."

"You're welcome. Glad I could help. But now, I'm off for food and more beer." Mack slapped Jay on the back and headed for the kitchen where he found the chef making mini burgers of steak or chicken, and meat skewers.

"Wow." Jay heaved a deep sigh and slowly drifted past Ari to the window, watching the view of twinkling lights dancing across the skyline. "Wow."

"You sound as if you seriously can't believe he'd do that, instead of worrying about the fact he's clearly suffering from burnout." Ari stood beside him and rubbed his back. "It's his choice. Not yours to be disbelieving over."

"Yeah." Jay tilted his head to look at her. "But you don't get TV gigs that pay you one million an episode very often. If ever. That's something you hang on to for as long as you can because not even movies come along that often. It's taken me two years to get a movie, let alone a mill a week TV gig."

"This isn't about you, though," Ari reminded him and rested her cheek on his shoulder. "It's about your best friend and what he wants and needs. You just need to be the supportive best friend I know you are and be there for him to encourage whatever choice he makes."

Jay's grin was tired, but soft and full of love for her. "Yeah, you're right. It's not about me, and I shouldn't foist my insecurities onto my friends. Let alone my best friend. I need to be supportive of him."

"Exactly. That's the way BFFFEs should be."

"BFFFEs?" Jay's brow furrowed as he tried working it out.

"Best friends for fucking ever," Ari filled in the blanks.

Jay laughed. "That's good. Yeah, that's good and I like it. Okay." He kissed her temple. "Let's get back to mingling."

After mingling, drinking and eating, chatting and singing carols, they were in a good mood until the doorbell rang.

"I'll get it," Ari yelled and went to answer to door. The grin on her face fell away when she saw who was standing on Jay's stoop. "Gloria!" She looked past Jay's ex to see Denver was idling behind her. "What are you doing here?"

"We're here for Jay's party," Gloria replied sweetly. "Can you let us in?"

Caught by surprise, Ari had no idea what to do. But considering what Gloria had done in the last month alone, she was reluctant. She also knew Jay had not invited them.

The sweetness and light act slid from Gloria's face. "Well. Let us in."

"No." Ari slammed the door in her stunned face and locked it. "Shit. What the fuck!" She released the handle and turned to find Jay coming down the hallway towards her.

"Who is it? I thought everyone was here." He noted Ari's

white face and the shock rolling over it in waves. "You okay? You look like you're going to faint."

The bell rang and someone pounded on the door.

"Are you going to let them in?" Jay asked.

"It's Gloria," Ari blurted. "With Denver. Said they're here for the party."

Jay's brows slowly furrowed. "What?"

"It's Gloria and Denver. She said she's here for the party, and all but demanded that I let her in." Ari stared up at him, seeing the emotions fly over his face. Her stomach was in knots. This is not what she wanted for their Christmas party.

Jay took a slow deep breath. "Okay... This is interesting. *No*, she wasn't invited. And *no*, she's not allowed to be here *un*invited. And yes, she'll do nothing but ruin it for everyone. So I have two choices. Let her in to ruin the party. Or tell her to leave because she wasn't invited."

The bell rang and someone pounded on the door.

Jay finally looked at Ari. "What should I do? Do you want her here?"

"Fuck no!" Ari spat. "She'll ruin everything."

"Okay, then." Jay opened the door. "Gloria. You weren't invited. Leave now."

"Oh, Jay, about time you answered the door," Gloria replied. "We're here for the party." She put on her best smile, beaming it at him while suggestively letting her fur coat slide off a bare shoulder.

"You're standing on *my* doorstep flirting with *me* while the boy child *you* cheated on me with is right behind you, and you want *me* to let you into a party that *you* were not invited to. Is that it?" Jay kept a firm hold on the door. He watched her smile fall and the coat slide back up. "Leave, Gloria. You weren't invited, and as a part of the contract you signed, you aren't allowed to be here unless you are. You weren't. Leave now, or the police and my lawyer will be seeing you tonight."

Gloria scowled. "You piece of piss weak shit," she spat and spun on her heel. "Come Denver, we'll go and find another party elsewhere." She rushed past him on her way downstairs.

Denver glanced at Jay and shrugged before following her.

"A piece of advice, Denver," Jay called. "Stop letting her lead you around on the leash she has you on. It's emasculating you." Jay closed the door and locked it before turning around. "There. It's dealt with." He grasped Ari's arms and pulled her close, resting his forehead against hers, breathing in her scent. "I don't need her here tonight, and neither do you."

"Nope. I don't." Ari slid her arms around him and breathed in his spicy cologne, trying to relax against the onslaught of emotions Gloria stirred up in her. Fear seemed to be the most common one. Fear that she would ruin everything that was happening, just as she had ruined Jay's life and career. And she wasn't about to let that happen to her. She squelched it down. "Let's get back to the party."

The party was in full swing by ten-thirty with carols and rock music blaring from the system, alcohol and food being passed around, and a few who stepped out on the back porch to do the drug of their choice.

Ari was in the kitchen munching on a mini chicken burger when she thought she heard the doorbell. But after checking the time, she shrugged and finished her burger, knowing that everyone was there. Wiping her face and hands, she moved over to the drinks bar where she obtained an ice-cold Pepsi Max on ice and turned to see where Jay was. But something by the front door caught her eye all the way down the hallway.

Gloria and Denver removing their coats and handing them to the wait staff who had clearly opened the door to them. "Jay," Ari called out and stormed down the hall, grabbing hold of the staff member who had their coats and spinning her around. "*They were not invited.* They need to leave," she told her. "Give them back their coats. Gloria." They stopped in the entrance way. "We had this discussion an hour ago. You weren't invited. Get out. Here are your coats." Ari pulled them from the stunned girl's arms and threw them at Gloria and Denver. "I told you. *Jay* told you. *Get out.*"

Gloria glanced from Ari to her coat pooled at her feet. The disdain on her face said it all, and she waved her hand for Denver to pick them up. "For a house guest, you're not very polite."

"Don't care what you think of me," Ari replied. "This is Jay's house; I'm invited, as are his other guests. *You* are not. Get out." She indicated for the staff member to open the door. "Escort them out. I'll get Jay."

"Going to tell on us?" Gloria mocked and watched her ex walk up behind Ari. "Well, hello again, husband."

"Ex," Jay spat. "And stop disrespecting your boy child the way you disrespected me. I haven't been your husband since I divorced you for cheating on me, and yet, here you are using the word to mock me in my own house, in front of the boy you cheated on me with."

"He's not a boy," Gloria informed him, her face screwed up as if she'd just sucked a lemon. "He's more man than you'll ever be."

"Then one, why are you here at your *ex*-husband's house, and two, why do you keep him on a leash like you tried with me in our final years of marriage?" Jay asked and turned his gaze to Denver. "I feel sorry for you. I truly do now that I've seen it. I see how she talks to you and treats you. Just like before when you turned up, just like now. She's with you, but she keeps coming back to me with her digs, and her lame-ass insults, and court battles, and boo-fricken-hooing about me not being the man and paying up what I owe while she's home fucking you for the fun of it because her pussy needed a new toy to play with. So don't worry, when she's done with you, she'll move on, just as she did with me, and you'll finally be free of her, just as I am."

Gloria stepped closer to Jay and glared at him in contempt. "You have no idea what you're talking about," she spat. "You're just the schmuck who couldn't be a husband."

Jay glared back. "And yet I fucked you enough to get you pregnant. Twice! If you didn't want kids with me, Gloria, you could've had an abortion, your tubes tied, or just stayed on the pill. Better yet; not fucked me at all. Yet you didn't. And now you're in *my* house, *uninvited*, and being a bitch, as always. So how do you want it? Cops? Arrest? Lawyers? Apologising on TV…*again*."

She stepped back and calmed slightly, glancing from Jay to Ari to the living areas. Seeing some of her friends, she calmed right down, and the sweet smile slithered its way across her lips. "Please, Jay, it's Christmas. Let's not fight. Our friends are here."

"*My* friends," Jay corrected. "They weren't yours before and aren't yours now. And *none of them* are on your side."

"We'll see." Gloria smirked. "I promise to behave myself tonight—"

"And the kids are where?" Jay asked. "Clearly not here,

unless you've left them alone."

"At my parents' place for the night to celebrate Christmas a few days early." Gloria sidled over to the living room doorway. "They're fine, let's party." She wandered into the room and called out to an old friend.

"Fucking hell!" burst out of Ari and she exhaled. "What the fuck, Jay?"

Jay looked from her to a very quiet Denver and waved his arm in Gloria's direction. "You may as well follow. Just remember, for the court case if there is one, *neither* of you were invited to this party. And *neither* of you are wanted here *at* this party *nor* in my house. Behave yourself and keep that bitch in line. Because if you don't, I might do something I will never regret, but will probably pay for for the rest of my life."

Denver silently nodded and followed Gloria.

"Doesn't say much, does he?" Ari had watched them all closely. "Very...timid? Shy?"

"Ball-busted," Jay supplied. "She's got his balls in a jar on her bedside table that she'll point at to remind him of what his role in her life is. Just like she did to me. And then she'll put that jar in her handbag and make him carry it around when they go out, but snatch it back to smash him over the head with it when he does something wrong in her eyes."

Ari wasn't sure if he was kidding or not, so she said nothing about it. "What do we do? You're obviously letting them stay, which kinda ruins our night."

"Oh, Ari, my girl. I'm so sorry." Jay sighed. "I don't need the cops and lawyers and everything that goes along with Gloria wherever she goes getting in the way. But I know this was our party." He pulled her close. "I'm sorry. But in letting her stay, I'm hoping she'll be ignored by my friends and leave pretty quickly."

"They're all on your side?"

"They were my friends before I met her, and we got involved. And after the cheating and divorce, they were still my friends."

"But we'll see how they react to her." Ari pulled out of his arms and sighed. "Not much I can do, or you can do, except throw her out."

"Just watch and observe and stay out of her way."

"Or shut her down when she's a bitch." Ari could feel the twisting in her stomach; the warming of her blood. She knew that anger was rising, and that anger could burst out at any point moving forward. "I'll warn you now. If she starts in on me, she's done for. I won't tolerate it."

"Considering you're my guest, and she was not invited, feel free." Jay kissed her forehead and pulled away. "And away we go." He led her into the living room, and they chatted with their guests while watching Gloria.

Denver was always two steps behind her, hands in pockets, not saying much, only speaking when spoken to.

Gloria was animated and very touchy feely with those who were never her friends, before or after the divorce. She took up conversations, interrupted conversations, and generally left everyone with a sour expression. They were polite to her but kept their hands to themselves. No one reciprocated the touching, they stepped away when she got handsy, and no one walked up to her to start a conversation. It was her intruding on them, inserting herself into their conversation or taking over, making many guests walk away from her so she had to move on to the next.

"See, she's going to run out of people to talk to in a moment," Jay said quietly in Ari's ear. "No one's interested in talking to her."

"Then let's hope she leaves as soon as she's through," Ari replied. "I'm going to freshen up and hope she'll be gone by the time I get back." She hurried up the stairs to her room and locked the door behind her. Sighing, she let her body relax and spent a moment slumped against the door. "I so don't need this," she mumbled and hurried for the bathroom. Once done, she sat on the side of her bed looking out the window, breathing deeply to relax her body and calm her mind. The quiet enveloped her, calming the chatter in her brain, the ringing in her ears, and the ache in her jaw. She knew what that meant. That she was stressed and had been clenching her jaw in anger and frustration.

"I will be calm," she murmured. "I will be calm and not let her bother me." She rubbed her jaw muscles and checked her watch. It had been twenty minutes since she'd rushed upstairs, and she knew she needed to go back down. Hauling herself to her feet, she closed the door behind her and walked downstairs. She didn't hear yelling or shouting, and didn't hear anything breaking. Glancing into the living room, she turned and walked down the hall, running into Jay at the doorway to the dining room.

"Hey, there you are." He pulled her close and kissed her gently on the lips. "Merry Christmas. Everything's fine, no deaths yet."

She giggled and kissed him back. "Good to know. Are we expecting one to happen?"

"Very possibly. She's gone through everyone, and no one is interested, but they're all talking about her when she moves on. I've had some *interesting* conversations."

"Care to share?" Ari snuggled into his arms.

"Maybe tomorrow. Because the party is over at twelve, and once the caterers are gone it'll be our time to party." His lips caressed her cheek. "I have something very special planned for you, Ari Travers. Planned for *us*."

Warmth sped across Ari's face and her smile was soft. "Do you now? I can't wait."

"You'll have to because we have another hour at least to go." He let her go and indicated to the waiter. "When was the last time you ate?"

"Before bitchface got here," Ari replied and slid her arm around his waist as they moved into the dining room. She caught a glimpse of someone over Jay's shoulder, watching them from the doorway at the other end of the hall. The flash of red sequins told her it was Gloria, and she vaguely caught the anger and contempt on her face before they turned away. "Uh-oh. We've been spotted."

"Huh? What was that?" Jay handed her a mini burger before shoving one into his mouth.

"Gloria saw us from the other end of the hall." Ari bit into her burger and watched Jay's face. A few expressions fled over it as he chewed, and she could tell he was considering things.

He swallowed and said, "Don't care. My house, my guest, my date. Whoever I kiss is my business. Let her rot in her anger. It's none of her fucking business."

"Fair enough." Ari had a second bite and chewed thoughtfully. While Jay was right, there was something about Gloria that reminded her of a cut snake. She was not someone Ari wanted to be on the wrong side of and she thought through the various ways she could stay out of it and stay away from Gloria.

"Mmm." Jay picked up a second burger. "Keep these coming, man, they're great," he told the chef, and motioned for a waiter for drinks. "Is everyone eating them? Are we running out? What?"

"Everything's good, Mr Daniels," the chef told him. "We have plenty to go around as we also have prawn skewers and shish kebabs."

"Yeah, I saw those." Jay mumbled through a mouthful of food. "Can I get some of the prawns? And what's on the kebabs?"

"We have chicken, beef, or vegetable being prepared on another pan for those who don't eat meat."

"One chicken, one beef, for each of us." Jay pointed between them. "Damn, I'm hungry."

"Haven't you eaten?" Ari asked and picked up the prawn skewer. She bit into it. "Oh yum."

"I haven't eaten since those horse's doovers earlier, but now I'm starving." Jay ripped off some chicken from his kebab as Ari giggled at the joke. "Mmm, this is good too." They ate for a few minutes as others came and went. The kebabs and prawns were now more popular than the burgers. When they were sated, they washed it down with their drinks and Jay moved into the lounge room to mingle. Ari stayed chatting to Babette London, an old friend of Jay's who attended the same acting classes.

"I see that *bitch* Gloria is here," Babette muttered and glared at Gloria in the living room. "The *nerve* of that woman. She cheats on Jay, takes up with the toy boy, and then has the gall to do everything she's done. Still trying to cash in on her fame, not that she ever really had any. You know," Babette leaned closer, "no one wants to work with her, or deal with her. That's why some of her shows have flopped, or not been given the greenlit these last couple of years. And the current movie she's trying to get lit and star in, they can't find a lead actor to work opposite her, because every time they find out who the female lead is, they turn down the role. Years back, before the divorce, and after the kids, her career became red hot again, but after the divorce, it took a downward slide, and with the way she's been acting lately, it's getting worse."

"All of her own making by way of that video." Ari sipped her drink and glanced at Gloria who was clinging to Denver's jacket and kissing him passionately. Everyone had turned their backs on them, and Ari did the same. She turned around to face Babette. "She's only got herself to blame and is clearly out for attention. *Especially* tonight. Not that Jay or I have any idea why she's here."

"To spy on *him*, and to check *you* out," Babette replied. "She probably also thought she'd score points with his friends, and it's clear that's not happening. None of us wants to know her. We haven't been near her, spoken to her, or worked with her since the cheating scandal and divorce." She sipped her champagne and eyed Ari. "I did hear her mention how she's channelling something called BDE these days. You don't happen to know what that is, do you? Is it a new drug? Typical of her if it is."

"I think she's referring to what the younger generations call big dick energy," Ari said.

"Big dick energy?" Babette glanced Gloria's way. "I have no idea what that is, but no, I can't see it. The only thing she seems to be channelling is being a bitch and that's normal for her."

"She's definitely channelling something, but big dick energy ain't it," Ari quipped.

Babette giggled behind her glass. "What she put poor Jay through… Jesus. He's definitely changed since he met you, though."

Ari blushed and took a sip of drink. "So I've been told."

"And it's definitely for the better," Babette added and glanced towards the lounge room. "Oops, here she comes. I'm off outside for some fresh air." She turned and slipped out the door before Ari could open her mouth.

"Well, what do we have here?"

The words chilled Ari to the bone, and she stopped breathing.

"So *you're* Ari Travers. The big-time author Jay helped publicise." Gloria stood in front of Ari, so she was facing her and the lounge room. She could see Jay talking to his friends, and Denver was chatting to someone by the Christmas trees.

Ari breathed in and let it out. "Gloria. Enjoying the party you weren't invited to?"

"Yes, I am." Gloria grabbed a glass of champagne from the waiter and took a sip. "Enjoying living in Jay's house that he bought with my money?"

"Was never *your* money, it was always his," Ari retorted, glaring back but keeping her cool.

"Mmm." Gloria eyed her up and down, taking in the Christmas themed red and green outfit Ari wore. "Money will never make you look good, though. I hear you scored an apology from Ken J. Jamison for his little comment about Jay fucking your pussy in return for making you famous. How much *did* you get for that?"

"The answer to that is none of your business." Ari tried

not to break the glass that was being gripped to death in her hands. "Once the divorce was final anything to do with Jay, his friends, his family, his guests, or anyone he cares to help all became *none* of your business."

"Except the kids. *They're* his family, so you're wrong on that count. They bind us together for an eternity." Gloria took a step towards her. "*I* have his children. *Me*. It would seem he'll never have children with you because you're just too old to have any. In fact, I'm surprised Ken even bothered making the comment about your pussy because it's probably dried up and useless. Has Jay even taken it for a spin yet? That's *if* he even can. God knows why he would. I mean seriously, who do you think you are? You're nobody special."

The words ripped through Ari's ears and into her brain like daggers. The syllables, the letters, each inflection of vocal tone tore through the delicate inner workings and into that very large part of her brain that kept telling her she wasn't good enough for a megastar like Jay Daniels.

The words drummed, banged, reverberated around and around...*who do you think you are, are, are, you're nobody special...*

The thoughts changed, became ones of rage, and she thrust her hand forward. The contents of her glass flew into Gloria's face. The cola streamed down her neck and into her décolletage. The ice cubes hit her in the eyes and landed either in the bust of her dress or on the floor.

"Oh my, God," Gloria screeched, dropped her glass, which smashed all over the kitchen floor, and swiped at her face. "You bitch. What have you done? My make-up." She flapped her sodden hands and madly grabbed at the napkins the wait staff handed her. "You fucking bitch. Just wait until my lawyer hears about this."

"Yes, let's just wait," Ari declared loud enough for every person at the party to hear. "Let's *see* how the court will look upon you inviting yourself to your ex's party and returning when you'd been told to leave, even *though* you signed that damn contract to stay away unless invited. *Which you were not.* Let's wait and see how they like it when I repeat this conversation to them where you're just the angry dumb cunt of an ex-wife who thinks her own shit doesn't stink and that she can go around verbally attacking and abusing her ex-husband's guest. *No one* wants you here, Gloria. *You're* the cunt who cheated on their friend and then fucked him over when he left and divorced you. *You're* the cunt who keeps on fucking him over by taking him to court time and time again. And *you're* the cunt who's done nothing but make herself look bad here tonight by *being* that dumb cunt. Well, Gloria Hannaford, since I don't have to worry about dealing with you, I'll say this…" Ari placed her right hand on her hip and waved the glass in her left hand. "I don't give a fuck about you. I never have and I never will. You're a worthless piece of shit, and if I had a gun right now, I wouldn't even bother wasting my bullet on you. And I sure as hell will never let you ruin my life and what's becoming of it, and while I'm here, I'll be backing Jay all the way. Just like his friends. So, since you and your dumb fuck toy boy weren't invited, you can get the fuck out of this house and don't fucking come back. Because if you do, *I* will be the one calling the cops on you. *You got that, bitch?*"

Wild applause flew around both rooms and out on the back porch. Caterers and wait staff stood silently by, but Jay's friends were showing Gloria what they all thought of her.

Jay came to Ari's side. "You got that, Gloria? Time to leave."

A growl came from Gloria. "Oh, I'm not leaving until this mess is cleaned up. I'm going to use the bathroom."

"It's under the stairs." Jay told her and watched her walk off.

Ari followed, sensing it wasn't the bathroom under the stairs she was going to. She saw Gloria pass the door and head down the hall and hurried after her. "Oh, no, you don't, you bitch, the bathroom's back this way."

"I'm using the master bathroom," Gloria declared and grasped the banister rail.

"The fuck you are." Ari grabbed her arm and pulled her off the stairs, getting a few foul words screeched in her ear. She saw several guests watching from both doorways. "There's no way in hell you're setting foot above this floor to do damage. The bathroom's under the stairs. Use it." She pulled open the door and shoved a screaming Gloria inside. "Don't be long, we want you gone." She slammed the door shut and hurried to retrieve their coats, finding Denver standing in the doorway near the entrance. "Here." She threw them at him. "What the hell do you see in her? You *chose* to cheat with a married woman with children, and then stayed with her when her husband divorced her. Why? What the hell do you see an in angry old bitch like that? She's ten years older than you and has two kids. I get it, she's still gorgeous, but fuck, what a bad attitude she has."

She watched his face and couldn't tell if he was depressed or just naturally looked that way. "What in God's green earth do you see in her? Look at you." She waved her hand at him. "Slumped over, barely converses, hands in pockets most of the time. Were you like this before you met her? Before you fucked her behind her husband's back. Because, quite

Anything for You

frankly, shit like that says you haven't got any morals. No principles, no standards, no code of ethics for yourself. Is *that* the sort of person you want to be like, because apparently you *are* like that to cheat with a married woman in the first place. But as for what you are now…" She waved her hand again. "It ain't that good, mate. You look like a hollow, sucked dry version of yourself. And that's a real damn pity because you *used* to be good."

"Denver, what's she saying to you? Let's go." Gloria strode up to them and grabbed her coat. She turned to Ari and opened her mouth.

Ari threw up her hand. "Don't even bother, Gloria. I am so not fucking interested. But since everyone's watching feel free to *keep* making a dumb cunt of yourself. They didn't like you anyway."

Gloria's ears went back, and she seethed. "Denver, let's go."

Jay magically appeared in the doorway and opened it for them. "Nice having you here, seeing you on the ass-end of an ass whooping for once, and not by me. I quite enjoyed it, as did all of my friends." He waved them out and locked the doors behind them. "Can someone keep an eye out to make sure they leave? And then I think it's time for everyone else to have their last drink or burger and leave as well."

The crowd that had gathered in the hall and doorways dispersed to see what they could finish off and congratulated Ari on her performance with Gloria. She was told she should be an actress in dramas because the hatred coming from her pores would reflect well on screen. As would her quick wit. But her twisted and knotty stomach and nervous system told her otherwise. Her anger had got the better of her and she didn't like it. She didn't know if it would have an effect on

Jay and his relationship with his children.

Jay paced back and forth between the kitchen and the front window to make sure Gloria had left. When the food was eaten, and the drinks drunk, they waved goodbye to their friends who were all getting home in chauffeured cars. The catering company took care of the leftovers, wiped and swept, and took out the garbage.

Jay locked up behind them when they left and slumped against the door. "What a night!"

"And I'm a combination of exhausted and exhilarated." Ari leaned on the stair railing watching him. "But didn't you have something planned as an after party? Do we have the energy?"

The grin shot across Jay's face. "I did, I did. Let's just see how cleaned up they made the place." He hurried into the living room and looked around. All of the mess had been cleared away, and the kitchen was as spotless as it had been when the caterers had arrived. "Okay, well that's less work for me. But I did some of the work before, so it shouldn't take long to set up. I'm going to go and freshen up and get ready for bed, and you should too. Then when everything is ready, I'll come and get you. Okay?"

Ari tilted her head. "What are you up to, Jay Daniels?"

"A little secret, Ari Travers," he replied and herded her towards the stairs. "Let's go and freshen up."

Jay changed in his room and then rushed down to the basement and hauled up the double layered air mattress he'd blown up that afternoon. He laid the rubber sheet on the floor between the two Christmas trees and set the bed on it. The bottom fitted sheet was already on it, so he quickly rushed down to the basement for the rest of the bedding. When he finished dressing the bed, and getting a few other bits and pieces ready, he rushed upstairs and knocked on Ari's door. "Are you ready? You haven't fallen asleep have you?"

Ari opened the door and grinned. "I nearly did I'm so damn tired after all that excitement." She saw he was in his robe and wrapped her red poinsettia print robe more tightly around herself. "What are you up to?"

"You'll see." He grinned and held out his hand. "Shall we?"

She took his hand and they walked downstairs, but the door to the lounge room was closed. "Hiding something from me, are we."

"Of course. Close your eyes." He stood in front of her so she wouldn't see. "Are they closed?"

"They're closed. Would it help if I put my hands over my eyes?"

"Yes, it would. Do that," Jay said, and watched her cover her eyes. "Okay. Here we go." He reached behind him and slid the doors open, then took Ari's arms and guided her into the room, closing the doors behind them. "Okay, now you can open them."

Ari opened her eyes, blinked a few times, and looked around. "What is the…oh…" She saw the bed with its rich green and red coverings placed between the trees. A strand of mistletoe hung between them, and both trees were still turned on. "Oh…"

"Now, the curtains are shut tight, as are all of the doors to keep the room cosy, and the only lights are the tree lights." Jay's face was lit up as bright as the trees. He'd planned this for a while, and it was now coming to fruition.

The night he and Ari consummated their love.

"Oh…" Ari's breath caught in her throat. She knew this

night was going to happen. The night they made love for the first time, but she hadn't expected it in the lounge room between the trees. "The bed looks... Is that safe to...you know..."

"Make love on," Jay supplied the words. "It's the biggest blow-up bed I could find, and it should be quite safe."

Nerves got the better of Ari. Her hands clamped on to each other and her stomach twisted in knots. As much as she wanted to, she was nervous as hell.

"You okay?" Jay gently rubbed her back. "I don't want to overwhelm you or rush you. We'll just take our time, okay?" He indicated for her to move, and she put one foot in front of the other and walked over to the bed. The covers were already pulled back, so they climbed on and sat side by side.

"This is...a bit too much a bit too soon," Ari muttered. "Let's just take things easy."

"Of course." Jay slid out of his robe and threw it over an easy chair. "Let's just lie here and enjoy the trees and relax." He reached for her robe, and she untied the belt and slid it off her shoulders, lifting herself for it to slide out from under her.

She grabbed the covers and pulled them up, lying back against the pillows, looking at the lighted trees. After a few moments, she said, "This is nice."

Jay slid his arm under her neck and pulled her close as she adjusted herself, his head resting against her. "Yeah, it is." A long pause. "You know, I was so proud of what you did tonight. She must have said something pretty vile for you to go off that way. And everyone else thought it was fantastic. Did you hear that applause?"

Ari grinned wryly. "Yeah. I did. And yeah, she did. My

anger got the better of me. I hope it doesn't hurt you with all of the court cases she brings against you."

"Don't worry about her. I'm dealing with her." His right hand slid down her right arm until it found its mate and lifted her hand to his mouth. He kissed each finger, each knuckle.

"I just hope she doesn't make things worse." Ari found herself becoming quite comfortable and very aroused. "That won't be fair. To either of us."

"Mmm." Jay's lips moved up her arm to her shoulder, and he turned to face her, his lips moving to her neck and face. "I love you, Ari. Let's forget about Gloria."

A soft sigh escaped Ari as Jay took her into his arms and kissed her passionately. She kissed him back with fervour to equal his, her hands and tongue roaming and exploring. She welcomed him when he slid over her and lay full out. Their mouths didn't stop. Their hands didn't stop. Their night attire came off and was thrown on the floor. Jay nestled between her legs, his arms either side of her. Her arms were around him, clinging on tightly as he made his way inside. Their passion exploded into a billion stars, rocking Ari as Jay rocked her. Small sounds came from her lips as he moved against her, inside her. Her legs locked around him, keeping him against her. Her tongue was played with, her face caressed, her breasts devoured until the explosion inside of them rocked them both.

Ari found herself drifting in and out of slumber. Wrapped in Jay's arms, a light was beckoning her to wake, prying at her eyes with their twinkles. She slowly opened them and saw where they were, and a smile slid across her lips as she breathed in Jay's scent. Manly. Masculine. Jay. She rubbed her face into his chest hair and then tilted it back to look at him.

L.J. Diva

He was sleeping, but his eyes moved behind their covering.

She snuggled into him and ran a hand over his flesh. Flesh she had craved since she had known him. Since before she had known him. Since she'd first developed her crush on him and had wanted to know every part of him. Her fingers came across a lumpy bit of flesh and she pulled back to look at it. A small crescent shaped scar was under his left arm pit. Her fingers traced it back and forth, imprinting it in their memory.

"That's the only scar I have," he mumbled. "And I've never told anyone how I really got it."

"Why not? Wouldn't your parents' know? Your sisters?" Ari's fingers slid over it.

"No…because it was too embarrassing, so I lied about it." Jay's eyes looked at her. "I've never told anyone."

"Would you tell me?"

Jay gave her a lazy smile. "Sure, Ari, my girl. I'll tell you. Just promise not to tell anyone. Especially my family."

"I promise."

He shifted his head and explained. "It happened one day after high school. My dad had to take me to the emergency room."

"What! It was that bad?" Ari asked. "What happened?"

"Well, it was high school, puberty was happening, and body hair was growing. And I stupidly decided to shave my armpits. But I got into a mess straight off and cut myself pretty damn badly instead. I was so embarrassed, and tried to mop the blood up, but it kept gushing out, and I was wrapping it up and then Dad came into the bathroom and asked what had happened. I told him some boys had threatened me with a knife and nicked me under the arm, so he rushed me to emergency. It took twenty stitches and days of painkillers. I had to keep the lie going and say I hadn't seen the boys before and didn't know who they were."

"Sounds like it would've been so much easier to just tell the truth and it would've been all over and done with," Ari suggested.

"In hindsight. Which is a wonderful thing. I never bring it up, and neither does anyone else."

"Is that the only thing you have? The only mark? Any moles or birthmarks? 'Cause you know I have plenty." Ari's hand slid slowly over his chest.

Jay sighed and grasped her hand. "The only other thing I have is a mole on my left foot. Same side of my body. Left under arm and left inner foot. I have no other scars or marks."

Ari threw her leg over and straddled him. "I'll just have to see about that myself." She shifted down his body and ran her hands through his chest of hair. A manly chest with manly hair on full manly display. Hair that led to the playground she was going to enjoy again. "Look at you, you hot hunk of furry man meat."

"What about me?" Jay gripped her legs and enjoyed the games her hands were playing.

"That's a fine chest of hair you got there, Jay Daniels. Very fine indeed. In fact, it looks familiar."

"Unless you've seen me without my clothes on before, which is entirely possible considering I've been shirtless in a few movies, how does it look familiar?"

"Mmm," Ari pursed her lips together in thought, crossed her arms, and tapped a finger to her chin. "I know where I've seen this chest before. In an ink blot!"

Jay's brows furrowed. "An ink blot? What the hell?"

"A Rorschach ink blot. You know, those cards that shrinks use. Your chest hair is like one of those. Perfectly symmetrical."

Jay burst out laughing. "You're kidding me? A Rorschach ink blot. Oh, Ari, where do you get these things?"

She shrugged and tweaked his nipples. "I write novels, so everything comes from my imagination. It's true though. You do look like one." Her hands spread across his collarbones. "This here is the smattering of hair that leads to every wild jungle on the planet." Her hands travelled down to the thick curls that spread across his chest from nipple to nipple. "And that leads us down to every wild forest on the planet." Her hands moved down the narrow path of hair to his hairy abdomen. "And there is the magical pathway that opens up to the Garden of Eden and all of its *very* unearthly delights." Her hands enmeshed themselves in the fur she was sitting on and squeezed. "*Very* unearthly delights."

He grabbed her and rolled over, trapping her beneath him. "You know what we need to do? We need to fuck and fuck a lot. Because it's about time that we did. Fuck. *A lot*. And not just fuck. We need to burn this motherfucking house down with our motherfucking fucking. What do you say? Ready to fuck 'n roll all night long, Ari Travers?"

"I say, fuck yeah, Jay Daniels," Ari replied and hung on tight.

Chapter 11

The few days leading up to Christmas were hectic in the Daniels household. Last minute presents were bought, plans made, and Jay picked up the kids for Christmas Eve.

Andrew was grumpy as always, but Marisol was happy.

"Merry Christmas," she told everyone when they arrived at Jay's sister's house for the night-before festivities. "Merry Christmas." She and Andrew hurried to join their cousins in the den while Jay hung his and Ari's coats.

"Oh, God, I'm exhausted already," Jay complained.

"The kids can't honestly be that bad?" Michelle said, leading them into the lounge room for drinks.

They saw the rest of the family were already there and greeted everyone.

"Oh, they always are. Especially Andrew." Jay accepted a glass of eggnog, but Ari politely declined. "But you know it's Gloria's fault. Have we told you about my Christmas party, yet?" He launched into the whole sorry saga of the party and Gloria showing up uninvited with Denver in tow. "The sheer nerve of that woman pisses me off. I can't believe there was something inside of her for me to love and fall *in love* with. She's so completely different to how she was, and now she's done a number on the kids."

"Is she not having them for Christmas?" his mother asked and motioned for Ari to join her on the couch. "Has she dumped them on you for the rest of the holiday? Not that I don't love seeing my grandkids, but it makes me wonder if she even wants them at all."

Ari sat beside her and sighed. "She gets them back tomorrow afternoon so they can spend time with her family for Christmas dinner."

"And New Year?" Jessica asked. She handed around nibbles and gave her brother a hug. "Who gets them then?"

"She does. I won't see them until the day after. Which is fine by me. I have plans for that night anyway. Big plans." He sipped his drink and casually glanced at Ari.

She raised a brow. "Anything I need to know about, so I can make my own plans?"

He gave her a brow wiggle in return. "No. Because my plans involve you."

"Ah…do they now," she said and turned to Melinda. "He never tells me anything. Always wants to keep everything a surprise."

"And there's nothing wrong with that," she replied and patted Ari's hand. "It's not often Jay gets excited about someone, and he's very excited about you."

Ari remembered their nights together and blushed. "Oh… he can get *very* excited. But I never know from one day to the next what he's going to do. Or where he's going to take me."

"Sounds exciting," Jessica quipped.

"Sounds romantic," Michelle countered.

"Sounds like none of your business," Jay told them both, getting a laugh out of them before turning to Ari. "But yes, I

Anything for You

do have New Year's plans for us. Not only you and me, but for all of us, since I already knew we'd be spending it together."

"What plans? Tell me!" Ari demanded. "I need to know what to wear."

Jay chuckled. "You'll need to wear your best party gear and rug up. We'll be spending New Year's out and about, and then in an establishment."

"Ah…sounds intriguing. Any clues?" Ari asked.

Jay shook his head and sat on the arm of the sofa beside her. "Nope. Not a one. But it will be the biggest night of your life so far."

"What? Compared to the night of your Christmas party?" Ari looked up at him and blushed. "That was quite a big night."

"Mmm…" Jay wiggled a brow. "It certainly was."

"Is there something we need to know?" Jessica watched the two flirting and nudged her sister in the ribs. "You two up to something?"

"No. Just thinking about how sexy it was when she stood up to Gloria. Damn that was fabulous." Jay shook his head at the memories. "So damn fabulous seeing someone else have a go at Gloria and put her in her place for once."

"That wasn't the intention, though. She wasn't invited but turned up anyway. And your son is too kind hearted and let her stay," Ari said to Melinda. "Gloria got bitchy, and I let rip."

"You never did tell me what she said." Jay rested his hand on her shoulder. "It was clearly bad."

Ari bit on her lip and thought back. "Yeah, well. She thought she'd run with the whole Ken J. Jamison thing and continue his line of bullshit. I didn't let her. I didn't tolerate it from him, so why the hell would I tolerate it from her."

"That was bad," Michelle said. "I was listening for your interview and what he said was just disgusting."

"Agreed." Jessica crossed her legs and leaned back in her chair. "Vile. Misogynistic, revolting. I would have punched him in the face if he said that to me."

"No, you wouldn't've," Melinda told her. "We didn't raise you that way."

"But *I* certainly felt like doing it." Jay rubbed Ari's back. "I heard the whole thing and was onto the lawyers immediately, but Bobby had beaten me to it. It was revolting, all right."

"And not something I want to keep talking about, especially at Christmas." Ari changed the subject. "Are you guys handing out presents to the kids?"

"We are," Melinda said. "Simply because the girls are spending tomorrow with their in-laws, so we thought it best to let all of the kids have them now."

"Oh, that's right." Ari remembered. "Jay said we're heading to Jessica's house, because that's where you guys are staying."

"That's right." Jessica thrust herself up off the couch. "We'll be seeing the in-laws for lunch, but Mom and Dad will be home to entertain you guys. I'm going to check on the food. Ari, Mich, come with?"

Ari startled. "Ah…sure." She followed the girls into the kitchen and watched the food be removed from the oven. "What do you need help with?"

"Oh, not really help. Just a chat." Michelle gave her a secretive smile and glanced over her shoulder to the others in the living room. "So…you and Jay, huh?"

Ari paused and her jaw dropped slightly. "Huh? What do you mean?"

"Oh, come on," Jessica nudged her. "We see the spark

between you two. It's brighter than it was at Thanksgiving, and we reckon you two have got it on since then. Maybe after Jay's party?" She exchanged a giggle with her sister. "Not that we'd mind. You're a lot better than the last one he dated."

"And definitely a lot better than the last one he divorced," Michelle added and spread the juice over the turkey rolls in the pan. "She was great to start with but turned into quite a bitch not long after." She glanced at Ari. "Not that we think you're a bitch. We don't. It's just that we've only met a couple of times, and he talks about you a lot, but we just don't know what you'll be like in five years' time."

"Five years?" Ari frowned. "Why are you talking about five years? What's five years got to do with anything? I'll be going home around this time next year. The plan is to stay for a year or so." She rested a hand on her hip and leaned against the island bench. "Who's talking five years?"

Michelle exchanged a glance with Jessica. "Oh, it's just that the two of you seem so close, and Jay seems so happy."

"And he doesn't stop talking about you when he calls," Jessica added.

"And he hasn't been this happy or relaxed in…" Michelle thought about it. "Since before Gloria turned into a cow."

"So we just figured that the two of you had got together," Jessica said. "Romantically, I mean."

The creeping blush rose up Ari's neck and across her cheeks and she avoided their gaze. "Well, things may have progressed slowly…in that direction." She glanced at Jay in the lounge room who was quite animated in his conversing with his parents and brothers-in-law. A soft smile lifted her lips. "Yeah…"

The girls chortled.

"I knew it. Told you I was right," Michelle told her sister. "They *are* doing it."

Ari's blush deepened. "Couldn't've come up with a better phrase than that?"

"I could have." Michelle sniggered and placed the pans back in the oven. She closed the door, but her hand lingered on the handle. "You know…it wouldn't be so bad if you and Jay got together permanently. But what about the kids?"

"What about them?" Ari asked.

"Would you want to be a stepmom?" Jessica asked, filling a couple of bowls with decorative cranberries. "His kids are a little…" She glanced at her sister. "What's the word I'm looking for?"

"Like their mother?" Michelle replied.

Jessica laughed. "No, that's not a word. Oh, I can't think of it, so the word shitty will do." She looked around for the kids but didn't see them. "How do you get on with them?"

Ari glanced over her shoulder before answering. "Marisol's all right, a little forthright at times, but Andrew's a little—"

"Shitty version of Gloria in the making," Michelle supplied and wiped her hands on a kitchen towel.

Ari lowered her voice. "I know he wouldn't have been like that his whole life, and from what Jay has said, it's probably just since the separation, and the divorce would have made things worse. But Gloria's selfishness about putting herself first seems to be damaging those kids and she doesn't care."

"She is a true narcissist," Michelle said. "Always puts herself first."

"And her sexual needs, clearly," Jessica added. "How will you deal with all of that?"

Ari considered her thoughts and chose her words. "Carefully.

If at all. Again, I'm only here for a year or so. I have no idea what'll happen with Jay and me, let alone what'll happen in a year from now. How much longer?"

"Half an hour or so. Enough time for the presents to be ripped open." Michelle walked out of the kitchen and into the den. "Present time!"

The kids came bolting into the living room and gathered around the Christmas tree.

Michelle followed them. "Half an hour till the food's ready. We may as well get the presents over and done with now."

"Okay, my darlings." Melinda stood in front of the tree and started handing out presents. "Don't make too much of a mess." She watched as they ripped into their brightly wrapped bundles and boxes and saw the delight on their faces.

Ten minutes later, the room was awash with paper, boxes, and battery packaging, and the adults were next.

Presents were exchanged between Jay and his sisters and then all three and their parents. Since Jay had the money in the family, his gifts were higher end and extravagant, and he enjoyed the smiles on their faces when they opened them. He sat on the sofa arm and leaned down to whisper in Ari's ear. "You'll be getting some of yours tonight. And then some in the morning, and then some more tomorrow night."

The blush rapidly spread across her face, and she suppressed a smile, making little huffy sounds instead. They had the kids; she hoped Jay's present wasn't too overboard. Or noisy. She glanced up at him and her smile broke free. "What are you up to?" she whispered back.

"You'll just have to wait and see," he replied.

Everyone thanked each other for the gifts and were soon headed into the dining room for the feast the girls had prepared. Marisol sat next to her grandmother and chatted away, Andrew excitedly gabbled on about the games he got with his cousins, Michelle and Jessica kept pulling Ari into conversations about New York and places to go, and Jay watched all of it quite happily until it was time to clean up and leave.

He piled the kids and their presents into the car and turned to his family. "Thanks for the food, sis. Have a good day tomorrow with your other fam, and Mom, I'll see you and Dad tomorrow at Jessie's. Jessie, have a good day tomorrow, too." He hugged them all and watched Ari do the same, being pulled into the family's clutches before he bundled her into the car. "See you tomorrow, guys." He pulled away and drove off, winding his way back home to find the kids were on the verge of sleep when he stopped the car.

"Okay, let's get you guys upstairs." He lifted Marisol out and took Andrew's hand. "Ari, can you get the presents?"

"Sure. I just need to freshen up first." She followed him inside and hurried to the bathroom. When she was finished, she set the doors back in place so they wouldn't slam shut and hurried to the car to carry piles of presents inside. Once the car was empty, she locked it and hurried inside, closing the doors against the cold flowing in.

Jay came downstairs. "Hey." He kept his voice low. "They're absolutely dead to the world." He stepped off the last stair and sighed. "That was a day, huh?"

She smiled softly and moved into his arms. His went around her and he held her tight. "Yeah, it was. But it was okay. Right?"

"Yeah," he agreed and rubbed his face into her hair. "Better than okay. Andrew wasn't such a shit once we got there, and he's pretty happy now."

"At least he liked the presents he got." Ari lifted her head to look at him. "But what about the ones you give him tomorrow?"

Jay groaned and rubbed her arms. "Yeah. I'm hoping Gloria hasn't got them the same things, so they end up with doubles. But after all these years, I learned that her trick is to buy everything on the list and leave nothing for me to buy. So I side-step her list and get other things instead. It's worked so far."

"Did you do that this year?"

"I did. And I guess I'd better lay them out, so it looks like Santa has come." He let her go and hurried upstairs to his room where he'd kept their presents.

Ari turned on the living room light and hurried into the kitchen. She needed a drink and a pill for the headache that was coming on.

Jay came silently down the stairs and placed the two heaving bags on the floor before closing the door behind him. "Don't want the kids coming downstairs and seeing this," he told her and started pulling out present after present and placing them under the trees.

"How many did you get them?" Ari looked into the bags to see if they had magic bottoms. "They just keep on coming."

Jay gave her a low chuckle. "About ten each. But then some of it's clothing, some of it's for school, and some of it's just for fun."

"So they get a bit of everything?" Ari nodded. "Great idea."

"I thought so." Jay stood and dusted off his knees. "Plus it keeps Gloria sidetracked trying to figure out what I'm buying. I change it up every year to annoy her."

Ari's smile wavered and she swallowed the lump in her throat that had suddenly appeared. "Everything always comes back to Gloria, doesn't it?"

"Yeah, well, it does sometimes. Especially where the kids are concerned." Jay folded the Christmas sacks. When Ari didn't reply, he looked at her and saw the expression on her face. "Hey." He reached out and touched her arm. "I don't mean anything by that. It's just the way it is. It's not meant to hurt you, or upset you, or anything like that."

"I'm not." Ari breathed in. "I've just noticed that almost every conversation leads to whingeing about Gloria. Gloria this, Gloria that." She saw his brows furrow and went on. "I know she's your ex, I know you have children with her. But I am *really* sick and tired of every fucking thing coming back to fucking Gloria. It's Christmas Eve, I've been here eight weeks, and I think every week has been marred by Gloria herself, or a conversation about her. And quite frankly," she huffed, "I'm fucking sick of it." A deep sigh left her and she turned and walked over to the couch, slumping down on it heavily.

"Hey, hey, Ari." Jay rushed to her side and took her hands in his. "It's okay. I don't always talk about Gloria, and yes, she's a part of my life, we have kids, but she's not *in* my life. You are. I love *you*, Ari, my life is about *you* now. Making *you* famous, and rich, and happy."

"Is that all," she scoffed lightly and glanced away. "I'm so fucking tired of Gloria. We're so much happier when she's not mentioned. And, as you've said to me before," she glanced at both doorways and lowered her voice to a whisper, "we're happier when the kids aren't around either."

He nodded and kept his voice low. "That's true. We are.

Anything for You

But what's got into you, baby? You've been happy today, haven't you? What's happened since we got home?"

"Ah…I…" She shrugged and shook her head, looking back at the trees with their abundance of presents. "Maybe I'm just not dealing with this as well as I thought I would. Your sisters asked me if we were doing it, for God's sake. And they've figured out we pretty much are."

"They are very nosy people," Jay said.

"And then the presents were handed out, and I was fine. And then dinner happened, and I was fine. And then we came home, and I was fine. But then I see you unloading the presents and up comes Gloria again and now I'm not fine. And if you've got something planned for tonight I don't think it should happen because the kids are here and *they* don't know we're doing it, so we shouldn't sleep in the same bed, let alone the same room for the night. And *that* pisses me off, but it needs to be done, otherwise they'll burst in on us and it'll be awkward with what Andrew said at Halloween because of Gloria, and then what Gloria said at the party the other night, and then it'll just be this big shit storm of hatred and anger and vitriol, and I'm resenting you having her for an ex. And I really wish right now in this moment that you didn't have kids, and you were single with no problems in the world other than how we're going to spend this night together. And I know I'm sounding really damn selfish right now and I don't know where it's coming from." She gasped for air and stared at him guiltily. "I'm *really* over Gloria."

Jay stared back, taking in every word she'd said. He contemplated it all and finally sighed. "I know, baby. I'm sick of her, too. And you're right, I hadn't thought about tonight and where we'd be staying. I mean, hell, it's my house and we're dating, you should be able to stay in my room if I want you to. But you're right, I have the kids and I'm kind of regretting it myself right now." He rubbed a hand over his face and into his hair, ruffling it as he thought things through. "I don't know. I guess tonight's plans are on hold as is sleeping together. Which sucks. But I can still give you your present and we can still have a few quiet moments together before bed, and tomorrow after lunch they'll be gone, and we can make up for it."

"I'm going to sound like a right bitch, right now, but you once said to me that you're so much happier when you don't have them." She saw the look in his eye. "So why don't you let her have them full-time and not see them at all? How do you plan on having relationships with them here, or fear they'll see something they shouldn't? How do you plan on maybe moving a fiancé or future wife in if they're here and you worry they'll send back information to her? How are you going to live your life, Jay? Because that's what I wondered tonight when your sisters had their chat with me. My plan was to only be here for a year. What happens if something happens between us in the next year? Not that I'm saying it will, but with the way things are going, if I decide to move here in a year because we're still together, what then? How do we live then? Do we hide in separate rooms from your children then?"

Jay leaned his elbow on his knee and rested his hand on his mouth. He stared at her, first with horror, then with wisdom, then with knowing. "Yeah…you're right. How the hell will I do that? How will *we* do that? She didn't stop to care about moving Denver in once I threw her out and filed for divorce. She moved into the apartment and moved him

Anything for You

right in. She didn't care about what the kids thought. Or what *I* thought, for that matter. She didn't care what anyone in this world thought except herself." He sat up straight, his hand dropping as he glanced around the room in semi-horror. "God... I've been holding back all this time because I didn't want problems from her. Because I didn't want to cause a rift with her. Because I didn't want the kids to take back information to her and then for her to drag me through the court over it. But she did all of that anyway."

He lifted her hand to his lips and kissed it. "You're right, Ari. It is all about her. And I'm sick and tired of it, too. I'm sick and tired of her, and if she thinks she's going to chase you away, fuck no am I going to let her." He pulled Ari to her feet and into his arms. "I'm not going to let her, *or* the kids, ruin this for us. I promise. And it starts tonight. We'll sleep in the same room, and I don't care what gossip the kids take back to her because she's living with Denver, and did the same with him, so she can go to hell." He nodded in time with his words. "Times are changing, Ari. You're in my life and this is the way it's going to be. You've been in my bed since the party, and you'll continue to be in my bed until the end of time."

"Oh, well, I don't know about that," she said and laid her hands on his chest. "Look, Jay, I didn't mean to cause any issues. I have no idea where all of this has come from. Maybe it's because I'm just emotional about being here for Christmas, and not back in Aus. Maybe it's because I don't have any one to exchange presents with, maybe it's for an entirely different reason. But I don't want to cause issues or problems and I don't mean to upset you."

"You haven't upset me, Ari, my girl. I love you, and

you're right. And no, you're not a bitch for saying what you feel and think. You're right. I need to get on with my life the way I want to and not be so damn scared because of her. So…" He hurried over to one of the trees and pulled a small box from a branch. "This is for you." He presented it to her.

"Oh, okay." Surprised, Ari lifted the top and pulled out a black velvet box. "Mmm, what could this be?" She prised the lid up and saw a gleaming heart-shaped pendant full of emeralds and rubies on a gold chain. "Oh…Jay…" Her head shook slightly. "You shouldn't have."

"Why not? It's Christmas." He gently removed the necklace and clasped it around her neck. "Merry Christmas, Ari, my girl. I love you." He kissed her cheek and squeezed both shoulders.

She held it lovingly in both hands and moved it around to catch the light. "It's stunning. It really is." She spun in his arms, threw hers around his neck, and kissed him. "Merry Christmas. I love you, too. But I didn't get you much because I didn't know *what* to get you."

He shook his head. "You didn't need to get me anything, so it doesn't matter what you did get. All that's important is that we're here, together, and you're spending the night in my bed because this is *my* house and you're *my* girl and that's just the way it is."

She gazed into his eyes, searching for something. "You sure?"

"Absolutely, without a doubt," he replied. "And I say we go up to bed now, so we still have some time to enjoy ourselves."

"I'll have to stop off at my room first, to freshen up and get your present, but I'll be up shortly after that."

"I'd say that's a plan." He kissed her gently, and after

turning off the lights, they went upstairs.

*****

They needn't have worried about the children. Andrew and Marisol headed downstairs the moment they woke. But Jay knew what they were like and had set his alarm to be up early with them. By the time Ari woke, hurried to her room and quickly showered and dressed, the kids had already ripped everything open and were watching a Christmas Day parade on TV and munching on breakfast.

"Hey, guess everyone got their presents opened." Ari saw the mess on the floor and an even messier trio of Daniels on the couch. She grinned. "Having fun?"

Jay grinned back, hair askew, and robe falling loose over his t-shirt and tracksuit pants he'd slipped into when he'd woken. "Yep. There's coffee, and bagels from yesterday. They soften up if you throw them into the microwave."

"I'll do that then." Ari hurried into the kitchen and made herself a bagel and orange juice. Still full after last night's dinner, she didn't want too much as she knew there'd be more at lunch with Jay's parents. She sat at the table and ate, leaving Jay to spend the time with his children. Regardless of last night's conversation, she still didn't want to intrude into his moments with his children and figured they could be conditioned to her being there a little longer before letting them know.

"Come join us." Jay waved her over.

Ari shook her head. "No, it's okay. Spend the time with your kids. I'll clean up." She rinsed her plate and cutlery and wiped her hands.

Jay turned up behind her and spoke in her ear. "Come and join us. It's time you did." He took her hand and led her back to the couch, pulling her down next to him. "We're just watching the repeat of the parades. There's not much on TV Christmas Day, but sometimes you'll find good stuff."

They sat in silence. Jay's arm around Ari, her hands firmly in her own lap. Out of her peripheral vison she noticed Andrew giving her a few side-eyes, but he had the decency to not say anything.

Unless his father's said something, Ari thought and kept her eyes on the screen.

After breakfast, Jay and the kids showered and dressed while Ari cleaned up the mess. She didn't mind. It gave her twenty minutes of peace and quiet. The TV was still on but turned down. There were no cars on the road to break into the silence, and no one in the street. She gathered the kids' toys and set them neatly to one side, so they weren't stepped on, and gave the place a quick tidy up.

It was not the way she thought she'd be spending her first and only Christmas morning in New York. Her first and only Christmas morning away from Australia. But, in the grand scheme of things, it wasn't so bad. She and Jay had made love for hours last night, and she'd given him the watch she'd bought him with Bobby's advice. He got up with his alarm for the kids and she slept in, missing the warmth of his hairy body beside her. A hairy body she was getting very used to sleeping beside.

She glanced at the clock and saw it was only two more hours before they would be at Jessica's house having lunch with Melinda and Ben, and then two hours later the kids would be dropped off at their mother's. A sigh left her. When she'd decided to come to New York, it had been purely for selfish reasons. She wanted to see it, Jay was paying for it, and it would get her away from her situation back in Australia to let her be free to be who and what she wanted to be. The rent and board she was paying Jay was almost nothing, and while she'd desperately wanted something to happen between them, she hadn't counted on it *actually* happening. Thinking about the end of her year and what was going to happen was exhausting. As were Gloria and the kids.

"Hey." Jay walked into the living room and saw her handiwork. "You didn't have to tidy up." The kids came in behind him. "Kids, do you want to play with your toys for another couple of hours, or pack them up for the trip to Aunt Jess's? Because once it's all in the car, I'm dropping you off after lunch."

"Can I leave my presents here, Daddy?" Marisol asked and picked up a current trend doll she had received.

"If you do, you won't see them for a while. You know I only get you every now and then. What if you want them when you go home?" Jay asked her.

Marisol thought about it. "I guess. What do we pack them in?"

Jay looked around and saw the Santa sacks that he'd stored the presents in. "Here." He picked them up and shook them open. "Pack them in here and then everything will be together."

They packed their presents and left the bags by the couch, sitting down to watch more TV until it was time to go.

Ari pulled Jay aside in the kitchen. "Are they okay? They're really quiet."

"Yeah, I noticed that," he whispered and opened the fridge

door. Bending down, he pretended to look for something. "Where's the…ah…"

Ari leaned down. "What?"

"I don't know if their mom said something to them, or my family did." Jay kept his voice low. "But they're definitely different. Oh, there it is." He pulled out a container and lifted the lid. "Ew, yeah." He screwed up his nose. "I thought it was old. I only remembered it was in here last night and wanted to check the date. Yeah, definitely past its used by." He threw the container in the bin and turned to Ari, leaning down and kissing her on the cheek. "I think someone said something to them. Or they're just warming to you."

"I highly doubt that, but I'll keep my fingers crossed for it," she murmured and kissed him back.

"Mmm," Jay mumbled. "Well, Andrew's throwing dirty looks this way, so maybe not."

"Oh, well." Ari pulled back. "We'll have to get another one if you still want it."

"Oh, I definitely still want it." Jay slid his arms around her and pulled her close. Hiding behind the fridge door now forgotten. "I can't wait until later."

She snorted. "Anything else you want to throw out?"

"Oh, there's plenty that I want to throw out." Jay nodded as each thought flew through his mind. "Plenty. I still need to go through my stuff in the basement and try and set up my office. I have awards and stuff somewhere that I want to get into the display cabinet."

"I can help with that. You want to do it this week?"

"Weren't you doing the after Christmas sales?"

"I was, and am, but can still help you with your stuff."

He thought about it. "I probably should get to it. There's

some other things I need to find, and can't, so yeah, you can help. That would be great." He kissed her.

"Get a room, you two. That's sick and disgusting," Andrew called from the lounge room.

Ari pulled away in shock. "Wow!"

"And the silence is broken," Jay said. "Okay, Andrew, I'm only going to tell you once." He let go of Ari and walked over to his son, stood between him and the TV, and stared hard at him. "This is *my* house and who I see in it is *my* business. Not yours *or* your mother's. She's been seeing Denver; do you say the same thing to her? No, she wouldn't tolerate it, and I won't either. Ari is a guest in my house, and I've fallen in love with her, so we're going to kiss and do other things that adults do. And you have no say in the matter, because we're adults, and you're not. We're not affecting you in any way, shape, or form, and again, you have no say in the matter. So be kind, as we raised you to be and say nothing." He watched his son intently. "Got that?"

Andrew sulked and crossed his arms. "Got it."

"Good." Jay looked at the clock. "I know we weren't supposed to be at your aunt's for another hour, but I might ring and see if we can come early, so you can spend some more time with your grandparents." He turned to Ari. "Does that sound okay?"

"Sure. Whatever you want." She had no right to disagree; it was his family.

Jay hurried upstairs for his phone and made the call. His mother had no problem with them coming early and he went downstairs and told them. "Pack up your stuff and get your coats. Make sure you don't leave anything behind."

They collected their coats, bags, and phones, and when

they arrived, Melinda and Ben took over the children and kept them entertained in the kitchen remaking the leftovers for lunch. Jessica and her family had left a couple of hours earlier, so it was just them.

Jay and Ari sat on the couch and watched and listened as his parents instructed the kids, so they could have a few moments to themselves.

"Your parents definitely know how to deal with them," Ari told Jay.

"Years of practice with me and my sisters," he replied, crossing his legs and swinging his left leg. His right arm was around Ari, and he was sipping a beer.

"At least they're not complaining." She listened to the conversation and Gloria didn't come up once. "Good to know your parents can steer the conversation away from their mother."

"Yep. 'Cause I don't want to hear her name right now."

The hours went by quickly, and soon they bundled up the kids to take them home. Melinda and Ben hugged and kissed them, wished everyone a merry Christmas, and waved them off when they left.

Jay drove the kids to Gloria's apartment and then drove home. When they set foot in his brownstone he locked the door, slumped against it, and cocked his ear.

"What?" Ari asked when she saw him. "What's wrong?"

"You hear that?"

She looked around, her ears straining for a sound, but she heard nothing. "No, what?"

"Silence."

"Oh." She giggled. "Yeah, it does sound good, doesn't it?" She held up the shopping bag Melinda had given her. "Just gonna put all of this food in the fridge and then we can relax."

They deposited the leftovers in the fridge, got themselves drinks, and settled on the couch. But after a few moments, Ari shifted and touched the seat of her pants. "What's…? Is the couch wet?" She smelled her hands. "It smells like… Pee? Ew." She bolted off the couch and looked at it.

"What's wrong?" Jay pulled the cushion away and saw the puddle that had been hidden by blankets and pillows. "Wait… That little shit! Andrew! He was sitting here; he must have peed on it. Damn it! He just never lets up with his bullshit." Jay flung the cushion onto the floor and ran both hands through his hair. "You know, when you said last night, why didn't I just give the kids to Gloria and not see them. Well, believe me, in times like this I want to."

While Ari went and changed her pants, he switched out the seat cushions, and took the wet one down to the basement to be cleaned.

"Damn that fucking kid!" he mumbled when they slumped onto the couch a few minutes later. "I'm sorry, baby. I didn't even realise he'd done it. He's ten for Christ's sake. He shouldn't be pissing himself, let alone on my fucking couch."

"I have to wonder if he did it on purpose after you told him off. He didn't look happy."

Jay pondered a moment. "I wouldn't be surprised. He did used to piss himself a lot as a kid. But only when we moved and then he'd settle down."

"So either he's still doing it, or he did it on purpose," Ari said. "Time the kid grew up. And if the divorce is affecting him, it's time to get him a shrink."

Jay deflated with a sigh. "Yeah. I have a feeling the bitch would make me pay for that, too, even though she's the one who's caused the damage."

Ari changed the channel and tried to change the subject along with it. "So, what are the plans for tonight? It's still afternoon, we have the whole evening and the rest of the week. But what's for tonight?"

A wicked grin slid across Jay's lips and his eyes flashed darkly. "Oh, Ari, baby, you'll just have to wait and see what I have planned for you tonight. It's Christmas and I'll be celebrating *very hard*. Inside *and* outside of you."

Her mouth opened and she blushed at the thoughts coming thick and fast.

Chapter 12

The days after Christmas were filled with holiday sales and sorting out Jay's office. It was at the back of the house on the ground floor, off the dining room. While it was half the length of the brownstone, it also meant it cut into the building next door.

Ari thought this odd and queried Jay about the layout. "It cuts into the place next door, isn't that weird? I didn't think brownstones were shaped that way. That means they have a room at the front of their house but not the back."

"Yeah, it is strange for old New York b-stones. But I think the developer made them that way on purpose when he renovated. To give each an extra room. Not sure how it works logistically. But it works well for an office space." Jay opened the final box that he'd lugged upstairs from the basement. "I have no idea what's in which box, but now that they're open, we can see it all and I can start sorting." He picked up an old high school trophy. "I guess I can display these."

Ari looked around the room. "It's a decent space, you have a full wall of shelving and counter space, plus shelves underneath for books all on one wall, and you have cupboard space for storage under the massive TV sitting on this wall."

"Yeah." Jay sighed and glanced around. "But I have no idea where to start."

"How 'bout this? We put all of the same things in certain spots and then see whether it needs to be moved or not. For example, all of the books in front of the low bookcases, your trophies, photos, and knick-knacks on the display shelves and then we'll organise from there."

"Sounds good. And I think each box is labelled, so there are multiple boxes of books, and we can start with those." Jay slid two boxes over to the shelves.

"And I'll unload your trophies and awards." Ari picked up one box and set it on the counter between the display cabinets. She quickly found the other boxes and pulled out the awards. Organising would come last.

Jay continued with the books, moved other boxes aside that could be stored away in the cupboard under the TV, found some of his high school stuff, and a box of framed photos. "Oh, these can go on a shelf, or wall, if there's space."

Ari dropped another empty box onto the pile in the hallway. "Okay. You have three display cabinets with counter space and blank walls in between, so I think all of your TV awards should go in the middle cabinet, your school stuff could go in another, and the rest of the stuff you want to display could go in the third where you have some stuff now. Once we have that done, then you'll see what space is left. But judging by everything we've set out…" She glanced over the counter top and saw how full of stuff it was. "We should probably offload the books first. How many boxes do you have?"

"Twenty boxes of books. Jesus." He shook his head. "Didn't realise I'd collected so much stuff. Just as well a lot of things are still in the basement at Mom and Dad's house."

"Do you want them all, and does it matter how they're set up? As in by colour, genre, author?" Ari walked over and looked down at a box. "Books are faster to unpack."

"As is everything," Jay replied and cocked his head to look up at her. "How many boxes of yours are downstairs?"

She smiled. "Too many, but I don't need to unpack them, so let's get into yours."

A half hour later they had organised the books onto the lower shelf space along the wall. They fitted nicely, and there was even room for more.

"That's done." Ari rose from the floor and brushed off her hands. She spied the boxes in front of the TV. "What's in those?"

"Stuff. And I'm not sure I want it, so I might leave it in there." Jay crawled across the floor and looked through them. "Yeah. Don't really need this stuff on a daily or weekly basis. It's just old scripts, files on movies…stuff."

"Any of them from the shows you won awards for?" Ari leaned over his shoulder. "We could display them with the awards."

"Ah…" Jay flipped through the scripts. "Yeah, some of them. But most are from movies that I made, or scripts that were sent to me to see if I wanted to be in the movie. Just a lot of paper, really."

"We can still display them, but you should probably get some kind of proper box or container to file them away in. Do you have a filing cabinet?" She looked over at the desk space to see if there was one. "You should keep them documented properly."

"Meh." Jay pulled out three scripts that had won him

awards and packed up the rest into the box before shoving the box into the cupboard. "No need. It's just paper." He quickly went through the rest and Ari added the three scripts to the display counter. "That's it. I don't need any of that stuff and it all fits into the TV cupboard." He got up and moved to Ari's side. "What now?"

"Now you start on that cabinet," she pointed to her left, "and do some sort of display for your school trophies. I'll start on your movie and TV celebratory cabinet."

"Ah…can't you do them?" Jay asked. "You like to display things, and you do a really good job of it. Whereas I can bang nails in the wall and hang pictures, so I'll do that."

Ari looked at him and sighed. "Only if you do lunch because I'm getting hungry."

Jay checked his watch and saw it was close to lunchtime. "I'll order pizza and help you out while we wait." He gave Ari his award-winning smile and quickly called the local pizzeria with their order.

"Huh," she mumbled and turned to the middle cabinet, waiting for him to finish the call. "Okay, here we go. In order of win please, start handing them to me."

Jay handed each one over and Ari placed them in chronological order until all of them were on a shelf. She spread them evenly throughout the cabinet, interspersed them with knick-knacks and scripts, and anything concerning the shows and movies, and then the cabinet was done.

"Wow." Jay looked at it in surprise. "You really do know how to lay out a display."

"And now we do the next one—" Ari was interrupted by the doorbell. "Pizza's here and I need a drink."

She hurried out to fix the table for lunch and Jay went to

pay. They took a half hour break and then got back to work with Ari starting on the second display cabinet.

She laid out Jay's trophies, awards, knick-knacks, and photos from his school years to when he started acting school and had the odd job working at places and clubs. "And we're done with that. Now we have the cabinet behind your desk."

She walked over and saw that he already had books, files and photos in it. "I'll just sort this out and add some more things and you can hang the photos that are left, and we'll organise the counter space." She opened the doors and quickly organised the display before adding a few things and closing the doors. "And done." She heard him bang a nail into the wall and saw him hang the last photo. "You're only hanging a few?"

"Yeah, the rest can just sit on the counter. Are we done?"

They stood back and looked at the wall.

"Wow, you do have a knack for layout and display. It looks great, Ari. Thank you so much. I love you for it." He slid an arm around her and pulled her close, kissing her cheek in the process. "It looks so good."

"And the lighting system in the cabinet helps highlight the awards." She stared at the middle cabinet and all of its sparkling shiny jewels. "You've got quite a few awards there, Jay Daniels. Emmys, Globes, People's Choice, Critics Choice, producer and director awards. Jesus. That's quite a heavy metal ensemble."

He chuckled lightly. "Yeah. Most were for that TV show I created. I also got some Razzies for a few movies. Are they in there?"

"They are. I found them and put them in since they were for your acting. Didn't you win big for any of your movies? I noticed there weren't any for those."

"No. Just the TV gigs. But that's okay. It made me a lot of money, gave me a lot of success, and won me a lot of awards." His smile drifted away. "But none of that matters a decade on, does it? Gloria got a chunk of it, I slowly fell out of favour with Hollywood, and stopped getting the calls."

"But that's changing." Ari laid her hand on his chest. "You're making a comeback with the new movie, and making me a famous author, and if we can get the movie up and going, it'll all change. Besides, you still have plenty of friends. They've been helping you out with parts in their shows and movies, haven't they?"

Jay's gaze wandered over the wall before them, taking in his last four and a half decades. He wondered if he should get the rest of his stuff from his parents' house, but then figured it would just sit in the basement. "Yeah…" he finally mumbled. "They've been good enough to do that. Asked me to produce or direct, or do some acting in. I just hadn't had a movie until now."

"At least you still have friends and still got to work. Producers and directors make money, don't they?"

"They do. And it was a regular income and great to work behind the scenes. You've done a great job, Ari. You even plumped the cushions on the sofas."

"Someone had to. They were pretty sorry looking before I got my hands on them."

"Yeah." He grimaced. "I picked those out before you got here. I didn't do a good job of it, did I?" He inspected the brown leather couch with its colourful cushions that he'd chosen months earlier and wondered why he'd picked such Godawful colours.

"They're cushions. They can be changed, or you just get new covers." She walked over to the cabinets and turned off the lights. "If we're done, I'd like to veg out in front of the TV for a bit and relax. Do you have anything else to do, besides packing up the boxes?"

"Boxes? Aw! I have to pack them up," he complained.

"Yep, they're yours, not mine." Ari pulled the curtains across the window facing the back yard. "Time to veg out." She followed him out the door, and while he dealt with the boxes, she went to the lounge room and flopped down on the couch. Putting her feet up, she flicked through the TV networks to see what was on.

"And for everyone's entertainment, we have Denver, with his new smash hit song that was written just for his girlfriend, actress Gloria Hannaford. Take it away, Denver," yelled Hoda Kotb from *The Today Show*.

"When the hell was this on?" Ari muttered and turned the volume down so Jay wouldn't hear. "It had to be some time in the last couple of weeks. It's Thursday afternoon, so not live…" She read everything on screen and realised it must be a repeat to fill in time before the next show. "Better change the channel."

"Ari, do you have any idea…" Jay walked into the living room and stopped, staring at the TV, Denver, and Gloria, who'd just flashed up on the screen. He turned and snipped at her, "change the channel."

Ari changed to another network and said nothing, waiting while Jay closed his eyes, clenched his jaw, and breathed through his issues.

Finally, he took a deep breath and opened his eyes. "Do you have any idea of how many boxes you have down in the basement?" He walked over and sat beside her. "You still have one hundred. How many did you unpack?"

"I think I only did about ten, so far. Just work stuff, files, folders, notebooks, some bits and pieces. I'm like you, if I need it; I'll go looking for it and will only unpack the box it's in."

He nodded and glanced at the TV. His eyes glazed over. "Yeah." A long pause. "I kinda feel sorry for him."

"Who?"

"Denver."

A surprised brow rose. "Why?"

A deep-seated sigh. "Because he has *her* to deal with."

"But he conspired to cheat with a woman who was in a committed relationship."

He countered, "To which *she* had no problem saying yes."

"Are you saying you've forgiven him?"

"Fuck no! I don't condone cheating of any kind, and just as you said to him the other night, it shows he hasn't any morals. But regardless of that, four, five, however many years it is in, he's turned into something, *someone*, he isn't." He turned his head and looked at her. "Remember how he looked before? You brought it up to him the night of my party. He's changed. I did too. That's what Gloria Succubus Hannaford does to men. She drains us of everything. Our energy, our love, our money, our strength, mental *and* physical. You saw him, he's a simpering weak imitation of what he once was. And unless he gets away from her, or she dumps him, he's going to wither away to nothing. He needs to leave and regain himself. So yeah…I kinda feel sorry for him in that sense."

The surprised brows furrowed deeply. "Mmm, well, you seem to have changed your tune."

"Not really. I hate him for his lack of morals, and he deserves all he gets, but I also feel sorry for him and the way he's turning out. His music won't save him from her."

"And Gloria?"

"What about her?"

"Anything to say about her today? Other than adding the word succubus to her name."

"No, why would I?"

"Normally when you see her, hear her, or hear about her, you go off."

A shake of the head. "Not today. I'm training myself to stay calm and breathe through my anger."

"Uh-huh. We'll see how long that takes."

Jay grinned softly. "Yeah. We'll see."

Chapter 13

New Year's Eve was a rush of activity.

They lunched with Jay's family at his sister's house and then everyone headed into the city to meet up with friends. Jay had booked out a restaurant close to 7th Ave and West 43rd Street months previously, so everyone had constant food, drink, and a bathroom to use, and they partied until it was time to go.

"Okay, everyone. We've got half an hour to get out and enjoy the place before the ball drops," Jay yelled over the hubbub. "I've got plans for afterwards. Has everyone got the address we're going to after the ball drop?" He received a chorus of yeses in return.

Ari turned to Jay. "We're not going home after the ball drop? What have you got planned?"

He grinned and slid into his coat. "You'll just have to wait and see, Ari, my girl, because this night is for *you*." He took her coat from her hands and opened it for her to slip into. "You'll just have to wait and see."

"Ah-huh," she mumbled. "How long do you plan for us to stay out?"

"Oh, for another three hours, maybe."

"We're going to be completely buggered by the time we get home, you know. Do you have the kids tomorrow?" she asked.

"I told Gloria I'd pick them up for lunch with the family at one." He waved his friends on. "Come on, you drunken bums, let's get going. We've got a new year to celebrate." He corralled everyone out of the restaurant, thanked the staff for staying, knowing his massive tip would get them through, and saw how crowded the streets were as people came to watch the ball drop. "Looks like we can still get closer. Let's go down a block."

They walked towards One Times Square until they were half a block away and found some space for them all to see the building clearly. With ten minutes left, they kept themselves entertained by taking photos with anyone in the vicinity who asked, and posting to their own social media accounts.

"Oh, wait, here we go," Jay yelled, and they all pointed their phones at the ball.

It slowly descended with the countdown and lit up the sky after one.

Jay took Ari into his arms, cocooning her within them away from the world that was just for a moment, and kissed her passionately; a precious memory made in that moment.

Their lips parted and hers slid into a smile. "Happy New Year."

"Happy New Year, Ari, my girl. I love you."

"I love you, too," she whispered before pulling away and blushing. All of the phones had been turned to them and Jay's friends were cheering. "Oh, God."

Jay laughed and waved them away. "Okay. Time for the

next part of tonight's entertainment. We're going to have to walk a bit more, but it'll get the blood pumping. Come on." With his arm still around Ari, he led the way down W43rd Street to the *Lyric Theatre* and greeted the man at the door.

"What are we doing here? Are we seeing a theatre show? Are they working on New Year's?" Ari asked, her eyes taking in all the magic of the lobby.

"Someone is. And I have a special night planned for you and everyone else. We're going back to the '70s for New Year and we have the balcony seats. Just give me a minute." Jay went over and spoke to a man who had waved him over. They conversed for a few moments before Jay walked back. "We need to follow this gentleman and he'll show us to our seats. Apparently everyone else is waiting."

"Who's everyone else?" Ari asked, following Jay and the man. They walked through a door and down a hallway to where the man stopped and waved a hand for them to enter. "What's going on?" Ari entered the private box and saw a good few thousand people down on the main floor. "What is all of this? What are we seeing?"

Jay helped her out of her coat. "You'll have to wait and see. I heard it was going to happen, so booked the place out for us. We've got the balcony seats. You'll love it." He made sure his family and friends were seated before taking his seat beside Ari. "I know you're missing home, so I thought I'd do this for you."

Her brows furrowed and she shook her head slightly. "*What* is going on?"

He grinned and crossed his legs. "You'll just have to wait and see."

Within moments, the theatre went dark, and a man came

over the speaker system. "Ladies and gentleman, for one night only, we're going back to the 1970s. This is a special production of a movie that Ms Ari Travers watches every new year back home in Australia, and actor Jay Daniels thought he'd make her feel more at home here in New York by bringing it to life. From the small screen to the big stage, put your hands together and welcome the coming to life of *You Can't Stop The Music!*"

Ari's hands had flown to her mouth at the sound of her name, and upon hearing the title of the show had come to the brink of tears. Shocked, her eyes widened, and she turned to Jay. "What…?"

His smile was ear to ear and all for her as he slid his arm around her shoulders. "Happy new year, Ari, my girl. I love you, welcome to New York."

The tears flowed down her face as she turned towards the stage that was set up as a '70s disco and saw the movie roll onto the screen above it. The words popped along under the movie for everyone to sing along to, and as each member of The Village People turned up on screen, they also did on stage.

"Oh, my God, is that them?" Ari cried and leaned forward in her seat.

"Yep. This is a singalong movie stage show," Jay said in her ear as the first song burst out of the speakers. "Get up and dance."

Ari watched the actual Village People, along with other actors, singing the song on stage as it was being sung in the movie on the screen behind them. The audience on the floor were standing and singing along, as were Jay's friends and family.

Stunned beyond belief that this was happening, Ari watched in silence for the rest of the show until the finale was ready to go, and that's when Jay pulled her into the hallway.

"What's going on?" she asked as he led her along the hall and down a flight of stairs. "Where are we going? We'll miss my favourite song."

"No, we won't." Jay came to a stop outside a door and knocked. "Just you wait and see. You worry too much."

The door opened and the man who had escorted them to their seats led them backstage.

"Oh, my God." Ari gripped Jay's hand with both of hers. "We're backstage. We're gonna see this from backstage. Oh, my God." Her insides giggled like a little girl, and she danced lightly on the balls of her feet. "Oh, my God, oh, my God."

"And now, to end this show, a very special performance of the last song. This song is Ms Ari Travers' favourite song of ours, and she watches the whole movie every year just to see it and turns the volume up all the way to hear it. So for this last performance, we're going to invite Ms Ari Travers, and Mr Jay Daniels, on stage for the show of a lifetime."

"What!" Ari stood stunned and rooted in place. "What!"

"Come on." Jay pulled her on stage and over to the band, introducing everyone to Ari, and Ari to them.

"Ms Ari Travers and Mr Jay Daniels, everyone." The Village People applauded them and directed them to stand in line for the song. "Okay, everyone, get on your feet and dance this one out. It's the extended mix just like the movie."

With the lights shining brightly in Ari's face, she stared across the sea of people looking back, and her gaze slowly wandered to the balcony where Jay's family waved madly, and then on to Jay himself who stood three feet to her left.

She could barely breathe; the intensity was overwhelming.

The strains of *Can't Stop the Music* came on and the lights dimmed. Ari breathed, looked at Jay, and felt the fear slowly drip away. He danced beside her, wiggling his brows and blowing kisses to her, making her laugh, which in turn loosened her up.

The next fifteen minutes was the best fifteen minutes of her life. She danced. She sang. She put her all into that song and that dance and made it her own, and by the end of it, she had the arms of The Village People around her and was being cheered.

It was a damn good night indeed.

Coming off stage, she almost shrieked with laughter and nerves. "Oh, my God, that was freaking awesome," she sang and jumped on Jay.

He wrapped his arms around her and swung around; not caring if he hit anyone. "It was baby, it was. Did you enjoy it? Did you enjoy your first New Year's here in New York? Are you having fun? It looks like you're having fun? Are you having fun? Did you have fun?"

"Yes," she cried. "So much freaking fun." Ari flung her head back and realised how hot and sweaty she was.

The band came up to them and thanked them for coming.

"We hope we made your night," the construction worker said.

"We hope we made your year," the biker replied.

"You made my entire freaking lifetime," Ari old them. "I will never forget this in my entire life. Thank you all so much."

"Not us." The cop patted Jay on the shoulder. "This guy here wanted to set this up to welcome you to the Big Apple.

Do you really watch it every year?"

"Absolutely." Ari nodded. "It's on every New Year's Eve in Australia and has been for almost thirty years. I watch it every year just for the fun of it, *and* that song."

"That's fabulous, darling." The Indian kissed both of her cheeks. "I'm off to keep on partying, and I hope you will, too. Toodles, darlings." He waved both hands, blowing kisses as he went. The others wished them well and followed him, leaving Ari and Jay backstage watching the other actors and crew run around. The manager came up to them and escorted them back to the balcony where they caught up with the rest of their party.

"Oh, my God, that was awesome," Jessica sang and hugged both Ari and Jay. "You looked so good up there."

"But terrified," Michelle added. "Until Jay started acting the fool and then you seemed to loosen up."

"I *was* terrified." Ari took her coat and bag from Jay. "But when I saw him dancing, I couldn't help laughing."

"He does look ridiculous when he gets that look on his face," his mother said, patting his cheek. "But it did earn him millions of dollars, so he can look after all of us."

"Gee, thanks, Mom. Is that all I am, a money machine?" Jay mocked but grinned anyway. "Is everyone ready to go? We'll grab something to eat and drink if anything's open, and then we can all head on home."

They filed out into the street to see it still buzzing with hordes of people, and that meant that cafés and restaurants were also open. They found one that wasn't too full and spent the next hour eating and drinking before taking taxis, or the subway, home.

"That was one hell of a night." Ari sighed as Jay locked

the front door behind them. "I haven't partied that hard since we used to line dance in the '90s."

"What? Out all night boot scootin'," Jay joked. "Didn't think they did it so hard."

"*Line dancing*, and yeah, sometimes we did." Ari slid off her coat. "I'm in need of a long shower and a scrub, and then a good sleep-in tomorrow morning."

"That would be later this morning." Jay took her arm and led her upstairs. "But I'll need to get up at twelve to get the kids at one, and it is now," he glanced at his watch, "four in the morning. So that's…eight hours I might get."

"Might?" Ari opened her door and dropped her bag on the end of her bed. "I'll be up soon. Try not to fall asleep without me."

He grinned and kissed her lips. "I'll try not to, so don't be long."

She hurried to shower and change and made her way up to Jay's room.

He came stumbling to the bed, slurring his words. "I'm dead to the world, but if it's one thing I'm gonna do before falling asleep, it's fuck my girl." He fell flat on the bed on his face and was fast asleep in seconds.

Surprised, Ari could only watch him snore and chuckle. "Oh, okay, not getting any sex then." She covered him over, set the alarm, and turned out the lights.

*****

Later that day, Jay collected the kids, and they spent the day at his sister's house. Everyone watched the footage of the night before. Many of them had filmed it, but Jay had gained permission to professionally film the entire show and the manager had given him the disc before they'd left.

Marisol danced with her cousins, Andrew sat and scowled at it, but everyone else enjoyed seeing it again.

Ari blushed and covered her eyes at the part when she was onstage but enjoyed the overall emotion of the moment. Jay had done something magical for her. Something no one else had ever done, or probably ever would do. And if it weren't for him getting that role in the Russell Crowe movie, and being in Australia, in her state, in her town, at her writers' group, then none of this would have ever happened. And she knew she would be eternally grateful for the stars aligning and all of it happening. Snuggling under Jay's arm, she glanced up at his smiling face. He looked back and gave her a peck on the lips.

Yeah, life is pretty freaking awesome right now, she thought. *And it can only get better.*

Chapter 14

"You've certainly outdone yourself this time, Mr Daniels." Ari slid into the chair Jay held out for her. She placed her clutch on the table and settled herself, sneaking quick glances around the luxurious restaurant they were in.

"I thought we should spend Valentine's Day somewhere special." Jay sat in the chair to her right so they could look out the windows at the city.

"It certainly is," Ari murmured and then sighed. It was her first Valentine's Day with a man. A man who loved her, and a man who had given her some extremely extravagant presents. First thing that morning, Jay had woken her to breakfast in bed, and a beautiful pair of pink and blue diamond drop earrings.

For lunch he had taken her to *Electric Lemon*, atop the *Equinox Hotel*, and given her a necklace to go with those earrings, and now they were dining at the *Liberty House* restaurant with magnificent old charm and views of the city.

She almost expected another piece of jewellery to go with what he'd already given, as he knew she liked to make up sets of jewels. But she was trying not to get ahead of herself.

"Would you care for entrée and a drink?" the waiter asked.

"Ah, yes, thank you." Jay ordered for them and waited until the waiter left before reaching for Ari's hand and bringing it to his lips. "Well, what do you think?"

Ari's lips curled into a soft smile. "I think it's beautiful and the view is magnificent."

"Mmm, the view *is* magnificent," Jay murmured, turning her hand over and brushing his lips against the soft skin of her palm. "Very magnificent."

The blush swept over Ari's face, and she glanced away shyly. "Should you be doing that in here?"

Jay glanced around and saw the part of the restaurant they were sitting in was fairly private, and no one was looking their way. "No one saw anything, and you're my girl, so of course I'm going to kiss your hand, your cheek, your lips. It's also Valentine's Day, Ari. I have every right to kiss you. Which I've been doing all day."

The blushed deepened. "Yes, I know, and believe me I've enjoyed it." She glanced over her shoulder to make sure no one was watching. "But in public, it's just a little…oh, I don't know. *Public*."

Jay flashed a grin. "I know. But I want to show my love for you because I'm sick and tired of hiding it in case you-know-who sees or finds out. We decided at Christmas to stop doing that. Remember?"

A coldness swept over her. "Yeah. I know. And I know we've been out and about holding hands and putting our arms around each other. And we both know that when I start doing interviews for the new book in March that I'll be asked about it. I denied it before, but *now*…"

"I know. And we'll come up with something simple, such as, we didn't know it was going to turn to love. Or everyone saw it before we did. We'll keep it simple because it's no one's business." He brushed his lips against her palm and rested their hands on the table. "You know, I like not hiding anymore."

"Did we really hide before, though?" Ari paused while the waiter placed their entrées and drinks on the table. "Thank you." She smiled and waited for him to leave. "I mean, you only told me in November that you loved me, and we kept it on the down-low then. And it was only December that you decided to hell with it, we're going public, without actually going public with it. And since then, well," she shrugged slightly, "you've been all over me like a rash since. Not caring that we're out in public. It's almost as if you want Gloria to see it."

Jay inhaled sharply. A part of him had wanted that exact thing, a revenge tactic on Gloria, and that's what part of the plan had been. But he'd tried not to involve Ari in his thoughts or practices. "I know that somewhere under all of the emotions I'm having about you, that somewhere there was a part of me that wanted to get back at Gloria. You're right. Maybe a part of me wanted her to see the photos and news stories and gossip about us. Maybe I wanted her to see that I'm finally happy without her and that she doesn't matter anymore—"

"Yet you *always* talk about her. And she *is* the mother of your children, so in those cases, she *does* seem to matter," Ari said.

"No, I don't." Jay let go of her hand to pick up his drink and took three sips. "I hate her guts. But yes, she *is* the mother of my children. And if something happened to her, I'd have to take over and be in charge of them. So, yeah, to a certain extent she *does* matter in my life. But in my personal life…hell no does she matter. I loved seeing you rip her a new one at my Christmas party. That was fun to watch. For once she was getting it back and she couldn't do anything except leave." He took another sip and set the glass down. "I don't want her ruining our relationship, Ari. I'm working my ass off to make sure she doesn't."

"And yet, when she calls, you go running." Ari sipped her mocktail and watched his face. "She seems to be using the kids to make you run to her. That's control."

Jay pondered the comment. "Yeah, in a way. And believe me, I hate that, too. She's done it how many times now?"

"About once a fortnight, so three times this year, already. And it's always the kids. I've noticed that she stopped whining about herself. There's no more *I want this* or, *I want that,* or *I'm taking you to court.* It's all about the kids when *they're* in trouble, *they* need this, *they* need that, *they're* sick." She picked up her fork, but it paused in mid-air. "She's changed tack."

Jay's phone rang and he pulled it from his jacket pocket. "Gloria! Why the hell would she be calling? She doesn't have the kids tonight because she didn't want them and fobbed them off on her parents." He denied the call and put his phone away.

"And now we have the fourth call." Ari finally took a bite of her seafood entrée.

"Well, it can't be about the kids, so no need to answer. Besides, it's Valentine's."

"Exactly why she's calling. To interrupt our plans," Ari said as his phone rang again. "Persistent bitch, isn't she?" She sighed.

Jay checked it and denied the call. "She is." He left it on the table and kept on eating. "I'm not going to let her ruin tonight."

"But what if something *has* happened to the kids? That's the problem, isn't it? The last three calls she's claimed the kids were sick or wanted you to read them to sleep. Which, as you said, made no sense because they hadn't wanted that since going to live with their mother, and she's turning them against you anyway. She's using the kids to interfere with your life, to screw you over, and to ruin the new relationship you're in. And sadly, it might work."

"What! No! I won't let it." Jay grabbed her hand and smashed it to his lips. "I won't let her ruin us, Ari. I love you and that's all there is to it. She doesn't get a say in this."

"She's already having her say," Ari told him. "By ringing, especially at night when she knows we could be out, or in bed. She's making you come running. Three times already. And you turn up and the kids are fine and don't want you there. She feigns sickness or lies, that the kids wanted you there, and then you return. But if you don't go, then the kids could really be sick, or in an accident, and you'll think she's crying wolf and not go, and that's the time it could be serious. It's a double-edged sword between a rock and a hard place. You go, and are used in the process, or you don't, and something happens to your kids."

He sighed and released her hand. "Yeah, you're right. So what do we do?" His phone beeped and he looked at the message. "She says the kids are sick and she needs me to collect them from her parents' house as her parents can't leave. What sort of bullshit is that?"

"Call her parents and find out," Ari told him. "They'll

either lie or have no idea what you're talking about. She clearly just wants you to make the trip all the way out to their house and waste your time *and* ruin your Valentine's."

"When no one can ruin *her* Valentine's Day," Jay mocked and dialled his ex-in-laws. "Not even when we were married." He waited for the maid to pick up. "Hi, this is Jay Daniels. I need to speak to Marilyn or Godfrey about the kids. Thank you." He waited till the maid handed the phone off to Marilyn. "Gloria has been ringing me, but just left a message asking me to pick up the kids because they're sick. Are they?"

"Why would she do that? No, they're not sick. They're perfectly fine and we have them until tomorrow. Why would she tell you that? It sounds like complete nonsense," Marilyn replied.

"Then so's the text message your daughter just left me asking me to pick them up. You're daughter's the liar, Marilyn, not me. If my kids are fine then they can stay there. And if Gloria rings, tell her she doesn't run my life." He hung up and pocketed his phone.

"And if she calls again?" Ari finished off her food and took a sip of drink.

"I'll let her know. But her mother's probably ringing her about my call. That'll really piss her off." His smile beamed. "I'm all for that."

Ari set down her glass and dabbed at her lips, then folded the napkin back across her lap. "I know it's not my place, but I'm going to say it. I don't like the fact she's doing this. I want her to stop. But I also know your kids are a priority and will always come first in your life."

Jay let out a long slow sigh. "I don't know about that anymore. I mean, I appreciate you thinking that, and yeah, they're my kids. But I really don't know…" He slowly shook his head and stared out the window. "They *should* be. And I *think* they are. But slowly, slowly, they're just not. Maybe it's because Gloria has them most of the time. Maybe it's because she's controlling their thoughts and feelings about me and turning them against me. Maybe it's because she's worn me out and I can't deal with any of them anymore. And now that I've met you…" He grasped her hand. "I have other priorities. Such as you, and my career. I really want to get that back and resuscitate it to what it used to be. When I made movies and earned millions. When I had fun working with friends and making TV shows and movies I liked, because I worked damn hard for twenty years to do so and make a name and reputation for myself. That's the reputation that my ex tore to shit when I divorced her. I want all of that back, Ari. I want it all back thanks to you."

He held her hand to his lips while his right hand slid into his jacket pocket. "I want my life back. I want the energy you've brought into my life, so I can reclaim what I had and move forward with freshness and a renewed vigour I haven't had in years. And you've done all of that, Ari. You've brought all of this into my life, and in these last few months especially, you've brought love and passion back again when I didn't think I'd ever feel it again. I love you, Ari, I'm glad I met you, and I'm not letting anyone take you away from me. Or me away from you."

He slid a huge pink and blue diamond ring onto her right-hand ring finger. "I hope this shows you how much I love you and appreciate that you're in my life."

Ari's eyes grew wide. "Oh, my God, Jay, oh…" She pulled her hand closer to stare at the massive emerald cut pink diamond. It was surrounded by sparkling blue diamonds and matched her earrings and necklace perfectly. "Oh…I thought I might be getting a bracelet to match the other pieces. I wasn't expecting a ring. Oh, this is way too much. You've spent way too much on me. These can't be cheap."

"Ari." Jay frowned and leaned on the table towards her. "Money's not a problem. I can afford it. And I wanted to spend my money on you to show my appreciation for you, and your love, and creativity, and everything you've brought to, and back into, my life. I love you, Ari Travers. I wanted to give you something special for Valentine's. Our first of many together."

"Oh…Jay…" She sighed. "Oh…it's beautiful." Ari turned it on her finger. Hitting all of the lights in the restaurant, it sparkled like the jewel it was. "It's stunning. And in my two favourite colours."

"I know. It was made for you." He grinned and knocked back his drink, before waving at the waiter for another.

Their main meal arrived, and they ate in relative silence, just gazing at each other over the candlelight. Ari smiled shyly, and Jay wiggled his brows or blew her kisses. They held hands through dessert and had one last drink before leaving.

While Jay paid the bill, Ari went to freshen up, but when she walked up to him she saw he was shutting off his phone. "Is she calling again?"

"Screaming at me because her mother rang her about my call. Pathetic really. But it's a voice message, so I'll forward it onto Merrick and he can use it for the next court case she brings."

"Do you think she will?" Ari slid into her coat that he was holding out for her.

"She hasn't since she signed the contract. But as we said before, if she's using the kids now, she might try and get me as an absentee father, or something. Who knows? She'll use them against me at some point if she can't get me herself." He adjusted his coat and took Ari's arm in his. "The car's ready. Are you?"

"I am. Are we going home?"

"I thought we'd take a tour around the city first. I know we've done it a few times, but it never gets old showing you around your new city."

She blushed and clung to his arm as they walked out to their chauffeured car.

They drove around for half an hour before crossing the bridge into Brooklyn and arriving back at Jay's.

"Would you like anything before bed?" he asked when he closed the door.

"You," she replied, sliding her arms around him and kissing him. "Let's go to bed."

They walked up the stairs arm in arm to Jay's room. Ari had moved her belongings in just after New Year's Day. They'd moved her desk and shelving unit into her old room which was now her office, and she still used her bathroom and closet spaces to shower and dress.

They undressed each other slowly in the semi-darkness of the room. Coats slid to the floor. Ari's pumps were left by the end of the bed, her dress pooling on top of them. Jay's jacket and pants, and then his shirt, joined them. Their underwear fell from their bodies, and they made their way to the bed where Jay grabbed the covers with one hand while the other lifted Ari onto the mattress and laid her down. He laid on top of her, their bodies never parting, their lips never breaking contact. Arms around each other, they joined as Jay settled himself on top of her and Ari moved to accommodate him and the pleasure he brought.

They didn't stop until he had poured every ounce of energy into her, and she cried out in rapt explosions of shuddering fireworks.

It was like that every time. Every time they made love. The fireworks, the cheering, the applause. Every single damn time. And Ari knew it was what she wanted for the rest of her life.

Chapter 15

Two weeks later, on the first of March, Ari put her new book up for pre-order on the sale sites she sold on. She'd spent all of February perfecting the proofs and getting all of the publicity ready. Blog posts, social media headers, book quotes, and character lists. Jay had sent copies of the book out to his friends with the same plan as last time, and now it was ready to go out into the world.

Ari kept her dashboard open to see what the pre-order status was like as she sent videos out via her social media accounts. She'd already been talking about it since January and was now seeing the results of her plan.

By five that night, there were a hundred thousand pre-orders. Today, was only day one with eighteen more to go.

"You're going to have another smash hit on your hands, Ari, my girl." Jay straightened from leaning over her shoulder and cracked his back. "My friends'll start reviewing and talking it up on their socials in the next three weeks and it'll start rolling in. Just like last time."

"Yeah." Ari pushed back from her desk and sighed. Her energy had been sagging for a couple of hours. It was mainly due to having worked so much in the lead up. Now the book was finally up, and she'd updated all of her websites, she could relax a little. "I don't have much to do for a while." She checked off her publishing list. "I'll just talk about it each day on socials, and don't need to worry until the actual sale day. I get to have a bit of a break."

"Great, so you can log off and come and eat dinner?" Jay pulled her to her feet. "You look a little worn out."

"Yeah, but I've been working long hours, plus we're in spring now, so the change of season is making me a bit tired. I'll close up shop and not worry about this until tomorrow."

"And I'll go and get dinner started." Jay kissed her cheek and left her to shut down her laptop.

Ari sorted through her paperwork, crossed off what had been done, highlighted what was to be done next, and mentally prepared for the interviews she had coming at the end of the month. She'd already booked Zennith's radio show again, plus at least eight daytime talk shows there in New York, and another five radio shows. None of them was Ken J. Jamison's, thank God.

She made her way downstairs to hear Jay arguing and saw him on the phone when she walked into the kitchen.

"No, Gloria. I *do not* need to come and see the kids. It's not my time, you know that." He glanced at Ari and rolled his eyes.

She raised her brows and sighed. *Here we go again*, she thought, and looked around for the food. Jay pointed to the oven, and she looked inside to see a sizzling roast.

"No, Gloria. I'm not coming." Pause. "Are the kids *actually* sick, or are you lying again like you did on Valentine's night?" Pause. "Don't bullshit to me, Gloria. You lied and told me to pick the kids up because they were sick. I called your parents.

They weren't." Pause. "No, Gloria – Gloria – hello Marisol, are you actually sick, sweetie?"

He listened while she hoarsely told him she couldn't swallow and how sick she felt. "Well, I'm sorry you're ill, Mari, but me coming to look after you would make me sick, too. It's best for Mommy to look after you at this point." Pause. "I know Mari. I know. Put your mommy on." Pause. "Listen, Gloria, Mari being sick doesn't mean I should come and get sick too. You're already there dealing with it, why do *I* need to come over and deal with it? Or do you just want me as a babysitter, so you can run out and party with Denver?"

"How dare you insinuate such a thing," she screeched loudly enough for Ari to hear when Jay moved the phone from his ear.

Ari pulled a face and moved away.

"They're your children too, Jay Daniels, and if I say you need to come over and help look after them, you'll fucking well come over and help look after them."

"The hell I will," Jay cut her off. "You don't get to dictate when I see my kids; you're not going to control me when I don't. You have primary custody, Gloria. If they're sick then you deal with them. Because let me tell you, if I came over, and you ran out, I'd leave too. I'm not playing your games. If they're really sick, get a doctor, and then that doctor can call me to tell me what's wrong with them. Not you." He hung up and sighed. "Jesus fucking Christ that woman can ruin things. She just doesn't stop."

"Are they that bad? Maybe you should go," Ari said, getting the plates from the cupboard. She set them down on the counter and looked at Jay. "When was the last time they were sick? Did she call you then?"

Jay thoughtfully chewed on his bottom lip. "They're kids. They get sick every six months or so usually because they've picked up some bug from school. Colds, flus, sniffles. And no, she's never called me except to pay for their medical bills."

"So why now? It's the first of March. Why today? Valentine's I get, it was a big celebratory day. Our first together. But why today?" Ari asked.

Jay's head shook slightly, and he gazed around the room. "I don't know…" His gaze finally landed on Ari. "Unless it's to do with you."

Ari's brows furrowed. "Me! Why me?"

"It's your big day, *again*. Another book up for pre-order. You're successful in your own right now and you've been churning it out on social. Gloria's probably been stalking you." He leaned against the kitchen island and crossed his arms. "She's probably envious."

"Of me?" Ari questioned and scoffed, pointing to herself. "Me? She's envious of me? I don't think so."

Jay shrugged. "I wouldn't put it past her. You stood up to her at the Christmas party, you had a go at Denver, you were on TV and radio last year, and will be again this month. You're also in my life, and she's clearly pissed about it."

Ari pulled out the cutlery drawer and collected what she needed. "I don't know… It just seems too ridiculous that she would be envious of me." She closed the drawer and started setting the table for dinner. "I don't believe that. I think she's still pissed at you and so I'm copping it by default."

"Could be that, too," Jay said and heard his phone ring. "Oh, God," he complained. "This had better not be her again." He checked it and became puzzled when he saw a number he didn't recognise. "This is new. Hello?"

"Hello, Jay, it's Denver."

Jay's brows rose in shock, but he kept his voice calm. "Denver? Why the hell are you calling?"

"Since Gloria's flown off the handle about you not coming, I thought I'd take a quick moment to call you to let you know, that yes, Marisol is sick. It's only a cold or flu, something she gets often. She's seen the doctor, and so has Andrew as he complained of a sore throat as well, but there's no need to come over. Gloria and I were going out tonight, but when Mari came down sick I chose to stay in. Gloria demanded we get you here to look after the kids, so we can still go out. There's no need. The doctor suggested we all stay in, anyway."

Jay was dubious, but the kid seemed sincere. "Well, thanks for letting me know Mari's seen the doctor. I guess it's best to stay away for a while. I'll call Mari in a week or so to see how she is. Tell her not to talk to save her throat."

"Will do… Bye, Jay." He ended the call.

Jay stared at his beeping phone for a moment. "Huh!"

"Jesus! What did he want?" Ari stood beside Jay and watched his face. The expressions flew past as he thought things through.

"Just to let me know Mari's seen a doctor and it was Denver who cancelled tonight's plans with Gloria. Gloria wanted me to come and look after the kids, so they could still go out."

"Well…" Ari took a deep breath. "That's weird that he'd bother doing that."

"It certainly is." Jay frowned and slid his phone into his pocket. "I didn't think he'd do something like that."

"Maybe he's seeing Gloria in a whole new light," Ari suggested.

"Ha! What? After the ribbing you gave him at the party? Yeah, that'd be weird."

"Why? Because it wouldn't give you a reason to hate him anymore."

"Oh, I still hate him. But as I said, I also feel sorry for him." Jay checked on the roast and turned the pan around before closing the door. "No. While I may offer sympathy to Denver on occasion, I still hate him for having the morals of an alley cat and fucking my wife while she *was* my wife."

"He clearly didn't care that he was ruining a marriage and family."

"A marriage and family that Gloria was already ruining." Jay placed his hands on the bench and stared straight ahead. "That damage was already in the making. I just didn't know it."

"And he exacerbated it." Ari carried the plates to the table and set them in place. "How much longer?"

"Ah, half an hour, I'd say." He checked his watch. "Yeah. It's been an hour now."

"I meant with Denver and Gloria." Ari turned to him and saw his surprise. "How much longer do you deal with this?"

Stumped, Jay could only stare at her.

"Until the kids are eighteen? Is that the legal age here in the U.S.? Until they finish college, move out of home? Until you don't need to legally support them anymore? How much longer will you have to deal with this? With the kids? With Gloria and Denver? With the divorce, the court cases, the lies and manipulations? How much longer?"

"Oh, Ari..." Jay shook his head. "Baby, I don't know. Ah..." He walked around the island and reached for her, rubbing her arms for some form of comfort. "I don't know.

Until they're old enough, I guess. Until I'm no longer financially supporting them. I don't know. Maybe when they're eighteen Gloria will leave me alone. I just don't know. But until then, I'm dealing with this the best I can, and hopefully Gloria's going to calm down with that contract in place. But I just…" He shrugged. "I don't know."

"That contract's been in place since October and it's now March. It hasn't done a lot to stop her from being aggravating." Ari chewed on her lip. She didn't want to put demands on Jay, and she hoped she wasn't. But figuring out how long this would go on for was important. Important to her and her thoughts on staying in New York with Jay, and maybe one day being his wife. She didn't know if she wanted to deal with Gloria for the next ten years until the kids were old enough. She didn't want to deal with Andrew the mini-Gloria, either. Denver was of no use to her, and Marisol could be reformed. Besides, she'd always wanted two kids, one of each, but especially a girl. And since she was too old to have any of her own, Marisol would make a great stepdaughter. If she could be converted.

"It's tough on you, I see that." Jay pulled her into his arms and held her tight. "I'm sorry. I know I keep saying I'm dealing with her, but now that we're together, that means you have to deal with it, too." He kissed the top of her head and sighed. "Maybe I should have another chat with Merrick about what I can do to stop her calling. Maybe I could have a restraining order against her for harassment using the children."

"But as we talked about, those kids are still yours and what if something bad *does* happen to them one day?"

Jay rubbed his face in her hair while he considered the

thought. He'd once loved his kids dearly, but the divorce had taken them from him, and his emotions, and the energy spent fighting for them had taken a toll. The time spent with them took more energy than before, and with Gloria influencing them to hate him, it just seemed a better choice to not see them as often. But that meant he was missing out, as were they, and something told him, they just didn't care anymore. They preferred Denver. Denver was the dad of that family now. The one tucking them into bed, the one telling them stories, or singing to them.

That thought made his blood boil to the point he gripped Ari a little too tightly.

"Ow." She pulled away. "You okay?"

"Sorry, baby. I didn't mean to clench you like that. Just thinking."

"Gloria, no doubt."

"The kids and not seeing them, or getting to tuck them into bed, or sing to them the way I used to. It's all about Denver and has been for the last four years." He wearily slumped into the kitchen chair at the end of the table. "I'm sorry. It really does keep coming back to Gloria, doesn't it?"

"Yep." Ari sat beside him and rested her hand on his knee. "I'm sorry."

He gazed at her through weary eyes. "Why?"

"Because some women are absolute cunts and put men through hell. And any children suffer from the consequences. Gives the rest of us a bad name."

"I could say the same about men being absolute cunts and putting women through hell." Jay kissed her hand and rubbed it gently between both of his. "Gives the rest of us a bad name, too."

"Yeah…"
"Yeah…"
"I'm sorry."
"So am I."
She kissed him on the lips and went to check on the roast.

*****

March the nineteenth rolled around quickly, and Jay threw Ari a lunch date for her latest book launch at a posh bar and grill atop one of New York's highest buildings.

"Love the view, but hate the height," Ari told him as they walked out of the elevator that had taken them sky high. "Oh my, so many people." She saw radio and TV show hosts, celebrities, and people she didn't know.

"I set this up since I didn't get to do it last time," Jay said in her ear. "You know that competition you ran on your website, for people to win an opportunity to come…well the winners are here."

"I remember, but I didn't realise you'd invited celebrities and hosts as well. I thought it would just be the winners and a little more quiet and private." Ari smiled and nodded at the people she passed. She saw Merrick, Bobby, and someone she knew as Ross, Jay's manager, but whom she had never met.

"We need to hype this thing up, baby." Jay moved her towards the stage to the right of the rooftop. "And you need to say a little something. We also have photographers to catch the moment for you to put up on socials and your website. We need to promote this thing." He escorted her up the stairs and stood in front of the microphone which he tapped. "Is this thing on? Great. Hello, ladies and gentlemen, thank you for coming to today's book launch of Ari Travers' new novel, *The Author*. We're here for a good while, so be sure to get plenty of photos with Ari as well as chat to her about the book. I see many of my friends have come along; great to have you here. A lot of radio and TV show hosts who were really supportive of Ari when she released her last novel are here, and you've all booked her for this time round." He scanned the crowd and added, "Enjoy yourselves, and make merry, but most of all, let's celebrate Ari Travers and her new novel, *The Author*, which is already number one on all the book charts. She's a best-selling author again, ladies and gentlemen. Congratulations." He stepped aside to wild applause and Ari stepped up to the mic.

"Oh, thank you, please, don't be silly." She waved a hand to make them stop. "Thank you so much for coming. I didn't realise Jay had set up such a wonderful party for me and for the launch, so much of this is a surprise. It's good to see you all again, and congrats to the winners of the competition we ran for this launch. I'll come and chat to you and sign your books and whatnot. And if I haven't met any of you yet, come and chat. Thank you for being here." She nodded and stepped back, reaching her arm out for Jay who escorted her from the stage. "This is overwhelming."

"Don't let it be. I'm here for you. Bobby's here for you, and Merrick will help if you ask. My manager Ross is here, and he can help if need be. I know the competition winners will come first as they were organised and everyone else was not; they were my surprise for this. But we set up an area for photos and book signings, so everything will be okay." He stopped and faced her. "I know you get overwhelmed, but just breathe. We're here for you."

Ari watched his warm sparkling eyes and did as she was

told. Breathed. Dressed in a royal blue pantsuit with a bright pink and blue top, she'd matched her outfit with the jewellery Jay had given her for Valentine's Day. "Okay. I'm breathing. Where do we start? I've never had a book launch before?"

He looked around at the hundred-strong crowd. "Let's mingle first and meet and see everyone, and then we'll set up the signing table."

"Okay, I can do that." Ari tried to calm the butterflies in her stomach fighting to get out, but she held them in. "I can do this."

They mingled for the next hour, meeting the competition winners, catching up with Jay's friends who'd come, and schmoozing with the radio and TV hosts. She'd be on their shows in the coming weeks and wanted them to have something good to say about it.

After an hour, Bobby led her over to the area where they'd set up the step and repeat backdrop for photos, and the book signing table. The photos were taken first, with everyone quickly lining up to have theirs taken with Ari. Phones were also out in force and social media was being besieged with pictures of the event.

Once they were finished, Ari took her place behind the table and started signing the limited-edition copies of her book that the competition winners had brought along, plus the regular copies they were giving away to everyone who didn't have one. Since Jay's friends already had their signed copies, they partied while everyone else joined the queue.

After four hours, a tonne of photos, and more schmoozing, the party ended with a round of applause.

"Thank you all so much for coming," Ari told them. "This has been incredible. I've never had a book launch before. It's been a lifelong dream to launch a book in person and have a party for it, so thank you all for wanting to come and join in on the festivities and make this one of the most incredible days of my life. Thank you so much." Ari stepped away from the mic and swiped at a loose tear falling down her face. Smoothing her hair to cover the action, she applauded along with everyone else before stepping down from the stage.

Jay was right behind her. "We can stay and mingle and thank everyone as they leave; or leave first."

"Oh, I think we should wave them off," Ari replied and saw Zennith coming towards her, arms open. They air kissed.

"Ari, darling. Thank you so much for inviting me to your new book launch. I cannot wait to have you back on my show next week to talk about it."

"I'm just happy to have a show to be on," Ari said. "Please, have a safe trip home and thank you for coming. Hope you enjoyed yourself."

"Oh, I did, darling, and we'll be talking about it next week. Toodles." Zennith waved her fingers and slinked off for the elevator.

Ari and Jay said goodbye and thank you to everyone else and finally made their way down to their waiting car.

"Well," Jay huffed when he relaxed into the back seat of the limo. "What did you think of your first actual in-person book launch?"

"Exciting *and* exhausting." Ari breathed out and tried to relax. "I didn't realise it was going to be so big, but then you did say you had a surprise for me."

"Of course. I couldn't let you go without like last time." Jay reached for her hand and squeezed it. "You deserve the world, Ari, and I'm going to give it to you." His phone rang and he checked it. "Damn! Gloria." He turned it off. "We're headed home, but I'm thinking we can relax a little, maybe have a nap," he wiggled his brows at her, "and then go out to dinner, which I also planned to celebrate this momentous occasion."

"A nap, huh?" She raised her brow in amusement. "Is that what you're calling it now?"

His lips curled up. "Just a short one. Since dinner is for seven."

Ari glanced at her watch and saw it was nearly four. "Time has definitely flown today."

"It has," Jay agreed and saw they were already pulling up to their home. "Time for that nap."

She snorted and took his hand to alight from the car. They made their way inside and upstairs where their nap lasted for two hours, meaning they had one hour to freshen up and get to the restaurant which sat on the top floor of a converted warehouse. The views were spectacular, and the colours of the sunset dazzled as they disappeared beneath the horizon and the twinkle of the city lights came into full force.

Jay seated Ari then himself. "Okay. This is your special book launch day dinner. Another best seller for best-selling author, Ari Travers." He opened his menu, but his eyes stayed on Ari. "You know. This is two in a row, so I'm going to plan your next book launch now. September, right? You can pick the restaurant, we'll book it now for the nineteenth, we'll come up with a guest list, and maybe make it different than today's, come up with another competition for your readers to attend. That went well, I thought. There was what, thirty or forty of them?"

"Mmm," Ari, murmured. She'd been absently looking at the menu, not really seeing what was written there, and only half listening to Jay.

"Ari...? Earth to Ari."

"Mmm?" She glanced up and blinked a few times, waiting for her vision to focus on him. "What?"

"What indeed," he replied. "Where were you? Thinking about today?"

"Mmm...but not today, more like our non-existent nap this afternoon." She saw his lips turn to a grin. "Since I didn't get to *actually* sleep, I can feel myself flaking out and I know I'll be getting a decent sleep tonight. It was actually exhausting. Who knew that talking to people for four to five hours was so exhausting?"

Jay chuckled. "Yeah, it can be. But the good news is you don't have to do it again for another six months. Is that going to be it for the year? Just these two books?"

Ari's relaxed composure and the candlelit atmosphere of the restaurant was making her sleepy. "Yeah, just these two. *The Lover* will be next since it's the sequel to *The Author*. And then no more books until next year."

"March again? Are you releasing every six months?" Jay sipped the beer that the waiter placed in front of him.

"No, maybe once a year. I have a few more books, but there's no need to release two a year, unless it's something that will keep the momentum going. But if I don't start writing, I'll run out of books to release within a few years." She sipped her tropical mocktail, but realising how thirsty she was, decided to just drink the lot. "I'm going to need another one. Man, am I dry! What are we eating?"

While Jay waved at the waiter for another drink, Ari

Anything for You

checked the menu and decided on the grilled chicken and vegetable platter, with a prawn salad for entrée. Jay chose the chargrilled steak and potatoes, plus a clam chowder for entrée, and they chatted while waiting for their first course. Jay's phone interrupted them.

"Gloria. I'm not answering." He turned the phone down and slid it into the inside breast pocket of his blazer. "Not interested today."

"And if it's important?" Ari knew better. Knew that it was always about the kids.

"Then I will answer it *after* we eat and *not* before," Jay said more tersely than intended. Gloria brought out the worst in him and he always tried not to show it in front of Ari. But that was hard to do.

"And if it's an emergency?" Ari pushed.

Jay took her hand and kissed it. "*She* has primary care. I don't have them today. What I'm doing is for you and she *will not* interrupt it. For *anything*," he stressed. "She does not get to run my life when she has the kids. And the kids sure as hell don't get to run my life."

"But what if they're in the hospital?" Ari suggested. "It could be bad."

"And what?" Jay scoffed. "They just happened to be in the hospital right now, tonight, while we're having dinner? No." He shook his head in disagreement. "I don't believe it. She would've watched social media all day. She saw the book launch hashtags we set up and told everyone to use. She would've seen who was here and she would've spat fire with envy. She would've then come up with a plan to ruin what other plans we had for tonight." He played with her hand. "I know Gloria, Ari, you don't, although you've seen what she's about, and I know how her brain works because she was doing this before you came to town. She's not about to stop, she's only ramping it up. And it *will* get worse."

Ari sighed and rested her chin on her left hand. This wasn't the first time Gloria had interrupted their dates, or nights together. But Jay had woken up to her and stopped taking the bait. The problem was, if something actually *did* happen to the kids and Jay wasn't there, then what, and how would that make him look?

"I know what you're thinking, Ari." He rubbed his lips across her hand. "And yes, it could be an *actual* emergency. But I'm not going to let her interrupt our time together any more. Not since Valentine's Day. I won't do it. I won't let *her* do it. I got sucked in and conned back in January, but no more. If the kids are really sick, then boy child Denver can call me, or I don't let her calls interrupt what I'm doing, and I finish doing it before answering. We are here to eat a lovely dinner and celebrate your victorious new book. She *will not* interrupt that. I'll call after."

Another sigh. "Fair enough." Ari leaned back for the waiter to set her plate on the table. "Thank you." The aroma of the warm prawn salad hit her full on and she salivated, having not eaten since the launch party, and even then it had been nibbles and drinks. "God, I'm starving."

As they ate, they watched the view and listened to the pianist at the other end of the restaurant. He was having a red hot go at *Bohemian Rhapsody* by Queen and doing a pretty good job of it. Their mains came, and they continued to relish in their time together and spoke quietly about the launch. But before they could order dessert, Jay's phone vibrated in his pocket.

He sighed. "What now?"

"It could be anyone. Like Bobby." Ari finished her drink and ordered a third.

Jay checked his phone. "Gloria, not Bobby, but he has been calling and texting." He bypassed the call and scrolled through the messages. "He says Gloria called and Andrew's in the hospital with a broken arm and concussion after an incident at school. He's at the hospital for observation."

"Oh, Jesus, Jay. See, this is what happens when you don't answer her calls. The one time it actually could be important—"

"I get it, Ari," he snapped and glared at her. "*I get it*. No need to keep going on about it." He went back to scrolling to see that even Denver had left him a message. But there were about ten from Gloria, all calling him names and hurling abuse.

Ari smarted and breathed deeply; shocked that Jay could raise his voice to her. *At her*. She knew Gloria wreaked havoc on his life, and now hers since she and Jay were a couple. She remembered Jay telling her Gloria had run off the last woman he'd dated. While Ari didn't want to run, her instincts told her in times of overwhelming emotion, *to* run. To a quiet space so her brain could calm down and think things through rationally.

She wanted to run to a quiet space now.

But damn if she was going to let any man speak to her that way.

"*So* sorry that I was right," she said, glaring at the table in front of her. "But don't ever snap at me like that again. I *will not* be your verbal punching bag in place of Gloria. You have children, Jay Daniels, you'd better start caring."

She managed a smile for the waiter who brought her

another drink and took a sip before Jay spoke.

"I'm sorry. You're right." He sighed and ran a hand through his hair. "She gets… Ooh." He growled deep and low in his throat and reached for Ari's hand which she reluctantly held it out. "I'm sorry, Ari. Baby, I'm sorry. I need to keep my temper in check, and I shouldn't take it out on you."

"No, you shouldn't," she replied and finally looked at him. "Don't do it again. Because I see where this is going, and I don't like it." She nodded at the phone. "Do they all say the same thing?"

Jay gave a slight shake of his head. "Denver's and Bobby's texts are the same, Gloria's are just abusive."

"What are you going to do?"

"If I call Gloria I'll just get screaming. If I call Bobby I'll just get the version she told him."

"Call Denver."

"Oh." Jay sighed and leaned back in his chair. "Really?"

"If you want someone who knows the whole story and will be calm and not abusive, call him." Ari pulled her hand back and straightened her blazer. "You need to find out what's *actually* going on. Without the screaming histrionics."

Contemplating speaking to the enemy, Jay ground his jaw and chewed on his lip. "Ah," he growled, "all right." He hit redial on Denver's last message.

Denver answered in three rings. "Jay."

"How bad is he?"

"Right arm broken in two places and in a cast. Concussion from hitting his head when he fell. The doctors have him under observation and want him to rest. They also want to keep him in for a couple of days to make sure there are no clots or other issues."

A sigh escaped Jay as he contemplated more. "Is there *any* need for me to come?"

"Only if you want to be seen as the caring father."

"But am I?" he asked. "They've seen more of you in the last four years than me, thanks to Gloria moving you in and cutting off my visitations. I know they see you as their father."

"That's not true, Jay, and not something I'm getting into over the phone. I've always been here for them, but I also encourage them to see you because you're their father. I think you should at least come and see your son, even if you don't stay long. Gloria's putting on enough of a show for everyone."

"Oh, nice," Jay said sarcastically. "So I'll get the Gloria show when I get there. Great."

"Do I tell her you're coming?"

"No. I'll just turn up. Where's Mari?"

"She's sleeping in Andrew's room while Gloria's sobbing by his bedside."

"Then I guess I get to be the big rescuer who comes in to save my daughter, at least." Jay looked at Ari and she mouthed, *go*. "I'll be there soon. Don't tell Gloria." He pocketed his phone and sighed. "Andrew's broken his right arm in two places and has a concussion. He'll be in the hospital for a few days."

"Go, now." Ari waved him on. "It's important."

Jay mused it over and reached into his pocket for his wallet. "We haven't had dessert yet and I don't feel right leaving before our meal is done."

"It's your son, and he's hurt himself. For *real* this time. Go and see him. Besides, we had all day together to celebrate. How long before visiting hours are over?"

Jay checked his watch. "I think they usually stop at ten

and it's nine now."

"Then go. I'll eat dessert and see you at home later."

He looked at her and sighed. "I'll leave money for dinner and a cab home. Unless you call Bobby."

"I might just do that," she said and took the wad of bills Jay handed her. She slid them into her purse and snapped it shut. "Go and take the car."

He rose, leaned over and kissed her, then left.

She watched him go, and when she couldn't see him anymore sighed and muttered under her breath. "Fucking bitch. She probably broke Andrew's arm herself and cracked him over the head just for attention."

The manager came rushing over, looking worried. "Ms Travers, is everything all right? We saw Mr Daniels leave."

"Not quite." Ari barely managed a smile. "He had to rush off to an emergency and told me to order dessert. So I want a big piece of chocolate cake like that lady over there is having." She pointed two tables over and behind her. "It looks delicious, if you have any left."

"I believe we do, and I'll get you a piece personally." The manager nodded and hastened away.

Ari placed a quick call to Bobby. While she was supposed to have found her own assistant, she'd never got around to it. "Jay's rushed off to the hospital and I'm left here all alone. Care to join me for dessert and a chat?"

He arrived ten minutes later and joined her. "I'll have the grilled seabass with vegetables, thanks," he told the waiter when he approached the table. "Followed by the chocolate mousse cake you're famous for, and a light beer."

"You clearly know the menu if you can order without it." Ari sipped her drink to wash down the last of the cake she had savoured with every bite.

"This is one of the restaurants Max and I come to quite often. It's close to where we live, and Max knows the owner. So…" He shrugged lightly. "What can I do and are you paying?"

"Jay left me five hundred to cover the costs, so I guess *he* will be. But what I want to know is, do you know a well-respected psychic?"

*****

Jay rushed down the hallway of the children's hospital and saw Denver, who noticed him, and pointed to the room in front of him.

Jay barrelled through the doorway and saw Mari sleeping on the couch opposite the bed, and Gloria at Andrew's bedside, holding his hand and sobbing.

"Cut the act, Gloria, it's pathetic," he muttered and walked around to the other side of the bed to lean over his son. "Andrew. It's Dad," he said softly and stroked his son's forehead. "I'm here, buddy." For all the rush to get there, for all the thoughts he'd had from the past, the present, and the future, as he stood staring down at his son, he realised, he truly did not have any feelings for him whatsoever.

How bad was that? Pretty damn bad. But hatred, on behalf of Gloria, had sabotaged his son into hating him, and in return, Jay had become so exhausted fighting Gloria, that he'd actually stopped caring about the boy he helped make and raise and had once loved. Yes, he'd loved Andrew from conception, but the last four years had drained that from him. The anger, the hatred, the hateful words that were his mother's but came from his mouth. Jay knew it wasn't Andrew's fault, but he also knew that hate can exhaust even the most emotionally and psychologically strong person. And he realised in that moment, looking down at his ten-year-old son, a son he had barely spent enough time with in the last four years that he was done caring. He was empty. He felt nothing. No grief, no care, no love.

"I'm so sorry, Andrew," Jay whispered, stroking his son's face. "I'm so sorry it's come to this."

"You finally turned up," Gloria spat, rising to her feet to level off with him, still clutching Andrew's hand. "I've called you for hours."

"And so has Bobby whom you also harassed," Jay said to her. "But I was busy all day and then out to dinner. You don't run my schedule, Gloria. All you needed to do was send a text telling me the details and that he was okay. I came when I could."

"That's not good enough," Gloria spat.

"I don't fucking care." Jay leaned over the bed towards her. "I don't fucking care about you, or your demands, or your needs, or your wants. You don't call and demand what you want out of me. You send me a text and let me know, *like a civilised adult*, what has happened and where to come. *That's it!* We could actually get along better if you did that, but you refuse to and always want to make a scene instead, because, oh, poor Gloria, woe is me." He rolled his eyes. "I don't fucking care, Gloria. I'm taking Marisol home and tucking her into bed. Andrew's fine. He's going to be just fine and dandy." He walked over to his daughter and lifted her into his arms.

"Daddy," she murmured and wrapped her arms around

his neck, snuggling her face into it.

"I'm taking you home, Mari. You'll be in your own bed soon." He rubbed her back and walked out the door.

"You get back here Jay Fucking Daniels," Gloria screeched behind him, finally letting go of Andrew's hand and racing out the door. "You don't get to take my daughter and walk away."

Denver glanced from Jay to Gloria. "I'll be going too, love. There's no need for me to stay here all night."

"What?" Gloria spun around. "You're leaving me too? How dare you!"

Denver saw the fire in her eyes and knew it well. He also knew not to play the game. "You don't need me here, Gloria. Just like you don't need Jay or Marisol here. She needs to sleep, just as Andrew does, and he doesn't need you vying for an audience because you want attention. I'll be back in the morning." He walked off and managed to catch the elevator going down.

"Waking up to her, are you?" Jay asked.

"Was always awake to her. She's just changed."

"She changed when she met you."

Silence

"I'm sorry."

More silence.

The doors whooshed open, and Jay strode out the door to the car he'd had wait for him. "I'm taking Mari back to Gloria's so she can sleep in her own bed. You're welcome to hitch a ride, and then look after my daughter as you always do." Jay managed to climb in without letting Mari go.

Denver got in behind him and sat against the door.

The drive back to Gloria's was quiet, as was the elevator

ride up. Jay put Mari to bed and tucked the blankets around her, waiting a few minutes until she settled in. Then he kissed her goodnight and turned off her light. He closed the door and realised, that, while he no longer had feelings for Andrew, he still fiercely loved Mari. She was his little princess, and he wasn't about to let her go easily. He saw Denver hovering in the hall off the kitchen doorway. "She's asleep. You look like you need some." He walked for the door.

"Jay. I truly am sorry."

Jay's hand froze on the door handle, but he didn't turn around. "For what?"

"The way this has turned out. I wouldn't want to go through what you're going through."

Jay scoffed. "A little too late for that." He opened the door and left.

Chapter 16

A few weeks later, after finishing up with some interviews for her new book, Ari made her way down one of New York's busiest streets. "It must be around here somewhere," she muttered, checking the GPS on her phone, trying to find the stationery store that had just opened the week before. She had decided to walk there, potentially a big mistake, but she was toughing it out.

Looking up at the street sign, Ari checked her phone a third time and found she was way off course. "Three streets over and two streets right. Jesus. Why did I decide to walk?" The palm of her hand slapped against her forehead. "Ugh, but I don't have to, do I." She spun around, looked for a taxi, and madly waved one down. When she climbed in and gave him directions to the store, he made small talk by asking about her day as he found his way to the address. Once there, she paid and thanked him for the ride, then alighted and stood in front of New York's latest emporium, dedicated solely to stationery of all kinds from all over the world, and stared at the shop windows for a few moments. "Love it!" she said and slowly walked through the door.

Ari stocked up on all she needed, and when she checked

her watch, she realised three hours had passed since her arrival.

"Better get home or Jay'll be wondering where I am."

Not that he would be. Really. He'd been distracted since the emergency with Andrew and had gone every day to see Marisol and spend time with her. He'd only gone back to the hospital the day Andrew had been discharged, three days after the accident, to take him home and get him settled. But then nothing. He'd say hello when he picked Mari up but he didn't spend time with his son. He had no idea how his son felt about it.

Jay told her all of this every night when he came home, and they were relaxing for an hour before bed. He'd speak animatedly about his time with Marisol and what they did. He thanked God that Gloria hadn't been pushing things or making things worse. And while Ari was glad he was spending time with his daughter, he hadn't been the same with her.

Things were a little tense, but at least he hadn't snapped at her again. Sex was a little rougher and faster than usual, with Jay mainly serving himself, but it wasn't anything she couldn't handle. He was distracted, and Ari knew he'd just be thinking about his kids and how to be a better dad to them. That was important to her. She knew they came first. Knew they would always come first. Knew they had to. Who was she to say otherwise? She'd been encouraging him to go every time Gloria had called. She wanted him to see his kids more than he did and she knew he would be a great dad again, if only Gloria let him.

But all of this just made her wonder if she was making a big mistake trying to be the other person in his life. She would not come first, so maybe this wouldn't work after all.

Doubts plagued her on the days he spent with his kids. Doubts plagued her on the days he spent with her. Doubts could make a person crazy. And she didn't want to be crazy.

Ari wandered down road after road heading in the general direction of Brooklyn, but soon she found herself on a smaller, less busy street, less packed with cars and people. She checked her phone for her location. "Ah, bugger!" She'd turned around and should've taken the next street right instead of this one. "Why don't I just take taxis?" she chided herself. "It would be so much easier and less time consuming." But she knew it was because she wanted to see the neighbourhood in all its spring glory. "Better take one over." She came to a stop at a walk way and waited while the few cars on the road rolled on by.

A massive neon sign, in the shape of an arrow pointing down and ninety degrees to the right, was hanging from the building across the road from her. It flickered green for a few beats, then turned itself on.

Someone behind her made a noise. "Well, if that don't beat all."

Ari glanced over her shoulder. "Excuse me?"

"That." An elderly man pointed. "The arrow. It hasn't worked in the ten years it's been here. Basically stopped right after they put it up. Nothing wrong with it apparently, just won't work. But now here we are…and it suddenly springs to life."

Ari looked at the sign and saw the word *psychic* was written in neon above the arrow.

That could not be…

"Seriously," she muttered, her brow furrowing. *The word psychic with a neon arrow. It's like the world is trying to tell me something.* She hadn't been to a psychic yet. Bobby had laughed at her when she'd asked at dinner that night, and then saw she was serious. He'd come up with a list of people his friends and co-workers had used and given it to her. *"Don't know if they're reputable, but my friends swear by them,"* he'd said when she took the list.

Quickly digging out her day planner, Ari found the list, but when comparing the names to the street sign she didn't see it on there.

"Almost like the universe trying to tell someone something," the old man said.

The light changed for them to cross, and Ari kept an eye on the sign as she walked towards it. It flickered off and on rapidly, as if trying to catch her attention, and just as she and the man passed, a loud grinding sound happened behind them and then a smash of metal on the ground.

"What the fuck!" Ari cried and ducked down, rushing a few steps forward before turning around.

The sign had crashed down just as they'd walked under it. The neon arrow was still pointing down the side street towards the psychic, still trying to tell someone to go and see them.

"Oh, that's definitely a sign," the old man said, looking at Ari. "And we were the only two walking under it."

She returned his look. "What? Are you saying it's meant for one of us?"

"Wouldn't be me, darlin', so it has to be you." He tipped his hat and moved on down the street as if nothing had happened.

By now store owners and the few people in the street had stopped to inquire if she was fine, and someone called emergency services to let them know.

Anything for You

Ari stood staring at the sign, blinking off and on, trying to get her attention, and as stupid as she thought it all was, she decided to just go.

"Oh, all right." She marched off down the street and found the smaller, matching sign on a store front on her left. The word *psychic* above a green arrow flickered to catch her attention, and she stood staring at it, contemplating whether to go in.

"Don't go and see him; he's a charlatan."

Ari spun around to see a withered old lady with white hair wrapped in a bun. "Excuse me?"

"That boy is a charlatan." The old woman wagged her finger at Ari. "I should know. He's my grandson."

"Grandma, what are you—oh, sorry, I didn't realise." A younger woman stopped beside the elderly lady. "Grandma likes to talk to strangers. She thinks it gets the customers in."

"And the one behind me. She says he's her grandson and a charlatan." Ari pointed at the store over her shoulder.

"That's my brother," the woman said. "And I tend to agree. Do you need to see a psychic?"

"Well, the sign out on the street fell down and I figured it was *literally* a sign when it didn't crush me like a bug." Ari pointed back to the main road. "You'll need to get that sorted."

"I'll let my brother know. Unless I let the police do it. Might serve him right."

"Come, child, let me do a reading for you. You're troubled." The old woman held out her hand to Ari.

"Aren't all people who see a psychic?" Ari replied and allowed the woman to lead her across the road to her own shop.

They entered, and the old woman gestured for Ari to sit

down at a round table in the back room. "I'll just prepare myself." The woman wandered into a side room and let the curtain close behind her.

Ari glanced around and asked the younger woman, "Are we allowed to record these sessions?"

"You can record the voice, but not the picture," the woman told her and lit a couple of candles around the room. "Grandma believes the soul disappears if footage is taken."

"Oh…" Ari glanced away and saw a small animal skull. "Okay." She saw the old woman come into the room wrapped in a red cape with glitter stars on it. *Mmm-huh*, she thought, *she might be as big a charlatan as her grandson.* Saying nothing, Ari checked her phone's battery usage, and seeing it was low, quickly pulled out her charger and plugged it in. She tapped on the record button and set them on the table. "Your granddaughter said I could record it."

The old woman nodded as her granddaughter placed a pack of tarot cards in front of her. In front of the cards sat a crystal ball. She picked up the cards and shuffled them deliberately, cutting them into two, and shuffling again. She finally placed them on the table. "Cut the cards."

Ari had played cards with Jay, so she did what she was told and watched the woman shuffle them again before finally placing one face up on the table.

"Mmm…" The woman laid a few more and stroked her chin. She set the cards aside and stared into the crystal ball, and a few moments later motioned for Ari to give her hands to her.

"Ah, okay." Ari laid her hands in the woman's, who started tracing the lines on her palms.

"Mmm…" The woman looked to the ball, then to the cards. "Yes. I see."

"Mind telling me then?" Ari said, trying to hide her laughter. This was worse than she'd expected.

"He will never put you first until the ones who are, have disappeared."

Confused, Ari's brows furrowed slightly, and she tilted her head. "Excuse me?"

"Your man," the woman said. "The man you lie with every night and consummate the devil's relationship with. He will never put you first until the ones who are first have disappeared. You will always come last. Behind all of them. His anger is too strong; it is taking all of his energy, his anger, his will. They all come first. They all come before you. They always will until they have disappeared, and you move to the head of the line." She flung Ari's hands away and gasped. Her head fell back, and her body jerked.

Shocked, Ari drew her hands to her chest and stared, wide-eyed, at the woman. "Is she all right?" she whispered.

"She's fine." The young woman watched her grandmother closely. "It's all part of it."

The old woman threw her hands in the air and wavered back and forth in her seat. "He has vengeance on his mind. He will take it when he can. He will take it because he must. He will take it because he cannot afford to lose you. He will take it when the time is right and then, and only then, will he be with you fully. Completely. Until then, you lie in the bed of the devil who seeks vengeance."

Her hands fell to her sides and her head fell forward. Her breathing was ragged, but she managed to raise her arms to the table. "Here lies the death card. It signifies the death of one so another can rise. Here is the fool, which you are, but don't know any the wiser. Here is the magician. You are wilful, willing to make new things happen, but that won't be up to you. The high priestess shows a time for learning, for using your intuition, but you will not. The lovers show imbalance, one-sidedness, and disharmony, that all comes from him. Your relations are one-sided in and out of the bed of the devil. An upside-down hermit means loneliness, isolation, paranoia, sadness, and you will feel all of it. An upright wheel of fortune means chance, destiny, fate, karma, turning points, life cycles, of which you are going through and think the devil is the answer to all of it. A reversed justice is injustice, dishonesty, lack of responsibility, deceit, negative karma that all comes from him. And here he is, an upright devil, trapped in bondage, addictions and depression, negative thoughts and betrayal. All him. All of it is him and you are in the middle of it, you stupid girl."

She dramatically swept her hand over the cards. Some were brushed aside, and others fell onto the floor. "You must leave him. You must leave now before you are too far gone. Run, run away, run so far away. He is bad for you; he is wrong for you. He is the devil incarnate. Leave, go now, go now go back to where you came from before it's too late." Her voice rose until she was shrieking.

The young woman quickly gathered Ari and hurried her from the shop and onto the street. "I'm so sorry. She normally doesn't do that."

"Do what? Freak people out?" Ari held her phone to her chest. It was still recording but she didn't notice. She was too busy trying to calm her heart that was beating hard.

"Normally she doesn't." The woman cocked her head in the direction of the store. "She seems to have calmed down. But this has never happened before, so you won't have to

Anything for You

pay. I'm so sorry about this."

"Ah, thanks," Ari said weakly. "I better go." Without a backward glance, she hurried to the main street and flagged down a cab. Once she'd given her address, she finally released her phone, turned off the recorder, and quickly checked the recording that was made. Hearing the old woman's voice, an ice-cold shiver fled down her spine, and she turned it off and shoved it into her bag.

The ride back to Brooklyn took twenty minutes and her heart had slowed to normal by the time she entered the brownstone. "Jay…you here?" She paused but heard only silence. "Guess not." She hurried up to her office and left her shopping on the floor before returning to search the house for Jay. She checked every room and found no one. Not even a note. She noticed the clock on the wall said it was nearly six, but since Jay wasn't home, and she'd had no messages from him all day, and he didn't pick up her calls, she decided to go out to dinner instead.

After calling for another cab, she freshened up and waited for it. Twenty minutes later, she was sitting in one of Brooklyn's most famous pizza shops waiting on her two slices. She checked her phone. Still no messages from Jay. She texted Bobby, asking if he'd heard from him.

No, I haven't.

Do you know where Jay is?

No, I don't.

What are you doing for dinner?

Meeting Max at El Gardos.

Ari sighed and threw her phone into her bag as the waitress set the plate in front of her. With a large ice-cold cola on the rocks, it was the perfect indulgence meal; especially with the way she'd been feeling lately. A little bloated, and a little ignored.

She enjoyed the atmosphere of the restaurant as she ate. She listened to the conversations going on around her, the fun and frivolity of the other customers. She missed Jay and his fun and frivolity, and eventually decided to go home. As she dug around in her bag for her phone to call another cab, she heard shouting towards the front of the restaurant and turned around in her booth. Two masked men were waving guns at the girl at the register, demanding money. Screams sounded through the room, sending Ari into a panic. Not knowing what to do, and keeping her eyes on the two men, she slid under the table and curled into a ball. "Don't kill me," she whispered over and over, clutching her bag to her chest and rocking back and forth. She crouched against the wall as far from the walkway as she could, hoping they didn't come to the back of the restaurant, hoping they didn't bend down to look under the tables, hoping they didn't see her.

But someone saw the men because men shouted at them and before Ari knew it, it was all over, and someone was yelling that they were gone, and everyone could come out from their hiding spots.

Ari waited, unsure about moving, until the voice calmly walked through the restaurant telling them it was okay, the men were gone, the police had taken them, and they could come out. She slowly poked her head over the seat and slid upwards. She saw other patrons doing the same, and knew she had to get the hell out of there and back home.

The restaurant owner and his family hailed cabs for the people who wanted to leave, and Ari was among them. She got her ride back to Jay's and hurried inside, locking the doors securely behind her.

"Where have you been?"

She screamed and spun around. Seeing it was Jay, she clutched her chest. "Don't do that to me."

"I asked you a question." His speech was slurred, and he was wearily leaning against the doorjamb of the lounge room, a glass full of amber liquid in his hand.

"I was out for pizza, since you weren't here when I got home, and the place was just held up at gun point." She brushed her hair out of her face. "Where have you been all day?"

"None of your fucking business," he growled and turned around. "You need to stop eating junk food. You're getting fat."

Shocked, Ari bristled at the insult and her fear slipped away. "*So what* if I've gained weight? I was a hefty girl when you met me, and a hefty girl when you first bedded me, and *now* you're complaining? Maybe if you didn't keep taking me out to all of the restaurants you do I wouldn't be gaining weight. Either way, my weight is none of your fucking business."

He spun back around and waved the hand that held the glass at her. "You're getting fat; do something about it. I don't like you fat."

"Well, I don't like you drunk," she yelled. "Which you are right now. And you're being an insulting pig, which I don't care for. You've never worried about my weight, haven't even worried about me for the last couple of weeks, so why do you fucking care right now? You weren't here when I got home, just like most days lately, so I went and found something to eat to get out of this depressing house. Because that's what this is now. Since Andrew's accident and you spending time with the kids... I have no problem with that, but it's clearly affecting you in other ways. *Like insulting me.* And never mind the fact I almost got clobbered by a falling sign earlier today, or that the restaurant was held up at gunpoint, oh, no, you just fucking worry about complaining about my fucking weight and how it's affecting *you,* poor old fucking Jay. Well, *fuck you,* Jay Daniels." Ari stormed up the stairs to Jay's bedroom, collected her things from her bedside table, and stormed back down to her old bedroom, slamming and locking the door behind her. "Fuck you, Jay Daniels," she spat.

"Ari?" Jay stumbled up the stairs to his room. "Ari?" He saw her open bedside table drawer and stumbled back down to her room, banging on the door. "Ari? Let me in. Ari, I know you're in there. Let me in."

She hurried into the bathroom and closed the door, wanting a moment of peace and quiet to cry in.

"Ari," Jay raged and backed up. He came at the door and kicked it hard. It shattered off the jamb and bounced back against the wall. "Ari."

Ari hurried from the bathroom and saw the wood splinters on the floor and the raging redness of his eyes. "What the fucking hell are you doing, kicking in doors? Fuck you, Jay. Get a fucking grip. You're drunk."

"I'm not going to lose you," he yelled and grabbed her roughly by the arms. "You're my woman, Ari, and I'll be damned if I'm letting you walk out of here." He paused and stared at the terrified expression on her face, his foggy brain remembering something she'd said earlier. "You said a sign fell on you. Are you all right? You could have died."

"Like *you* care. But I'm fine. It missed me." She tried

pulling away, but his grip was too tight. "Let me go."

"And you said the restaurant was held up by two gunmen…" He pulled her to his chest, smashing her against him and encaging her within his arms. "I could have lost you, Ari. I could have lost you."

She struggled against him and the suffocation overwhelming her and managed to break free. "No thanks to you. I wouldn't have been there if you were home, and we were eating here together. Where the hell were you besides getting plastered?"

"I wasn't out getting plastered," he slurred and pulled her closer. "I only drank when I got home, and you weren't here."

"So why didn't you bother texting me, or calling me, to let me know what was happening? Not even Bobby knew where you were," she accused.

"You knew I was going to spend time with Marisol. We've been out all day and I didn't think it would be right to make calls while spending time with her."

"Then call me when you drop her off and let me know you're on your way home," Ari said. "You didn't even bother doing that."

"I'm sorry, Ari," he sputtered, on the verge of tears. "I don't want to lose you now. I can't lose you now."

"Then don't insult me, either." She scanned his face to see if he was being real. But he was an actor, so she really didn't know sometimes. "My weight may be getting higher, but it's all the food we've been eating. It can't be helped. I'll just have to cut back. But that doesn't mean you need to be mean and rude over it. You said that didn't matter to you."

"It doesn't," he sobbed and fell to his knees, his arms locked around her legs. "I'm so sorry. You're right. I'm drunk and trying to get a grip on things. Gloria got into it with me, and I got angry and came home and drank. I didn't eat anything and made it worse. I don't have the right to attack you. I'm so sorry. I'm trying to sort this out, I really am. But it's going to take time."

Ari stood in the middle of her room, her hand on Jay's head, giving it an absentminded pat. She didn't know what to do. She didn't know how to handle this outburst, didn't know how to handle any of them at any time, except to just be there and be supportive. She remembered back to the psychic and what she'd said. She really needed to listen to that recording again.

"Don't insult me again, Jay. I won't tolerate it. Regardless of what Gloria does to you. Because this is not the first time with Gloria, and it won't be the last unless she's out of your life permanently."

"No, baby, no, Ari. I won't, I'm sorry," he sobbed into her crotch. "I'm so sorry."

Ari glanced down at him. So was she.

She thought about the psychic's last words to her.

Chapter 17

May was coming on bright and spring-like, and it was not only Ari's birthday month, but the first anniversary of them meeting.

"Hard to believe it's almost a year since we met," Ari said one morning over breakfast as she was rinsing dishes at the sink and gazing out at the glorious spring day.

Jay seemed back to his old self and was rather cheerful. "It is and I have something very special planned, so keep the date free." Turning the page of the newspaper, he read something about a house fire at the bottom of the page.

"It's free. So's my birthday which is coming up."

"Mmm? Did I hear something about a birthday? Whose birthday?" Jay briefly glanced at her before continuing to read.

"Funny," Ari said dryly and wiped her hands. "If you're not interested then I plan on spending the day blowing up your credit card."

"You don't have my...wait," he turned to her, "is that where it went? I couldn't find it in my wallet."

"Calm down." She sat beside him. "I don't have it, my birthday's not until three weeks' time, and a week later is our anniversary. Your card should be in your wallet unless you lost it."

"It is. I'm just joking." He grinned and folded the paper up. "Listen. I know things have been bad these last few weeks—"

"More like two months," Ari muttered.

He sighed and took her hand. "I'm sorry. I know it's been rough since Andrew's accident and that was back in March, but things calmed down during April, you know. We did the Easter hunt with the kids, saw the Easter Parade, had lunch at my folks' house. Things have come good in the last month. And I've apologised profusely for insulting you about your weight and for being an asshole that night. I shouldn't have done that. I was just under a lot of stress at the time, and things really got to me, and I stupidly drank on an empty stomach. But the last three or four weeks have calmed down and things are great again." He kissed the palm of her hand, knowing it made her melt. "You know I'm sorry, Ari. I love you and would never hurt you."

Ari breathed calmly, trying not to let the emotions of the last six weeks start up. "I know. And just like you, I'm sick and tired of Gloria and her phone calls. Personally, I wish she'd just drop dead. Which is a really bad thing to say, especially as she's the mother of your children, and at one point, you did love her. But I've never met anyone who makes the anger and hatred rise in me as much as she does."

"Now you know how I feel." Jay caressed her hand with his lips. "It can be hard to keep your anger under control. Hey, maybe we should go to *The Chop Shop*. I did a couple of times when things went to shit back in March. It helped release everything I was feeling. Maybe we should go together."

"And maybe Gloria should just drop dead," Ari muttered

more to herself as she gazed off into the distance.

"I wish." Jay thought about the plan he'd started manoeuvring into place. "I know she and Denver do drugs every now and then. She did it with me when we were together, but more so now; maybe I could have her arrested for it."

"And then you'd get the kids permanently. How would you feel about that?"

He thought about it and shrugged. "Don't really have a problem with it. With Andrew, yeah, but not with Mari. She's still Daddy's little princess and me spending all that time with her has proved it."

"But Andrew? And having the kids full-time?"

"It wouldn't be a problem, would it?" He watched her face for a sign of anything. Something.

Thoughts passed through her head. "Marisol, no, but Andrew…"

"Yeah…" Jay murmured. "Andrew…"

"Let's change the subject. My interviews are all over and I have nothing booked until September and October for the next one, so we have all of summer free, well, except for August when I'll need to make sure everything's in place for the book launch, but we could do stuff, travel, go overseas, Hawaii, visit some cities we haven't been to. I'd love to see Chicago, Vegas, New Orleans, Miami. Maybe go somewhere for my birthday, and our anniversary," she said, watching his face. "We haven't really had any holidays yet and I've been here since October. It's been all about New York or states adjacent."

"We could." Jay nodded in agreement. "I don't have custody of the kids for summer, but Gloria usually dumps them on me so she and Denver can fly off to wherever they go. We could set up a couple of holidays, maybe one long one…a month…then come back, rest up, and fly off again, so we're not always on planes, or travelling."

"Sounds good. It's my first summer here in New York, my first summer here in the U.S. I want to explore before winter kicks in again."

"And before it's the first anniversary of you being here, which will come around quickly enough," Jay added. "It's your seventh month being here. Should we celebrate the anniversary?"

Ari snorted. "Hardly, considering we have our one-year meeting anniversary. What are your plans for it?"

"My plans are…" His gaze darted away. "Top secret. I cannot tell."

"Are we going to let Gloria ruin them?" Ari didn't know why she kept bringing Gloria up when she was the one who kept telling Jay not to. Except for the fact she was a part of Jay and the kid's lives, just as Ari was a part of theirs, and that made Gloria a part of hers.

Jay sighed. "Ari! You used to tell me off for bringing up her name all the time, and now you're doing it."

"I know, and was just thinking that, and I don't know why except for the fact she's your ex-wife and a massive pain in the arse of our lives. And she ruins everything. Especially this year. Ever since the Christmas party when she saw us together, she's been trying to pull us apart, and it seems to be working. In March we did *so* well," she said sarcastically and sighed. She rested her chin in her hand. "Sorry. I've become as bad as you, bringing her up all the time. I just want her to go away."

"So do I and believe me I'm working on it, but it's going to take time." Jay slumped in his seat and clasped his hands in front of his face, elbows on the table. "I've come up with a solution to the problem. I don't know how long it will take. But it could work. It just needs time."

"How much time?" Ari asked wearily.

He looked at her. "I don't know, baby. I just don't know."

*****

Ari thought about Jay's comments for days. She thought about them while shopping, while eating, while trying to bang out five thousand words of a new story she'd come up with, and all of them distracted her. Distracted her from working, from playing, and from doing. Anything.

What was Jay up to? What was going to take time? A plan to get rid of Gloria? To get her out of their lives forever?

She thought through her feelings on the situation. She'd come to feel as much anger and hatred towards Gloria as Jay did. That wasn't healthy, emotionally or psychologically, and it was reflecting in their relationship.

The last two weeks of March had been harrowing but had smoothed out by April. And May was shaping up to be better. But all of it left Ari feeling uneasy. So did Jay being gone every day.

Not that he needed to be there every day. He'd played host and tour guide enough for her to be able to get around the city without his help. He claimed he was working on the movie of her book. But that had been happening since last year, so why was that taking so long? The kids were in school every day, and he wasn't spending a lot of time with them, but he did have his finger in a few pies directing and producing for his friends, so maybe that was it.

And maybe it was Gloria.

The thought chilled Ari to the bone.

Was he getting up to something with Gloria?

Nothing according to the latest gossip articles.

Gloria was travelling with Denver and the kids on weekends to music festivals or concerts. What she was doing during the week, Ari didn't know, but supergluing herself to Denver would probably have been it.

No, Jay wouldn't be seeing Gloria.

Maybe he was seeing Merrick, or Ross, trying to figure out ways of legally getting rid of her. Because *illegal* ways of getting rid of her just wasn't Jay's thing.

Was it?

Ari thought seriously about it. Would Jay illegally get rid of Gloria? Did he think the only way out of their situation was to…*murder* Gloria?

Oh, hell no, Ari thought, trying to justify his absences every day. *There's no way Jay would stoop to murdering his ex. The mother of his children…*

Would he?

The question hung heavy in her brain. She dare not say the words out loud for fear they might come true. But something nagged at her. Something in the way he brushed off questions about it when she'd asked. It nagged at her when he just left without saying where he was going, or what he was doing. Nagged at her repeatedly.

Where the hell was he going every day?

Thrusting herself up from her desk, she marched downstairs to his office, making sure he wasn't home along the way, and walked right in.

"Okay, Jay Daniels, where are you today?" Ari made her way to his desk and scanned it for his planner, hoping he'd left it behind as he sometimes did. She found it shoved to the side under some papers and opened it to that day's date and checked. She checked the previous days. She checked the days going all the way back to March when Andrew's accident had happened.

Isn't that when Jay said he'd been trying to figure something out and had a plan?

She noted what he'd written down. *Direct ep of NM* was written across every day for a week and nothing else. Another week had notations for getting in a script for a friend's show which needed to be finished. Another week had notes about catching up with *FD about BE*, and *RT about GH*.

"No idea who or what they are," Ari muttered and flipped through the last eight weeks of pages. They were all the same. She turned a page and saw a note. *JG at EW.*

"Wait…didn't I see that before?" She went back to March and slowly looked through each week. "Here it is. *JG at EW.*" Flipping another page, and another, and another, by the time she was done, she saw Jay was meeting *JG at EW* every Wednesday. She flipped through the rest of May and saw the same notation, and the same for June, July and August. It was the same for the rest of the year, but there were question marks besides those notes.

"Who the hell is JG?" Puzzled, Ari scanned the rest of the year for other notes, but besides scribbled bits about directing or writing, the only other note was about JG.

She sighed and closed Jay's planner, sliding it back under

the papers. Wednesday was yesterday, so she couldn't find out what he was up to until next week. And while she didn't know where Jay went, she did know what time he needed to be there as he'd noted it down.

*****

Thinking things through was one of Ari's strong points. She did it for her novels, and now she did it for how she was going to follow Jay. She'd thought back through the last few weeks to when he'd left the house. There was no specific time, so she couldn't follow him without being obvious.

She'd thought of using Bobby and had asked him if he knew where Jay went every day because she was worried about him doing something stupid to Gloria. When Bobby said he didn't really know, she specifically asked about Wednesdays, and said she wanted to plan something for him. But Bobby said he had no idea.

"Would you tell me if you did?" she'd asked.

"Obviously not," he'd replied. "Confidentiality and all that."

"Would you help me if I asked you to say nothing to Jay?"

"Help you with what?"

"Finding out where he goes each day?"

"Spy on him, you mean?"

"If that's what you want to call it," Ari said. "I'm worried he's getting into something he shouldn't be trying to find a way to get rid of Gloria."

"Oh, that could be bad," Bobby murmured. "Look, I dictate his schedule when it comes to interviews, publicity, etc. What he does on his personal time is his, but..." He flipped through his calendar. "I don't have him down for Wednesdays."

"Would you help me on Wednesday? You'll need a car he doesn't know."

"So we are spying on him?"

"I guess you could say we are."

"Okay. Let me know when you've figured out how we're doing it."

After that conversation, Ari had gone to an electrical store and bought a few things she might need in order to follow Jay. It was funny how easy it was to buy tracking devices in order to know where people were at all times. So it turned out, she didn't need Bobby after all.

A week later, on Wednesday, Jay was in the kitchen when Ari came downstairs. "Hey, you're not going out today?"

"I am, but not until eleven." Jay bit into his jam smeared toast. "Why?"

"I just need to pop out and get some things. Will you be home for lunch or dinner?"

"Dinner. Are you planning anything special?"

"Mmm, I thought roast beef…"

"I meant for the day, besides popping out and getting some things."

"Meh." Ari lightly shrugged a shoulder. "Who knows what the day will bring once I set foot out in it? It's nice today. I might shop all day."

"With *your* credit card, right?" Jay drawled.

"Ha-ha," Ari replied and set to work preparing her breakfast.

She left just after nine and took the taxi she'd called into the city to do some shopping. That shopping was for a wig. She already had the big black glasses, and had brought along a black long-sleeved top to change into before she got back to the brownstone. She just needed a change of hairstyle.

An hour later, she walked out of the store wearing a black, shoulder length wig that matched her top and jeans. Donning her glasses, she glanced at her watch and hailed a taxi, making her way to Queens and the car rental company. She paid for the day and drove home, pulling over to the kerb down the road in time to see Jay's car pull out of the driveway. She watched for a few seconds, until he was down the road, and then followed.

She followed Jay around the city and into upstate New York, hanging back when necessary, losing him when she thought he'd caught her. But she didn't worry. She'd attached a tracker to his car a few days ago and had the GPS of it on her phone, so she could see where he was going. And where he was going was a surprise.

She pulled under a tree in the foliage lined street, opposite an impressive building. A sign reading *Elderwood Way* was bolted above the double metal gates and she saw Jay's car parked out the front of the main door. But she didn't see Jay.

"What the fuck…" she muttered and gazed over the building. Impressive in its construction, *Elderwood* was clearly built in the previous century. It sported turrets at both ends of what was a good half-mile long building, and it was a good four storeys high.

"How the fuck am I supposed to find out why he's here?" Rubbing her eyes, she sighed at the prospect ahead. "Okay, get a grip and let's google the shit out of this place." She went to work, and for fifteen minutes read all about *Elderwood* being a sanatorium for the bat shit crazy. "Nice," she muttered. "But how do I get in?" She checked the map of the sanatorium's layout and saw it was surrounded by forest. "I could go for a walk…"

Grabbing her bag and her bottle of water, Ari locked her car and walked down the street, keeping her eye out for Jay leaving, or anyone else walking in the area. She tried not to act suspiciously and kept on until she saw the fence line through the trees.

The sign on the fence read *'electric fencing, do not climb'*.

"No plans on that," she said and had a drink before moving on. She walked another few hundred yards down the road and then slipped quietly into the woods, doubling back towards the fence. Staying hidden by the trees, she followed the fence down the side of the property until the back of the building came into view. A wide terrace held seating for many, and quite a few were seated there. Three wide steps led down to a lush, neatly clipped green lawn which continued until it reached the lake beckoning all to come and swim in it.

"Nice." She hid behind the trees and slowly made her way along, scanning the crowd for Jay. She thought she saw him, but wasn't sure, so she pulled out her phone and tapped on the camera app, using her fingers to zoom in so she could use it like binoculars. She scanned the crowd and found Jay sitting at a small old-fashioned metal table on the lawn with an elderly man, who was leaning towards him. The man's back was to her, and she couldn't see who it was to figure out if she knew him or not.

Studying the tree line to see if she could move on along the perimeter, Ari saw there was about five metres before the trees cleared and she would be seen. Keeping low, she sneaked through the foliage and hid behind a massive bush growing around a tree. She retrained her camera on Jay and the elderly man, and hit the record button, waiting for Jay to move, or both of them to move, or for something to happen.

She was well hidden and out of anyone's eye range but standing close to a tree she hoped wasn't poisonous. She didn't need a rash at this point in her life for Jay to figure out she'd been here, especially if the tree was native to only that area. *Fuck!* she thought. *This has gone beyond ridiculous.*

Watching the time tick by on the camera, she periodically glanced around in case someone was approaching. After another fifteen minutes, the elderly man stood to leave, and glanced around before laying a hand on Jay's arm and leaning in close. He gave Jay's shoulder a gentle squeeze before walking inside.

Ari watched until an orderly in a white uniform escorted Jay inside and out of view, and then decided it was time to leave. She slowly found her way back to the street, casually popped onto the sidewalk, and proceeded back to her car, looking out for Jay's along the way. But his was gone from the parking lot, and when she finally got to hers, she slumped in the seat and shivered.

"What did I just witness?" she asked herself, breathing slowly as she tried to figure out what she'd just seen. But she couldn't. She watched the footage and her brows furrowed in frustration. "Who the hell were you talking to? And why were you talking to him? What the fuck is going on, Jay?"

*****

When Ari finally made her way home it was just after six and Jay was cooking the beef. She stopped off in her office to hide her bag with the wig in it and freshened up. After hours of trying to figure out what was going on, Ari hadn't come up with anything to say to Jay when she saw him. She had no idea who he'd been talking to, or why he'd gone there, but she'd also argued with herself as to whether it was even any of her business. Sighing, she walked down the stairs and into the kitchen.

"Hey. I didn't know what time you'd be home, so I did my own recipe and shoved her in." He closed the oven door and looked up, seeing her slowly walk into the kitchen, a deep frown on her face. "Hey. What's wrong? Did something happen?" Moving quickly to her side, he held her. "Hey, baby. What happened? Did something happen? Tell me."

Not knowing what *to* say, she made up something on the spot. And what mumbled out of her mouth was, "I think I saw a crime."

"What? What crime? Did you report it? Did you film it? Where was it? Have you called the police?"

He stared so intently into Ari's eyes she had to look away and close her own. "No, I said I *think* I saw a crime, but I don't know. I don't know if it *is* a crime, I don't really know what was happening. I just…" She sagged against him, her head falling to his chest, her hands sliding their way around his waist. "I don't know. It was weird."

"Tell me about it. I can tell you if it's a crime or not."

"No…just…hold me." She moved closer into his arms, and her hands slid under his lightweight sweater and t-shirt and found their way over his body. "Just hold me," she murmured, rubbing her hands over his skin. They briefly brushed the scar under his arm pit and kept on moving. "I need to feel you." She felt it several times before sliding her hands away and sighing. "It was just… I don't want to talk about it."

"But baby, if it was a crime you have to tell the cops." Jay pulled away.

"But that's just it." She looked into his brown eyes. "I don't know if it was. It was just a very weird experience that happened, and since I have no idea what the laws and rules are around here, it could have actually been nothing." Her fingers lingered on his skin, and she realised as he watched her that she didn't know if this was something to worry about. She either had to let it go or get to the bottom of it, even if she didn't like the end result.

Chapter 18

Ari's birthday celebration started off with a bang.

Jay let poppers go in their bedroom in the morning, waking Ari from a deep slumber. "Good morning, good morning, it's time to wake up the birthday girl. It's your birthday, it's your birthday, all around the world," he sang.

"Hardly," she mumbled and wiped her eyes before burying her head back into her pillow. "What are you doing?"

"Celebrating your birthday." He brandished a huge bunch of red roses and presented them to her. "It's your birthday, it's your birthday, all around the world."

"Not quite but thank you for the flowers." She sniffed them and set them on the bed. "Is this all I'm getting?"

"Ha! Of course not. I'm going to shower you with gifts all day. I'm also going to make you breakfast in bed because it's Sunday and we have it alone and together."

Gloria was off with Denver and the kids and that meant Ari and Jay were free for a weekend of festivities.

"You know I don't do breakfast in bed. Too many crumbs and shit." Ari rolled onto her back and stretched. "Just another day in New York City."

"It's not just another day, Arial Travers. It's your birthday and here's your first present."

"As long as it's not your dick in my face, I might accept it," she murmured.

"Well, that's just insulting, but no, it's not my dick." Jay set a brightly wrapped present next to her head. "Here. It's not cock-a-doodle-doing."

She sniggered and turned her head. "It's not what?"

Jay grinned and waved at the gift. "Never mind. Just open it."

Ari pulled herself up and opened the present. It was a thousand-dollar gift card to one of her favourite stationery shops in the city. "Ooh, nice. My fave store. I can buy up big."

"I should think so. You've been writing a lot lately. Figured you'd need supplies." Jay slid off the bed, rushed over to the window, and flung back the curtains. "It's a lovely May morning here in New York City, and it's time to get up and enjoy it."

"Why can't I sleep in on my birthday? It's Sunday you know." Ari slid back down under the covers.

"Nope." He threw the covers back and grabbed her hands. "Unless you actually *do* want breakfast in bed, you're getting up. Come on. Time for a fancy breakfast I'm ready to prepare you."

Groaning, Ari let him slip her robe around her and pull her downstairs. When he'd seated her at the table, he started pulling out pots and pans from the cupboards, and food from the fridge.

She surveyed the kitchen bench. "You're not going to make a mess are you? I really only need my normal omelette wrap."

"Normal omelette wrap," Jay mocked. "This is not the day for normality."

Ari watched him whip up pancakes and waffles. Not from

scratch; he had the waffles and pancakes ready to go. But he finished off those suckers with maple syrup and the bacon and eggs he made as a topping.

She thought about Jay and their life together. How it might be destroyed by Gloria, or, from the inside.

He placed the plate in front of her and Ari breathed in the aroma. It made her stomach gurgle and retch. "No." She grabbed her mouth and rushed for the toilet under the stairs, vomiting into the sink before she could shut the door. "Er, no," she managed as last night's dinner came up. "Ugh." Shuddering, she finished off by rinsing her mouth out. "Ugh."

"Baby?" Jay was there by her side. "You okay? Did you eat too much last night? It was the pizza toppings, right? Or that weird dessert?" He got her a fresh hand towel and led her back to the table. "I've moved the plate. Is it the bacon and eggs? I don't think they're off."

"I think it was the combination of the bacon and eggs on the waffle and pancake stack." Ari sat carefully at the table. "I'll just have some juice for now. And maybe scrape the bacon and eggs off. I'll try the waffles and pancakes on their own."

Jay fixed the meal and handed back the plate. "You don't have to eat it. Do you think it's food poisoning?" He sat beside her and moved his plate away from her. "Will you be okay? I'm taking you out all day, and we'll be eating lunch and dinner out."

"Let's just take it one meal at a time." Ari carefully munched on a small forkful of pancakes. It tasted okay, and she felt okay. But she knew she wouldn't be eating much.

"Do you need a doctor?" Jay had already devoured half of his food.

"No, my body just needed to get rid of whatever was

making it sick." Ari carefully ate another bite. "I should be okay. I feel okay now. Just keep bacon and eggs away from me. Do they smell okay to you?"

Jay sniffed what was left. "They smell okay and did when I was making them. Must be your stomach."

"Yeah," Ari mumbled and dismissed the thought. She knew what it was, and it wasn't the food.

*****

Jay took her to a light lunch at the latest hot spot on the best restaurants to eat at list, and then they freshened up at home before heading out to dinner.

He'd showered her with presents all day. Jewellery, a pair of Nike sneakers in blue and pink glitter, her favourite picture of New York that she'd taken, and he'd had blown up and framed, gift cards to more of her favourite stores, and finally a digital photo frame full of pictures of the two of them.

Dinner was at *Lombardo's*, one of the hottest nightspots in New York laid out over multiple levels. On one floor a nightclub, on one floor a bar, and the top floor a restaurant that wound its way up to the rooftop so you could eat inside or out.

"How come we haven't been here yet?" Ari asked as they made their way to their table. "This is incredible."

"Because I was waiting for a special occasion." Jay let her go so she could take the chair the waiter had pulled out for her. "And because I was too busy taking you everywhere else."

"Well…" She rolled her eyes. "I guess one could call a birthday a special occasion."

"Ah, yeah, I think you could," Jay agreed and took his

seat. He thanked the waiter for their menus and glanced out at the view. "It is disgustingly incredible."

"Disgustingly amazing," Ari added. "And disgustingly breathtaking." She gazed across the skyline of Manhattan and followed it out to the Statue of Liberty she saw in the distance. "Just stunning."

"Now *that* the view definitely is." Jay leaned on the table towards her. "I definitely agree with that."

She smiled and turned her head to see him watching her with a smile to match her own. Everything from the past few weeks slipped away. "I love you."

"I love you too, Ari." Jay took her hand and kissed it. "And it's your birthday, so tonight, we celebrate."

"Mmm." She breathed in slowly and tried to work out what food she could have. Eggs and bacon didn't work, but pastries did, so nothing too full of protein. Some of the aromas that had attacked them when they'd walked in had made her salivate, and not in a good way. She scanned the menu and decided on fish, but then thought better of it and chose a vegetable-based meal instead. "I might keep things easy tonight, just as I did for lunch."

"Still feeling ill?" Jay closed his menu and waved their waiter over. "Do you want an entrée?"

"No, I'll just have the vegetable stir-fry. Let my stomach have a rest from all the food it's been consuming. Just one more reason why I've gained weight the last couple of months. It's almost summer, time for a dietary rethink."

"Don't take it too seriously." Jay gave the waiter their order. "There are plenty more restaurants we haven't tried yet."

"I'd better cut back and really go on a diet then." Ari handed her menu over and turned to stare out the window.

"It's a stunning view."

"It is, but it doesn't need to be on a diet."

A soft smile curled up the corners of her lips. "No, maybe not. But I had lost weight before you met me, and it looks like I've gained it back."

"I'm sorry about my comment. I always will be. I didn't mean it. It was just a bad time in our lives."

"I know. It always will be as long as Gloria is around."

"And I'm fixing that, believe me. I've come up with a plan and I'm trying to execute it."

Ari wondered if it had anything to do with the man at the sanatorium. "How?"

"Best you not know such things in case I'm arrested and charged," Jay joked and took a swig of beer.

"What!" she cried out in alarm. "Jay, are you joking?"

"Of course I am," he quickly placated her. "Of course I'm joking. I won't do anything stupid, Ari. It was just a joke. But I *am* trying to fix it. It'll just take a while, that's all."

Her racing heart calmed. "A while is too long and I don't want to talk about her tonight. We've managed not to do all day. Let's not do it now."

"Fine by me. Let's talk about us."

"Do you want more kids?" popped out of Ari's mouth.

"What?" The words didn't register in his brain as he'd been thinking about what he was going to do to Ari that night.

"Do you want more kids?" she repeated.

"Fuck no!" Jay replied, then saw her semi-horrified expression. "But that could just be because of Gloria and the way she's ruined things, ruined the kids, and ruined my relationship with them. I mean if *you* could have kids…that might be a thing down the road. But you're older than me and have said that you won't be having them simply because of your age. I'd like to think we could." He softened. "But I know it won't happen."

Ari noted the softness to his voice and face. His eyes searching hers for something made her search her soul for it too. She wanted him. She wanted this life with him. She wanted babies with him. But she knew that wasn't going to happen. And she knew the rest of it wasn't going to happen while the babies he did have came first. She sighed and changed the subject.

They talked through their meal, with Ari able to eat hers, and made it through dessert, holding hands, and making gooey eyes like lovesick teenagers, before his phone rang.

"Argh!" Ari growled and her head dropped. "It had better be an actual emergency."

Jay looked at the caller ID. He frowned and made a growling noise in his throat. "It's even worse when Denver calls. Hello."

"Mari just wants to say goodnight to her father before she goes to bed." Denver handed his phone over.

"Hello, Daddy. I'm going to bed now and wanted to say goodnight."

Unable to help himself, Jay smiled at his daughter's voice. "Goodnight, Mari, my little princess, sweet dreams. I'll see you during the week."

"Okay, Daddy. Night."

"Night, Mari."

The phone went dead.

"What? No Gloria screeching down the phone like a banshee?" Ari asked, startled that the call had gone better than expected.

"Yeah, I was surprised by that, too." Jay put his phone away and reached for Ari's hand. "But we made it through, Ari, my girl. We made it through another night and another dinner without her."

"Just," Ari quipped and squeezed his hand. "And it's still my birthday. So what plans do you have now, Mr Daniels?"

"Oh, just you wait and see, Ms Travers. Just you wait and see." He gave her a cocky grin and winked.

Chapter 19

A week later they were celebrating their one-year anniversary of meeting. One year of knowing each other. One year of Jay helping Ari to become famous. One year of her being physically close to the man she'd had a major crush on. And one year of her falling in love with him.

"Ari, my girl, are you nearly ready?" Jay called from the bedroom. He rooted around in his closet drawers and found the small velvet box buried underneath his sweats. His gaze lingered on the box a moment before he placed it in the inside pocket of his blazer.

"Nearly there." Ari applied the finishing touches to her make-up and sprayed her favourite perfume over herself. She pulled on her sequinned top, added her jewellery, and slid into her shoes and blazer, then checked herself in the mirror and walked through the closet to the bedroom where Jay was waiting. "Done. Where are we going?"

His lips curled into a huge smile when he saw her. "Somewhere *very* special. It's our anniversary, after all."

"Yeah. Just the anniversary of us meeting, though. Nothing fancy." She brushed off his blazer and rested her hands on his chest. "I mean, our anniversary would technically be

Thanksgiving, or Christmas, wouldn't it?"

"Why wait?" he asked. "Yeah, Thanksgiving is when we declared our love for each other, and started dating. So yeah, that's another anniversary. And yeah, Christmas is when we first did the wild thing, so that will be *another* anniversary." His fingers slid over her forehead, pushing aside the curl that was draped across it. "We can celebrate everything we've done."

"That leads me back to my original question, where are we going?"

"And that leads me back to my original comment, somewhere very special. So we'd better get going." He escorted her downstairs and into the waiting limo that took them into the heart of Manhattan.

"This is not where I was expecting." Ari craned her neck to look up at the high rise building they were standing in front of. "You know I don't like heights. How many floors?"

"Oh, we're not going in here." Jay turned and pointed to the building three doors down. "We're going there."

Ari looked to where he was pointing and saw a mid-sized high rise lit up on every floor. "Okay. A quarter the size. I take it it's a restaurant?"

"Oh, it's more than a restaurant," Jay said mysteriously. "Just wait and see."

They walked down the street and entered the building, giving their coats to the girl at the door.

Jay took her arm in his and guided her down a hallway towards the back of the building that opened to a view of the river and skyline, and a bar. "It's a multi-level playground like the restaurant we went to for your birthday."

"Nice." Ari took in the view. The bar was at one end and

ran the length of the room, a dance floor was at the other, and small, round tables with chairs sat in between. She looked up and saw three more floors wrapped around an atrium of greenery and fairy lights. She heard birds tweeting. "Are there birds in here?"

Jay followed her gaze. "There are. And I thought we'd have a drink here and then move on to the next floor."

"And what's on the next floor?"

"You'll just have to wait and see," Jay told her.

The maître d' escorted them to a table near the window and they ordered their drinks before taking a spin around on the dance floor. Returning to their tables to take in the sparkling lights along the river, they sipped their drinks and chatted until they'd finished.

"And now that phase one of our night is done, let's move on to phase two." Jay took her hand and led the way to the elevator where they went up to the next floor.

The doors opened to a more laid back and relaxed atmosphere. The floor was forest green carpeting, the walls were red velvet, and gold metal detailing was in every other aspect. Thick green vines and branches wound around the atrium, holding up bird cages and fairy lights to give an ethereal forest atmosphere.

They were escorted to a table near the window and given menus to peruse.

"Thank you." Jay smiled and leaned in to Ari. "When this place opened it sounded amazing. It definitely looks it."

Ari glanced around at the luxury on offer. "Is this the dining room? It's rather informal."

"Oh no, this is just the entrée level." Jay read a few things off the menu.

Ari frowned and her gaze darted around. "What do you mean *just* the entrée level?"

Jay chuckled. "That's the concept of the restaurant. Each level is a part of your meal, and so a part of your experience. It also helps get people through more efficiently since not everybody eats entrée or has drinks."

"Wait." Ari leaned towards him. "Do you mean that each level of the restaurant is each part of the meal? So when we want our main meal, we go up to the next floor?"

"Yep." Jay flashed his grin at her. "Great, isn't it? Such an unusual concept. I'm glad I waited to come here with you."

Ari leaned back in her seat and took everything in. "I didn't know restaurants like this existed. Definitely unusual and very popular I see." She saw several celebrities around the room and wondered what the prices were like.

They ordered their entrées and made small talk until they arrived. Ari kept to vegetables and pastas, food that wouldn't make her sick as she was still experiencing nausea from certain foods, and Jay went for the seafood.

When they were finished, they moved up one floor to the main dining room, which was even more luxurious than the entrée room, and were seated at the window which had a slightly better view than the other levels.

Ari glanced around the floor and then up at the atrium. "Two more levels. So…dessert level and rooftop restaurant?"

"You'll just have to wait and see," Jay replied. "So…Ari… how are you enjoying your night so far?"

She gave him one of her looks, as if to say, *what are you up to*. "Why?"

He shrugged lightly. "No reason. It's our anniversary, and I wanted to make it special. I'm wondering if you're enjoying the evening."

Her lips curled into a soft smile. "Yeah. I am. But it's just a restaurant. We've visited a lot over the last, what, seven months."

Jay nodded. "Mmm, has it only been seven months since you've been here? Wow, time *has* flown, hasn't it?"

"You know full well it's seven months." Ari sipped her mocktail. "What are you up to?"

Another shrug. "You'll just have to wait and see."

"Ah-huh, so you keep saying," she managed before their meals were placed on the table.

They ate in relative silence, except for murmurings of appreciation over the food and surroundings, and when the meal was over, they moved up to the next floor.

"What in the hell!" Ari exclaimed when the elevator doors opened.

The whole room was full of desserts. From cooking areas with chefs in white hats and coats, all whipping up sugary delights for their guests, to ice-cream stations, candy stores, and all kinds of decadent cakes.

"What the actual hell!"

"It is *literally* dessert heaven." Jay gazed around the room. "Any dessert you want, one of their chefs will whip it up, or you can make your own." He pointed to their left. "There's a candy bar, and an ice-cream bar next to that with about a hundred toppings, cakes of all kinds. You want it, they probably have it."

"I'm definitely going to be so sick after this." Ari groaned. "I'm already full. Maybe we should have skipped the other levels and just come here."

"I thought about it, but considering you've been sick lately,

I thought you might need some solid food in you first. We can roam the room and see what they have before deciding. And they have tables near the windows so we can sit and enjoy our food."

"A little bit of everything," Ari murmured and licked her lips. "Just a little bit."

They moved towards the left and followed the path around the room, picking and choosing what they could sample.

"Okay, I see a lot of things, but I only want a little bit of each," Ari said when they came back around. "And I can't wait, so let's go."

They accepted plates from the staff and started loading them with the small bite-sized pieces of decadent desserts, pies and cakes, mainly, as Ari bypassed the very sugary treats of cotton candy, candy apples, and the like. She added small dollops of ice-cream on the side, and they finally made their way to an empty table at the window.

"The view is even better from here." She set her plate down and slid into the chair Jay held out. "This has been quite a meal."

"It has been. We definitely need to come back a few times to really soak it all in." Jay took his seat, and they slowly made their way through their food. "Did you get some of the melted chocolate?"

"From the fountain? I drizzled it over the cheesecake pop." Ari bit into the one-inch sized ball and it melted in her mouth. "Oh," she mumbled around her food, eyes rolling skyward. "That'sh sho good."

Jay grinned and slid his key lime pie into his mouth. "Mmm, so's this."

They worked their way through the food, sipping their

drinks, and gazing at the view until done.

"And now?" Ari asked, looking up at the ceiling. "I know the atrium has been getting smaller and smaller, and it looks like that's actually a full roof and doesn't wrap around like these floors."

"You are correct, and it is the final stage of this momentous meal and all its trimmings."

"Then you'd better show me, and I hope there's no more food involved because I *am* absolutely stuffed." Ari discreetly rubbed her stomach. "And getting bigger with every meal. I'll be the *Stay-Puft* marshmallow man before long."

A guffaw burst from Jay, and he quickly covered his mouth. "Oh, Ari. That's funny. But no, there's no more food, so let's go and explore what is level number five." He held out his hand and escorted her to the elevator where they went up to the final floor.

When the door opened, Ari saw that the floor was solid marble, and led to the magnificent view seen through the floor-to-ceiling windows. Just like the other levels, they ran from one side to the other, but they boasted even more magnificent views of the city.

"Oh, wow," Ari said softly as she stepped towards the window. "Better with every level. But what do we do here?" She looked around and found no food and no waiting staff. "What is this floor?"

"This floor," Jay said, "is the penthouse suite where you can recover from the exorbitant amount of food we just had. It's where you can make memories and moments, and dance the night away in relative silence and just breathe." He took her into his arms and gently moved back and forth. "Let's dance the night away, Ari. Let's make more memories to live by."

She snuggled into his arms and rested her cheek against his, letting out a relaxed sigh.

"I love you, Ari."

Ari heard those words. She thought about the last year of her life, and tried to figure out if she wanted it moving forward.

"Ari…"

"Mmm?"

"I love you."

"I know. I love hearing you say it. I love you, too."

Jay bent his head and nuzzled her neck, planting soft kisses along her collarbone. "I love you, Ari. I love you so much that I want to show you how much."

"Ah…" She pulled her head away. "Are we allowed to do that here? You can't wait until we get home?"

He chuckled. "This is a penthouse and I've booked it for the night. So believe me, we will be doing a lot of it here. But that's not what I wanted to say." His phone rang and his expression fell. "Not now," he muttered.

"You'd better answer it," Ari told him.

"I'm in the middle of something very serious here."

It kept ringing.

"It could be about the kids."

Jay slid his phone out of his pocket and looked at the caller ID. "Gloria. Nope, not tonight." He threw his phone over his shoulder, and it landed on the couch. "Tonight is special and not going to be ruined by her and her needs. Now, Ari. There's something I want to tell you. Something very special. That is why we're here at this magnificent penthouse with this magnificent view." He swept his arm out in front of him before taking her by the arms. "I want to talk about the last year we've had together. We met one year ago today. I knew then, the same thing I know now. I needed you in my life. I still do. And it's become more and more obvious to me as the months have gone by, as you've moved here to have a life, as you've felt the same way about me as I do about you." His phone rang and his head fell forward. "No, I'm not going to let it interfere."

"It could even be your parents, or sisters." Ari moved over to the phone and picked it up. "Nope. Still Gloria." She set it down on the coffee table and walked back to Jay. "Should we put it on silent, or something?"

"We could turn it off," he suggested. "Or break it. Anyway, back to what I was saying that is being rudely interrupted. You feel the same way about me as I do about you and that is, I love you and you love me. And I want us to be together, Ari. I don't want you to go home. I want you to stay here and I want to love you and make love with you and make you happy. You make *me* happy, and I want you here. I don't want you going home and so I never see you again. I love you." He got down on one knee and pulled the box from his jacket.

Ari gasped, covered her mouth with both of her hands and stumbled backwards. "Oh, my God…"

"Ari, will you—"

His phone rang.

"Not fucking now," he growled at it and turned back to Ari, his anger slipping away as fast as it had risen. "Will you marry me?"

Ari stared at the huge emerald ring in the box, but the insistent ringing pulled her attention away. *If it's the kids, they'll come first. If something's happened, they'll come first.*

Because they always will. But you love him, oh, God yes I love him. But can you tolerate this, moving forward? Gloria will just get worse, not better. Not until something is done about her.

"Ari?"

Ari's gaze moved back and forth between the ring and the phone.

The phone won.

She hurried over to it. "It's Denver. That means something's serious." She put it on speaker and turned to Jay, seeing him reluctantly climb to his feet. "It's Ari, and you're on speaker."

"Ari, Jay, Denver. Something's happened and both of the kids are in the hospital. The nanny, well, there was a fire and the kids suffered smoke inhalation and the apartment's ruined, but the kids are in dire straits. Can you get to the hospital? Same as last time, emergency. Gloria's been calling, but I know you hate answering her calls."

"Ah, yeah, okay. We're on our way." Jay took his phone and hung up. "Well don't that beat fucking all. The one night we have—"

Ari cut him off. "It isn't as important as the health and well-being of your children." She glanced at the ring box still in his hand and a mixture of emotions went through her. "I'm sorry."

"For what? You didn't do anything." He saw the tear slide down her cheek and pulled her close. "Hey, hey, this has nothing to do with you. You have no need to be sorry for anything. Oh, Ari, my girl. I love you. And I want an answer before I go."

"Before *we* go, and no, you're not getting an answer," she told him. "Even I know this moment has been ruined by this and we may not get it back. And even though I know the time and place isn't really important in the grand scheme of proposals, there are two things that are far more important than me and your proposal and my reply right now. And they're called Andrew and Marisol and we need to get to the hospital. So put that box away and let's go." She pulled him towards the lift, and they collected their coats on the way out. Since the limousine had left, they hailed a cab to the hospital.

Making their way into Emergency, they saw Gloria pacing back and forth, biting on her lip and fingernails while Denver stood silent and patiently by.

Gloria spotted them. "Where the hell have you been, you fucking bastard?" she screeched. "Our children could be dead, and what," she flicked a hand at Ari, "You and your whore were out to dinner."

Ari responded to that comment with a lightning flash of movement. She cracked her hand across Gloria's face with precision, making her physically spin around. When Gloria turned back, both her hands were over her cheek. "Don't you *ever* fucking call me that again," Ari said in a low deadly tone, her right forefinger thrusting into Gloria's face. "I *am not*, and *never* will be. But *you* are responsible for this catastrophe, so shut the fuck up and keep your fucking temper to yourself. Because it was *your* nanny who was looking after your kids while *you* were out. This is on *you*, Gloria. The police will want to speak to *you*. The court will see what *you* did. This is what *you're* responsible for. Jay isn't responsible for *any* of this. Leave your anger for me the fuck out of it because I'm here in support of Jay and the kids. *Not* you!"

Stunned, Gloria could only stare wide-eyed from Ari to Jay.

Denver hadn't even bothered moving to her side or saying anything. He knew better than to interfere. He knew Gloria made enemies wherever she went and had made an enemy of Jay from the moment of their affair, and of Ari from her arrival on Jay's doorstep. This, he was staying out of.

"Where are the kids?" Jay asked quietly, stunned at Ari's attack, but secretly gloating that Gloria had got what she deserved because he'd never been able to do it.

Denver supplied the information. "Still being checked by the doctors, on ventilators to help them breathe."

Jay didn't bother with Gloria, but spoke directly to Denver. "Do you know what happened to start the fire?"

"We don't know for sure," Denver replied. "We know there *was* a fire that spread quickly, and the neighbours called it in after hearing the alarms go off and seeing smoke under the front door. The nanny's unconscious and is being checked over by doctors."

Jay nodded and looked around for his children. "Are they in a cubicle, or a room? I want to see them."

"A cubicle. And we can't see them until the exam is done and the doctor comes out." Denver shoved his hands into his pockets and went back to being silent.

Gloria's lowered her hands from her face and sniffed. Her eyes had watered at the slap, but she wasn't about to show either of them that they were tears. "When I couldn't get you on the phone, Denver offered to call. I see you come running for his calls."

Jay and Ari both shot her warning looks and she closed her mouth.

"That's because, *unlike* you," Jay spat, "*he* doesn't behave like a screaming banshee making demands."

Gloria blushed and folded her arms tight against her chest. As much as she wanted to rip into Jay, she knew that doing so wouldn't look good for her. Because Ari had been right, and while that made Gloria hate Ari even more than she already did, spouting her mouth off could actually get her into more trouble than she could already be in. She'd known the nanny did drugs. Hell, she and Denver did drugs. So, if they were found in the apartment, the kids could be taken from her and then where would she be? She'd be royally screwed and worse off than she wanted Jay to be. She saw several officers coming down the hall towards them. *Shit!*

The curtains were flung back, and the doctors emerged from the cubicles. "Mr and Mrs Daniels?" They looked between all four of them.

"I'm Jay Daniels." He stepped forward. "What's wrong with my children?"

While the others walked off, the doctor consulted his folder. "Smoke inhalation, their lungs and airways have swelling, which we're treating, they're both on ventilation tubes and will need to be here for at least three days so we can check on them and make sure the swelling has gone down. They can go home after that."

Jay inhaled a shuddering breath. "Okay. Okay. But they're both okay or will be okay?"

The doctor glanced among them. "They'll be just fine. It wasn't too bad, but enough to affect them. Their recovery should be quick, and we'll have them taken up to the children's wing shortly." He nodded and walked off.

"Oh," Ari let out a gush of air. "That's good, right?"

"Very good," Denver agreed quietly. "Gloria?"

"Mmm" she said distractedly, hoping the officers weren't there to speak to her. However, they hadn't budged from their stance behind them.

"Mr Daniels. Ms Hannaford. We need to have a word."

Everyone turned around to see the two officers waiting for them.

"Guess I'll take a seat while you have a chat," Ari told Jay and wandered over to the waiting area with Denver.

"Mr Daniels; Ms Hannaford. Your nanny was home with the children, yes?"

"*Gloria's* nanny was home with the children. We've been divorced for two years. She chose her," Jay said and cleared his throat. "I was out with my partner when I got the call."

The officer, who had spoken, nodded. "Right. Ms Hannaford, where were you when the fire broke out?"

Gloria licked her lips and tried to get a story together. "I was out to dinner with my partner, Denver, the singer and musician." She saw Jay rolled his eyes and turn away. "The building's concierge called me after it happened, and we rushed back home to find the paramedics loading my children into the back of the ambulance. The fire department was wrapping things up, and there was smoke billowing everywhere. It was awful."

"Okay." The officer made notes. "And did you know your nanny did drugs? There was paraphernalia found lying around. It looked as if she was trying to make something in the kitchen, which is what started the fire."

Gloria couldn't look them in the eye, but she tried to remain stoic. "We thought she might be doing them in her own time. But we have never seen her high and haven't found anything lying around the house before. Nothing. So we couldn't be sure if she was or wasn't."

"And do you and your partner do drugs, Ms Hannaford."

Jay inwardly grinned at that. Of course she did.

Gloria riled up a little. "My partner and I smoke marijuana on the odd occasion, but that's it. We don't pop pills, or snort, or smoke anything else. And we certainly don't inject."

"So if there was anything else found in the house, it would be yours or the nanny's?"

Gloria's back straightened as if a rod had shot up it. "As I said, we smoke pot, nothing else. So yes, we do have a small supply of it at the moment. Whatever else is in my apartment will be the nanny's. Maybe she had a boyfriend over and he brought it. I don't know what she gets up to when we're not there and my children aren't awake for me to ask them." She spun around to face her children in their beds. Both were resting, with tubes down their throats doing the main work. "I mean, look at my babies. Look at what she did to them." She lunged for their beds, sobbing over Andrew's supine figure.

Great, throw the nanny under the bus, Jay thought and rolled his eyes. He looked over at Ari who rolled her eyes and shook her head in disgust.

Denver's furrowed brow gave his thoughts away and he watched Gloria intently. She was putting on a show to save face and he didn't like what he saw.

"Look…" Jay distractedly scratched the top of his head. "Do you have any more questions? The kids are going upstairs soon."

"Not for now, Mr Daniels," one officer said. "We heard that the children will be here for a few days, so we'll be back if we have any more questions."

"Okay, fine." Jay turned his back and stood watching his children as the orderlies prepared them for transportation.

The officers watched, along with Ari and Denver, as they were moved into the elevators and taken upstairs. They watched Jay and Gloria go with them, and then turned to Denver and Ari. "And now we talk to the two of you."

Stunned, Ari could only say, "Why? I wasn't there. And I need to be with Jay."

"Just a quick recap of who you are and where you were, please." The second officer pulled out his notebook. "We'll start with you." He pointed to Denver.

"I'm Denver, partner of Gloria. We were out to dinner when she received the call, so it's just as she said. We thought the nanny might have done drugs, but never saw proof, and kept her on anyway."

The officers exchanged a glance and nodded. "And you." He pointed his pencil at Ari.

"Ari Travers. I was with Jay at dinner when he got the call. I've never been to Gloria's apartment, and have never met the nanny. And now I'm going upstairs." She rushed off before they could stop her and made her way into an elevator that opened right on cue. Denver was a beat behind her.

"That was weird," she muttered when the doors closed. "What did they need to know that for?"

"Witnesses, I suppose."

They found the children's ward and Jay and Gloria.

"Hey." Ari rubbed his back and watched both Marisol and Andrew being hooked up to the new machines. "There's no point me staying here, so I'll bring you some clothes and stuff tomorrow. I know you'll be staying the night."

Jay turned his attention to her. Gloria's carelessness had

interrupted their night; the big night he had planned for months to propose to the woman he loved. "Hey," he said softly and moved her away from the kids. *And* Gloria. "I'm so sorry this didn't turn out. I planned it for months and made sure it was going to be special."

"Shh." She put her finger over his mouth. "Don't. The kids always come first. And this *was* important."

Jay sighed and leaned on her a little as he physically deflated. "*Tonight* was important. But Gloria was still responsible for the nanny and her bullshit ruined our night. She threw the nanny under the bus."

"I heard." Ari's arms were around his waist, holding him up.

"I'm so sorry, Ari. I'm so sorry our big night was ruined. But you can still give me your answer." He looked hopeful, giving her his best puppy dog expression he knew she loved.

She smiled lightly and closed her eyes, not wanting to look into his. "Not now, Jay. This is too important. It can wait. Is there something you want me to take home, so no one sees it, or you don't lose it?"

"The ring?" he murmured and carefully pulled the box from his jacket pocket, keeping it out of Gloria's line of view. "I want you to look at this all night and tell me tomorrow you want to."

She opened her purse and put the box in. "I'll look at it. Don't worry. What *is* important are the kids. So when they wake, give them my love, and I'll bring you an overnight bag tomorrow. I take it you'll be staying here until they go home?"

"I don't know." He ran a hand through his hair and over his face. "A couple of days until they're out of the woods, maybe."

"And where will they stay when they get out?"

"Gloria's."

"Which is apparently destroyed by fire."

"Ah…"

"Yes. Ah."

"They can get a hotel room or buy another apartment. This is on Gloria. Not me. But if I have to take the kids for a while, that won't be a problem, will it?"

"Of course not. They're your kids. They come first." Ari kissed him and moved out of his arms. "I'll see you tomorrow. I'll take a taxi home."

"Okay." He pulled her back and kissed her passionately. "I love you."

She sighed, gave him a small smile and walked off for the lift, meeting Denver there.

They rode down in silence and went their separate ways without acknowledging one another.

Arriving at Jay's, Ari slumped against the front door when she closed it. Worn out from the last twenty-four hours, she wandered up the stairs to their bedroom and sat on the side of the bed.

"What the fuck am I going to do?" she whispered and took the box out of her purse. Holding it under the lamplight, she examined the ring. It had a massive emerald, God knows how many carats, in a heart shape, with diamonds around it. Millions of dollars' worth, no doubt. A part of her wanted to slide it right onto her finger. But another part didn't want to jinx anything until Jay put it on himself. Not that he'd be doing that now.

"Ah…what the fuck am I going to do?" She let out an exhausted sigh and left the box on the bedside table under the light. It twinkled merrily as she watched it, mesmerised.

"I can't do this. Not anymore."

She knew, in her heart, that she desperately loved him. Was desperately *in love* with him and wanted to make a life with him. But she was sick and tired of coming second. And it only took so long of coming second before it was time to say no more. She feared that time was upon them. Life would never be the same after tonight.

She walked into the closet and made up a bag for Jay with jeans, t-shirts, and underwear. She added his toiletries, a pair of sneakers, and a jacket. He couldn't stay in his suit for three days, or however long he planned on staying.

And how long was that? Until the kids were released from the hospital? The doctor had said a few days, so he was probably staying a few days unless he decided to come home sooner and once they were out of the woods as he'd suggested.

Gloria will probably be there the whole time to make herself look like the doting mother. Ari grimaced at the thought, knowing that she would for fear of going to jail. But smoking marijuana wasn't a crime in the Big Apple; neither was having it in your home, so they would be safe from any charges concerning that. Unless there were other drugs…

That thought led to thinking about what Jay had said a few weeks earlier. He had come up with a plan and was making it happen. Was this it? Or a part of it? Or not at all? If this wasn't Jay's plan, then what was? What was he trying to do to get Gloria out of their lives?

"I have no idea," she murmured and changed into her nightie and dressing gown. She got into bed, rolled onto her side and slid down until her eyes were level with the ring.

It was beautiful, and one she would proudly wear on her finger as Jay's wife. But regardless of how much she loved him, she had also overlooked a hell of a lot. His anger issues, mainly concerning Gloria. His insults about her weight, his lack of love concerning his children until recently and now only for Mari, and his seeming distaste for having any more. Unless it was with Ari.

And what do I tell him about that? What do I say to him tomorrow? Or the day after, or the day he comes home? He's going to need to spend time with the kids, to be the doting dad. Gloria will no doubt let him in, so she looks like the responsible parent and not the one the children need to be taken away from. She knows full well the money she gets out of Jay is something she can't lose. That means he's going to be spending a lot of time with the kids. A lot of time I can't afford to lose.

Sighing, Ari seriously contemplated trying the ring on, in case Jay never got to propose again. But if she put it on, she might never take it off, and that would tell Jay that her answer was yes. As much as she wanted to say yes, there was also that part of her saying no. Not yet. Not while Gloria was in the way and the kids came first. Because she was sick and tired of not coming first. She remembered her visit with the psychic, and scrolled through her phone for the recording, playing it, remembering her exact words. *"He will never put you first until the ones who are, have disappeared."*

The pain of those truthful words, and her own personal history, racked her with sobs.

*****

The next morning, Ari went back to the hospital. She found Jay beside Marisol's bed and Gloria beside Andrew's. Denver was sitting quietly on the couch on the opposite side of the room.

"Hey. I brought you a bag of clothes." Ari set it by couch. "How are they doing?" She saw Gloria's filthy look, but ignored it, and Gloria said nothing.

"They woke early this morning, but are resting again," Jay told her and reached out for her hand. "How are you? And thank you for bringing me a change of clothes." Because of his position by Marisol's bed, it was Ari's left hand he took a hold of and noticed there was no ring.

"Of course," she replied, and kissed him. "Anything you need."

"I need you to leave," Gloria muttered.

"I need you to go fuck yourself," Ari slammed back. "But you've pretty much done that with your nanny, your drug stash, *and* the cops."

The shock that crashed over Gloria's face made Jay laugh and he pulled Ari onto his lap. "Fast as a whip, my Ari is."

Ari smiled and moved her gaze to Marisol. "They're going to be okay."

"They are," Jay said, watching his daughter. "They both are, but it'll take some time."

"Mmm...time," Ari muttered. Sitting on Jay's lap she wanted his life with him. She wanted to be a part of it for the rest of hers. But he had kids. And this shit kept happening. "So you'll be here all day, then?"

Jay wearily yawned. "Yeah. I'll be here today. If they're better in the morning I'll pop home for a bit before coming back. I just want them to wake up and be themselves before I leave."

"The doctor said three days before they could go home,

right? They'll need extra care once they're home." She brushed his hair back and tried to wrangle it.

"They will. It's just a matter of whose home." Jay glanced from Marisol to Ari to Gloria. "We'll have to have a chat about that."

"There's nothing to chat about," Gloria boldly told them. "They'll come home with me. I have primary custody."

"To a burned-out apartment?" Jay asked. "Or are you planning on moving them?"

"I have a house out in the Hamptons. We'll go and stay there. It's May, the kids are out of school soon, and anyway, we can start off summer there and see where we go. We may even travel, so they get out in the fresh air," Gloria stated, almost petulantly.

Jay studied his ex's face, not sure if she was serious or just still trying to get one over on him. "Or you could just rent an apartment near your old one, or in Brooklyn. Then I could see the kids every day."

"Or you could just get the hell out of my life and stay as far away from us as possible and stop making my life difficult," Gloria shot back.

Denver finally piped up. "I don't know about the Hamptons, love. You know I have a series of shows to do this summer. I'll be all over the place. I think it best if you and the kids weren't on your own, or so far from the city."

Gloria turned her gaze to her toy boy and put on a syrupy sweet smile for him. "Then we'll come with you. Get out of Dodge, so to speak."

Denver shook his head. "Not sure that's a good idea. I don't like the thought of flying the kids around when their lungs are so fragile. They'll need lots of rest and recovery time. Days by the beach, lots of fresh air."

"And that's exactly why the Hamptons would be perfect." Gloria's arched brow and snippy tone told them the conversation was closed.

Ari saw the muscle under Jay's right eye twitch, as it always did, when he was trying to control his temper over Gloria.

Luckily, the doctor took that moment to arrive, and their attention was diverted.

An hour later, Ari said her goodbyes and Jay followed her out of the room.

"Hey." He hugged her tightly and breathed in her scent. "I see you're not wearing the ring."

With her arms wrapped around his torso, and her face pressed against his neck, she chose to say nothing.

"I also see that your eyes are red and puffy. That means you were crying last night."

Ari knew that any word was going to make her start again, so she chose to change the subject. "Just call if you need anything and either I'll bring it, or Bobby can get it for you."

"I don't need anything except my future wife," he murmured against her hair. "I love you, Ari. I want you to marry me. I know I didn't finish last night, but I still got down on one knee and proposed. Why aren't you wearing the ring?"

She managed to disentangle herself from him but couldn't look him in the eye. "I'm not talking about that right now. You have other things on your mind and I'm not one of them. Neither is that ring, or the proposal."

"Ari!" he said sharply. "You're everything to me, and always on my mind."

"But the kids need to come first. Not me," she told him. "I'm going and I'll see you tomorrow. Let me know if you're coming home for a shower and change, or not." She turned and hurried away, trying desperately not to cry.

Jay stood there, frustrated. His feelings for Ari were everything, and yet here he was in the hospital with his children that Gloria couldn't even look after properly. For all of her whining, Gloria could still not actually look after her own children and be there for them when she needed to be. And now, that meant *he* needed to be, and the bitch was going to take them up to the Hamptons which was even farther than the city.

Fucking Gloria!

He breathed deeply, trying to get a grip before he went back into their room. He was not going to lose Ari over this, but he knew the more Gloria wreaked havoc, the more it was tearing them apart. And it had been tearing them apart for months. That was one reason he had proposed to Ari on their anniversary. To keep her there. Show her she was of the utmost importance to him and took precedence over Gloria and the kids. Unfortunately, the kids seemed to be taking precedence over Ari, and that's not what he'd wanted. He wanted and needed her in his life and be damned if that wasn't going to happen.

I'm trying to fix it, he thought. *I just need to fix it faster. But there's only so fast I can go with the plan. It needs to be slow and steady and set in place perfectly. Unfortunately, it's taking longer than I anticipated and that means Gloria will be around for a lot longer. And did Denver say he had shows this summer and wouldn't be around? At least he suggested the kids stay here and not fly off around the world, so they'll be with Gloria every second unless she dumps them to run off with him. And she has a house in the Hamptons, huh? Didn't know about that one. I'd better find out where it is and see what the security's like on the house and property.*

He took a deep breath and walked back into the room.

*****

Ari busied herself with cleaning up her office, throwing out anything she didn't need, and tidying the rest. Every motion was filled with thoughts about Jay, the ring, the proposal, and that fucking bitch, Gloria. She went out to grab some things from the store and found herself in her favourite stationery shop stocking up on supplies. But every motion was filled with thoughts about Jay, the ring, the proposal, and that fucking bitch, Gloria.

Fucking Gloria, and those fucking kids.

Ari sighed. It wasn't the kids' fault; she knew that. But they didn't make it easier. They just made it so much damn harder. And that meant her decision was so much damn harder to make.

She spent the rest of the day distracting herself, but everything always turned back to Jay and thoughts of their life together. She also ignored his calls, and texted Bobby to deal with whatever he needed.

Come six o'clock, she was sitting in the living room in darkness contemplating her future and feeling like a complete and utter selfish failure.

Selfish, because she wanted Jay to herself. A failure; because she didn't want to give up the one thing she wanted. She was so busy sobbing she didn't notice Jay standing in the doorway.

"Ari." He rushed to her side and enveloped her into his arms. "Oh, Ari, what is it? Oh, my girl."

She sprang back and quickly wiped her eyes. "I didn't know you were home," she gasped

"I thought I'd come back for a couple of hours to see how you were." He wiped her wet face and felt the tension in her furrowed brow. "What is it? Tell me."

She shook her head. "No. This isn't about me. How are the kids?"

"Ari." Jay sighed and slid down a little on the couch. "They're fine. I'm here to see you and ask why you're not wearing my ring. Why aren't we engaged?"

Ari glanced away and took a deep breath. "Because last night was interrupted. Because Gloria exists. Because the kids come first. Because I'm not sure it's a good idea. Because the timing is wrong. Because, because, because." She flung her hands up in despair.

"Hang on." His fingers massaged her neck and shoulders. "Let's break that down. Yes, Gloria and the kids exist, and yes, I know Gloria makes life a living hell. And yes, last night was interrupted so the ambiance dissipated, and it went to shit. But how is us not getting married not a good idea? How is the timing wrong? Because we were interrupted? Tell me, Ari, because I'm a little confused right now."

"It's been one year. And with everything else going on, it's the wrong time for all of this to happen." Ari felt his hand take a hold of hers and squeeze. She squeezed back. "I love you, Jay, but the timing of everything was just shit. And now I don't know if it's a good idea while all of this is happening." She didn't dare mention her other thoughts on the matter.

He sighed and slid his arm around her. "Oh, Ari. I'm so sorry. The one time a man proposes to you it's interrupted by a phone call about his kids almost dying and being in

Anything for You

hospital on ventilators. That sucks. I get it."

Ari arced up at his proposal comment, and pain seared through her chest at having been single for so long, but she decided to let it go. "And they're going to need care for some time, while they're recuperating. And what happens if Gloria takes them to the Hamptons? Or Gloria flies off with the kids to see Denver?"

"Yeah, I've been thinking about that. I made a call to Merrick to track down Gloria's house there. I think it'll be good for the kids to get away, but it means travelling almost two hours to see them instead of twenty minutes to the city. The selfish bitch doesn't want to stay in the city."

"Fair call. The kids need clean air, not stinky smog." Ari wiped her face free from all remaining traces of her tears. "I'm just being stupid and selfish. But I do think you need to be with the kids. They could've died."

"No thanks to Gloria and her stellar child-rearing ability."

"Is it her fault, though?" Ari asked. "Or her nanny's?"

"Both, I'd say, and dickhead Denver did nothing except perpetuate the problem by smoking pot in the house. And Gloria already smoked it with me—"

"While the two of you were together and the kids were being born," Ari interjected. "Can't really blame her. What if it had happened when the kids were young and the two of you were smoking it? What then? You might've had the kids taken away from both of you."

Jay glanced at her profile in the darkness. "Are you sticking up for her?"

"No, just stating a very long history of pot smoking, and the involvement of another person. The nanny."

"Fair enough," Jay mumbled and frowned. "Ari, what's

going on? Really."

She didn't answer right away, just sat there thinking the same thoughts she'd been having for the last few weeks. "A lot."

"Care to tell me? I might be able to help."

She shook her head, but he wouldn't have seen it in the dark. "No. I need to figure this out for myself."

"You sure?" He stroked his fingers along her back.

She shivered at his touch. "Yes. I need to figure this out and make my own decisions."

"Okay. Well, I'm going to grab something to eat and freshen up. Then I'll head back to the hospital." He pushed himself up and blindly made his way into the kitchen where he turned on the light.

Of course you will, Ari thought despondently. *Because that's where you need to be.*

*****

Jay spent the next two days at the hospital, and that gave Ari more time to consider everything that was going on. She knew a choice needed to be made, and knew she had to be the one to make it. It wasn't up to Jay or Gloria, or anyone else, only Ari. And it wasn't one she could deal with. She listened to the recording of the psychic over and over, made copious notes and then shredded them so Jay wouldn't see them. She considered the pros and cons of saying yes, and the pros and cons of saying no, and then the pros and cons of staying or going. By the end of the third day, her eyes were permanently red and puffy from crying, but she knew her choice had to be made.

Jay came home on the fourth day; the day of the children's release from hospital.

"Hey, baby." He took Ari into his arms and held her close. "God I've missed you. You feel and smell so good." He buried his face in her hair and neck, breathing her scent, feeling her shape against his body. "I've missed you so much. Missed this, missed us, missed the feel of you."

"I've missed you, too," she murmured, wondering how she was going to tell him. "How are the kids?"

"Leaving for the Hamptons today, which means I'll have to organise my visits with them." He kissed her and led her over to the couch where he slumped down and pulled her into his arms. "I'm ready to put this whole thing behind us and get back to our life. How 'bout you?"

I wish, she thought. "I'd like to."

He contemplated her words and tone. "Is that all?"

"Is that all what?"

He cocked his head to look at her. "Is that all you have to say about us finally getting back to our lives? *I'd like to.*"

She lifted her head from his chest. "What do you want me to say, Jay? Yee-haw, we can finally get on with it? Can we? Can we *really* just get on with it? *Our* lives, *our*… whatever…" Words failed her, and she stopped, heaving a sigh of defeat instead.

"What the hell is going on, Ari?" Jay twisted his body around, so he faced her. "What the hell is going on with you? Why are you talking this way? What do you mean *you'd like to*? No, we *are* going to get back to our lives when this is all over—"

Ari cut him off. "But that's just it; it'll never be *all over*. As long as Gloria is alive and not burning in hell, she'll forever interfere with you and your life, and so with me and us and my life. As long as she has those kids to ruin and interrupt everything, she'll have power over you, us, me. I'm sick of it. I didn't realise getting involved with you would be such a fucking nightmare. And I've lost count of how many times you've told me you were dealing with it. But here she is, *still* causing trouble and you *aren't* dealing with it."

Ari heaved herself up from the couch and wandered over to the front window, staring out at the Manhattan skyline. She was done with Gloria wreaking havoc on their relationship, and that meant there was only one solution.

"Ari." Jay grabbed her roughly and turned her to face him, making her gasp. "Gloria *will* be dealt with. My plan needs to take time, but believe me, it's going to happen and then we can be truly happy."

"But how much longer will that take?" Ari cried, flinging her arms up to force his off. "How much longer do I have to come second, no, *third*, to Gloria and the kids before I'm truly happy being with you. How much longer will it take before you stop talking about Gloria and letting her interrupt our life together and just worry about you and me and us?" She breathed in and wiped her face. "Do you remember when you said you were bringing me here and I told you it was going to be hard living in your life? You didn't understand, so I said it was because I was walking into *your* life, moving into *your* life, that I'd be living in *your* life. Well I've lived in *your* life, Jay, for seven months now, meeting *your* friends, *your* family, dealing with *your* ex-wife and her partner, and *your* kids, and *their* problems and *your* problems. And while I've done a few things for myself and had some success, and met people and gone places, *your* life has been absolutely fucking exhausting, and I just can't fucking do it anymore."

He forcefully took hold of her arms. "Ari, where is this coming from? I thought you were happy here with me—"

"I *am*. I *was*," she said. "But Jesus fucking Christ it's so fucking exhausting. Gloria's taking up most of our time and I'm done with her. If murder was legal I'd kill her myself, just to get rid of her." She shook him loose and moved away. "I can't keep doing this, Jay. I can't keep worrying about her ringing in the middle of something we're doing. I can't keep worrying about her taking you away because she cries wolf about the kids. I just…" She deflated on the inside and slumped onto the couch, her head in her hands. "I can't keep doing this."

"Okay, okay." Jay hurried to her side and rubbed her back. "My plan is in motion, Ari. The kids are out of the hospital and she's still adamant about taking them to the Hamptons. I know it's a longer drive to see them, but I can cut down my visits to once a week and eventually go back to my previous visitation times. It's just for now, while the kids recover."

Ari wiped her face and sniffled. "And how long do they need to recover?"

"The doctor said today that it'll take anywhere up to a month for them to be fully fit. But that doesn't mean I need to be there the whole time. Besides, she won't want me there. But I did have an idea. How about we go and rent a house in the Hamptons and have a holiday for the month? Or until Gloria moves back into her apartment."

"*Is she* moving back into her apartment? Or will she go off and buy another one? And Denver's not going to be there most of the time…"

"I don't know. She hasn't said anything since the other

day when you bitch slapped her in the hospital. Did I congratulate you for that? That's something I've wanted to do since she started treating me badly. And when I found out about Denver, whoo wee." He rubbed a hand over his face. "Man I have wanted to slap her so bad."

"I don't need to be congratulated for one, *physically* slapping your bitch of an ex, and two, *verbally* slapping your bitch of an ex. I've had an absolute gutful of her, and the bitch can rot in hell. I just wish she'd hurry up and do so. When is she back in her apartment?"

He shrugged. "I don't know. If it needs a major overhaul, it could take months, or the rest of the year."

"She could be in the Hamptons for the rest of the year, then?" Ari rolled her eyes and looked away. "And that means chasing after her and the kids for another six fucking months. But then again, my year here in New York will be up by then."

Jay's ears picked up on that last sentence. "What's that supposed to mean? You're still leaving? You can't leave. I've proposed to you, you're staying here, *with me*, and making a life, *with me*. What the hell, Ari?"

Her fingers rubbed over her brows, trying to ease the tension building there. "I have a contract. *We* have a contract. A contract that says I'm only here until the end of December. The rest was up to me. It seems to me that Gloria and the kids are taking all of your time and there's none left for me. So what's the point me being here anymore." Her voice cracked and she hurried into the kitchen for a drink. She poured herself a juice and sculled it back before Jay even made it to her side.

"What the fuck, Ari?" he raged, the shock rolling over

him in waves. "I don't give a fuck about the contract. What are you saying? Are you saying you want to leave? Are you saying you want to break up with me? What?"

"I don't know," she cried, unable to look at him. "I don't know. What I *do* know is that Gloria and the kids always come before me and I'm sick and tired of it. I know they're your kids and they need to be first. But I'm sick and tired of *not* coming first. *With anyone.*" The tears flowed heavily down her face, and she swiped them away. "I want to come *first* for once. Just for fucking once."

"Ari." Jay slid his arms around her. "You do come first with me, baby. *You do.* I'm doing all of this for *you*."

"All of *what*, Jay?" she asked, finally looking him in the eye. "*All of what*? All of letting her interrupt everything. All of letting her use the kids to break up our relationship. What? Well guess what? It's worked." She rushed from his arms, through the kitchen, down the hall, and made it to the staircase and up three steps before Jay caught up.

"Ari," he bellowed, panicking at the thought of losing her. He grabbed her hand that was grasping the railing, his eyes as wild as his tone. "Don't you dare tell me you're leaving," he threatened. "You are *not* leaving me. That cunt will not win. She is *not* winning. You'll stay here in New York and marry me, and we'll live our lives happy and together. *Do you understand me?*"

Her body buzzed with fear and anger; a sad mix that threatened to make her unleash the gates holding back the tears that threatened to blast it open.

Jay saw her bottom lip quiver and felt his anger flow away. "Ari," he said softly. "No...what are you saying? Are you saying you're leaving me? Leaving us? New York? Don't leave me, Ari. I love you. I want you to be my wife and my lover, and I want to grow old and grey with you."

"I'm sorry," she whispered, the tears overflowing anyway. "I'm so sorry. I love you, I do, so much. But I can't take it anymore. I can't take her, or the kids, or you running off to see them because she says jump and you say how high. I'm so sick and tired of coming second, or in this case third, or being sacrificed for everyone and everything else. And I know your kids need to come before me. I get it, I do." She caressed his face and felt the stubble growing nicely into the beard she loved seeing him with so much. "Believe me, I understand how much your kids need to come first. And maybe it was my fault for letting myself fall in love with a man who already has kids, but we can't help who we fall in love with. And I thought maybe I could deal with it, and at first I could, and things were okay. But then they got worse and worse, and she wouldn't let up."

"Ari." Jay moved around the railing and fell onto the step at her feet. "Don't leave me, Ari. I love you. I'll fix this. My plan is in motion."

"I can't deal with plans that aren't happening, or motions that aren't moving, or with time that's not ticking, Jay. I just don't have it in me anymore. All my life I've come second or third or fourth, or not at all. Not one person has ever put me first before everyone and everything else. And I don't expect you to, but I also didn't think this was going to be so hard. All I want, for once in my life, is to come first. To be someone's first and only and not be sacrificed. To be put above everyone and everything else in their life. And I know that might be unreasonable to expect, but it's the way I feel. I need to be first, Jay. Just for once in my life."

"No, Ari," Jay sobbed. He wrapped his arms around her legs and buried his face in her crotch. "Don't leave me. You can't leave me."

Her tears didn't let up. They kept on sliding down her face and wetting the neck hem of her top. But that didn't matter. What mattered was that she was already packed. What mattered was that she always knew Jay would not change where Gloria and the kids were concerned. What mattered was that she knew it was time to go and take a break to mentally regroup. Because that's what she needed to do.

She stroked his hair and face and then slid her hands under his arms and pulled him to his feet. "Jay…" A defeated sigh left her. "Nothing has changed. It's only got worse. And I can't deal with it anymore. I love you, oh, God help me I love you with every fibre of my being, but I refuse to deal with Gloria and the kids anymore, and I refuse to come third in someone's life. I want to be first in yours. I want to be your only. The only one in your life. But that won't happen. I'm sorry if all of this hurts you, but maybe we're not meant for each other. Maybe your life is just way too complicated for you to date anyone while Gloria's around and the kids are in your life." She cupped his face, her thumb stroking his cheeks. "I love you. Oh, God, I do. And if things hadn't been going the way they were and they were so much better, I would have said yes to your proposal in a heartbeat. But your life isn't easy to say yes to. And until it is, I can't say it. I'm sorry. I'm going back to Australia to take time out from this and regain some emotional stability. Because right now, I just don't have it anymore."

Horrified at losing the love of his life, not only back to her homeland, but possibly forever, Jay rallied. He sniffed, wiped his face, and adjusted himself, his mind wildly running through ideas to keep her there. Rambling thoughts came tumbling out. "Okay then, the timing is wrong. I get that may have been where I went wrong. But I thought our anniversary was a good time to propose. And I get that Gloria is a pain in my ass that'll never go away unless I make her. And the kids, well, they're kids. But I love you, Ari, and I won't let you go. So I propose another contract if you will. A contract that I'll sign in blood because I'm not willing to let you go forever and I promised you I was going to sort out Gloria and deal with her and by God I will. I swear to you on my grave I will. So the contract is this. Six months. Give me six months to fix this. To get rid of Gloria and deal with the kids. Six months is all I ask before I propose again, and you say yes." He reached out and slid his hands around her arms, holding her gently.

"I would do anything for you, Ari. *Anything*. Anything to be with you, anything to bring us back together as a couple, and a family. *Anything* it takes. *Anything* for you. I promise. I would do *anything* for you, Ari. I'll make this happen. I promise. Know this, understand this. I'll do anything to bring you back to me. Anything to bring us back together. Anything to get me back to you. I'll do anything to have you, have us, have the life we're meant to have. I promise you. I'll make it happen. I will make *us* happen; *this* happen. Because I will do anything, *anything*, and I mean I will do anything for you. Understand that now. I *will* do *anything* for you."

She dried her tears before cupping his face. Her feelings of fear and sadness perked up slightly at the thought of trying again. "Okay. Then I'll give you six months. I'll wait six months for you to resolve this and come and get me. But after that, I'll know it wasn't meant to be if you don't turn up."

He agreed with a sharp nod. "Six months is more than enough time to make this happen. I love you. I'll do anything to bring us back together. Because I *will* do *anything* for you, Ari. *Anything.*"

They were interrupted by a knock at the door.

Ari pulled away and checked her watch. "That's the movers," she murmured and looked at the door. "I already booked them to take my stuff today."

"You're already packed?" He frowned. "When?"

"Yesterday. Everything else is in the basement, remember." She sighed and opened the door. "Hi, come on in. Most of my stuff is in the basement, but there are some boxes upstairs."

The lead man nodded, looked from her to Jay and startled. "Oh, right. We brought your things here last year. Leaving again?"

"Yes," Ari replied. "Back to Australia. The basement door is down the hall." She pointed and waited for them to disappear down the stairs.

"Ari." Jay pulled her into the lounge room and closed the door behind them. "I don't want you to leave." He hugged her tightly.

"I know. But it will give me time to get my shit together and be away from Gloria. That woman does my head in."

"Oh, don't I know it," Jay said and heard the men wheel the first load of boxes outside. The fact she was leaving terrified and infuriated him at the same time. He'd finally found a woman to love him for him and not cheat on him, and she was leaving because of the cunt of an ex-wife. *She needs to be dealt with now,* flitted through his mind.

It took the movers two hours to pack all of Ari's

belongings into their truck and wave goodbye. All she had left were the six cases and two bags she'd arrived with, and they now stood in the entranceway of the brownstone.

"You're leaving me today?" Sadness overwhelmed him once more and he didn't stop the tears.

She breathed in unsteadily. "Yeah. I thought it best while the kids were heading off to recuperate. This way you can go to the Hamptons for a while and spend time with them and not worry about me or deal with me and my needs."

"Ari." Jay frowned at her choice of words. "That's not—"

"I know." She waved a dismissive hand and glanced away. "I was planning to go after you'd gone. But you mentioned both of us going there and I just can't. I know Gloria will think she's won, but since we're giving it six months, just tell her I had to rush home for a personal emergency. She doesn't need to know I packed up my stuff and moved back."

"You could have left your stuff here and come back in six months," Jay offered. "You could have just gone for a six-month holiday."

"No." She shook her head. "This was going to be a clean break. Then you came up with the contract and I chose to agree to it. I'll be in a holding pattern for six months from today. No more, Jay. I don't have more time to waste on Gloria and the kids."

He nodded and wrapped his arms around her, the tears flowing freely down his cheeks and into his t-shirt. "I love you, Ari, my girl. And I *will* come for you."

"I know," she said, hugging him back just as hard. "I know you will. Because that's the way you are. That's what you'll do."

"Yes." He rubbed his chin in her hair, his brows deeply

furrowed. "That's what I'll do."

Ari saw the taxi stop outside and pulled out of his arms. She slung her handbag over her shoulder and grabbed the handles of two of her suitcases. The bags were attached to the top. "I need to go, taxi's here."

He nodded and followed her out with the other cases, loading them into the trunk and back seat before kissing and hugging her. "I love you. Don't forget that. And I *will* come for you in six months, Ari. And I have your phone number and Skype and Zoom and Facetime, so I'll be contacting you to see how you are. And I'm following you on your socials, so I'll be watching you."

"I'll be taking a break from socials. Pretty much cutting off any and all contact. I just want some time alone and peace and quiet by a nice beach."

"The Gold Coast?"

She nodded. "That's where I'm headed."

"Okay. Then I'll know you're spending time where you want to be and it'll be good for you. The beach and Aussie life. You love it there, and hopefully it'll regenerate and invigorate you."

"That's what I'm hoping." Her lips lingered on his cheek. "I love you. Come for me," she said before pulling away and climbing into the back seat.

"I will." He closed her door and planted his hands on the window. "I'm coming for you, Ari. In six months. Send me your address so I know where to come."

She gave him a small smile and placed her hand on the window.

The taxi drove away.

Jay stood watching until it was out of sight then trudged

back inside. He closed and locked each door. Heard the silence that came with the emptiness. Didn't like what he heard. He also *saw* the emptiness. And that emptiness gutted him to his core.

His sobs came thick and fast, and he grasped his face and crumpled to the floor. He stayed there until he was empty of all the anger and pain he'd felt for four years. But the hatred remained. He got to his feet and walked down the hall to his office, standing in the doorway with his hands in his pockets, wondering what he was there for. He saw the way Ari had decorated the room with his things, making the centre display cupboard in front of him the prime cabinet for awards. He saw the Emmys on the middle shelf calling to him.

His feet moved one in front of the other over to the cabinet, and he looked at them. At all of the awards he'd won for his roles in movies and TV. The awards he'd won for his comedic abilities and dramatic overtures. The awards he'd won that looked like lethal weapons if the desire so overtook him.

In one swift movement, he opened the double doors and picked up two Emmys. He felt the weight of them in his hands as he lightly bounced them. He spun them in his hands with one lift in the air, so they faced downwards, and he caught them and stabbed one, then the other, at the ground as if stabbing his enemy. Gloria. His long-held deep-seated anger overtook him, and he lurched hand over hand towards the floor, stabbing her with every movement, seeing her face as the wings of the woman on the award stabbed the bitch in the heart over and over. His hands moved faster and faster, stabbing down one after the other in a frenzy of blood lust until his energy was spent on four years' worth of hate.

He breathed in deeply, waiting for the whiteness in his eyes to dissipate. It was something that always overcame him when his blood boiled white-hot with anger and hatred and made him feel faint. It also made him think strange thoughts in that whited out moment, as if he were on hallucinogenic drugs, and sometimes he wanted to act on those thoughts. Just as he did now.

His arms fell to his sides, sweat dripping from his brow. They'd make great weapons. If the need arose. Which it definitely had. He spun them back around in his hands and replaced them on the shelf, making sure they were in their right place. The place Ari had put them. He flicked on the display light and watched them shine for a few moments in their spotlights before closing the doors. He stood still, listening, hearing nothing. Watching, seeing nothing. Breathing, smelling nothing. Ari was no longer there. Her scent, her body, her presence. All no longer there. All because of fucking Gloria!

His fist balled up and thrust forward. "Gloria, you fucking bitch, you'll pay for this," he growled as the glass tinkled to his feet and scattered over the floor. His anger calmed, as did his pulse. "Well, there's only one thing to do then…" He turned around and heard it under his feet. Saw the glass on the floor and realised what he'd done. Knew what needed to be done with the other things in his life. All of his messes needed to be cleaned up. And that started today.

PART THREE

Chapter 20

Ari slowly walked down the hallway and into the light, bright room. It was spacious, with warm sand-coloured floors, and floor-to-ceiling French doors in the middle of two bay windows, all of which spanned the length of the room. A mirrored piano sat in the bay window to the left, and a wooden bar with shelves of coloured glasses and bottles of alcoholic fuel sat in the bay window to the right. A brick fireplace with a mantel covered the wall to the left, with a huge TV above it, display coffee tables sat in front of turquoise couches with tropical cushions scattered over them, and soft white curtains billowed gently in the warm summer breeze.

Ari stood in the middle of the room, surveying all around her. The peace and quiet wrapped around her like a safe haven. She felt the privacy it had afforded her in her time of need. And she'd needed that privacy, and peace and quiet desperately, when she'd returned to Australia, heading straight for the Gold Coast in Queensland. She'd taken refuge at a private hotel resort until she acquired a car and home. Upon finding the perfect home surrounded by palm trees and situated on one of the many river inlets, she'd stolen away into it seeking the tranquillity she now had.

She'd refused to use social media, hadn't called or texted anyone, had barely watched TV, kept away from all entertainment shows, and she'd done so for the six months she'd been back.

Ari breathed in slowly, catching the tropical scent of the trees and river she resided alongside. The beach was a short distance away and the saltiness wafted into the house.

She breathed out slowly, letting the stress of the last six months flitter away. She wished New York was a distant memory. But it wasn't. Neither was Jay. Neither was their time together. Neither was their love, or what they'd created.

Neither were Gloria and the kids.

Ari had tried to keep Gloria and all of the pain she'd caused out of her head. The destruction that one woman could cause was beyond comprehension. The narcissism and entitlement, the arrogance and ego that had made her hate Jay so much had fuelled her obsession to destroy him and everything that made him happy, including new relationships.

She thought back to the times she'd been mere feet from Jay's ex and had felt the hatred that oozed from every pore in Gloria's body and was glad she'd defended herself and fought back. Gloria hadn't expected that, and that put Ari in first position.

Just not first position in Jay's heart or life. And while she understood that where the kids were concerned, she was fed up with Gloria and the issues with his ex coming before her.

She sighed and closed her eyes. She hadn't come first in Jay's life, and that hurt. But he'd vowed to her on her last day in New York that he would come for her in six months. He'd begged for the time to deal with Gloria and the kids once and for all, and since she'd not been online or watched TV, read magazines, or even checked her phone, she had no idea whether that had happened. She preferred the silence and the peace and quiet over the bickering and hatred. She preferred to be creative with her hands and mind and fill her time the only way she knew how. She also would have preferred to be with Jay and be a family and had barely survived all the lonely days and even lonelier nights. Her dreams had been invaded by him and what she'd wanted with him every single night that she'd been gone, even more so recently.

Because the six months were up.

Rubbing her weary eyes, she glanced out into the soft fading light of the afternoon and the shadows it cast as the lazy summer rays filtered through the palm trees that lined the side of the house and the back terrace. She gazed at the meandering river floating past the back of the property, passing her by just as her life was, and she wondered where Jay was in that moment.

Probably spending the winter with his kids, she thought. *It's nearly Christmas. He'll be getting their presents and arguing with Gloria to spend time with them. Unless he doesn't want to spend any time with them. Maybe things have actually changed…and maybe they haven't.*

Six months were up.

The front gate buzzer rang out, startling her and her two Cavoodle puppies who barked up a frenzy. "Quiet!" she snapped, and they shushed. Her head turned to the door. "Who the hell could that be?" They rarely had visitors. Only the supermarket delivery trucks turned up. Her mail was sent to a P.O. box which she checked once a week on her weekly trip to the beach to sit under a palm tree and watch the waves crash in. Other than that, she rarely went anywhere.

She hurried to the front door and clicked the button. "Yes?"

"Ari…it's Jay…" the disembodied voice came over the speaker.

Stunned, Ari could only stare at the camera attached to the front gate intercom. "Jay," she whispered. "Jay?"

"Yeah, baby. It's me. Let me in."

She buzzed him in and unlocked the hardwood main door, standing in front of the screen door while he walked up the short driveway into the courtyard. He looked mentally exhausted and physically worn out. So did his clothes. Old faded blue denim jeans, a light grey t-shirt, and a battered blue denim jacket hung from his frame. Badly scuffed cowboy boots were on his feet, and he dropped an old overnight bag beside them.

"Jay?"

He smiled wearily at her. "Ari."

She opened the screen door and he reached out and cupped her face with both hands. "Jay?" she whispered, her eyes searching his body and face for recognition.

He responded by planting his chapped lips on hers and kissing her passionately.

Ari responded in kind and clawed her way up his tall, thin frame, clinging to him as to a life raft before pulling away. "Jay…" She gazed at him. "Is it really you? Are you really here?"

"Yeah, baby. I'm here with my girl." He pushed her hair back from her face and gazed deeply into her eyes. "It's over, Ari," he said, taking in all of the fine details of her features. "It's finally over. The years of Gloria berating and insulting me are over. Gloria's gone. The kids are gone. Denver's gone.

We can finally be together. Just you and me, like I promised. I'm finally with my girl. I'm finally here. Didn't you believe me?"

"I…" she began, but swallowed and glanced away.

"Ari?" He gently lifted her face, so she had no choice but to look at him. "What is it?"

A tear rolled down her cheek. "I wanted to believe so much that you'd come. But I also didn't want to allow myself to believe in case you didn't. I've been stuck between wanting to and not wanting to for six months. I wanted this so badly, I wanted to believe it would happen so badly, and now I'm not sure you're even real."

"I'm real, baby. I'm real." He kissed her lips and settled his forehead against hers so he could look into her eyes. "It's me, Ari. I told you I'd sort this out and I have. It's done. Gloria and the kids are out of our lives forever. It's just you and me now. Just you and me."

Ari blanched and pulled back. "Let's get you inside." She grasped his right hand and he bent and grabbed his bag before she pulled him into the house and shut both doors, locking them tightly against the world. She ushered the dogs out of the way and led him to the lounge room and offered a drink. "Do you want something to eat? I don't know when you ate. Did you eat on the plane? How long have you been here? When did you get in?"

"I'm okay, but I could do with a stiff drink if you have one. I ate on the plane, and I've come straight from the airport, so I got in a little while ago."

The sun was setting over the houses across the river and glinting in through the terrace trees and curtains as she poured him a drink. "Here." She handed over a glass of whiskey.

He sculled it down in two gulps and winced, coughing as the liquid hit the spot.

"You okay? Do you want water or juice instead?" Ari moved to his side and gently clapped him on the back.

"I'm fine." He handed the glass back. "Just haven't had a stiff drink in a while. Went down the wrong way." He looked around the room while she set the glass on the bar. "I like this place. You found a really nice house to live in. Did you buy it?"

"I did." She slid her arms around his waist and worried about how much smaller it seemed. He was decidedly thinner than six months ago, and she wondered what had happened for him to lose so much weight. "Are you okay?" she ventured. "You seem a little gaunt and—"

"I'm fine." He brushed it off and left her embrace, walking around the room, studying the pictures on the walls, and the knick-knacks on the mantel and shelving units around the room. "Did you have all of this before?"

"Most of it, yeah." Ari took a few steps towards him. "I've bought a few things since and added those."

"I don't remember these." He gestured to a wall where framed photos of New York hung. "Did you take them?"

"I did." She nodded. "Found them on my laptop and had them printed out and framed when I unpacked and started sorting everything into its own space. I think I took about a million photos while I was there. Maybe more."

Jay picked up a snow globe from a shelf and studied it before replacing it and picking up another, and then another.

"You okay? You can look at my stuff tomorrow." Ari was puzzled. Why would he want to look at her belongings instead of talking? She tried to bring him out of it. "So, what

Anything for You

happened? You said to give you six months and you'd deal with Gloria and the kids. Did you? Is that why you're here? Are we finally free to be together?"

"Mmm?" Jay glanced up and put down the snow globe. "I just want to refresh myself with you and your belongings. It's been so long, Ari." He straightened and moved over to her, taking her into his arms. "I've missed you. I've missed everything about you. I don't think I truly appreciated it before. Truly appreciated *you*. I love you, Ari. I never should have taken so long to say it, or make it happen. Six months is far too long to make things happen."

Ari sighed and relaxed a little into his arms, resting her chin on his shoulder. He smelled different. Not the normal cologne, or body wash and sprays he usually used, but a scent she couldn't put her finger on. *Maybe it's from being on the plane so long,* she thought. "Okay, look…" She pulled back. "Let's get you settled and then we can have something to eat. It's nearly tea time."

"Tea time?" His brow furrowed. "What's tea time?"

"It's what some of us call dinner," she told him. "I've been eating around six. Is that okay for you if you want to eat?"

"Okay." He gave a weary sigh. "That's fine, but I'm not really hungry."

The cries of a baby came from the second floor.

Their heads cocked to listen.

"You have guests? Someone else is here…with a baby?" Jay asked, looking towards the entrance way stairs. "Am I intruding? I didn't know you'd have guests."

Ari contemplated her next words. "No. Not guests. Just a baby."

"Whose baby?"

She bit on her bottom lip and glanced away.

He read the signals. "Wait… *Your* baby?"

She nodded, unable to speak for the swiftly forming lump in her throat.

He took an uncertain step back. "Did you adopt?"

She shook her head slowly.

He took another step and his head pulled back slightly. "*You* had a baby? When? Whose?"

Hurt by his actions and words, she grasped her hands in front of her. "*Yes*, I had a baby. She came in September. She came early."

Jay frowned, his brain trying to figure out the timing. "Wait…is she *my* baby?"

"Do I seriously have to explain it to you?" she asked. "I wasn't sleeping with anyone else at the beginning of the year." The baby's cries continued. "I need to go and check on her." Ari rushed out of the lounge room, up the stairs, and into her bedroom. "There, there, my baby, it's okay. It's okay. Mama's here. Yes, Mama's here." She picked up the infant, whose cries stopped the moment she was in her mother's arms and held her to her chest. "There we go, my baby. There we go." She patted and rubbed her back, soothing her until she cooed.

"Ari?" Jay stood in the bedroom doorway watching them. "Oh…Ari…" His Ari was patting and rubbing the back of his baby. "A baby. Oh…Ari. I…" His feet managed to move in her direction, closer to the woman he loved and the baby he hadn't known existed. "A baby."

"Yep." Ari curiously watched him. There was a deep vibe she was picking up, and she didn't like it, or feel comfortable about it. "A baby."

Anything for You

"*Our* baby…" Jay stood by their side, watching the baby's expressive eyes darting back and forth from him to her mother. "A baby." His hand rose to gently touch her chubby cheek. "Our baby… What's her name?"

Ari's gaze didn't leave him. "Lilly."

His eyes lit up. "Lilly. Hello, little Lilly, how are you? I'm your daddy." He gently stroked her head. "Hello, little Lilly, hello."

Lilly gurgled and tucked her head into her mother's neck.

"She needs her tummy filled and probably a change. Why don't you go and get some food sorted for us and I'll be down in a bit." Ari laid her daughter down in her cot and started prepping for a change.

"No. I want to help. She's my baby too." Jay watched Ari prepare the change table and gently lifted Lilly into his arms. "Hello, my baby. Daddy's here. Yes, that's right; I'm finally here with you and your mama." He laid her on the table and handed Ari what she needed when she asked for it, and then picked up Lilly when she was done. "That wasn't so bad, was it, now, my baby." He held her up against his chest and rested his lips on her head, watching Ari tidy up. "My Lilly," he murmured. A dazed expression glossed over him. "My little Lilly. Your daddy's home. Yes, that's right. Your daddy's home and I finally get to be a daddy. Yes, I do. And I get to be a daddy to the most precious girl in the world. Yes, I do."

As Ari cleaned her hands with an antiseptic wipe, she stared quizzically at him. Those words didn't make sense to her. He was finally getting to be a daddy? What about Marisol and Andrew? She frowned and threw the wipe into the small bin by the change table. "It's time to eat. She needs her tummy filled, and I'm getting pretty hungry myself."

Jay stood gazing into the distance having not heard Ari. He just murmured to Lilly and kissed her head.

"Jay?" she called and tapped him on the shoulder. "Time for tea."

He came to and turned his gaze to her. "Mmm?"

"Time to eat." Ari steered him out the door and downstairs into the spacious kitchen, seating them at the small table and chairs. She quickly fed the dogs and laid out bowls for her two missing-in-action cats in the butler's pantry, and then pulled a few items out of the fridge, setting them on the island bench before she put a bottle of milk in the microwave. "You can put her in the bassinette."

"No. I'll hold her. Can I feed her, too?" he asked, still holding Lilly to his chest. "I don't want to let her go."

Ari watched his interaction with his daughter and saw the bond that was growing with her. She smiled wistfully, having been unsure of what his reaction would be when he found out she'd been pregnant when she'd left and not told him. That she hadn't told him in the last six months. Nor had she told him his daughter had been born. "You seem to be taking this well."

"Mmm?" He looked up as she placed the milk bottle on the table in front of him.

"You seem to be taking this well," she repeated and waved a hand at him. "You need to move her so you can give her the bottle."

"Mmm? Oh, right." He gently moved Lilly so she was lying in his arms and snuggled against his chest. She gurgled and clasped her hands together, eliciting a smile from him. "Look at you, Princess Lilly. Ready for a feed?" He picked up the bottle and gently rubbed the teat against her lips.

She opened her mouth and greedily took it, closing her eyes as the warm milk went down into her stomach.

"You seem okay with this." Ari pulled out a chair and sat down. "I didn't tell you before I left because I didn't want to risk losing her, and then I'd have to tell you *that* and we'd be grieving. So I kept it secret." She gazed down at her hands, a touch of shame flitting over her. "Then when I came home and things were okay, I still didn't tell you because we weren't together. And then everything went haywire because she came early because I was a geriatric pregnancy, and she was in a humidicrib for a few days, and we didn't come home for a week."

"Ari." Jay finally lifted his head to look at her. "It's okay. I get it. It was all about Gloria and the kids and you were suffering. I'm okay. It's okay. You're okay, and Lilly's okay. We're together now. *Everything is okay.*"

Puzzled by his lack of anger, or emotion of any kind, Ari stared at him. A niggle was chewing away in her gut, telling her something was wrong. But she couldn't put her finger on it and didn't have the energy right then to figure it out. "You want anything to eat or drink? I'm just going to heat up a meal."

"Not right now, thanks." He slowly swayed side to side, holding the bottle to Lilly's mouth, waiting patiently for her to finish. A small smile curled the left corner of his lips, and he couldn't take his eyes from her. He wouldn't take his eyes from her ever again. She was his little girl and he'd never take his eyes off her again.

Ari watched as she made herself a small meal and sat at the table to eat. Watched as Lilly finished her milk and Jay shifted her in his arms to burp her. Watched as Jay gently patted her back, and wiped the milk that came up with the towel she handed him. Watched as Jay gently settled his daughter back into his arms and rocked her off to sleep.

"She'll need another change or two before bedtime and will probably be hungry again by midnight." Ari finished off her food and kept watching.

"That's okay. We'll do it," he murmured, never taking his eyes from his daughter.

Slightly disturbed by his nonchalant attitude, Ari washed up and ushered them into the lounge room where they sat in relative silence, under the soft glow of the lamps either side of the lounge suite, listening to the trees rustle outside the French doors. It was quiet and peaceful in that moment.

Too quiet and peaceful.

"Is there anything you want to ask?" Ari ventured, picking at a knot in the fabric of the couch seat. "Anything."

Jay's glazed eyes looked at her before returning to Lilly. "No. I'm good."

"Well…I have questions."

"I don't want to talk about Gloria or the kids," he said, his finger stroking Lilly on the cheek. She gurgled and shifted her head, then calmed.

The niggle in her gut grew. "Well I…" she took a breath, "want to know what happened."

Jay sighed and lifted his head. "Ari. Nothing happened. Gloria, and the kids, and Denver have been dealt with. There's nothing to talk about. Not anymore. It's just us now. I get a second chance at life being here with you, and now Lilly who was a big surprise, and all I want to do is be with the two of you and not talk about Gloria. Okay?"

Ari considered his words, and the niggle grew bigger. Maybe him not telling her was saving her from knowing. In that case, did something bad happen and he didn't want to talk about it? She thought back to all the times Jay had said he was handling it, but never seemed to actually do anything. She thought back to the sanatorium and Jay meeting with the old man. Did he have something to do with it? What had Jay actually done to deal with it? Because she'd refused to watch TV and be online, she had absolutely no idea what had happened. So maybe it was time she got one.

They sat in relative silence for a while longer, and Ari let the dogs out for a late-night pee before heading up to bed. She carried Jay's fairly light overnight bag, making her wonder what was in it, and Jay carried Lilly all the way to her crib where he set her down and covered her in a light blanket.

"There's my girl. There's my little Lilly. You sleep now, because Daddy's here and I'm going to protect you, and love you, and raise you like the daddy you deserve. That's my little Lilly." He stroked her cheek and head until she was soothed, then stood staring at her.

"Do you want a shower before bed? I've put more towels and whatnot in the bathroom. Your bag's pretty light. Did you bring enough clothes?" She waited for him to turn, but he didn't. She waited for him to speak, but he didn't. "Jay?" When he didn't reply or move she walked over to him and lightly grasped his arm. "Jay?"

"What?" he snapped, yanking his arm from her hand. "Don't grab me like that. I don't like it."

Stunned, Ari stepped back, and that niggle grew to a large gaping sore. Something was seriously wrong.

Seeing her expression, he softened. "Sorry, baby. I'm sorry. I was…" He waved his hand near his head. "Somewhere else and thinking something else. I didn't know it was you and didn't mean to snap." He reached for her, but she backed away. "I'm sorry, Ari. I don't want to ruin our first night together. Our first night in six months. Baby." He smiled and stepped towards her. "Please. It's just been a rough six months and a rough four years dealing with Gloria. Let's just relax and be together, and let this night just be for us."

Ari softened slightly, but the niggling remained. "Okay," she finally relented. "But it looks like you'll need more clothes, and we need to have a chat about things. So let's start fresh tomorrow. You're probably tired from the long flight, and you didn't even tell me where you were coming from. Whether it was New York, or some movie set. You could've been on a plane for a whole day for all I know. So go and have a nice hot shower and we'll chat more tomorrow. Bathroom's that way." She pointed to the opposite side of the bedroom. "I've put green towels out for you."

"Thank you." He kissed her cheek, slowly picked up his bag, and wandered into the bathroom, closing the door behind him.

Letting out a deep breath, Ari sat on the edge of the bed and questioned everything that had happened from the moment Jay had arrived. He wasn't himself. That was clear. He didn't want to talk about Gloria and the kids. That was clear. And that was okay in her book. He just wanted to concentrate on her and Lilly and their future together.

But whatever happened in the last six months was important and she needed to know what had happened where Gloria and the kids were concerned in case they came

Anything for You

back into their life. She didn't need Gloria following Jay down to Australia just to keep up the harassment. Or Gloria deciding she wanted to foist the children upon him for any length of time. She didn't need more of the hell Gloria had inflicted for the seven months she'd been in New York. She didn't need Jay clamming up and not talking to her.

A sigh left her. Jay's demeanour was quiet, closed, and that wasn't him at all. Not the Jay she'd known from when they'd first met. Not the Jay who'd come and whisked her away to New York for seven months. No, this Jay was different, and she needed to get to the bottom of it so she could help him if need be.

She heard the shower turn off and walked over to the French doors of the balcony. She breathed in the scent of sea and salt mixed with hibiscus as she waited for him to finish up. It wasn't too late, only around ten or so, which gave them time to be together before sleep hit. Her stomach clenched and there was a sharp intake of breath.

Did she want to be with Jay in that way? To make love as they hadn't in six months.

Her memories weaved back through time to their last night in bed; the night before Jay had taken her to the restaurant and proposed in the penthouse—the night before the kids ended up in the hospital with smoke inhalation. They hadn't had sex during those few days, with Jay spending most of his time with them and coming home to shower or change. She'd left the day they got out of hospital and Jay was going to spend time with them in the Hamptons.

The Hamptons…

She remembered he'd suggested they go for the month and make it a holiday. She remembered Jay saying he'd go back to his normal custody visits within a month. That would have been five months ago. What had he done since then?

The door opened and Jay emerged in a pair of shorts and a t-shirt. "I guess I'm going to have to get some more clothes after all." He dumped his bag beside the bed. "Is this my side?"

Ari turned and studied him, a frown causing her brows to downturn. "Ah…yeah. I'm on this side to be close to Lilly." His mannerisms, his face, his body, his gait—he seemed exhausted. They would definitely be talking tomorrow. "I'm going to have a quick shower." She gave a half smile and entered the bathroom, locking the door behind her. That was stupid because it was Jay. But the niggle in her stomach told her to, even though that left her daughter in the bedroom alone with him. Disturbed by that thought, she quickly stripped off and showered, getting out in record time to rush into the bedroom.

Jay was standing over Lilly's cot, murmuring something.

"Everything okay?" She walked around the bed and stopped by his side. "Is she okay?"

"She's fine. Cried out a little, but I sang her back to sleep." Jay reached out and touched Lilly's chubby cheek. "She's so beautiful Ari. And we made her."

"Yeah." Ari couldn't help smiling as she stared down at her baby. "And I'm so glad I was able to have her." She reached up and rubbed his back. "Ready for bed?"

His lips curled into a soft smile. "Yeah. I'm exhausted. I might fall asleep the minute my head hits the pillow."

"That's okay. We don't have to be intimate tonight if you don't want to. If you're too tired, we can just sleep." To say she was disappointed was an understatement. She'd missed Jay for six months, wanting his body beside her, on top of her, inside her. And now he was too tired. Maybe it was for the best, considering her earlier thoughts.

"Intimate?" He turned from Lilly to look at her. "You want to be intimate?"

Puzzled, she said, "Well, yeah. It's been six months, Jay. Don't you want to? I thought that would've been the first thing you wanted to do when you came through the door."

Jay thought it through. "No, you're right. I'm sorry." He grasped her hand and kissed it. "I'm just so tired, and the flight was long, and it's been a long couple of days. I'm not thinking straight. Of course, I want to be intimate. Let's go to bed." He pulled her towards the bed, and they climbed in, lying down and wrapping their arms around each other.

Their lips found the other's, hands found their way over bodies, and limbs found themselves entwined.

Ari wrapped her arms around him, her hands skimming over his back. His bones peeked through a little, and she made a note to get him eating so he could fill out back to his old self.

Jay shifted on top of her, her legs wrapped around him, and he moved against her.

Ari slid her hands under his t-shirt and lifted it up.

Jay did the same with her nightie.

Ari moved her hands into his shorts and pushed them down.

Jay did the same with her knickers.

Ari guided him inside her and Jay moved back and forth.

Except it was not Jay. Not the Jay Ari knew. Not the passionate lover he had been in New York; the passionate lover who had dressed up an inflatable bed for them to make love on for the first time between the two lounge room Christmas trees. Not the lover who had made her cry out as wave after wave of explosions erupted inside of her.

No, this was not the Jay she knew at all.

When he was done, he rolled off and she lay there, barely panting, barely aroused.

He slid his shorts up and his t-shirt down and lay back against the pillows. "That was good, baby. That was good and I've missed it. God…" He rubbed his eyes and pulled the bedding over him. "I'm so tired. I'll see you in the morning."

Ari lay staring at him as he quickly drifted off to sleep. What the fuck had just happened? What the fuck did he think that was? What the fuck did he think he was doing? He'd been almost flaccid, had barely thrust till he came to ejaculation, but not enough for her to get off, and he thought it was good. This was a side of Jay she had never seen and didn't want to see again. What the fuck was going on? What the fuck did he think that was? That wasn't sex. It was a hell of a long way from lovemaking, but it sure as hell wasn't what she'd been waiting six months for.

Sighing, Ari pulled her nightie down and her knickers up. She definitely needed to get Jay into therapy because that most certainly would not do.

Chapter 21

The next day, Ari was holding Lilly and sitting out on the back terrace watching the dogs play with their toys when Jay waltzed outside and joined her.

"Hey, here are my girls. How about a swim? It's a beautiful day." He kissed Ari's cheek and planted a smooch on Lilly's forehead. "I cannot believe how fantastic this place is, Ari. You found an incredible home to live in, and I see you've unpacked everything." He took his place next to her in a chair and set his glass of juice down.

He's making himself right at home, she thought. "And how would you know that?"

"I had a peek in your office. You have a lot of stuff, and clearly unpacked it all after moving back."

She was riled at the intrusion but kept her cool. Jay was back with her, and things would finally get on track, so she had nothing to get upset over. But there was still something that niggled her. "You're being so nosy."

"I do live here now, Ari." He placed his feet up on the terrace railing and let his head drop back so his face could catch some rays. "It's my home now, too."

Something about the way he said that made her grit her

teeth. Something about him made her not want him there. She'd been awake most of the night trying to figure out how she was feeling. Whether it was just her, the amount of time since she'd seen him, the lack of sex, or Jay himself.

She was now uncomfortable with him being there, which was not how she'd expected to feel. If only she could figure out that niggling feeling deep in her gut. "So you're feeling better then? I let you sleep in and tried to be quiet when I got up."

"I'm feeling great. Fit as a fiddle, loads of energy. How 'bout that swim?" Jay dropped his feet to the floor and stood up, stretching his arms overhead. "It's a beautiful day and I'm going to take full advantage of it. How about you?"

"No, thanks. You go."

"Okay, then." He hurried down the terrace stairs and through the glass fence around the pool, stripped off his t-shirt, and dived into the deep end.

"He's chipper today. Unlike yesterday," Ari murmured and stared at Jay cutting through the water. "What's got into him?"

"Sure you won't come in, Ari? It's beautiful?" Jay called up to her as he trod water.

"No, thanks."

"Okay. I think I'll float around a bit and then lie by the pool." He swam a lazy backstroke as he watched her. "Care to join me for that?"

A crazy idea popped into Ari's mind, and she stood up. "No. I'll go and put Lilly down and then do a tidy up of my office. I was supposed to do it yesterday."

"Does Lilly really need to go back to bed?"

"Well, she is asleep." Ari looked at her daughter. "Babies sleep a lot, you know."

The comment didn't faze him. "Oh, yeah. I forgot about that. Guess I have a new baby to get used to."

Ari frowned at such a flip off comment. "You swan around the pool and relax. I'll put her down."

"Okay." He swam away and paid no attention.

Ari walked inside. She tried not to rush as she had a three-month-old in her arms, but she was eager to get upstairs. She settled Lilly down and peeked out her window to see Jay lying poolside, and then hurried around the bed and looked for his bag. She made quick time of searching for his phone, or an ID that he might have, and found his passport, his wallet with his driver's licence and some American and Australian dollars. There was nothing else besides a few pieces of clothing.

"What are you doing?"

Ari spun around at the question, dropped his t-shirt and grasped her pounding chest. "What? Jesus! Don't sneak up on people."

He inched closer; his brows furrowed so deeply the crease between them looked like a ravine. "What was it you were after, Ari? Are you spying on me?"

"Hardly," she scoffed. "I told you I was putting Lilly down, and I decided to tidy up and put your bag in the closet. You're going to need clothes and toiletries, so I checked to see what you have, and we'll make a list for when we go shopping."

He placed his hands on his hips. The towel he'd wrapped around his waist had barely dried the water from his body and he was dripping on the carpet. The frown slowly melted away and his demeanour changed. "Oh…okay. Yeah, I will need some new clothes, but I'll put my stuff away. Okay?"

Ari studied him, but that naggy little feeling flared up in her gut. "Fine. Did you come up for a reason? Because you're dripping water on my carpet."

He glanced down and saw the drops around his feet. "Sorry. I came up for a shower. I didn't want to burn like a lobster. Guess I'd better go and have it."

Ari watched him walk past. "Yes; and stop dripping water everywhere."

"Will do." He walked into the bathroom and closed the door behind him, leaning against it and sighing in relief as the tension from the moment slipped away. He'd heard her in the room and wondered what she was looking for. Not that he had much besides his wallet and passport, and a few clothes. He was rich enough to buy everything new and hadn't needed to bring much with him. So what had she been looking for?

Ari stood in the upstairs hallway, her hands in the pockets of her Capri pants, brow furrowed, bottom lip being chewed on between her teeth. She tried desperately to figure out what it was about him and why the nagging feeling wasn't going away. Everything about him was the same. Nothing had changed. His hair was the same shade and style, his eyes the same brown, except for the dead-looking expression in them. His height was the same as far as she could tell, and his weight a bit less than before. The magnificent forest of hair on his chest was exactly how she remembered it, and as much as she longed to bury herself in it, there was something so wrong. His long arms and legs were the same, his hands, except for the wounds she noticed that he hadn't mentioned.

The engagement ring!

Why was that not in his bag? Why had he not brought it

with him? Why was he talking about having a future, yet there was no ring in his bag? He'd gone on and on in New York about it not being on her finger, and yet, he didn't bring it with him.

Her frown deepened. What the hell was going on?

There was only one way to answer that question.

It was time to get back online and call Jay's people.

*****

They spent the rest of the day making lists and talking about their future. Jay refused to talk about the past, so Ari talked about her writing. It was something she was still doing; could easily do while Lilly slept. She talked about releasing *The Lover,* the sequel to *The Author,* in September, but had done nothing since as Lilly had come along and she'd concentrated on being a mother.

They had a light lunch and then a light dinner, spent time with Lilly when she was awake, and then went to bed around ten because Jay was feeling worn out.

But sex was as it had been the night before. Unfulfilling and disappointing for her, amazing for him.

Ari lay awake for a couple of hours, listening to Jay sleep. His breathing was even, his body unmoving, except for the light rise and fall of his chest.

When Lilly stirred, Ari took the opportunity to take her daughter downstairs and prepare her a bottle. The moment Lilly had the bottle in her mouth, Ari hurried along the hallway, shushed the dogs with a finger to her lips and pointed to their bed, glanced up at her bedroom door as she passed, and rushed into her office and locked the door.

She set Lilly in a bassinette that she kept there, pulled her phone from the drawer and attached it to a charger which she plugged into the wall socket.

With one hand holding the bottle for Lilly, she scrolled through her contacts and found Bobby's number.

"Hello?"

"Bobby? It's Ari. What's going on with Jay?"

"What do you mean, what's going on with Jay? He's missing."

"Missing? How can he be missing? He's here with me."

"How can he be there with you? He's supposed to be here in New York dealing with the fire."

"Fire?" Ari's brows rose. "What fire? Did something happen again?"

"Oh…shit… Sorry Ari, you better call Merrick for this, being Jay's lawyer and all. He can help straighten it out better than me."

She took down Merrick's private number and tapped it in once the conversation had ended.

"Merrick Statton, how can I be of service?"

"Merrick, it's Ari Travers. Remember me?"

"Ari, yes, long time no hear. What can I do for you?"

"You can tell me what the fuck is going on. Why did Bobby just tell me there's been a fire, and why does he think Jay should be in New York dealing with it when he's actually here with me in Australia?"

A long silence came down the line.

"Fuck! You're kidding! Jay's there with you? Fucking bastard. Why didn't he tell me, I could have sorted it out?"

"Sorted what out?" Ari glanced towards the door and heard a deep and heavy sigh on the line.

"The fire that killed Gloria, Denver and Andrew."

An ice-cold shiver fled through Ari, and she didn't think she'd heard right. "What?"

"It's been all over the news, Ari. Don't you watch it? Didn't you get it down there?"

"No. I haven't been on social media since I left New York, and I don't go online at all, or watch much TV. Jay hasn't mentioned anything since getting here. He just said it was all over and that we didn't have to worry about them anymore. What the fuck happened?"

"There was a fire in Gloria's Hamptons' house last week and it took their lives. The children were on the back lawn covered in blankets. Marisol was still breathing, but she's in the hospital hanging in there with smoke inhalation. Andrew needed resuscitation but didn't make it. Gloria and Denver were burned alive. We know that Jay left the set of the movie he was working on and hasn't been seen since, although a man of his description was seen in the vicinity of Gloria's house when the fire took hold. The cops want Jay for questioning, but can't find him, and he's not answering his phone. We've tried, Ross has tried. We even called Bobby and he has no idea." Merrick flipped through some papers on his desk. "They told me to let them know if I saw or heard from Jay. I'll let them know he's in Australia with you."

"Okay. What's happening with the burials? Has Andrew been buried yet?"

"Not yet. The morgue has the bodies until the autopsies are finished, and then they'll be released. But Andrew's body has to be released to Jay as he's the father."

Ari paused so long Merrick repeated her name several times.

Her blood had run cold. "What the hell is going on?"

"I don't know, but I'll let the detectives know he's there and they can contact the Australian police to come and see you."

"Good. Because I think there's something really bad going on and I don't think he's the Jay you and I know anymore. I think something happened, and I think he was that something."

Merrick tapped his fingers on his desk. "In that case, I'll tell the detectives to get onto your locals ASAP. What's your address? I'll pass along your phone number as well. And in the meantime Ari, check online. Entertainment Tonight has covered it more than the other sites. See what they've put up."

"Will do." She checked the time on her phone. "It's almost three in the morning here. I'll keep my phone on and wait for their call. Bye, Merrick."

She clicked off and quickly turned her laptop on, burping Lilly until it was booted up. Resting her daughter in her arms, she tapped in the website for Entertainment Tonight and searched for Jay Daniels. What she found horrified her.

"Brand new details about the fire in the Hamptons last week. The bodies discovered in the burned-out home were of actress, Gloria Hannaford, and her son, Andrew Daniels, as well as Gloria's partner, singer musician, Denver. Her daughter, Marisol Daniels is currently in the hospital with severe smoke inhalation. They had been staying there since May when Gloria's New York City apartment was set on fire by their nanny and the children suffered smoke inhalation then as well. Gloria moved them out to the Hamptons, and their father, actor Jay Daniels, visited them regularly. Gloria

Anything for You

and her family were yet to move back to the city apartment which had only recently been finished after renovations. Police are yet to determine the cause of the fire, but alcohol and drugs are the main factor. No word on where Jay Daniels is. He's supposed to be on the set of his latest movie, Gold Dust, but hasn't been seen since last week. Police want to talk to him as a man fitting his description was seen outside the house shortly before the fire. Now, onto the latest news about The Rolling Stones—"

Ari slumped back in her chair and stared at her computer. "What…" she breathed on the exhale. "What…oh…what the fucking hell!" *Gloria…dead… Andrew…dead… Denver… dead… Jay… They don't know where Jay is? Why wasn't he on his movie set? Where has he been? What did he do? Is this the plan he formulated to get rid of Gloria? But the kids? I mean, Andrew was a pain in the arse and took after Gloria, but he didn't deserve to die. Jesus. And Marisol. Sweet, adorable Marisol who could've been my daughter if given half the chance. But I blew that one, didn't I.*

"Jesus fucking Christ!" Ari rested her elbow on her desk and ran her hand over her face. "They're dead. All of them. Dead. And Jay? What the hell did he do for him to be missing since last week when the fire happened, yet he turned up here and hasn't said a fucking thing? Jay, what the fucking hell?"

She knew she had to do something, so she checked all of her emails and messages in case he'd contacted her in the last six months. Jay had sent her an email on the first of every month letting her know what had been happening, that he knew she may not read them, that he loved her, and couldn't wait for the six months to be up so they could be together, and he couldn't wait for his plan to play out. But he never mentioned what the plan was. He certainly didn't mention the Hamptons. And he hadn't been seen since last week on the set of his movie, around the same time as the fire. But he hadn't contacted her about that, either.

When she was done, she shut down the laptop and sat back, the time passing quickly as she thought things through. Finally, she pulled up the video on her phone to confront Jay with it. But when was an appropriate time going to be? Now? Later, when he was awake? She could hardly go back to bed with him now.

She'd avoided watching those shows for the last six months. Had avoided anything to do with celebrity gossip in her life. She didn't want to see, or hear, or read, about Gloria, Jay, Denver, or the kids. But the fire, and Jay turning up at her home, had changed all of that.

Ari drew a shaky breath and adjusted her daughter in her arms, snuggling her into the crook of her arm as she made her way back upstairs. Entering the bedroom, she turned on the light and saw Jay was still in the exact same position she'd left him in.

She placed a sleeping Lilly into her cot and rolled it into her walk-in closet, then closed and locked the closet door so she was safe.

Ari turned and saw Jay shifting. "Jay. I need you to wake up. Something's happened." She went over and pushed on his shoulder, waking him fully.

"Ari, what's wrong? Is it Lilly?" He rubbed his eyes and pulled himself up.

She realised in that moment that he hadn't even worn glasses in the last two days, and she hadn't seen any in his bag. "We need to talk. Something's happened."

"What, tell me? Is Lilly okay. Is it Lilly?" He looked around for her, but found her cot gone. "Where is she? Where's her cot?"

"She's in another room and just fine, but apparently your other children are not."

"What? What's this about? Is this a joke? Ari, what's going on?" He took her hand and brushed his lips along the top, eyes haunted with black emptiness that reminded her of death.

She took a breath to squelch the uprising of dread in her stomach and decided the only way to be, was blunt. "Jay, why aren't you in New York dealing with the death of your son? Why aren't you in New York dealing with your daughter who's in the hospital? Why are you here and not there?" She felt the stubble on his top lip and chin as he brushed them back and forth across her hand. Her brows slid down in a mix of emotions. After the news she'd just seen, something wasn't sitting right with her. "Jay, why aren't you on the set of your movie? Why aren't you in New York dealing with the death and burial of your child? Why aren't you talking to the police? I saw the story on an entertainment show. I saw stuff online. Why are you here when you should be there?"

His eyes were dead as they stared at her, making a quiver of ice shoot down her spine. In a very casual, low tone, he said, "I spoke to the police. They had no say in where I went."

"But there are reports of a man who looks like you being seen near the house when it happened," Ari said. "Was that you?"

"No!" Jay spat. "It wasn't. I came here for you, Ari, and

yet you're questioning me and my choice? They're dead, Ari. That's what we wanted. That's what the plan was. The plan was to get rid of them so we could be together."

Stunned, Ari pulled back and moved away. "What?"

Jay sighed, closed his eyes, and shook his head. "I'm sorry; I didn't mean it that way. It's just been really rough, you know. Dealing with it. I've been thinking non-stop about it since I found out and spoke to the police. It's over, Ari. They're gone. There's nothing I can do about it, except make the choice to be with the woman I love and want to spend my life with. The plan was to deal with them, and now they're dealt with. In a very unfortunate way, but that can't be helped. It's all been taken care of. We can be together now."

"Did you kill them?" she managed to ask.

He gazed at her for the longest time, etching her details into his brain, his expression cold and frozen. "No, Ari. I didn't," he said coldly. "And lots of men can look like each other. Just because a man that looked like me was seen in the area, doesn't mean it was me."

She swallowed the lump in her throat. "Why aren't you in New York with Marisol? She's in the hospital. She needs you."

"So do you and Lilly, Ari," he said. "Gloria's family is taking care of her; I don't have custody, remember."

She knew that was true, but it still didn't stop the icy shards shooting around her body. "Okay. Okay. So, now what? What does this mean? Are you here permanently? Here on holiday? What? Are you going back for the funerals? What about your family? How are they coping?"

He gave her a half smile and reached for her. "I hope I'm here permanently. From what I've seen, coming from the airport, it's as good as you said it was. Warm, tropical, beautiful." He slouched a little. "I think I'm going to love it here with my daughter and future wife, Ari Travers Daniels."

Her brows furrowed. "You always wanted me in New York."

He shrugged. "New York's not home anymore. It has bad memories, you know. I like it here."

She studied his mannerisms, his gestures. He didn't seem like the Jay she knew. But then, he had lost his son, and pretty much his daughter, so maybe he was in shock. Plus, the weight he'd lost could be from health issues, or the stress of the last six months in general, or maybe it had been for his movie role. His face was a little harder, a little weary; his hands a little rough and beaten up. She saw the half-healed wounds on his knuckles and wondered what they were from. "I didn't ask you how you did that," she said carefully, pointing to his hands. "Are they okay?"

He saw her watching him. "They're fine. Nothing I haven't had before. Ari, where do we go from here? I came here to be with you. It's six months since you left New York. Left *me*. We can be together now. You, me, our daughter. Why aren't you happier?"

Her face screwed up in anger. "*Because your son is dead, and your daughter is in the hospital, and you haven't even bothered telling me about it, that's why, Jay.* How do you expect me to be? How do you expect me to feel about you turning up on my doorstep barely a few days after you find out your daughter's in the hospital, and your son and ex-wife died in a fucking house fire, and you're clearly not giving a fuck? And you just want to pick up where we left off? How the hell do we do that, Jay, huh?" She shoved herself up from the bed and stormed over to the window, crossing her arms to ward off the very bad feeling that was snaking its way through her body.

"Ari." He came up behind her and rested his hands on her shoulder. She flinched. He settled them back. "Ari. I know it will take some time to deal with this. It's a tragedy that should never have happened. But it did. Gloria's screwing around made it happen. She was trouble, and I should have tried to get the kids from her and make them better off. But I didn't, and now they're gone. I'm sorry, I really am. I'm sorry that I'll never get to see my kids again. But I can't let that stop me from living my life with you. I promised you, Ari. I promised to make it better. To make her go away. And I did it."

Ari stepped out of his grasp and turned to face him. "And what do you expect me to do? Cheer and whoop and holler and plan a party while your daughter lies in a hospital bed fighting for her life, and your son is waiting in the morgue for his father to bury him?"

"What?" His brows furrowed slightly. "No, of course not. I just expect to get on with my life with you, and to deal with this over time. It won't happen overnight, Ari. It'll take time, and I can do it here with you. Wasn't that the plan? Isn't that what I told you?"

She shook her head and moved away. "Jay, I just… I don't know. This is too weird for me, and I only just found out. The cops said they haven't even spoken to you, that you haven't been seen on the set of your movie since last week when the fire happened."

He wondered how she knew that and spoke his lies truthfully. "That's because I was called away and didn't hear the news until a few days ago. That's when I came straight here." Jay moved to her side. "Ari, when I found out, the first thing I thought was, oh, those poor kids, how awful. The second thing I thought of was you."

"That doesn't comfort me, Jay," she retorted. "In fact, it just sounds crass. You were reconnecting with Marisol; you spent time at that home while they recuperated from the fire in May. You don't just think, oh, how awful. You *grieve* for your children. You know, the flesh and blood of your loins?" She waved his advances off. "Don't. I've just found out your ex and son are dead, and your daughter is in the hospital, and you're here instead. I need time to digest this and grieve for *your* children, even if you don't want to. Go to the police and let them know you're here. They're still looking for you."

"No. I've already spoken to the police in America; I don't need to do it here. I just want to relax and reconnect with my girl and grieve in private."

"And what about the funeral? What about Andrew's burial?" she asked.

"I took care of that," he said swiftly. "Before I came."

Puzzled, she stepped towards him. "How? Did you call your family? Your friends? *Gloria's* family?"

He turned nasty. "It was all taken care of, Ari, okay. I didn't fucking come here for the Spanish Inquisition. It's all been taken care of. Done. Dusted." He crossed his arms and waved them outwards. "Done. Now what I want is to reconnect with my future wife."

She shook her head and huffed in distaste. "You don't get to come here and dictate. I've spent the last six months trying to get myself into some decent mental shape after everything Gloria pulled. Waiting for the six months to be up so you could come and be with me, be with *us*. But not like this. Not with the death of your son and hospitalisation of your daughter hanging over our heads. You need to do better."

"Like what?" he sniped. "Ari, this is me, this is who I am. I made a promise, and that promise is fulfilled. We can finally be together. Be a couple, be a family. My God," his laugh was maniacal, "you didn't even tell me I had a child. I didn't know. Why didn't you tell me?"

"Because you said you didn't want any more kids, and when you saw the look of horror on my face you changed it and said unless it was with me, but since that was unlikely to happen, you didn't need to worry about it. And I thought I couldn't have any, but it looks like I was wrong. So what!" She waved a hand at him. "I told you this last night. And you made it clear in New York you didn't want kids. But now what, now that Andrew is dead, and Marisol has been taken in by Gloria's family, you want this baby? Is that it? A chance at redemption! Well, let me tell *you*, Jay Daniels, this ain't it. We're not going to be the happy family you were expecting, and I'm not going to jump back into bed with you and play house. You can damn well earn your way back into my life because what you're doing is atrocious."

"And what does that mean?" he argued. "Are you kicking me out? Are you saying you don't love me anymore? That this was all for nothing?"

"I didn't say that," she snapped. "But if this *is* what you really want, then you can stay in the spare room. There is *no way* you're coming into my bed again until things have settled down and all of this is sorted out, *and* you mourn the death of your children. Got it!" There was just something she couldn't put her finger on, and it was irritating the hell out of her. He was different, almost dismissive of his children, not quite the same with her. The feelings weren't there. Maybe it was her. Maybe she had fallen out of love with him. Maybe she didn't want this life with him after all. Maybe she didn't want *him* anymore.

Jay studied her and saw how serious she was. His emotions boiled on the inside, but he calmed himself on the outside. "Okay, Ari, I see that things are a little weird for you, right now. I guess they are for both of us. And you're right, I have my son to mourn, but I also have my new life to celebrate. My new daughter, my future wife, my life here in Australia. We can be the couple we dreamed of being. We can be *the family* we dreamed of being. Just you, me, and Lilly. I'll be the best husband and father I can be. I always will be."

"Spare room, nothing more," she said. "No more affection, no more kissing, no more touching, and definitely no more sex."

"Ari," he complained and threw his hands up in exasperation.

"No!" She pointed her finger at him, her eyes giving off a warning shot. "You *do not* get to dictate how this goes. It's been six months; a lot has changed. And now that I know what's happened, we are going to take the time to reconnect."

Sighing, Jay knew he just had to bide his time. The problem was, how much time did he actually have?

Sighing, Ari realised that time may have run out for them and the feelings they once shared just might not be there anymore.

She checked the clock and saw it was almost seven and the light was starting to infiltrate through the curtains. "There's no point continuing this for now. I'm tired and I need to get Lilly fed and bathed."

"I can help with that," Jay said softly. "Regardless of what happened in New York, Ari, I *am* here now. Just as I said I would be."

Nodding, Ari unlocked the closet door and pulled the cot back into her room. Lilly was just waking, a grumpy cry coming from her cherubic lips. Her tiny hands made fists and rubbed over her face. Ari bathed her, with help from Jay, and then showered before heading down to the kitchen for her daughter's first feed of the day, leaving Jay to his own devices in the spare room.

That feeling was still nagging at the back of her mind and deep in her gut but was interrupted by the buzz of the gate intercom. She hurried to answer it, her dogs bouncing at her feet. "Bed!" she commanded and pointed to the lounge room, watching them scurry back before answering. "Yes?"

"Ms Travers, my name is Detective Garmond, I have Detective Marblack and several officers here with me as well. We need to speak to Jay Daniels. We understand from his lawyer in New York that he's here."

"Yes, he arrived two days ago. Come on in." She buzzed them through and opened the door to see two cars drive through; a plain sedan with the two detectives, and a four-wheel drive cop car from which two officers alighted. "Wow," she murmured, her brow rising. "That's a lot of cops for a chat."

"Ms Travers." The two detectives approached the door.

"Yes." She opened it for them. "Come on in. He's upstairs having a shower." She waved them through to the lounge room and followed. "He turned up two days ago. I don't watch much TV, and haven't been on social media for months, so I only found out in the wee hours of this morning about Gloria and the children after ringing Merrick

Statton, Jay's lawyer, to find out what was going on."

"Yes, he rang us personally and told us what was happening, and we're following up for him. We called the NYPD as well, but we couldn't speak to the lead detective because he was out. We're waiting on his call. Meanwhile, we'll speak to Mr Daniels."

"I'll go and get him." Ari turned but didn't get to take a step.

"Before you do, Ms Travers, how is he?"

She turned back. "Meaning?"

"How does he seem? We know you were living with him in New York and left back in May. We know he'd been divorced from Gloria for two years and they had the two children. But he disappeared from his movie set last week, not long before the fire, and then poof," the detective waved a hand as if conducting magic, "he turns up here."

"And that surprised me, believe me, it did. When I found out this morning I questioned him thoroughly about it and didn't like his answers. I think he's disassociated himself from it. He doesn't seem to care." She frowned in thought. "I also think he lied."

"How so?"

"He told me the burial was taken care of. That everything was taken care of before he left. That Marisol was being taken care of by Gloria's parents. Not that I actually know that. He also hadn't bothered telling me yet. I had to find out from his lawyer this morning. And he said that he'd spoken to the police. But Merrick said the police were looking for him *to* speak to him."

The detectives exchanged a surprised glance. "But Jay told you he *had* spoken to them."

She nodded thoughtfully. "Yes. He did. I'd better go and get him." She hurried up the stairs and into the spare room. "Jay," she called and walked into bathroom. She saw him rubbing himself down and stopped short, glancing away.

"What are you looking away for?" he asked. "We made love enough for you to get pregnant. You've seen the package before." He sidled up to her and wiggled himself. "Come on, Ari, dance with me. You know my bits intimately."

She blushed and looked away. "Jay, stop it, it's not funny," she said tersely.

"Come on, Ari." He waved his hands in the air. "Dance with me."

Her brows furrowed and she glanced down at his package to see the same old Jay. Except he wasn't. He had a red mark on the inside right leg near his pelvis. "What's that? Did you hurt yourself?"

He glanced down and whipped his towel in front of him. "Ari, that's so rude. You know how I feel about that."

She picked up on that last line and it rang in her ears. "Feel about what?" Her gaze darted over his body as he wrapped the towel around his waist. It went to his underarm and she saw nothing but hair. Her heart raced.

"Funny," he quipped. "So, what were you saying?"

She cleared her throat and tried to speak calmly so as to not give herself away. "The police are here. They want to speak to you about Gloria and the kids."

His face turned to stone, and he remained silent.

"They want to see you downstairs. I said I'd get you." She watched him, trying to keep calm. "Hurry up." She left and walked into her bedroom, locking the door behind her, to check on Lilly, and then remembered that she was downstairs in the kitchen. She clenched her fists and muttered through gritted teeth, "Damn it."

She knew there had been something niggling her. Knew what it had to be. Memories flashed into her mind as she paced, scratching her forehead, trying to remember. Jay standing in her room dripping water on the carpet. Looking down at the floor and seeing his feet but not seeing the bigger picture. Now the mark on his thigh, and the lack of one under his arm. *Oh, my God...*

Ari carefully opened her door and found Jay's room open. He was nowhere in sight. She walked into the hall, gripped the banister, and took several deep breaths, knowing something was wrong. But how the hell was she going to convince them? Taking the stairs slowly, but surely, she stopped at the lounge room door to listen to their questions and hoped Lilly didn't cry out, warning them to where she was.

"So...where have you been, Mr Daniels?"

"Here, detective."

"I mean since you left your movie set last week? You turned up here at Ms Travers' house two days ago, didn't you? How long have you been here in Australia itself?"

"I flew in and came straight here."

"Mmm-hmm. And you know about your children."

"Yes."

"And your ex-wife?"

"Yes."

"And where were you when the fire happened?"

"Helping a friend who called for help."

"Ah-huh. And what did you do when you found out about your ex-wife and your children?"

"I dealt with my son's funeral and saw to it that Marisol

was being taken care of by her grandparents, and then flew here to be with Ari."

"And why was that?"

"Why was what?"

"Why did you just deal with your son's funeral and your daughter's care, and then fly here to be with Ms Travers?"

"Because Ari and I are in love. She flew to New York last year; we became involved and fell in love. I proposed back in May. Unfortunately, my children were injured in a fire thanks to my ex-wife's nanny, and they needed care. Ari had to rush back here to Australia for personal reasons. I've only just made it back to her."

There was a long pause and Ari could tell they were all weighing each other up along with the truth.

"Mr Daniels. We need to know what's going on. Your son is dead; your ex-wife is dead, along with her boyfriend, and your daughter is in the hospital. A man was seen in the vicinity of the house, and you were nowhere to be seen on your movie set. We've been asked by your attorney, Merrick Statton, to check on you. Ms Travers called him last night to let him know you'd turned up."

Shit! He shouldn't have said that. That's given her away.

"She called my lawyer?" Jay said calmly. "How sweet. It was nice of her to let him know I turned up. I haven't had my phone for a few days now. I lost it somewhere at the airport when I was flying out. I haven't thought of calling anyone as there was no one *to* call."

Ari remembered not seeing his phone in his bag. She took a deep breath, prayed that Lilly didn't cry out, and walked into the room. "Why not? Have you even called Bobby? You can use my phone if you don't have one of your own. And what about your family? They should know where you are. They'd be mourning your children as well. You really should let them know." She motioned to her dogs to stay as she bypassed the detectives and Jay who were standing in the middle of the room, and stopped near the terrace doors, resting one hand on the piano, the other on her hip.

"I'm surprised you haven't done that yourself," Jay mocked, his gaze boring into her. "You called my attorney."

"Yes," Ari replied. "They haven't heard from you either. And since I was so surprised at you turning upon my doorstep and not telling me anything, of course I was going to ring them and find out what was going on."

"Of course you were." Jay cast a sugary sweet smile on his lips and played up for the detectives. "See how wonderful she is." He gestured at her. "This is why I fell in love with her. She's so caring and considerate."

"Ah-huh," Detective Garmond muttered and glanced from Jay to Ari and noted she was as far away as possible from him. He cocked his head at his partner.

"No, ah-huh about it, Detective." Jay's eyes never left Ari. "She's the love of my life and I'll be thanking her later for calling Merrick."

Ari gathered her courage and hoped her voice didn't crack. "No, you won't be. Because I'm telling these officers that you're not the real Jay Daniels." Ari stepped behind the piano, keeping it between her and Jay. "You're an imposter; you're not Jay Daniels. Detectives, I want this man arrested and removed from my home."

The detectives looked confused, but Jay got a destructive, obsessive expression over his face. His head dropped a little, so he was looking at her under hooded eyes. It was how serial killers looked when you saw their arrest photos.

"Now, Ari, my baby. Why would you say something like that?" He took a step towards her, and Ari saw the detectives take a step towards him.

"Because I know for a fact you are not the real Jay Daniels. You showed me you weren't in the bathroom when I went to get you." She inched towards the terrace doors. "You're an imposter who probably killed Gloria and the kids and you're trying to frame Jay for it. What have you done to him? Have you killed him and are trying to take over his life? Is that it, you fucking bastard?" she screamed and bolted out the lounge room French doors hoping he followed, and Lilly was kept safe in the kitchen.

Jay took the bait and was right behind her, but the detectives grabbed him. He shook them off and lurched out the door after Ari. The officers also didn't react fast enough, and Jay slid through their fingers.

Ari ran screaming down the terrace stairs, around the pool, and down to the dock where she kept a large canoe moored.

"Get back here, you bitch," Jay yelled behind her.

The dogs ran after him, baring their teeth as they let their high-pitched barks loose on the new person in their life. Their mistress was in danger, and they needed to stop it.

Ari managed to slide the mooring rope off the wood pole and jumped into the canoe with enough force to push it away from the dock just before Jay reached her. She grabbed a paddle and started paddling as the officers ran down the dock and arrested Jay who was screeching obscenities at her. They shoved him down and slapped handcuffs on him.

"Ms Travers, look out," one of the detectives yelled and Ari spun around to see a motorboat slamming into her canoe's bow. The boat upended and she fell backwards into the water.

Detective Marblack ripped off his jacket and shoes and dived in after her.

She came spluttering to the surface, slapping it for traction and balance. The boat floated nearby, and she paddled over, grabbing it as the detective reached her side.

"Are you okay?" he asked, helping her onto the boat.

"Fine." She coughed. "That's not Jay. That's not him."

"We heard you," he said, trying to push the boat back to the dock. "But we reacted rather slowly, unfortunately."

They were helped out by Garmond and one of the officers.

"Ari," Jay yelled. "How can you say it's not me?" He struggled against the cuffs and the officer with the knee in his back and the barking dogs in his ear. "Of course it's me. You know me, Ari, it's me. We've made love the last two nights. Of course it's me."

"Yes, I *do know* Jay. And *you* aren't him," Ari told him. "I know Jay's body, and his *is not* yours. *You are not him.* I know that for a fact. And he's not a flaccid fish like you. What have you done to him? Where is he?"

The only reply she got was a snarl that turned into a hollow laugh.

The officers hauled Fake Jay to his feet and started up to the house, the dogs following as if they'd caught an intruder themselves. Ari and the two detectives followed.

"How do you know?" Detective Garmond asked.

"I'll tell you when he's not in earshot," Ari replied. "But I do need a shower and to check on my daughter. Can you keep him out of the house?" She looked at the detective in his sopping clothes. "Can't offer you a change, but I can offer you a shower."

"Just as well I keep a spare set of clothes in my boot then," he said.

A half hour later they were sitting in the lounge room, Ari and the detective freshly showered, and Fake Jay in the back of the cop car being watched by the two officers.

"All I know is, this imposter has a red mark on his inner right thigh. Jay doesn't. Jay has a mole on his left foot. The imposter doesn't. But I barely noticed that yesterday morning when he was dripping water all over my floor. I saw his feet but didn't notice that there was no mole. And it wasn't until I went to get him for you, that I noticed there was no scar under his left armpit. Jay has two marks on his body. A scar and a mole. This...*person* has neither but does have a red mark on his thigh."

The detectives had Fake Jay's bag at their feet and had gone through it. "The passport and driver's licence are pretty real looking, though. We have a lot of work to do when we get back to the station."

"Just as long as you keep him there. I have a daughter; I don't need him coming back to kill us like he might have done to Jay and his family." She gently rocked Lilly's porta-crib and received coos in return.

Detective Marblack glanced at the baby. "We'll keep him until someone from the U.S. police department comes and collects him. Meantime, someone needs to find the real Jay Daniels."

Ari looked up at him. "I just hope he's not dead. He was meant to come here after six months. We made that plan back in May. Six months, no more. If he didn't turn up in six months I'd know he wasn't coming, and it was over between us. He's not here himself, but an *imposter* is. This...*person* knows about Jay and me, our plan, our life, and behaved pretty much like Jay. Now Jay's ex is dead along with his son, and his daughter is in the hospital and could die herself and where the hell is he? Why isn't he here, or at his daughter's bedside?"

The detective could only stare back. "I don't know Ms Travers. I just don't know."

*****

Once the police took Fake Jay away, Ari locked every door and window in the house and closed the roller shutters. "No more outside pees for you two," she told the dogs when they stared forlornly at the disappearing outside world. She also called Merrick.

"What's going on? Where's Jay?"

"I have no idea, Ari, but I have detectives on it."

"The cops?"

"No, private. Figured we'd get a better answer than the lacklustre NYPD detectives could give us with their searches."

"Okay. Let me know if you hear anything."

"Will do."

After she had dinner and settled Lilly down, she spent the rest of the night googling Jay. Other than him leaving the movie set at the same time as the fire, and being mentioned in the news, there was nothing. No one had posted photos on social media, Jay hadn't posted to his accounts, and it was as if he had disappeared from the face of the planet.

Ari let out a whoosh of air and collapsed against her bed pillows. "What the hell, Jay? Where the hell are you?"

Chapter 22

The next morning, the Australian detectives contacted Ari.

"Ms Travers, Detective Garmond. We have a problem."

"And what problem would that be?"

"It would be the fact that the fake Jay Daniels has escaped our custody."

"What! How the hell did that happen?"

"We have no idea. He managed to get out of the cuffs and disable the officers long enough to get away. We have an APB out on him and we're sending a car with two officers to sit outside the front of your house."

"And what good will that do if the real Jay turns up? Or the fake Jay tries to break in my back door?"

"The officers have notes on Mr Daniels' marks for identification. And if you have roller shutters, keep them closed."

"Great, so now I'm a prisoner in my own damn home," she spat.

"Sadly, Ms Travers, you are. Until we find the fake Jay Daniels, that is."

"And do you have his real name? Who is he?"

"We still have no idea. The detectives on the case in New

York haven't called in yet. We're going to be calling again."

"You do that and get the real damn Jay back."

"I hope we can, Ms Travers. I hope we can."

News of Fake Jay's escape didn't thrill Ari; in fact it petrified her. With a baby to look after, and a psycho serial killer on the loose, it was the last thing she needed to deal with.

*****

Ari stayed frozen all day, sitting on the couch in the lounge room, scanning entertainment show after entertainment show looking for news of Jay. They all said he was still missing, that the police hadn't heard from him, and no one had seen him.

She called Merrick, Bobby, and Ross. Still no news.

Ari didn't sleep that night. She kept Lilly in her cot in her bedroom and kept all of the roller shutters closed. She heard odd noises, which the dogs perked up at, but wasn't about to go and look. If it was Fake Jay there was no way in hell she was letting him in. If it wasn't, she wasn't about to find out.

She scrolled through social media and found nothing except rumours and innuendo that he'd run off with another woman or killed off the ex and the kids to start a new life. Ari's name was never mentioned, but the idea that Jay had run off with someone else chilled her to the bone. What if it was true? What if he'd forgot all about her in the last six months? What if he'd moved on and fallen in love with some other woman he preferred over her? What if he—

"Stop it," she growled and threw her phone on the bed. "He didn't run off with another woman."

But what if he did? What if he'd found someone else in the last six months? What if she's better? What if she's gorgeous?

What if she does things to him I don't do?

"Fuck off," she muttered. "He loves me, and we *will* find him."

And if they don't?

*****

The next morning, the front gate intercom buzzed, sending the dogs into a frenzy.

Ari sent them to their beds before she rushed to answer it. "Yes?"

"Ms Travers, Detective Garmond. We need to come in."

She buzzed them through and opened the front door to see two plain sedans and two police four-wheel drives come through. "Doubles every time," she murmured.

The back door of a sedan car was flung open. "Ari!"

Her eyes moved towards the sound.

"Ari, oh, my God, baby." Jay ran for the door. "Ari, it's me, the real me, let me in."

Ari stared at him in shock and didn't move.

"Ari, come on, baby." Jay rattled the door handle. "It's really me. Let me in."

"It's okay, Ms Travers, it's really him," Detective Garmond said. "He flew here with two detectives from New York which is why they weren't getting in contact with us."

Ari's eyes finally moved to the others, and she saw four black suited detectives standing in her courtyard. "Jay," she gulped as her eyes moved back to him. "Jay."

"Come on, baby, let me in." He rattled the door. "It's me. It's really me."

Her fingers were stiff and fumbled with the lock of the

screen door, but when it clicked, Jay yanked the handle and swung it open.

"Jay…" Her lips trembled.

Jay swept her into his arms, hugging her with a ferocity he'd never felt before. "It's me baby. It's me. The real me."

She struggled out of his embrace and pushed him away. "Prove it. I want to see the proof."

He gazed at her, unsure, and then realised what she was talking about and pulled up his t-shirt, showing off the scar under his left armpit. "Here's my scar. I got it trying to shave my arm pit in high school." He let go of his top and pulled off his shoe and sock. "And here's my mole. It's me, Ari. It's really me." He slid his shoe on and shoved his sock in his jeans pocket. "It's really me."

She burst into tears and fell into his arms. "You're alive. You're really alive."

"Not for much longer," screamed out of nowhere. "Tell them you bastard; tell them this was all a set up. Tell them that you made me kill them. That this is all on you, Jay Daniels. You did this. You dressed up as an old man and came to the hospital and told me to do it. Tell them you set them up to die and you made me do it. It was all a set up and *she* was in on it."

Everyone looked around for the body that belonged to the voice. The detectives and officers had their hands on their gun holsters, ready for what could happen next.

Fake Jay came running past Ari's garage that he'd been sleeping behind, and across the courtyard. He reached for Marblack's gun and yanked it from the holster, lifted his arm, aimed the gun at Ari and Jay, who screamed and ducked down covering Ari's body with his own. But it wasn't Fake

Jay's gun that went off.

The four officers and Detective Garmond released their ammunition into Fake Jay, and he floundered, falling onto the stones mere feet from Ari and Jay who stared in horror at the dead body in front of them.

Jay pushed Ari into the house and slammed the door behind them.

Detective Marblack retrieved his gun, and the others holstered theirs.

Ari was plastered against the wall, a million memories flying though her brain. *Why had he said Jay had made him do it? Why did he say she was in on it? Did he mean me, or someone else? Who's she? What hospital is he from? Does he mean the sanatorium?*

The day she'd followed Jay's car to the sanatorium in upstate New York came back to haunt her. She'd seen him sitting there talking to an elderly man who got up and left. But Jay had stayed there a while longer before being escorted inside. She'd left before him. But now that there was a fake Jay, what if it wasn't actually Jay she was looking at that day? What if that was Fake Jay. Because Jay hadn't quite looked himself. He'd appeared silent and mentally distant. And the clothes he'd worn. The real Jay wasn't wearing the same clothes as the Jay at the sanatorium when she got home. His clothes were different. She remembered looking in his closet for those clothes and didn't find them. She'd even looked in the laundry room and they weren't there either. Had he got rid of them between the sanatorium and going home? What the hell became of them, and who the hell was the elderly man?

"Ari." Jay's words broke through her memories. "Baby." He cupped her face and kissed her gently. "I love you, Ari

Travers. Will you marry me?"

She pulled back; her eyes boring into Jay's. "That's hardly appropriate given all that's happened." She pushed him away and opened the door to see the officers had covered Fake Jay's body. "So what the fuck is going on?"

"Turns out, Mr Daniels here was off the grid," an American detective said. "I'm Lee Railgate, this here is Dan Castell." He motioned to his partner. "When these detectives rang and we had a chat, we told them we had the real Jay Daniels and would let him know. We spoke to Mr Daniels and immediately flew out of New York."

Ari turned to Jay and demanded, "Where the hell were you? *No one knew*. Not Merrick, not Bobby, not Ross."

"Did you call my family?" Jay asked. "Because I was with them."

Ari let out a deep breath and looked at his haggard appearance. "I didn't think to, no. And I don't have their numbers anyway. Why?"

"I left the set after I filmed my last scene. My sister rang me to say Mom had been hit by a car and I flew out immediately. I lost my phone somewhere at the airport but didn't realise until I'd got to the hospital. Mom was more important, so I figured I'd wait on getting one as we were in her room 24/7 and phones weren't allowed. The rest of my family barely turned theirs on. We didn't hear the news about Gloria or the kids until the detectives came to the hospital and told me about Mari and the Fake Jay." He took a shuddering breath. The last week had been harrowing, spending time in two hospitals dealing with the illness of two family members. His mother and his daughter. The shock of both, and then realising he'd also lost Andrew, his only son, had taken a toll.

"How is Mari? Is she still alive?" Ari asked.

"Yeah. My sisters are looking after her. When the detectives turned up and told me, my mom was doing okay. She told me to go and be with my daughter, so we rushed back to New York to the hospital."

"And how's your mum?" Ari's fingers laced with his and he lifted them to his lips.

"She's doing well but devastated about Andrew and Mari as are the rest of the family. That's why I didn't come, and didn't even think to ring, Ari. I was in the hospital worrying about Mom, and then in the hospital worrying about Mari, otherwise I would've been here."

"No, I get it." Ari sighed, her body deflating. "How did they find you?"

Castell spoke up. "We searched the airports, showed his picture, and found out from the lady at the desk that he'd bought a ticket for his home town. We were also able to trace his phone. Someone had dropped it off at lost and found in the airport, and when we turned it on we saw the messages from his sister and followed. We found him at the hospital and told him what had happened."

"So who the hell was at the house in the Hamptons that supposedly looked like Jay?" She pointed to the fake Jay lying in her courtyard. "Him?"

"More than likely," Railgate said. "Since we found out Mr Daniels was mid-flight when it happened, and he arrived at his destination, it can't've been him. He's in the clear."

"So Fake Jay set the fire and burned Gloria, Denver, and Andrew to death," Ari said, trying to piece it all together. "And put Marisol in the hospital."

"That's pretty much it." Railgate nodded. "Guess we'd

better wrap this thing up."

The sound of a baby crying filtered through the air.

"Fuck! Lilly." Ari rushed for the lounge room and over to her crying daughter.

"Who's Lilly?" Jay dashed after her and saw Ari holding a baby in her arms. "Who's that?"

"Hey, bubba," Ari soothed. "It's okay, it's okay, Mama's here." She rubbed her back lightly to stop her cries.

"Mama?" Jay stared, almost horrified, at the infant in Ari's arms. "Who the hell *is* that?"

Ari looked up apologetically. "Um…this is Lilly."

Jay looked at the curious blue eyes and little tuft of golden hair and felt himself soften. "She's cute. Did you adopt? I didn't know you were doing that. Or that *we* were going to be doing that."

"Um…no…I didn't."

He looked into Ari's eyes and saw her expression. "Well if you didn't adopt what…?" The light finally dawned. "What! But you said you couldn't."

"I said I probably *wouldn't* be having a baby because I was too old and probably had no eggs left." She blushed and glanced away. "Turns out, I had at least one."

Jay's gaze darted back and forth. "So…" He pointed at the baby. "She's yours?"

"Yes."

Jay thought a second more and pointed at his chest. "And mine…"

Ari smiled and turned back to the baby. "Hey, Lilly, say hello to your daddy. Your *real* daddy this time." She lifted the baby for Jay to see.

His heart was melting, and so was he, right into a puddle

of goo. "Another baby? With you? Is that why you asked me in the restaurant that night if I wanted any more children? You knew you were pregnant."

"Pretty much." She lifted the baby into his arms, and he took her with ease. "I didn't want to say anything, being a geriatric pregnancy and all, because I could've easily lost her. And then you know, Gloria, and the kids, and Denver, and you said fuck no to more kids." She nodded at the dogs in their beds. They were eager to run to the new man in the house and sniff him out, but they waited for their mistress to give them the go ahead. "We also have those two kids, and two cat kids that I never see except when they want food."

Jay chuckled at their vigorously wagging tails. "So this is what you've been doing for the last six months, huh? Playing house with dogs, and cats, and our baby."

She smiled at the love of her life holding her daughter. "Pretty much. What about you? What have you been doing?"

His sigh showed his exhaustion. "Ah…did a couple of movies, wrote a screenplay, still worked on turning your book into a movie. Wrote you an email every month, which I don't even know if you saw, prayed to God that we'd be back together ASAP. I saw the kids every week when I could, especially Mari, and tried to stay out of Gloria's way." He watched as Lilly wrapped her tiny hand around his finger and stared up at him with her big blue eyes. Unable to help himself, his lips curled into a smile. "She *is* adorable."

Ari raised a brow. "She bloody well should be. She's a Daniels."

He laughed and slid his arm around her. "That she is. And you know what else?"

"What?"

"I brought your engagement ring with me."

"Did you now? I wondered where that was when I went through Fake Jay's bag."

"I did. Because believe me, Ari Travers. I plan on proposing to you all over again."

"Ah-huh. Well, that will have to wait until the police have left."

It took another two hours before Fake Jay's body was hauled away in the coroner's van and the officers and detectives were gone. They were going to track down who he really was and get back to them.

When Ari finally opened up the roller shutters, and locked the doors and front gate, she sighed in relief and saw Jay was still holding his daughter. "I take it you're staying?"

Jay glanced up. "Well, the plan was to come and find you. I just got a little sidetracked by personal issues."

"And the plan didn't include Mari."

A blush crept over his face, but he kept his cool. "Not at the time. But considering what's happened, it will now."

"You'll be going home to get her?"

"I guess," he said, lightly bouncing up and down as he soothed Lilly. "She'll need time to recover."

"Just like in May."

"Just like in May," Jay replied. "And then I'll bring her with me when I come back."

Ari's brows rose in surprise. "Bring her here?"

He watched her. "Yeah. If that's all right?"

Ari kept her tone neutral. "Of course. Just wondering, since the plan was to kill off Gloria, Denver, *and* the kids. So who saved Marisol?"

Jay couldn't even hide his shock and his face quickly

turned red. "What? What are you talking about?"

Ari crossed her arms and chuckled. "Come on, Jay Daniels. I've been trying to figure it out for the last six months, and even before that. Trying to figure out *your* plan. It was so obvious with everything that'd gone on in New York when I was there. Fake Jay said plenty about it before he tried to kill us. I know about the sanatorium because I followed you one day and saw you, or him, or whichever one it was. And you went on and on about this plan of yours to get rid of Gloria."

Jay remained silent and the blush grew deeper, travelling down to his neck and chest. His eyes turned down and he concentrated on Lilly.

Ari noted his discomfort and knew she was close to an answer. "I mean, seriously, like I'm going to tell anyone. We *all* wanted something out of that plan, whatever it was. We *both* wanted Gloria out of the way, and dead was a good option. The *only* option. You wanted out of being a dad. I wasn't overly enthusiastic about killing off the kids as Marisol was rather endearing, so I'm glad she's still alive. At least Lilly gets a big sister."

"What makes you think that was my plan?" His anger seeped through to his words. "And who the hell are you to follow me?"

Ari took Lilly from his arms and rested her against her shoulder. "I'm your future wife, Jay Fucking Daniels, and don't you forget it. But I sure as hell won't tolerate any secrets. Especially from the man I'm going to marry and have a life with. We *both* wanted Gloria out of the way, and *you* promised to get rid of her. *You* had a plan. *You* were the man *with* a plan. So what was it? Who the hell is Fake Jay?

And who was at the sanatorium? You or him? And who was the old man talking to? You or him?"

She saw a flicker behind his eyes, and it all fell into place. "Oh…*he* was Fake Jay, and you were the old man. Which made it easy, because you're the big actor dude and know how to apply make-up and wigs and shit. That's why I couldn't find the clothes Fake Jay was wearing in your closet or the laundry. You didn't own them because he did. So that makes *you* the old man, and I didn't see you get out of, or into, your car at the sanatorium, or the house. Oh, you sneaky fucking bastard!" She glanced up at the ceiling and shook her head. "But that doesn't tell me who Fake Jay is? Or are *you* really Fake Jay and *he's* actually *real* Jay? Doppelganger? Twin? Twin dumped in a sanatorium seems much more feasible. And I know you were going to see him every week. It was in your planner as JG at EW."

"You looked in my planner? You conniving little—" Jay blurted out angrily as it all came tumbling out. "He's not my twin, just a patient I discovered while doing a community visit one day. They all thought it was hilarious, showing me this man who could've been my twin. But when Gloria started making our life hell, *I* came up with a plan. And the plan was to make that man do my dirty work and take the blame for it. You know, the lunatic escapes from the asylum to get revenge, or some such thing, believing he's actually me and actually has the life I have, but he doesn't. You know, obsessive compulsive, or something like that."

"And what's his name?"

"Jeffrey Gambon."

"And what did you do to him?"

He frowned. "Who said I did—"

Her laugh was mocking. "I know all about it, Jay. For the most part. Just face the facts that I figured out your plan and accept it. I sure as hell won't reveal anything. I wanted Gloria dead as much as you did. That *was* the plan, wasn't it? To *kill* Gloria; or have her killed. How did you convince Jeffery to do it?"

Jay took her by the arms and relented as he realised he had a co-conspirator who would never reveal the truth because she would lose as much as he. "I dressed up as an old man and told them I was his grandfather. They told me the first time I was there as myself that none of his family visited him, so I told them I'd only just found out my grandson was in a sanatorium. And then slowly, each week, I told him who he looked like and what I wanted him to do until he had it down pat and knew as much as he needed to. I worked on him to make sure he executed this plan perfectly, but I guess I told him too much, telling him over and over what he needed to do and how he needed to do it. It wasn't easy, you know, working on a guy who's only there half mentally."

"Half?" Ari queried. "I'd say he was a whole lot more there than half. He knew who the kids were, who I was, where I lived, how to get here. He sounded like you, looked like you, acted like you. He certainly figured out enough about us, didn't he?"

"Did he fuck like me, too?" Jay asked sarcastically.

"No, he didn't which is another reason I knew something was wrong. We had sex, because, oh, I don't know, I thought he was you!" She saw his horrified expression as he stepped back. "Oh, don't worry, he barely got it up and got it in. But now I'm going to have to see a doctor and get tested for all sorts of shit like HIV and other STDs. Fuck! I didn't know it wasn't you. I feel disgusted with myself for sleeping with someone I believed was you but was a complete and total stranger. Ugh."

"Yeah, well. I'm not happy about it," Jay grumbled, having not expected her answer. "I didn't sleep with anyone in the last six months."

"Oh, thank God for that," Ari muttered, sarcasm dripping from her words. "Guess I'm the only one at fault, but at least I'm not a murderer."

"Neither am I," Jay snapped.

"Aren't you? You instigated it, planned it, almost to a T. Guess you didn't plan on Jeffrey wanting revenge on you, though. Why *did* he want revenge?"

Jay rubbed the pounding spot on the top of his head. "I don't fucking know. The bastard got one over on me with that one. Coming all the way here, pretending to be me and fucking my future wife. I sure as hell didn't except him to fly here and track you down to take over my actual life and keep pretending to be me. I'm surprised he didn't try and kill me too, instead he just left me to deal with the deaths and the fire and probably thought I'd be the one arrested and sent to jail for it. Out of his life, and hence yours, forever. No more real Jay to worry about while fake Jay took over my life *and* my wife."

Ari rolled her eyes. "Well, don't worry, he's gone. Denver's gone, Gloria's gone, Andrew's gone, and now you can fuck me all you like, and we'll never have anyone bother us again."

His face softened and a sigh slid out from between his lips. "Look, Ari. I didn't know he'd do this, okay. Fly here to Australia and track you down, I mean. I didn't tell him that much about you *or* us. This wasn't supposed to happen. He didn't hurt you, did he?"

She watched him for a few moments before answering. "No, he didn't."

Calming slightly, Jay said, "Okay. That's good. He did say something, though, that I didn't put much stock into when he said it…"

"What?"

"That *she* was in on it. What do you think he meant by *she*? And who the hell would *she* be? Do you think it was Gloria?" His brow furrowed and he rubbed his hand over his mouth as he thought through possible suspects.

Ari glanced away and thought of all the times she'd visited Jeffrey in the sanatorium in May to find out Jay's plan, because there was no way she was going to let Jay have all the fun killing off Gloria and getting away with it. She'd wanted in on the plan too and added to that plan with a plan of her own. Because she wanted Gloria as dead and out of the way as he did. But Jay would never know that she'd done because she would never tell him. And he hadn't actually killed Gloria, so there was no need to admit to her part in it. What was that old saying? The couple that kills together stays together. She shook her head, disgusted that she hadn't realised it wasn't Jay when he first arrived. "No idea."

Jay pulled Ari and the baby into his arms. "Look, Ari. I think I've proved I can be the man you want who puts you first before anything and everyone else. The man who makes you number one in his life. I told you six months ago that I'd do anything for you, and I meant what I said."

"Yeah," she murmured and glanced up at him, knowing they'd both take their secrets to their graves. "You certainly did."

Epilogue

Jay's phone beeped and he looked at the text from his lawyer. He'd sent the police and coroner's reports via email and Jay needed to read them now.

"Who's that?" Ari asked, looking up from her daughter sleeping peacefully in her arms. They were sitting on the sofa in the lounge room, relaxing in the summer warmth; their fingers weaved together as they watched Lilly. Her engagement ring, the emerald heart that Jay had bought her, sparkled in the light streaming through the window, and the wedding and eternity rings nestled gently into it. They'd finally made it official on the first of the year.

"Merrick. He's sent through some papers. I'm gonna go and print them out. I might be a while." Jay kissed them both before hurrying into their shared office and booting up his laptop. He turned on the printer and added paper, and minutes later, they were printing out, but he waited until they were done and clipped together before he started reading.

The body of Gloria Hannaford was found in the middle of coitus with a male. She had drugs in her system, consisting of ecstasy and marijuana and may not have realised that numerous candles had been knocked over during sex. In doing so, she may have been slow to act, if she did at all, as both bodies were found still joined on the couch, fused together.

The body of the male was found to be that of Michael Denver Landon, who professionally went by his middle name of Denver. The tattoos found under the burned skin were a match, as were the teeth upon examination of dental records.

With drug paraphernalia lying around, boxes of unlit matches, lighters and candles, and bottles of alcohol found on the floor, plus the half empty bottles of cleaning fluid in the nearby kitchen, the fire had spread quickly. The fire has since been deemed accidental and the case has been closed. With the two adults being highly intoxicated, it is clear they would not have had any idea what was happening.

The children, daughter, Marisol, and son, Andrew, had been removed from the house. Both were found in the back yard covered in water-soaked blankets. Marisol suffered light smoke inhalation, but the son, Andrew, suffered chronic inhalation and severe burning as he may have been pulled out last or been closer to the fire, if not in the middle of it. Resuscitation efforts proved fruitless, and he could not be revived.

The person who pulled them to safety is yet to be found, although several men were seen around the house and in the vicinity, including one we now know as Jeffrey Gambon, an escapee from a mental institution, who was mistaken for Jason Daniels, the children's father, and Gloria Hannaford's ex-husband.

The other has not been clearly identified, but witnesses said he scaled their back fences with ease and appeared young and fit even though he was coughing chronically.

"Wait..." Jay whispered. His brow furrowed and he read over the section again. "So who got them out...? The guy jumping fences or Jeffrey? What the hell did he even do? Did he set the goddamn fire or what? What the fuck did she get up to, and how the fuck were the kids even *allowed* to be around that? Gloria! What the fuck did you do?"

"What's going on? Anything bad?" Ari asked from the doorway before walking over to Jay with Lilly in her arms. "What is it?"

"Just the police report about the fire, and everything." Jay waved it and then rolled the stack into a tube. "No need to worry about it."

"Did I hear you say something about Denver being in the house? So that *was* his body in the middle of coitus with Gloria?"

Surprised, Jay glanced at her. "Ah…"

"I heard." A wicked little smile slid over her lips. "That was Denver in the fire, and Jeffrey's dead, so all three major pains in our backsides are dead. Do we have any loose ends left?" she mocked.

Jay stared at her, the gears in his brain ticking over. "Not that I can think of. We get to keep the life we fought to have, because we fought hard for it, Ari Travers Daniels." He brushed aside golden-brown strands of her hair that she'd grown longer and slid his fingers over her cheek to her chin. Tilting it up, he added, "He was there with her, they were together, and now they're gone, along with Jeffrey. We know that for absolute dead set certainty."

Ari gently patted Lilly's back to quieten her. "At least Mari's still alive, which is nice."

A week after Jay had arrived in Australia; he'd flown back to New York for Marisol who was able to leave the hospital. He'd packed up their belongings and they moved over just before Christmas. Mari was thriving during the day in the summer warmth, but still having nightmares at night. She enjoyed being a big sister to Lilly, playing with Ari's dogs and cats that she'd sequestered for herself, and had just started at the local primary school where she was making new friends nicely.

"Do we know who got the kids out?" Ari swayed back and forth on the spot, more to comfort herself and not her daughter.

"No. It was either Jeffrey, or the young man seen jumping people's back fences. I can't believe all of the drugs they had there, and that they did that with the kids around. That's sick. The nanny's drug use was one thing, but…" Jay tilted his head in thought.

Ari brightened somewhat. "Consolation is that Andrew's gone. Although it can't be easy for Mari, losing her brother."

Jay nodded. "Consolation is that I don't have to put up with him anymore."

"Jay," Ari murmured. "Your son *is* dead."

"I know, I know." He pouted. "But why can you say something and not me?"

He'd laid Andrew to rest in the same coffin as his mother. He was the mini version of her, so he'd be with her for all eternity. Their remains had been cremated and scattered under the rose bushes in Gloria's parents' garden. The way Jay saw it, he didn't get to make her burn in hell the first time after all she'd done to him, so he made sure to send her a second.

Ari rolled her eyes at his childishness. "The other consolation is that you're off the hook for the part *you* played in it for the rest of your life."

Jay raised a brow at her. "The same can be said for you, my dear wife. And *we* have the rest of *our* lives to spend together as husband and wife." He pulled them into his arms and kissed her. "See, Ari. I told you I would do anything for you, and I meant what I said."

About the Author

L.J. has been writing since 2006, when her first of many novels, ***The Road To Vegas,*** was born. In 2016 she created the ***Porn Star Brothers*** series about three sizzlingly hot Australian born Greek Island raised brothers who became the hottest porn stars in '70s America.

L.J. lives in Australia, loves '80s music, disaster movies, and collecting Jackie Collins books as Jackie is her inspiration and mentor.

L.J. Diva is the adult pen name for author Tiara King. You can find more about Tiara on her website; follow her on social media, or visit her publishing house, Royal Star Publishing.

Socials

ljdiva.com

tiaraking.com.au

royalstarpublishing.com.au

Sign up for *Tiara's* Newsletter…

Make sure you're always in the know and never miss free exclusives, the latest news, book updates, and so much more with newsletters from…

tiaraking.com.au

Have you read these?

THE PORN STAR BROTHERS SERIES

Carlos: Book 1
Pedro: Book 2
Tomas: Book 3
Retribution: Book 4
Porn Star Brothers Forever
Love Never Dies
Stefan: The New Generation
DeLuca
Spiros & Jenny
And Always

Or these?

NOVELS

Anything for You
Falling for London
The Road to Vegas
Hollywood Dreams
The Billionaire's Dirty Little Secret

CPSIA information can be obtained
at www.ICGtesting.com
Printed in the USA
LVHW101105131022
730612LV00016B/281/J